THE RADIANT
FUTURE

Alexander Zinoviev

THE RADIANT
FUTURE

*Translated from the Russian
by Gordon Clough*

THE BODLEY HEAD
LONDON   SYDNEY
TORONTO

British Library Cataloguing
in Publication Data
Zinoviev, Aleksandr
The radiant future.
I. Title
891.7'3'4F   PG3490.I498S/
ISBN 0–370–30219–2

Originally published in Switzerland as
Svetloye Budushchee
by Editions L'Age d'Homme, Laussanne
World Copyright © 1978 by Editions l'Age d'Homme
Translation © The Bodley Head Ltd
and Random House Inc. 1981
Printed in Great Britain for
The Bodley Head Ltd
9 Bow Street, London WC2E 7AL
by Redwood Burn Ltd
Trowbridge & Esher
Phototypeset in V.I.P. Plantin by
Western Printing Services Ltd, Bristol
First published in Great Britain 1981

Once I happened to overhear a conversation between two Moscow intellectuals. One was a famous sociologist who had devoted titanic efforts to the development of Soviet sociology for the benefit of the party, the state and the people. Yet despite that, his group had been completely destroyed in the name of that same party, that same state and that same people. And he was left with nothing to do, grateful merely that they kept on paying him. The other was a famous painter who had put no less effort than the former into the task of raising the Soviet visual arts to a world-class level, but who in the course of twenty odd years had not been allowed to stage even a small one-man show. I set down their conversation in full.

'What a bloody awful life it is!'

'Oh, f—— it all!'

There can be no more definitive comment on the life we lead. And yet in that life we sometimes see some vague hints at something different. And those hints merit at least a moment's consideration.

Moscow 1976

Long live communism

Where the Avenue of Marxism-Leninism meets Cosmonaut Square, a great permanent slogan was erected reading: 'Long Live Communism—The Radiant Future of All Mankind!' The Slogan was erected at the request of the workers. It was a long time in the building, mainly in winter, when costs are higher. A huge amount of money was poured into it—no less (it is rumoured) than was invested in the whole of our agriculture during the first five-year plan. But today we are very rich, and such expenses are a mere nothing. We have spent even more on the Arabs without breaking ourselves. What we spent on the Arabs was a complete waste, while the Slogan is a source of undoubted benefit.

As might have been expected, the Slogan was of very shoddy construction. The paint began to peel even before the Slogan was put to use. The individual letters became progressively covered in a sort of grey grime, and fell to bits. Therefore the Slogan had to be completely repaired at least three times a year: once for the May-day celebrations, once for the November celebrations, and on every occasion when Moscow entered for the All-Union contest for the model communist city, and the multi-million army of Moscow office workers was driven out on to the streets to clean up the rubbish. As a result the maintenance of the Slogan cost the State several times more than its initial construction. And to judge by the vulgar graffiti which adorn the supports of the letters, the educational effect of the Slogan has not yet achieved even the half of its planned potential.

As the 25th Congress of the CPSU drew near, it was decided to put an end to this outrage. New letters for the Slogan were cast in stainless steel at the Brewery named in honour of the 21st Congress of the CPSU (formerly the Marshal Budyonny Brewery). They were cast by the shock-workers of communist labour in their overtime. The letters were made of bee . . ., forgive me, metal, which had been specially saved up by the workers in honour of the forthcoming Congress. The letters were mounted

(7)

on a mighty concrete pedestal. The concrete itself had been saved up by the construction workers of Moscow in honour of the forthcoming Congress. So, on this occasion, not only was nothing spent on the Slogan, there was even a profit, as the builders of the Slogan had saved up more than ten million roubles in honour of the forthcoming Congress. It was decided to spend these carefully garnered resources on the construction of permanent reinforced concrete frames to carry the portraits of the members of the Politburo, thus putting the crowning glory (as the newspapers said) to the splendid architectural ensemble of Cosmonaut Square and the wasteground adjoining it. Defending his idea about the portraits to the Central Committee, the chief city architect asserted frankly that by this means we would be able to conceal the ugliness of the wasteground from the eyes of the foreigners. For after all, we cannot rid ourselves completely of foreigners at the present time!

The official opening of the Slogan was a most solemn occasion. The Avenue was resurfaced. There were many foreign journalists and diplomatic representatives. Countless guests came from the friendly parties of Africa and South America, and there were also delegations from all the countries of the Socialist camp. There were also guests of honour from the lands of capitalism—the Italian actress Sophia Bordobrigida, that personal friend of the Soviet Union the American millionaire Hamson, the farmer Zdrast, the French singer Georges Ivanov, and many others. The ceremony was filmed. To the accompaniment of tempestuous applause from the representatives of the workers who crammed the Avenue, the Square and the wasteground, an Honorary Presidium was elected consisting of . . . and a telegram of greetings was sent to comrade . . . in person. A major speech was delivered by one of the secretaries of the City Committee of the party, Comrade Tsvetikov, who had recently replaced Yagoditsyn, who had been down-graded to some minor ministry on account of his boundless arrogance. Yagoditsyn had grown so insolent that without any reference to Mitrofan Lukich he had published an article in a magazine which Mitrofan Lukich himself had wanted to publish, and had thus completely discredited himself. So as not to fall flat on his face in the mud, Comrade Tsvetikov had learnt his speech by heart and delivered it almost withour error (if we leave aside mistakes in pronunciation). Then it was the turn of the cosmonaut Khabibulin, who said that from out in space Earth looks as it should look under communism: very round, and a kind of pinkish-blue. Then there was a speech from the representative of the freedom-fighting peoples of Africa. Dazzling the whole Square with his flashing, powerful white teeth, he said 'Tank yo' very moch!', which threw the workers' representatives into a frenzy. When the applause had finally died down and the well rehearsed spontaneous slogans had been shouted, Academician Kanareikin mounted the rostrum.

Kanareikin is the director of our Institute. In its time our Institute was in charge of the building of the Slogan. Members of the Institute delivered more than a hundred lectures on the theory of scientific communism for the builders of the Slogan, which won for them the challenge trophy of the Red Banner of the Regional Committee of the party. That was why Kanareikin was allowed to speak. Otherwise he would in no way have been permitted to mount the rostrum, since he should have gone out of print long ago and cleared the stage for young, talented and literate scientists (and most of all for Vladilen Makarovich Eropkin, a corresponding member of the Academy of Sciences, and son-in-law of Mitrofan Lukich himself). It was a great personal triumph for Kanareikin to be allowed to speak. The newspapers would report it. There would be a rumour that Kanareikin still wielded power. And his removal from office would be further postponed to some unspecified time in the future. And once he had got to the rostrum, Kanareikin knew better than anyone else how to exploit his opportunity. He rolled out a penetrating speech which consisted mainly of exclamation marks.

'The malicious enemies of communism and the so-called writer, the anti-Sovietchik Solzhenitsyn, expelled at the demands of the workers beyond the frontiers of our fair Motherland for his slanderous inventions, to find shelter under the wing of the worldwide imperialist bourgeoisie and its lackeys, who . . . Where was I? Ah, yes! And also that self-styled Academician, the renegade Sakharov, for whom too there is no place in our ranks, who gambles on the long-suffering and humanity of our beloved government and all our people . . . Just ask yourselves what more could this man want! The government had given him everything! A seat in the Academy. Praise. Awards. But it seems that all this is not enough! Now, what was I saying? Ah! So, they allege that the faith of the Soviet people in communism is on the ebb. What a vile slander!!! If they could only see with what love, with what enthusiasm, the workers of our region have built this magnificent Slogan!!! Completely without payment!!! Is not this an example of the new, communist approach to labour!!!? Does not this bear witness to the fact that, with every year, with every decade, our faith in communism strengthens and widens??!! The freedom-loving peoples of Africa . . . We have already heard what our comrade here has had to say about that . . .'

When the fountain of Kanareikin's eloquence had finally, with some difficulty, been turned off, Comrade Tsvetikov yelled all the appropriate 'long lives . . .' and 'glory tos . . .' and cut the ribbon. An avalanche of automobiles, from which could clearly be heard curses directed at the idiots who had organised this spectacle, poured on to the Avenue of Marxism-Leninism, heading directly for the yellow building which housed the Human Sciences Institute of the Academy of Sciences. Kanareikin tore off in his personal automobile. And I . . . Why the devil, I ask myself, have I been hanging about here if I haven't been allowed to say a single word! And I'm obliged to drag myself home on public transport, and what's more, with two changes.

I

Two changes! And I'm not just anyone, I'm the Head of the Department of Theoretical Problems of the Methodology of Scientific Communism, i.e. the Head of a department of the Institute whose director is still, for the moment, Kanareikin. I am a doctor of philosophy, a professor, a member of the editorial board of our leading philosophical journal, a member of countless Scientific Councils, committees, commissions, societies, the author of six monographs and a hundred articles. My textbook has been translated into all the semi-Western languages—Polish, Bulgarian, Czech, German, Hungarian. It's even about to be translated into Rumanian. It's generally accepted that at the next Academy elections I shall surely become a corresponding member. Even that scum Vaskin from the Higher Party School (HPS) is reconciled to this fact which is so disagreeable for him. Yet—two changes! No one would believe me if I told them. I could take a taxi, of course. But taxis cost a fortune. And prices are soaring every day. And what's more, you have to give the driver a tip, which is extremely humiliating. After all, no one gives us any tips! Again, I could walk. It's not very far. But that would be against my principles. A professor, almost a corresponding member—and walking home! It's ruled out by my rank.

Our institute and the department

Our Institute occupies the upper floors of the Yellow House. If you look from the Centre, our department is in the right-hand wing of the top storey. In the past, when the arrival of communism was expected from day to day, and the fall in prices of one kopeck per annum raised the hopes of even the unbelievers that it would happen any time (well, I'll be damned, they are going to build communism after all), our Institute was very small. In the days of Nikita, when the onset of communism was pushed a little further back into the somewhat ill-defined future of the 'present generation', the Institute doubled in size. And after Nikita was toppled, when prices began to rise irresistibly, and the promises of cost-free benefits came to be regarded by all as a mere joke, the Institute quadrupled in size. As a result of events which were well known to all, the sectors dealing with the struggle against anti-communism and revisionism, and with the development of Marxism by the brotherly parties of the West, East, South and North, were first established and then strengthened. And now, our Institute, in terms of the size of its staff (there are more than a hundred graduate students from the

(11)

non-Russian Republics alone!) has become one of the most powerful scientific organisations in the country. Five hundred quires of 40,000 characters each every year! If you reckon 20 quires to the average book, that means 25 fat volumes a year. Two hundred and fifty books in ten years!

'Now I understand why we've got such a paper shortage,' said Sashka, my son by my first (but, alas, not my last) wife, when he heard about this. 'You publish all this shit, and there's no paper left for anything decent.'

'You're just naive, Sashka,' said Tamurka (that's my present wife, Tamara). 'If you only knew how much paper is used for editions of the classics of Marxism and the speeches of our leaders, you wouldn't worry about a triviality like twenty-five books a year.'

'But it's just waste paper!'

'Of course it's waste paper. And we plan it ahead as waste paper.'

'So why spoil all that paper?' said Lenka, in astonishment. Lenka is my daughter by my second wife (by Tamurka, that is).

'Don't be silly! What about those obligatory minimum print-runs?'

'Well, why not say you are producing big editions, and print fewer? What difference would that make?'

'You'd lose your job for a start, and might even land in jail. Once anyone makes a speech, it's got to be a work of genius. Therefore you must print twenty million. And it's got to be put on sale. And its balance sheet has got to check out.'

'Surely no one buys these things?'

'Of course they do. The political education classes. The evening courses in Marxism-Leninism. Libraries, study circles. And look at all the students we've got. They've all got to be able to regurgitate this stuff in their exams.'

After a conversation like that, one could easily begin to feel pessimistic about the size of our Institute. And what can one say about the size of our department?! No more than fifty people altogether. But that does depend on your point of view. The department, one could say, is like my own child to me. I have spent almost twenty years of my life on its creation. When I first came to the Institute as a young Ph.D. candidate, the only people working on the methodology of the theory of scientific communism were three cretinous Stalinist yesmen in the Scientific Communism section. This section immediately grew into a department, but something a long way short of our department. With great difficulty I managed to get rid of one of these imbeciles, (catching him red-handed in immoral activity). The other two turned out to be quite bright lads and were easy enough to re-educate. Indeed, one of them went so far to the left that I constantly had to restrain him. I more than once had to tell him straight out that the criticism of Stalin wasn't to be taken seriously, but he didn't take my advice. Later he got rapped very sharply over the knuckles for his concessions to the Yugoslav revisionists. He was slung out of the Institute on the pretext of some injudicious remark about the Chinese. And then all trace of him disappeared. The rumour was that he'd been put into a psychiatric hospital. Today there are as many people in our department as there were in the whole Institute when I first went there. There's even talk about up-grading the department to an independent institute. But I'm in no hurry. I'm afraid that the same thing might happen to us as happened to the sociologists: as soon as the Department of Sociology inflated itself to eighty people, and then, when it split off from us as an independent institute, to five hundred, there was a massive pogrom against the sociologists. You've got to be careful. The business is far too serious to take unnecessary risks. But on the other hand you mustn't delay too much either. According to some certain unwritten laws of our life, if you want to hang on to what you achieve you've got to keep on pressing forward, i.e. ask for wage rises, plan new publications, get new sections set up, and so on. Otherwise you'll be accused of inaction and backwardness. How can one define the moment when one can say the time has come to make a move?

Many people confuse our department with the Department of Scientific Communism. But in fact there is a great difference between us. They have gathered together the most sombre figures of our national philosophy. The old ones are the 'escaped' Stalinists (that may sound rather comical, since the Stalinists were never victims of anything; the worst thing that happened to them was to be mocked a little in the wall newspaper). The young ones are cynical careerists who are prepared to do anything. And every one of them is completely, crassly ignorant. On the other hand, in our department we have the brightest and most capable representatives of our philosophy. Stupak, Nikiforov, Novikov, Tormoshilkina, Bulygin, and so on. There isn't a comparable constellation of names in any other philosophy establishment in the Union. It's no mere chance that we are so hated in the Academy of Social Sciences (A S S), in the H P S and in many other places. In comparison with us they feel themselves to be mere provincials and they accuse us of trying to turn Marxist theory into something elitist. But who stops them from writing good books themselves?!

The director of our competitor, the Department of Scientific Communism, is the most disgusting creature in our philosophy—that bitch, Tvarzhinskaya. For more than fifteen years she was the butt of all the sarcasm of the progressive young people of our Institute, but that is now all in the past. For some years now Tvarzhinskaya has been regarded as one of our leading lights! She used to be a close associate of Beria and an active agent of the secret police. Today she regularly travels abroad, and there's never been a single case when she's been refused an entry visa. Even prominent Western sociologists treat her as a colleague.

At home

When I got home I gave them a detailed account of the opening of the Slogan. My mother-in-law said that it was splendid. Sashka fell about on the divan clutching his sides. Lenka, without batting an eyelid, remarked that she would organise a trip from school to visit this remarkable monument of our culture.

'Nikita promised that communism would come within the lifetime of the present generation,' said Sashka. 'Who did he mean? His contemporaries, or newborn babies? Anyway, this promise has turned into a dirty joke. Now the date's been pushed back to some vague time in the future. That's easier to cope with. Anyone can always say that communism will come, and that we won't see any more of the scandals and outrages we see today. And for the meantime just hang on, because for the time being we've only reached a lower level. It may be the upper step of the lower level, but it's the lower level just the same.'

'Since the letters are cast in stainless steel,' said Lenka, 'your Slogan will stand there for ever. Shall I tell you a story? The President of the United States asked God when there would be an end to unemployment and inflation. "After you've gone," God replied. Our General Secretary asked God when communism would be built. "After I've gone," God replied.'

'It's easy enough for you to laugh,' I said. 'But I've got to earn your bread and butter at this business. Where do you think all this comes from—the apartment, the dacha, holidays, your transistor radios? Maybe we'll be able to buy a car soon.'

I need a car. I finally came to this conclusion on my way back from Cosmonaut Square. Close contact with the masses, who are particularly noticeable in public transport, causes me great irritation, and becomes offensive. Some old cow rammed her elbow in my side and then bawled me out on top of it. And I was so taken aback that I didn't even manage to pay her back in her own coin. Why are so many people unpleasant?

'Your father's right,' said Tamurka. 'Even a black sheep is worth fleecing. You get to be a corresponding member as quick as you can. I'm fed up with fighting my way through queues. And anyway, there's nothing decent in the shops these days.'

'Who are you calling a black sheep?' asked my mother-in-law.

'The Academy of Sciences,' said Lenka. 'Do you want a bet? They'll give the people who built the Slogan the Lenin Prize. It's as good as done.'

'Don't put yourself out on their behalf,' said Tamurka, who reckons that I should have been awarded at least a State prize long ago.

'Why shouldn't they get the prize?' said my mother-in-law. 'Building something like that isn't just writing some tatty little book. You need talent for that.'

(15)

The burden of glory

Dima Gurevich telephoned.

'Congratulations, old man! I have just seen your mug on television. It's true you were only one of a crowd, and you were only there for about a hundredth of a second, but it's something for a start. Now you've got it made—just let them try getting out of electing you.'

Then there were calls from Novikov, Nikiforov, Stupak, Korytov, Ivanov, Svetka, and the rest. The whole evening was ruined. The worst of it was that I didn't see myself at all: my mother-in-law was watching ice-hockey on the other channel. But on the whole it's a good thing that I've been seen on television. The news'll be round all Moscow by this evening, and it'll have its effect.

The last to phone was my old friend Anton Zimin. He said that he saw nothing at all funny in the story of the Slogan. Communism had been built here long ago, and it achieved its most classic form under Stalin. Today it had become somewhat less well defined under the influence of enforced contacts with the West. So the words: 'Long Live Communism' may be interpreted in the same sense as when we say 'Long Live the Soviet People', 'Long Live the CPSU', and so on. As far as the second part of the Slogan is concerned, it reflects an equally real phenomenon: this radiant future does indeed threaten all mankind. And it is no mere chance that the letters are made of steel: once installed, communism is here for ever.

'Certainly I congratulate you,' Anton concluded. 'But I must warn you: excessive glory gives birth to hatred and envy.'

Anton

Anton and I have a strange relationship. There is no single question on which we agree. But I find Anton's disagreement less irritating than the praises of others. My children adore him. All I ever hear is Uncle Anton thinks, Uncle Anton said,

What will Uncle Anton feel about that? Anton is the only one of my friends whom Tamurka does not despise. And she's got a remarkable flair for people. She even likes Natashka, Anton's wife, because Natashka doesn't make herself out to be an omniscient intellectual who understands everything; she considers her the ultimate authority on questions of food and fashion because Natashka manages to produce good meals and turn herself out well on Anton's miserable salary and her own even more miserable earnings.

Anton was arrested in 1945 and spent almost twelve years in the camps. When he came out I found him a job in the evening-class section of the philosophical faculty, and later as a junior research assistant in my own department. He was quite a bright lad, but a little bit cracked. He never managed to finish his thesis. He's submitted several articles to journals or symposia, but they have either been rejected or they've kept him hanging on (in other words, the pieces have been accepted but postponed from number to number and gradually 'forgotten'). So in the end he gave up. Then there was talk of firing him from the Institute. So I transferred him to a technical job consisting of preparing manuscripts for the press. Here he turned out to be irreplaceable. He re-worked the most stupid papers so that they became better than the best. Anton gained the reputation of being a first-class editor. The vice-president of the Academy himself tried to get him into his own editorial group, but he refused. He also refused to become assistant to the scientific secretary, even though his salary would have been almost doubled if he had accepted.

At the time when war veterans were given all sorts of awards, Anton became a central figure in the Institute: he has more military decorations than all the other Institute 'veterans' put together. Our 'veterans' almost all used to work in the political departments, on newspapers, magazines, special departments, 'smersh', and so on. But Anton never wore his medals, which always aroused Tvarzhinskaya's sincere distaste.

On one occasion the lads from the editorial board of our wall newspaper 'For a Leninist style' asked Anton to write an article for a special jubilee number. Anton described in detail the system of decorations which really existed during the war.

Then he told how one of the pilots in his regiment had become a Hero of the Soviet Union. According to him, it happened quite by accident. The deputy political commissar of the division, when he was censoring a report in the army newspaper, had tried to cross out the name of the man who was later to become a hero. But it looked as if, instead of striking the name out, the commissar had underlined it. And so the reporter who'd written the piece strengthened the passage in question by adding the number of missions the pilot had flown. As a result, the regimental and divisional authorities got excited and proposed the pilot for the decoration of Hero. Of course Anton's article was not published in the paper.

I've told Anton more than once that he is a cretin not to take advantage of all his possibilities. He merely shrugs his shoulders. I think that in the camps he must have gone off his head a bit. My hypothesis is clearly confirmed by the fact that Anton always brings any conversation on any subject back to the same theme: the way we live and who we really are. He gives the impression that he is pursuing some objective which only he can perceive, and that he doesn't give a rap for all our little cares and anxieties.

New times

The Institute brought out a special number of the wall newspaper on the opening of the Slogan. The front page had a portrait of the Leader, copied from the magazine 'Ogonyok'. The portrait turned out very funny. Beneath it appeared these lines by Tvarzhinskaya:

> Throughout the planet, the universe overall,
> Casting a chill fear on imperialism,
> Our deathless slogan propagates the call
> Long live communism!
> The freedom loving nations of the earth
> March on to communism cheek by cheek,
> Under the direction of our Central Committee of such
>   great worth,
> Which will be elected again at the Congress next week.

The entire Institute held its sides laughing. Novikov congratulated Tvarzhinskaya on her outstanding artistic success and advised her to send her verses to one of the major literary magazines. But Stupak said that the literary journals were all run by conservatives and that they would never publish verses of such bold poetic form. Tvarzhinskaya, who genuinely believed herself to be a true revolutionary in everything she undertook, grasped Stupak's hand with real feeling. When Kanareikin read the poem, there and then, standing in front of the newspaper, he held forth for an hour on the multi-faceted development of personality under communism. He ended his tearful improvisation with a quotation from another great poet:

> Sometimes tills the fertile loam,
> Sometimes writes a little poem.

Today it seems incredible that a mere five years ago this same wall newspaper published a 'philosophical poem'.

> Come, my sweetheart, come outside,
> Let's debate, my dearie.
> Everything can be explained
> By our Marxist theory.
>
> You've had your say, so now shut up.
> It's my turn now to natter.
> There's nothing in this world of ours,
> —Nothing, only matter.
>
> Come my sweeting, come my heart,
> Cease your girlish laughter.
> Existence came alone the first,
> Consciousness came after.
>
> Autumn nights are drawing in,
> The leaves are turning brown.
> The ideologue can grasp it all,
> Even upside down.
>
> The nightingale no longer sings
> In grove or bosky wood.
> Everything, both broad and long,
> Can be understood.

The faithful hound stands in the road,
And wags his faithful tail.
All agnostics must be crushed,
Rebutted without fail.

Do not kick me up the arse,
That tactic's had its day.
We must now approach the truth
The asymptotic way.

There's no way to get a drink,
It drives me up the wall.
Even the electron, so minute,
Does not reveal its all.

If I have to live with you,
I know that I'll be sorry.
Every intellectual step
Has its category.

Water from the dripping tap
Falls in an endless flow.
What is true and what is false
Practice will surely show.

In a side street t'other night
Some ruffians smashed my face.
The world exists in actual time
And, too, in actual space.

In the fields the gentle breeze
Sways the crimson flowers.
All is always on the move
In this world of ours.

No, my darling, do not err,
Nor yet doze off in dreams.
The only thing that moves the world
Is the conflict of extremes.

I simply can't get through your clothes
Your body's so encased.
Everything that's in the world
Is wholly interlaced.

If I ask for a fur coat,
It shouldn't give you pause.
There is not the slightest thing
Happens without cause.

Slow down, my little driver dear,
Speed is unavailing.
Quality can never come
If quantity is failing.

Beneath my window please restrain
Your fervent declarations.
One negation's followed fast
By yet more negations.

Give yourself a bath, my dear,
You don't smell too divine.
The world pursues a spiral course,
And not a direct line.

Take your hand from up my skirt
Your mind's always on sex.
Natural progress always leads
From simple to complex.

And will you leave my bra alone,
Stop fiddling with the thing.
All superstructures, every one,
From infrastructures spring.

I'm getting tired of all this crap
I babble as I sing.
It's class warfare, hard and sharp,
Keeps history on the wing.

Do not make me laugh, old girl,
With jokes of such inanity.
Individuals only thrive
As part of mass humanity.

Leave our girls alone, my friend,
Or else you'd best watch out.
The proletariat always leads
All progress without doubt.

What a load of crap you spout,
You're drunk out of your mind.
The proletariat always leads,
The peasants march behind.

Why do you roll your eyes to heav'n
Why wrinkle up your nose?
Leading on to victory
The workers' party goes.

My old woman's in a state
With anal embolism
Now Africa is haunted by
The ghost of communism.

No kisses now for me, my dear?
Don't stand stiff as a tree.
Papuans soon will make a leap
To the supreme degree.

Will you leave my tits alone?
Don't dare to slap my face.
According to our abilities
We'll soon proclaim our case.

Don't push me on the bed, you brute,
You know I'm wearing shoes.
When communism comes along
We'll scoff just what we choose.

Sit down, don't be in such a rush.
Don't take your boots off yet.
We'll gorge ourselves on powdered milk,
And eat all we can get.

You really are a funny girl,
You make me hoot with glee.
Every day we'll volunteer,
To work without a fee.

And your buxom figure, too,
Stands looking at, my love.
Every day we'll listen to
Directives from above.

(22)

In the fields the rampant weeds
Have still not turned to wheat.
But soon, my brothers, we will shit
Through a golden toilet seat.

That's my lot, I'll end my song,
My bladder's feeling sore.
The study of our theory
Will be our nightly chore.

It was that same Tvarzhinskaya, who had been dumped on our Institute from the KGB because she was useless to them, who declaimed from the rostrum of a party meeting her praise of the wall newspaper's editorial board for that 'philosophical poem'. The poem had made such a strong impression on her that it set her writing poetry herself. At this time it was I who was in charge of the wall newspaper on behalf of the party bureau. It was up to me whether I should allow her to go ahead or not. I gave her permission. Indeed, I could not have refused even if I had wanted to. Three years later the entire editorial board of the wall newspaper was dismissed for a completely anodyne edition. Again I was a member of the party bureau, and like all the rest voted for the censure of the editor. What else could I do? The editor himself was very happy to have escaped with a reprimand. At the party meeting the decision of the party bureau was unanimously approved, although there was a good deal of angry muttering in the corridors. And at the general meeting of the Institute, when a new editorial board was elected (which this time included Tvarzhinskaya), no one so much as raised a murmur of protest. And if someone had done so, what would have happened? Nothing special. The one who dared to protest would have suffered personally, and that's all. There would certainly have been no echo of public sympathy. So certainly we can be accused of cowardice. But does the problem lie there? I think not. Our problem is that in our circumstances it is completely nonsensical to exercise courage over trivia. And very few of us have access to genuinely important matters.

The decent soviet man

In the evening the Kuritsyns turned up at our place. They're
very decent people. Admittedly they're terribly grey, boring
and lifeless, but they are modest and honest. I've been friends
of theirs since my first year at university. They got married
during that first year. They are the only couple I know who
managed to avoid divorce. That pleases me, and I hold them up
to everyone as an example. Tamurka says that it's all a front,
and that in reality they sleep around like everyone else, except
that they do it on the quiet in their own gloomy way. And if they
don't get divorced, it's only because it's more profitable to stay
married. And at home they probably quarrel night and day like
cat and dog. But Tamara is a venomous, cynical woman,
although she isn't usually mistaken. I prefer to think of people
as being better than they actually are. It's more agreeable to live
among decent people.

Kuritsyn is a rather odd character. He's a keen motorist. He
puts his heart and soul into his automobile, but never drives it
anywhere. He's an excellent photographer, but the pinnacle of
his art in this field is a photomontage of a lavatory bowl and his
own grinning face. Recently he defended his doctoral dissertation. I was his official opponent. It was a very colourless thesis,
with ideas you could count on the fingers of one hand, but it was
conscientious, with no serious deficiencies—in fact, perfectly
acceptable. Kuritsyn had no pretensions to innovation—all he
wanted was to get the thesis accepted. After he was through,
however, his self esteem took an acute upturn. When I asked
him to act as official opponent of the thesis of one of my
students, he refused on the grounds that he was terribly busy;
then he changed his mind and agreed, thinking that I might still
be of some use to him. He said in his report that my student's
thesis was colourless, with ideas you could count on the fingers
of one hand, but that it was conscientious, with no serious
deficiencies, in fact, perfectly acceptable.

During dinner, the purpose of the Kuritsyns' visit became
clear. Their son was on the point of leaving school. He had

decided—he of all people!—to enrol in the philosophical faculty. I have a great deal of influence and good connections there. And the times are such that these days it is almost impossible for the children of intellectuals (the Kuritsyns—intellectuals!) to go straight on to higher education from school without some kind of pull. Of course, I'll do everything I can. But my Lenka's a problem as well. She still doesn't know where she wants to go. She's categorically rejected the idea of the philosophical faculty.

After the Kuritsyns had left, Tamurka declared that she never wanted to see these sickeningly decent friends of mine again.

'It's about time you revived some old acquaintanceships. Why have we never been to the Kanareikins, even though they've invited us quite often? And the Korytovs? Or the Ivanovs? I wouldn't even mind making our peace with the Vaskins. But you're always hanging about with drunks and very dubious characters.'

I muttered something about how bad I was at getting on with the right people. My mind was on the Kuritsyns. They really are decent people. And if they seem strange, it is only because they are Soviet people. Decent Soviet people. There's a strange phenomenon—a decent Soviet person. Take my sister, for example. She's a splendid woman, kind, receptive, honest, modest. You couldn't find a better person. Recently we exchanged our flat—to move in with my mother-in-law. The woman in charge of our flat-exchange looked very like my sister. At first I approached her with a smile, and she . . . b-r-r-r! It still gives me a chill to think about it. Oh, and then she had a really good go at me. Look at you, a professor, and you can't even fill a form in properly! Fine kind of professor you are! And suddenly the idea came into my head that my lovely gentle sister might be just as unbearable when she's in her own office. And one day I was able to see with my own eyes. She was totally unrecognisable. A minister! What am I saying, a minister? More like a militia officer. She spat her words out. And used expressions like 'Do you ever take the trouble to think?' or 'Are you going to stand there all day, or do you expect me to do it for you?'

We spend all our time complaining about something or someone. We are always looking for excuses outside ourselves, justifying ourselves by circumstances. But you only need to apply a little common sense, to observe the world about us, to perceive the simple truth: everything which we had or have is the product of our own existence. We have done, and do, everything ourselves—we, decent Soviet people.

On the other hand, how did we become as we are? After all it isn't inherent in our biological make up. In general terms there isn't any problem here: there was the human and social material handed down by history, and the Revolution opened the way along which the typical Soviet man and Soviet society were formed. But here there is a deeper problem: what is the mechanism for reproducing all this? The most interesting views on this matter are those I hear occasionally from Anton, or from my children, or from chance acquaintances, but never from professionals, neither from defenders of our way of life nor from its critics. I recently read a collection of essays called *From Beneath the Rubble*. I read it completely legally—behind an 'iron door', i.e. in the secret stacks of the library: I have a completely free access to literature of this kind because of my work. Shafarevich's article is interesting, but the rest is nonsense. Even that one article is clearly the work of a dilettante. It is said that Shafarevich was a great mathematician. Maybe. But as a social theorist he is nothing. It is ridiculous in our time to pretend to propound a theory of socialism without being a professionally trained specialist in Marxism and concrete sociology. It is odd how all the ideas put forward by our dissidents come to nothing, even though they are often wise and just. Yet even the most nonsensical ideas which swim along the channels of Marxism manage to survive and flourish. Why is this?

'For the very reason that the former are sensible and the latter nonsensical,' Anton once replied to this question. The former have no pretensions to exist on a scientific level. They remain in the sphere of ideology. And what ideology needs is specifically nonsense.

Lenka

Lenka read my article in the special number of the philosophical journal devoted to the Twenty-fifth Party Congress, or rather to the huge philosophical significance of its documents. It sent her into raptures.

'Papa!' she yelled all over our vast apartment, 'It's not all those people—it's you who are the real genius! You've got a wasted literary talent. You ought to be writing satirical pieces for the paper. No, even better; you should be writing complaints to the block management committee, or to the sanitary inspectors or to the Moscow fruit-and-vegetable-and-rubbish organisation about rotten potatoes and leaking taps. Just listen to what he's been writing: ". . . in the brilliant report of the outstanding leader of our party and of the whole worldwide communist movement . . . and of all progressive mankind . . . we have a brilliant general statement of the grandiose experience of the victorious and impetuous construction of communist society in our country, executed under the brilliant leadership of our communist party and personally of comrade . . . the brilliant successor and continuer of the work of the great Lenin, the outstanding theoretician and leader of our party and of the whole Soviet people, marching at the head of all progressive mankind . . . and all this expressed with a penetrating depth, breadth and extraordinary perspicacity . . ." No, Papa, you really ought to be writing novels. Tolstoi, Balzac, Dostoievski—they're all mere children compared to you. Why, given half a chance, you'd leave even Laptev way behind!'

'And who's Laptev?' I asked, wiping away the tears brought on by my hysterical laughter.

'He's never heard of Laptev,' cried Lenka, with some indignation. 'He's the greatest Soviet socialist realist. He only needs to scribble any old rubbish for everyone in school to be forced to study it as an example of socialist realism. He's won every prize five times—(from the Stalin to the Lenin). Hero of Soviet Labour. Delegate. Member of the Supreme Soviet and so on, and so on, and so on.'

'Very well,' I said. 'So I write a novel. What do I do with it then?'

'That's no problem,' said Lenka. 'The first thing is to hide it so carefully that no one knows anything about it. Otherwise the KGB'll sniff it out and you'll be done for. Or better still, get it circulated via samizdat or printed abroad. That's what everyone does these days. Since Solzhenitsyn got to be world famous, one in three Soviet intellectuals is either writing or planning to write something anti-Soviet.'

'Just you think what you're saying,' I replied. 'If I so much as had a thought of writing an underground book I'd be expelled from the party and sacked. And what'd happen to you? Sashka'd have to go off to Siberia, and you'd never get to see the inside of any institute.'

'If you've got any idea of attacking the system,' said Tamurka, 'don't behave like these idiotic dissidents. They spend all their time debating all these high-flown ideas like freedom of speech, creative individuality, and the right to emigrate, and never a word about what really matters—that there isn't a sausage worthy of the name in the shops.'

The guideline

That swine Vaskin has got in ahead of me again. While I was contorted with shame at the thought of the careerist speech I had dreamt up through the sleepless night, and which I was preparing myself to deliver at this meeting, Vaskin had the effrontery to ask to speak first, and blurted out the very thing that I had intended to say. In his concluding remarks he proposed the preparation of a collective work which would summarise the rules which had governed our progress towards communism in the period between the Twentieth and Twenty-fifth Party Congresses. And he drew applause from the audience. He's certainly a skilful rogue! But I did not lose my head. I spoke calmly at the end of the meeting, and said that our department had been maturing the idea of such a work for a considerable time. It was clear that rumours of our work had got as far as the Academy of Social Sciences (ASS) and the Higher Party School (HPS). And so responsibility for the preparation of the work was entrusted to our department. Of course, it was proposed that leading scholars from the ASS, HPS and other organisations should also participate. Vaskin was included in the editorial board.

On the way home my excitement at this victory began to cool off a little. And I told myself what a cretin I was. You've already got one epoch-making work on the methodology of the theory of scientific communism hanging round your neck, and that's not enough for you. What use will this one be to you? Still, taking on this job will mean that we should be able to argue for ten new posts in the department. We'll have to start a new section. The department will be huge—almost an institute in its own right. On the whole, I've done the right thing. Otherwise the work would have gone ahead anyway, except that it would have fallen into the hands of Vaskin and his band of idiots. Just imagine what kind of rubbish they'd have written!

While thinking along these lines, I was gripped by an access of honesty with myself. The period between the Twentieth and Twenty-fifth Party Congresses was truly remarkable. What possibilities opened before us! There is a school of thought which argues that the Soviet intelligentsia did not take advantage of these possibilities, or rather that they took advantage of them only to the extent of sorting out their own little personal problems. Of course, there is an element of bitter truth in this, but on the whole this opinion is unjust. We—(I am a typical representative of the liberal Soviet intelligentsia of this period, and so I have the right to use the word 'we')—we did achieve something all the same. And I think that achievement was not inconsiderable. We did what we could, what was within our strength to do. The fact that our strength was limited is another matter. But that was not our fault. The fact that we did not go to jail, that we did not immolate ourselves in public places, that we did not erupt in protest demonstrations and get beaten up, was not because of our cowardice and self-interest. It was more complicated than that. When we start work on our book, we shall have to go into this question among others. We must not go bull-headed at it, of course, but more subtly, so that no one will have anything overt to complain about, and yet in such a way that the intelligent reader will know what we are talking about. I discussed these thoughts with Novikov, the head of one of the sections of our department.

'Rubbish,' he said. 'We can have only one guideline: delay our completion date as long as possible, turn out some verbiage so that no one can start pestering us, hold a discussion meeting, thank everyone for their valuable comments, and screw another year out of them for putting finishing touches, etc. In general terms, we must do everything we can to ensure that those bastards from the ASS and the HPS don't devour us. You mustn't forget that for ages now we've had all the provincial universities, and all the chairs in the capital, in fact everyone who doesn't think of themselves as men of the sixties, the elite of liberal Marxism flirting with the West—we've had all that lot baring their fangs at us for a long time. My dear chap, at the present time we ought to be thinking about saving our skins rather than getting fat. We must just take care that they don't destroy us, like the pogroms against the sociologists and the historians.'

'I don't think that's likely,' I said. 'The meeting came out on our side. Look, all the important ideological posts went to our people.'

'That's of no consequence at all. Whatever happens they'll act according to circumstances, not because of any personal sympathies or antipathies or of past relationships. And the circumstances are against us. Our time is over. We might have a year or two still, because of inertia. Perhaps you'll even have time enough to make it as corresponding member: I hope to God you do! But we won't get anything useful done. So why the f—— are we beating our brains out?'

'I simply don't understand you. We've got our consciences and our duty. We must do something.'

'Absolutely! We must do everything in our power to do nothing.'

'What an attitude to start writing a book!'

'If it's the book that's worrying you, I can write that crap for you in six months from my left foot. I'm talking about our situation. What's the book got to do with it? We have to think about our situation, not about the book.'

'Our situation's excellent. Why worry about that?'

'As ever, your judgements are behind the times. In the past that worked to your advantage, because your lagging behind kept you on good terms with the Stalinists. But it's not like that any more. Now we're rolling downhill. Just watch out. From now on, delay will work against you. What you need now is to be just ahead of the times.'

Our paradoxes

From her earliest childhood Lenka acquired the nasty habit of disturbing me when I am working. She knows that it makes me angry, and that I enjoy being angry, and this pleases her. These moments are some of the most agreeable of my life. At this moment she is wandering around my study behind my back. She is very thin, very tall, and very sarcastic. And she is declaiming poetry in a voice which she thinks is very solemn, but which in fact is extremely comic.

> Let us end this empty quarrel for a space,
> And let all our unbelief be set aside.
> Let that Radiant Edifice now come to pass,
> Let the Pearly Gates be now flung open wide.

'We really are quite a family,' I say. 'A father who's an orthodox Marxist, one of the leading communist theoreticians. And children who are almost dissidents.'

'Oh, don't you worry,' says Lenka. 'Butter wouldn't melt in our mouths compared with Kanareikin's Mongrel.'

Mongrel is Kanareikin's son, a student in the philosophical faculty (Department of Scientific Communism, of course), an egregious idiot, but one who knows where's he's going. He is secretary of the Komsomol for his year.

'At home,' Lenka continues, 'he's got every recording of Okudzhava, Galich and Vysotsky. Books by Orwell, Zamyatin, Solzhenitsyn. And *Kontinent*. And *From Beneath the Rubble*. And *The Third Wave*. He's got two copies of *Gulag*.'

'Not bad,' I say. 'If they find out at the faculty, that'll be the end of him. You get put in jail just for reading *Gulag*.'

'Nothing'll happen to him,' says Lenka. 'His position's un-assailable: we must know our enemy thoroughly so as to be able to oppose him effectively! D'you know what his thesis subject is? "Dissidents in the service of imperialism". So there!'

Let the mighty trumpets bellow out their call,
When those in power above us deem it meet.
Let the fortunate elect come, one and all,
At Heaven's Gates shake their sins from off their
    feet.

'Who wrote that?'

'One of our lads.'

And in fragrance sweet of equity benign,
The true incarnation of Marxism's lore,
The leaders will address us gently, 'Swine!
Do you not take orders from us any more?
Don't just stand there, fool, get moving now, I
    tell ye,
And if you're guilty, then it's banished you shall
    be.
Come on into communism: fill your belly
With glorious sweetmeats all washed down with
    tea.'

'You know what,' I say. 'I'm not Kanareikin yet. So please don't bring any more of this anti-Soviet stuff into the house. If you go on like this, where will it all end?'

'Oh, heavens, I'm late. I'll finish it for you some other time. See you! I've got an important rehearsal.'

The surprise

This was before the meeting. I got a phone call from the police station asking me to go in on some important matter. I went into the office indicated, where I found waiting for me three men whose affiliation to a certain organisation was in no doubt at all. One of them introduced himself, showed me his ID card, and immediately handed me a thick file.

(32)

'Would you please take a look at this manuscript—just skim through it—and then tell us your opinion on a number of matters which interest us: (1) how does this manuscript relate to our ideology; (2) what is its scientific value; (3) what reaction could we expect to it in the West; (4) would it be wiser to prevent its publication or to permit it; (5) if it is to be published, what would be the best form?'

It was not the first time I had been asked to do this kind of work, so I was in no way surprised. I calmly opened the file and . . . felt petrified. The first page bore the words: 'A. I. Zimin. Communism—Ideology and Reality'. In utter confusion I raised my eyes to those of my interlocutor.

'Yes,' he said. 'This manuscript—or rather a photocopy—is by your colleague A. I. Zimin. But don't let it worry you. We won't report this fact to the Academy for the time being at least. Of course, if the book is published, then what happens after that will be entirely in the hands of your colleagues. For now, we're just interested in the questions I asked you.'

'But I can't determine the qualities and demerits of a manuscript this size just like that. Can you give me an evening at least . . .'

'Unfortunately that can't be done. So don't let's waste time, have a look at it now. As far as we know, you are already fairly familiar with the ideas anyway . . .'

I began to read. My forehead came out in a cold sweat. My hands trembled. The comrade from There told me to calm down and poured me a glass of tepid, stinking water from a carafe which clearly hadn't been changed since our last meeting.

We distinguish, I read, between real communism and ideological communism—not in the sense generally accepted by both the apologists and enemies of communism, that is to say in the sense that the reality of communism does not coincide with its ideological schema, but in the sense that the former is a certain real state of society, and that the latter is a certain aggregate of just as real texts. A classic example of the former is furnished by Soviet society, and particularly society during the Stalin epoch. In the post-Stalin period, under the influence of contacts with the West and the fear of the recent mass purges, Soviet society to a certain extent smoothed out its classic communist aspect. But this was only as far as certain extremes were concerned, and not in its essence, which now and ever more is condemned to be Stalinist (or Leninist, which is the same thing; but the former expression is more accurate). Communism is ideologically set out in the immense literature of Marxism, so it might seem that there is little need to say anything on this subject. But a brief note on it may be useful, for the following reasons. During the Stalin epoch ideological communism attained a level of striking clarity, which threatened to strip bare its essense and reveal it to the broad masses of the population and not merely to those individuals for whom it had already lost its fascination as the pinnacle of human thought. And the criticism of the Stalinist 'vulgarisation' of Marxism-Leninism had the practical aim of returning it to its former (pre-Stalin) confused state which was more in accord with the nature of the ideology. And in this respect the criticism achieved such significant success that now no trace remains of the former (classic) Stalinist clarity. We shall try to set out the bases of ideological communism (Marxism-Leninism) as closely as possible to their Stalinist models. The more so, since its post-Stalin 'development' has brought to it absolutely nothing essentially new or worthy of attention if we leave aside revisionist deviations from its general line.

We consider that communism as an ideology (Marxism-Leninism) is totally adequate to communism as a real social structure. But adequate not in the sense that science is adequate to the object it studies (Marxism-Leninism is not a science; it is an ideology, i.e. something different in principle from a science), but in the sense in which an ideology is adequate to the society in which it dominates. But we also consider that there is as yet no science dealing with communist society as an empirically given reality. A rich literature critical of the Soviet way of life has already developed. It is enough here to mention the works of Zamyatin, Orwell, Solzhenitsyn and many other authors of the recent past. This literature contains many true observations. But the sum of these observations and the generalisations drawn from them do not of themselves consti-

tute a science of communism in the true sense of the word
'science'. Here we shall attempt to set out at least the bases of
the science of communism (of the scientific understanding of
communism) as far as we have been able to identify them,
working, as we have been, in total creative isolation and in
conditions which seem to have been specially created in order to
inhibit the slightest attempts to acquire such understanding.

When I had glanced through the book, I said that the picture
was completely clear to me. The book was obviously anti-
Marxist, although superficially the author appears to have a
calm and respectful attitude to Marxism. And that was easy to
understand: at the present time Marxism in the West is
experiencing a new and powerful upsurge, and if the author
were to speak out openly as an anti-Marxist, he would simply
find no readers. The scientific value of the book was minimal,
as almost all its ideas had already been discussed in some form
or other in Western literature of a similar kind. But since the
book was by a Russian author, who during the Stalin period had
spent more than ten years in prison, and since it was written in a
lively and accessible style, it would arouse interest and would
probably be translated into western languages. So this was a
very serious matter, and if possible its publication Over There
should be prevented. I think that in fact this would be better for
the author himself.
    'You know Zimin. Might he change his mind about publish-
ing the book if we have a word with him? We could promise him
our help in getting a corrected version published here, and
having it accepted straight away as a doctoral dissertation. On
the other hand, if he published this book abroad, that might be
interpreted as a hostile act, with all the consequences that might
follow.'
    'Zimin is a determined man. I doubt whether he'd agree to
that.'
    'You see, very probably they'd be very enthusiastic about
this book Over There. I don't know whether we'd be able to
stop its appearance altogether. But at least there's a chance of
postponing its publication until after the Congress.'
    'Of course'—I heartily supported this idea. 'Before the Con-

gress, and even for some time after the Congress' (I should really have said until after the Academy elections, but of course I kept my mouth shut) 'this book could attract a great deal of attention Over There. It must be held back!'

'But we'll need your help.'

'I'm at your service. What do I have to do?'

'We think we've got a solution that might work . . .'

For several days I was completely under the influence of Anton's book. Although I had only had time to leaf through it briefly, I had seen a great deal in it. Anton and I had discussed these topics dozens of times. I was already familiar with everything in the book. But here everything had been brought together and set out systematically. The effect was devastating. It was the general method which produced the greatest impression. Anton did not criticise Marxism and the Soviet way of life in the way which is generally accepted everywhere. He accepted everything as fact. He even accepted our most extreme demagogic pronouncements as truth. He looked an even more orthodox Marxist than I. For example, we all moan about the collapse of agriculture, about rising prices, about waste in the economy and so on. But Anton accepted as truth the statements of our leaders (he even quoted from our newspapers) to the effect that Soviet society today is more monolithic than it has ever been socially, politically and ideologically; more powerful than ever economically, and so on. And he set out the bases of Marxism in a way which can only be described as brilliant. Clearly, briefly, convincingly. And that creates a feeling of unease. It was as if you were being flayed alive, leaving your body like one vast wound. You can't be touched anywhere without being in agony.

'There is one thing that worries us particularly in this case,' said the comrade from There. 'We have read the book very carefully. It seemed completely Marxist to us. But at the same time there is something deeply hostile in it, and we non-specialists find it very hard to see exactly what. That's why we asked you . . .'

If they only knew that even for me it's not too easy to sort out the answers.

(36)

I thought about everything except the moral aspect of what had happened. It was as if this side of things simply didn't exist.

Academician Kanareikin

Academician Kanareikin is a symbolic figure in our philosophy. He first appeared on the philosophical arena at a time when even in the Institute of the Red Professorate the statement that Stalin was a philosopher was greeted with laughter. Kanareikin was one of the first to recognise Stalin not merely as a philosopher, but as a philosopher of genius and a classic of Marxism. In return for this Stalin offered him (and a few other characters of the same mould) an immediate place in the Academy. The others accepted, but Kanareikin's excessive honesty and humility were his undoing. And he became a mere corresponding member of the Academy of Sciences, having neither a master's nor a doctor's degree, without even being a university lecturer. After that it took him almost thirty years to pay for these stupid scruples of conscience: he was not elected a full Academician until after Stalin's death. When he finally did become an Academician he made all speed to recover the wasted opportunities of the past. In a few years he delivered at least a thousand tearfully enthusiastic speeches, thereby winning for himself the reputation of a lyrical Marxist and a leading phrase maker throughout the entire socialist camp, and put his name to hundreds of books and papers, written for him by his subordinates (rumour had it that he had never learnt to write himself). Towards the end of the fifties he was appointed director of our Institute, with the result that the whole extraordinary upsurge of Soviet philosophy in the sixties was associated with his name. It was under his aegis in particular that the consequences of the 'cult of personality' in the field of philosophy were overcome.

Kanareikin's method of direction deserves a separate study. Here I shall confine myself to a very brief comment. By every means available to him, Kanareikin interfered with our work, delayed the publication of books, the printing of papers, the submission of theses, the organisation of conferences and our taking part in them and so on. And we did everything in our own way, as if he did not exist. And when we did our work, he praised us and turned our work to the benefit of the Institute he directed. For example, let us say we had completed a book. Kanareikin would take the manuscript and say that until he had read it, it should not be published. And then he immediately forgot about the book, since he was always deeply engaged in affairs of epoch-making importance. We submitted the book to all the proper authorities, printed it and presented a copy to him, with our gratitude. With tears in his eyes, he would thank us, praise our work, and rush off to the Central Committee, the Ministry, the City Committee or to any other responsible authority to disseminate terror with threats against revisionists, warnings that he would sweep away deviationists, and root out error. And things followed their course. And Kanareikin grew accustomed to everything going along exactly as he wished, and what he wanted was in complete accord with the directives from above. And indeed such was the case because such were the times. But those times have now disappeared irrevocably into the past. Kanareikin has become the object of general mockery. He will soon be removed and transferred to some highly paid sinecure.

Almost half of Kanareikin's published work has been written by me, or under my direction. So that when Kanareikin is denounced in my presence for his primitive approach, his ignorance and his stupidity, I sometimes feel ill at ease. On such occasions it seems to me that the company is giving me knowing looks, even though formally no one knows the measure of my participation in Kanareikin's work. And if they guess, then it is only on the basis of indirect hints: Kanareikin has always protected me. I have become so skilful at preparing work for him that it seems, even to him, that he has done it all himself. I have even developed a special Kanareikin style which is fundamentally different from my own. Not even a computer could detect my hand in Kanareikin's works. It seems that the authors of Stalin's works, too, were selected for their similar capacity for reincarnation. Of course they have been liquidated. And just try now to identify them! So, now and for ever more

Stalin goes down in history as the author of many books some of which are masterpieces of Marxist literature (whatever people say about them today). The same goes for Kanareikin. It is quite certain that a collected edition of his work will be published, and incidentally it will include what are far from being the worst texts in Marxist literature. And will there ever be a complete edition of my works? Are they significantly superior to those I have written in Kanareikin's name? He has the advantage of age and priority. And even the abject role he played in the establishment of Stalinism is to his advantage: at all events he remains a major figure, even though one with a minus sign. His descendants will be astonished when they read his works, and they will receive a totally distorted impression of our times, and of us who have played a part in them. Yet how can it be otherwise if even we, ourselves, have fundamentally distorted the picture of our own life? We are born in lies and evil. And in lies and evil we will pass into history. We even lie the truth, and do good as if it were evil.

'Explain to me,' Anton said once, 'how is this possible? Marxist-Leninist theory offers the most profound, the most exhaustive, the most correct, the most this, the most that, interpretation both of the general laws of history and the laws of our society, and still more so of the laws of their society Over There, and of the concrete phenomena of our existence, and self-evidently of all the concrete phenomena of their existence Over There. You have said that more than once in your own books. And you have taken a hand in writing the appropriate passages in reports at the very highest level. Isn't that so? And of course you sincerely believe all this. Yet at the same time you know perfectly well how our cadres of Marxist theoreticians are selected and trained. They are the inept, the self-seekers, the idlers, the lunatics, the villains, and what have you. Their education is a matter of cultivated ignorance. You often complain that you cannot find a decent graduate student. Yet every year we produce hundreds of little jackals ready to do anything to get their doctorates. And you've often said that our newspapers and journals are full of downright lies and blatant nonsense. We're up to our ears in lies and hypocrisy. How is this possible? How can it be that such human resources, working

(39)

under such conditions, can create this thing which is the most this, the most that, the most everything . . .?'

'Theory is one thing, and the people who preach it and defend it are another,' I said, uncertainly, since I had no real weapons to meet this argument. 'After all, the same kind of thing can happen in the natural sciences, when correct ideas are defended by cretins, rogues and careerists.'

'That does happen but it's quite a different thing. Once science becomes a social phenomenon of the mass, certainly there will be inept careerists who will milk it for all its worth. But if it is obliged to preserve its status as a science, it must necessarily contain a certain nucleus of able, literate and conscientious people. If not, it is not a science but an imitation of a science, of which today there are many. No, my friend, there's quite a simple solution. Your theory is in no way a science in the proper sense of the word. Even its pretensions to be "the most what-have-you", are purely ideological pretensions. And the atmosphere of lies is its natural milieu.'

Sometimes I wonder whether, if I had adopted Anton's position, I would have been able to produce anything like his book or not. When I listen to Anton, or other men of his kind, I understand everything. And at the time it seems to me that I could have come out with the same sort of thing myself. But in the depths of my subconscious I can feel that this is not true. I simply could not have done what Anton does. I do not have either the voice, nor the ear, for it. I do what I can. What I do I might have done better. Much better. But this is precisely the opportunity that I lack. I could have become brilliant and authoritative even in the ranks of the enemies of Marxism. I can feel that. But that is what my colleagues and my bosses of all ranks fear more than anything else. It would be easier for them to forgive me for revisionism (there's no need to make a fuss about it, we've seen this kind of thing before!), than for a vivid and talented defence of orthodox Marxism. This may even seem a trifle comical, but in practical terms I have fallen into the same situation as Solzhenitsyn in literature and Neizvestniy in art. It is strange that I find this analogy flattering. People say that the basic principle which drove Penkovsky to treason was that he came to understand that he could never realise his professional potential. I can just imagine what a rumpus would be raised in the West if I repudiated Marxism and began to revile it!

If only my colleagues suspected what thoughts wander round my head! Who am I in their eyes? I know perfectly well: benevolent, hard-working, not particularly stupid (but of course more intelligent than Kanareikin, which is the easiest thing in the world!); a careerist, with dreams of becoming a corresponding member, then an Academician, then . . .; but an individualist; a careerist typical of the sixties. Normal Soviet careerists move slowly from step to step, giving those around them an impression of complete legitimacy; while those like me skip some steps and rise thanks to their 'personal capacities', which irritates everyone, both their friends and their enemies.

The golden age

Our apartment is splendid. The Academy gave me a three-roomed apartment. My mother-in-law had a two-roomed flat to herself (her husband is dead and her daughters got married). Tamurka insisted that we should all get together, despite my opposition. These days everyone tries to live apart rather than join up. And they are right to do so. But anyway, we now have a five-roomed apartment, which for the average Soviet intellectual is something quite out of the ordinary. Apart from that, guests in our home are fed and watered very well, thanks to Tamurka. And so we always have guests, who usually turn up without invitation and often even without warning, quite impromptu. And that we like. Even my mother-in-law has come to like having people in and having a drink or two. She's even rather bored if no one comes by.

Today, Dima Gurevich and his wife turned up unannounced. Then Anton and Natasha appeared. Edik Nikiforov, a member of the department, telephoned. I told him to come round with his wife and, if he felt like it, to pick up another colleague Semyon Stupak, and bring him along too. So in the end we had quite a party.

Dima is an inveterate anti-Semite. It is the fashion in certain Jewish circles, in the same way that it is fashionable with some Russian intellectuals to vilify the Russian people. And anyway, if you've got a nose like Dima's it is permissible. But how about me?! Everyone is convinced that I am a Jew, or at the very least half-Russian and half-Jewish. Me, a product of the peasantry of Tula Province, and the face of a classic Ivan! That sod, Vaskin (who for sure is at least half Jewish!) started a rumour that it wasn't true that I was half-Russian, half-Jewish, but that I was half-Jewish and half-Jewish. Like every Jew brought up in an old Bolshevik family, Dima is an impassioned champion of authentic original Russian culture, which manifests itself in balalaikas, traditional wooden dolls, folk songs, carved window-surrounds and folk dances. When I said to Dima that the so-called Russian dances had been invented by Jews, and that as far as genuine Russian culture was concerned, the Russians had invented classical ballet, he almost had a stroke.

'Well, then, my friends, we'll probably be pushing off quite soon,' said Dima, after his second glass (after the first he'd started talking about balalaikas).

'To return to the land of your forefathers?' Anton asked.

'You must be off your head,' said Dima, indignantly. 'To Canada, or the States. Paris at worst. Such, alas, is the sad fate of the advanced Russian intelligentsia.'

Edik Nikiforov immediately dashed off an impromptu poem on the subject.

Now I can see what a fool I have been
To be born a mere Ivan; my God, was I green!
And it matters not how I trim my genitalia,
My attempts to be Moishe are, alas, doomed to failure.
No matter my rages, never mind what I do,
My passport will never declare me a Jew.
The secret police will not say 'He's a Yid;
There's no point nicking him, boys, whatever he did.'
But alas, I'm an Ivan, so I've got to stay,
Building heaven on earth for some subsequent day,
So my children may wail as they stand at heav'n's door:
'Why am I not a Jew, but an Ivan so pure?'

(42)

But if we're objective, there's really no doubt,
This whole sorry mess has been turned inside out.
'Twas not Moishe's idea, it was Ivan's device,
To think of creating this new paradise.
Yet in forging this heaven, for one and for all,
Our poor wretched Ivan ends up with f—— all.

'Not bad,' said Dima. 'But the situation's changed now. Have you heard the story about a Russian and a Jew applying for exit visas? The Russian got his but the Jew didn't, because according to his passport he was a Jew. Well, [and here Dima mentioned a number of typically Russian surnames] have got permission to leave for Israel. That is now the legal form of emigration. So if you're a Russian, and you want to get the hell out of it, declare that you're a Jew.'

Then we began to chat about our epoch-making collective work.

'Papa thinks this period is the Golden Age of our history,' said Lenka. 'He says that before it was worse, and it will be worse again afterwards.'

'That's quite something, coming from the leading Marxist-Leninist of the entire socialist camp,' said Dima. 'Don't you realise that that's the point of view of renegades and slanderers? And revisionists as well. And of pinkish Western communists who dream of setting up their own liberal model of communism with only three barbed wire fences instead of four, like we have. In our country, my friend, it has never been worse. It has always been, is now, and always will be, better.'

Suddenly Sashka, who normally keeps very quiet, broke into the conversation: 'This last, stinking, period of our history is justified if only by the fact that it has produced remarkable people, like Solzhenitsyn, Sakharov, and others, who have brought a faint light into many of our little minds, and also a faint hope that not all the humanising process applied to the two-legged genus will be lost in oblivion but may even produce a few results.'

'Your Solzhenitsyn is an idiot,' said Tamurka. 'He spends his time telling them Over There how they should live—as if they need his help to sort it out.'

Then we talked about Stalin, about the circumstances of his death, and about Khrushchev's secret speech. Stupak said that Beria had prepared this speech for himself, and that Nikita had grabbed it. And he talked in some detail about the behaviour of the leadership during this period. Where did he get it all from? He claimed that much of it came from the Western press, much of it from ours, much from unofficial conversation, and the rest by means of historical interpolation and extrapolation. And he gave a brilliant demonstration of this, using one example. He's a very able lad. But unfortunately he gets too bogged down in facts, and is too pedantic and preoccupied with minor detail. I do not see how we can use him on our book. He has suggested that he should take on all the factual side. Heaven preserve us! That is exactly what we don't need. After all, we are theoreticians.

'By the way, have you heard the latest?' said Dima, as he was leaving. 'They've closed the Central Swimming-pool.'

'Why's that?' asked Sashka, in surprise. 'I was there yesterday, and it didn't . . .'

'They're using it to develop a photograph of our leader,' said Dima, without the hint of a smile.

So you can see the difficulties of having a serious discussion in conditions like that! Then we walked everybody home. We all live in the same area. It's very convenient.

'Yes, very convenient,' said Anton. 'You only need to put barbed wire round the area, set up a few watch-towers and guards, and the problem of Soviet democracy would be solved once for all.'

I reminded Anton of his promise to let me have a brief summary of his thoughts on the period we were considering. As soon as our guests had departed, Tamurka and I immediately returned to our situation of mutual alienation and withdrew into our separate rooms. For a long time now we have led independent lives. As my intellectual mother-in-law puts it, we even sleep as separate members. I am completely indifferent as to how and where she spends her evenings, and sometimes her nights. From time to time she blackmails me by threatening to write a report to the party bureau, describing my real moral character. What is it that keeps her with me? Habit. Money.

(44)

The apartment. The villa. The hope that in the end I will become a corresponding member, which would give us access to the special food store for the privileged.

Anton brought the summary of his ideas round the following day.

New demands

As Marx put it, a demand once satisfied engenders a new demand. As soon as the citizens who live around Cosmonaut Square had had their fill of the delightful spectacle of the Slogan, 'Long Live Communism', they felt a new need—to mess it up. And soon the concrete pedestal was covered in coarse graffiti, among which figured prominently that world-famous four-letter word. According to Stupak, the Gallup Institute in the United States has established that not even the word 'sputnik' is more widely known throughout the world. And somehow or other the hooligans discovered a way of sticking their fag-ends and used matches to the steel letters. One letter was defaced to such an extent that it produced a spelling mistake. A group of old Bolshevik pensioners wrote a letter to the paper. Journalists rushed to the scene of the crime. A satirical article appeared about the way in which we defend our cultural heritage. The article reached the city committee of the party, who gave the go-ahead to the regional committee, the regional committee leant on the party bureau, the party bureau leant on the Komsomol bureau. A meeting of the Komsomol was summoned. And with great enthusiasm the Komsomol of the Institute took charge of the Slogan. A group of vigilantes was formed from the younger members of the staff. And the permanent guard kept watch over the Slogan every evening.

Of course those who stood guard duty were students and junior research assistants who, on account of their youth, were inclined to drunkenness. And since the Slogan was close to the 'Youth' café and a supermarket with a well-stocked wine and spirits department, the vigilantes didn't waste their time. For a start, when they had got themselves thoroughly drunk they picked a fight with casual passers-by. The police naturally took the side of the vigilantes, since the institute from which they came was a model of the embryos of communist democracy, of the communist organs of self-management (or domination) of society. And the affair was hushed-up. But soon the vigilantes got so thoroughly plastered that all of them, with just one exception, were carted off to the cooler. The exception was a lad who had fallen into the gap between two letters and was not discovered. When night came he was stripped by a bunch of hooligans. Following these events a considerable educational programme was started in the institute. The vigilante group was expanded to include a few senior research assistants who were party members. One of these was an old and experienced alcoholic. He set about teaching his young colleagues how to get drunk without getting into trouble.

'The main thing,' he told them, 'is to make personal friends of the police. On the day of the meeting when I was to be admitted to the party, I was put inside for fourteen days for a breach of the peace. Well, I was released simply on my word of honour. Those times have passed now, of course. So you see, lads, you have to know how to hold your liquor.'

Anton Zimin's reflections

The period of Soviet history which has just passed, wrote Anton, and which I shall call the period of Confusion and Stabilisation, was one of the most interesting periods not only of the history of the peoples of the Soviet Union, but also of the history of mankind in general. Chronologically the period extends from the Twentieth to the Twenty-fifth Congress of the CPSU. Of course these limits are not absolute: in certain spheres of Soviet life this period began a little before the Twentieth Congress of the CPSU, and in others rather later; in certain spheres it ended before the Twenty-fifth Congress of the CPSU, and in others later. The chronological limits I have referred to are arbitrary. But since they are official landmarks in Soviet history, they are convenient. And they are objective, since

(46)

in the Soviet Union real history in one way or another tends to become identified with the way in which it is officially represented, and for all practical purposes we have virtually no unofficial history. Soviet history really (and not merely apparently) is a history of congresses, meetings, plans, obligations, overfulfilments, conquests of new fields, new departures, demonstrations, decorations, applause, folk-dances, farewell ceremonies, arrival ceremonies, and so on; in brief, everything which can be read in official Soviet newspapers, journals, novels, or which can be seen on Soviet television, and so on. There are certain things which happen in the Soviet Union which do not appear in the media of mass information, education, persuasion, and entertainment. But all this represents in this context an immaterial non-historic background to real Soviet history. Everything which, to an outside observer who has not passed through the school of the Soviet way of life, may seem a falsehood, demagogy, formalism, a bureaucratic comedy, propaganda, and so on, in fact represents the flesh and blood of this way of life, in fact this life itself. And everything which may seem to be bitter truth, the actual state of things, commonsense considerations, and so on, is, in fact nothing but the insignificant outer skin of the real process. If that is not understood it is impossible to understand the essence of the Soviet way of life, this classic model of the communist system towards which, in one way or another, all mankind is tending to progress.

If, for example, we take such a striking fact of Soviet history of the previous (Stalinist, tragic) period, as the millions of victims on the one hand, and on the other the discussions about humanism, about the strengthening of socialist legality, about the battle against enemies of the people, and so on, which so saturated the spiritual atmosphere of the society, we will perceive that it is these apparently futile discussions which form a more dominant part of the corpus of Soviet history than the very real, and now quantified, purges. I have deliberately chosen this example, although it exposes me to the risk of being accused of Stalinist apologetics, in order to express my basic thought as trenchantly as possible. If you wish to understand what communism is, you must study its real and classic

(47)

model—Soviet society, i.e. start from a basis of fact, and not from abstract guesswork and pious wishes. And to be able to understand Soviet society precisely as a communist society, it is essential to consider it from the point of view of its self-sufficing realities and values, and not from that of external evaluations and comparisons. We need a specific method of comprehension. If it cannot be entirely scientific (because of internal Soviet circumstances which exclude any scientific examination of the society on a broad scale and in complete accord with scientific criteria), it should at least attempt to contain itself within the general parameters of a scientific approach. We must look at Soviet society at a conceptual angle and within a conceptual system which would be acceptable neither to the apologists of communism nor to its opponents. The former would reject our approach for completely comprehensible reasons, and the latter because, using our approach, the phenomena which produced the greatest emotional effect would tend to disappear.

I shall give two examples. The enemies of communism regard collectivisation in the Soviet Union merely as violence and an atrocity committed for the benefit of some ideological or political idea, while certain proponents of a reformed communism (i.e. communism without the negative aspects which it displays in the Soviet Union, for example without mass purges) regard it as a mistake, or at best an unsuccessful experiment. If this had really been the case, it would still have been a minor misfortune. But, alas, it was not a mistake. And not in the sense that it was justified, but in the sense that the concepts of 'mistake' and 'justified' are in no way applicable to events of this kind. We need other concepts, since collectivisation was a normal phenomenon in the life of this social organism which was in the process of formation. Nor are the concepts 'violence', 'atrocity', and so on, adequate to reflect the essence of the matter, if only for the reason that the vast majority of the peasants went willingly to the collective farms, and that any attempt to restore individual property on a countrywide scale would be condemned to failure even if it were attempted by constraint. It is not a matter of denying that violence was used (it was) or that atrocities were committed (they were), but of

(48)

saying that in this case the essence of the matter is entirely different. And if, instead of thinking of settling accounts with our painful past we seek, rather, to understand the substance of the Soviet (communist) way of life in the interests of the future, then we must radically alter our ways of seeing, and of course, our phraseology.

Another example. The defenders of communism say: Look, in the Soviet Union they have a free health service, cheap housing and transport, there is no unemployment, and so on. The critics of communism say people have to queue to get into hospitals, the treatment is appalling, apartments are cramped, public transport is overcrowded, wages are low, and so on. The critics, then, see communism from the viewpoint forced on them by its advocates. But in fact medical treatment is not free, since every citizen contributes to its cost by deductions from his pay and by higher prices for food whether or not he receives any treatment; there is no unemployment only because directors of firms are not allowed to dismiss superfluous employees, cannot increase productivity and rationalise their use of labour, are not allowed to increase the salaries of staff whom they would like to keep, and so on, so the circumstances which create unemployment still exist but operate in a different way (in the final analysis they lower the standard of living of the population). Here we need comparisons of a different kind; for instance, the relationships between different categories of the population as far as the distribution of wealth is concerned, i.e. internal comparisons which are much more relevant to an understanding of the general tendencies of the Soviet way of life. I may be told that everywhere there have always been privileged strata of society. Certainly. But the problem does not lie in this commonplace, but in the way in which our privileged strata are formed, whom they comprise, and where this kind of social stratification leads. It in no way follows from the fact that, in the West, there are rich men and paupers, oppressed and oppressors and such like contrasts, that Soviet society is not differentiated, and that this differentiation does not have its own specific manifestations and consequences.

But I think I have departed from my theme. What are the most interesting lessons to be drawn from this recent period of our glorious history? In this period there opened before the Soviet people real opportunities for a radical improvement in the social conditions of their existence, but they voluntarily and quite consciously let those opportunities slip. During this period the essence of the Soviet way of life and the innate character of the human beings who embody this way of life came into the open in all their cynical sincerity. Here the laws and the mechanisms of Soviet society revealed themselves with such clarity and simplicity that enormous efforts were needed from all strata of society (from the right and the left; from the advocates and the opponents) to avoid noticing them. During this period the idea that Stalin's regime had been imposed on the Soviet people by force from above was blown to shreds. The evident mechanisms of Soviet life operated at this time of their own accord with implacable strength, and despite the wishes of the leadership, of the people, the intellectuals, friends, enemies, wise men, fools, boors, the learned, the scientists, the ideologists, and so on. They operated as natural laws of nature and stabilised Soviet society in a state which would have been entirely satisfactory to Stalin and all his gang. During this period all the filth of the Soviet way of life came to the surface for all to see, and asserted itself as the natural milieu and the daily bread of any normal, healthy human being.

Of course there had been some opportunities to this end before. For instance, the writer I. P. Gorbunov observed the formation of the Soviet system, after the Revolution, in two parts of the country isolated from each other and from the centre. In neither of them was there a single Marxist. The authorities in these regions never communicated with the central power, but behaved as if they were acting directly under the instructions of Lenin. Even the percentage of exterminated enemies of the people coincided with an accuracy of hundredths of a percentage point with the general level throughout the country. But Gorbunov attributed no significance to this. He took it as an evident triviality, and like a typical educated cretin of our age, sought some profound and mysterious laws, inaccessible to commonsense and to ordinary native wit. That is why, later, he wasted more than thirty years of his life at forced labour in the search for twopenny-halfpenny secrets of backstage Soviet life. The period I have considered has at least the merit of allowing many things to be understood with the minimum of effort.

The beginning of an epoch

Anton, of course, is exaggerating. But there is in his words something both very disturbing and very true. His reflections are worth remembering for my personal use. But they are of course absolutely unsuitable for our collective work. How am I going to be able to use them? I think that he and I have slipped into a very unpleasant situation. The more so since the gossip in the Institute is that he is a supporter of Solzhenitsyn and Sakharov. Today there was a closed meeting of our management with representatives from the Central Committee. They warned us that if anyone in the Department applies for an exit visa for Israel, they will have to turn in their party card. So we should take preventive measures. Anton's name was mentioned. I said that he was the most Russian of Russians, profoundly Russian, a direct descendant of the Zimin who was quoted by the historian Soloviev. The instructor from the Central Committee said that that meant nothing at all. They (who are these 'they'?) know how to camouflage themselves. When I got home Lenka slipped me some little pamphlet or other. She said it had been specially written for me. This is what I read.

By this time no one had the slightest doubt that Stalin's days were numbered. Everyone was waiting for his death; they were fixed motionless in their waiting. But it was not the fate of a concrete human being which so preoccupied everybody. Long ago Stalin had ceased to be a human being for anyone. It was an unacknowledged feeling that some grandiose social event which affected everyone was moving towards its climax.

Rumours circulated in Moscow that Stalin had died long ago, but the papers kept on printing bulletins about his health. Some explained this by the desire of the Leadership to prepare the people gradually, others by the fact that a struggle was going on

(51)

within the Leadership for the now vacant throne. Yet at that time few people realised that the death of Stalin would mean a great deal more than the end of the life of a man called Stalin, that it would mean the conclusion of an entire period of Soviet history—a period of tragedy, of romance, of terror. Few people understood that the name of Lenin was connected only with the pre-history of the Soviet Union, its establishment and its purely physical survival of the civil war, and that its genuine immanent history up to the present time was linked with the name of Stalin, was incarnate in him, and was symbolised by him. Stalin was the very name and the very substance of this history. Everyone felt this but almost no one understood it. Those who had understood it were either rotting in their graves, or were in the camps awaiting their turn to rot, or were hidden away in the corners of Soviet life without the slightest hope of ever appearing on the stage of history.

And there were still fewer who understood that this period of Soviet history began to come to an end long before the imminent (or perhaps already accomplished) death of Stalin: that is to say, in the stupendous defeats of the beginning of the last war, when many millions of Soviet citizens seemed to awaken from an hallucination and acquire some grain of common sense. After this, the period did nothing more but pass through its last agonies. And who knows, maybe the same thing happened to the period as happened to Stalin: it had died long ago, but for some reason everyone concealed the fact of its passing both from themselves and from one another. They did not want to part with it. They felt sorry to part with it. Everyone felt subconsciously that the passing of this period would mean an end to their illusions about the Radiant Future of mankind, felt that this Radiant Future was a stupendous deception and self-deception. And they did not want to admit this. They wanted to delay as long as possible the difficult moment of recognition. And there were very few indeed who understood this.

Yet millions and millions of people awaited the death of Stalin like the greatest of festivals. Many of them did not acknowledge this fact. Many were afraid to acknowledge that they felt this way. Many were ready to forgive him everything on condition that he died soon and did really die. Many hoped for changes. Many prepared to make changes. This waiting for Stalin's death was like waiting for the end of a nightmare which for more than thirty years had tormented Soviet society. And the sea of tears which was shed by the Soviet people when the Leaders finally decided to announce that Stalin had died was not made up so much of tears of grief, as of tears of relief. And the Soviet people, trained by decades of lies and dissimulation, found no difficulty in transforming their emotions, willingly and freely, into emotions of genuine grief; just as only a short time later, with the same ease of well trained builders of communism, they would work themselves into a state of genuine anger about the crimes of their former idol and his abject gang of henchmen, about which crimes they had allegedly heard nothing, despite the fact that they themselves had zealously abetted their commission.

In the end, it was announced that Stalin had died.

This marked the beginning of a new and unexpected period in Soviet history, but a period which nevertheless many people did expect. And no one knew at the time, nor could they have known, that it was this new period, and not the past history of the world in general and of the Soviet Union in particular that would provide the key to an understanding of communism and the future prospects of humanity.

At that time neither did I know anything of the kind. At the time I was a sports-loving lad from a very well-to-do family. My father was an important engineer working for the Ministry of the Interior (the MVD) on the construction of concentration camps. In return he had been given a Stalin Prize, a splendid apartment in the house of the 'Generals' near the Sokol metro station, and a rent-free villa with a magnificent garden quite close to Moscow. Without any particular effort I got into the university Faculty of Physics. It is hardly surprising that a group of my friends and I rushed off to pay our last respects to the universal idol (and my idol too, of course). Somewhere near Trubnaya Square, we became separated in the crowd. This was the beginning of a stampede the like of which had never been seen before. No one will ever know how many volunteer victims Stalin took to the grave with him. I began to fight my way back through the crowd, and with great difficulty managed to do so.

Before my eyes, a young woman was crushed up against a wall. She slipped under the feet of the crowd. And no one paid the slightest attention. By some miracle I was pushed into a court-yard and dragged over a seething mass of human bodies. Then on all fours I crawled out of the crowd and into the paws of the police, the vigilantes and some soldiers. For some reason known only to themselves they were selecting from the crowd 'ringleaders' and some 'provocateurs' who could be used as scapegoats, beating them up, slinging them into army trucks and carting them off somewhere. I got a crack on the head and came to in the truck. We were taken to the outskirts of Moscow and dumped out in a yard surrounded by a high fence. I was like a madman. And I remember nothing of what happened to us until night fell. Then we were released and allowed to go home. Released, not put inside: that was the mark of the new epoch. But that didn't make me feel any better about what had happened. I was the son of a father who guaranteed me protection and dignity. I was practically beside myself with fury. I ground my teeth, and without caring who heard me, bellowed: Just you wait, you bastards! I won't forgive you! I'll get you for this!

My whole life was altered by those few minutes. Since then I have often wondered why they let us go home. Of course, it's easy to make all sorts of guesses about what concrete orders might have been given. But the essence of the problem is now clear to me: they had no one left to put inside! In that group of detainees along with me there were two Stalin Prizewinners, one Hero of the Soviet Union, one well-known writer—a Stalinist creep—four colonels and so on. The regime of the purges crumbled for the same reason—that the purges could now be turned only against that part of the population who were themselves the supporters, the body, the executants, the interpreters and the advocates and so on of that very regime of purges. The bonfire of Stalinism was extinguished not because the leaders of the party and the state decided that it should be extinguished but because every scrap of the fuel which had kept it going was now exhausted. There was nothing left to burn.

'Who is the author?', I asked.
'Zabelin, of course,' Lenka replied.

'Where did you get this book?', I asked.

'From Bob,' Lenka answered. 'His father gets this kind of book for his work. But you needn't worry about it. Half the town's read it already.'

'Half the town can read what they like,' I said. 'But I must ask you not to bring books like that into this house. It could cause us enormous problems. Listen to the radio, but don't bring books in. They're material evidence, can't you see? You're still only a child, and it's time you learnt to be more careful.'

A heart to heart talk

After my meeting with the comrades from There, I had a chat with Anton.

'Listen, Anton. We've known each other for a long time, and we understand each other. I've got a funny feeling that you've written a book. It'd be impossible for a man like you, with your principles, and who has thought so much about our problems, not to have written down the sum of his thoughts. And since you've written a book, you're determined to publish it come what may. Am I right?'

'Let's say you are.'

'Tell me frankly, have you already started trying to get it published Over There?'

'Yes.'

I pressed him.

'No results so far,' he added. 'The Western publishing houses I had in mind are under the control of one or another group of Russian émigrés. They refuse to publish because my conception doesn't suit them at all. That's a typically Russian phenomenon, by the way—intolerance of anyone who thinks differently from yourself.'

'Typically Soviet, rather.'

'Of course. And for the time being I don't want it to be brought out by any of the downright anti-Soviet publishers you know about. That would only be a last resort. And it'd be easy. They'd get it out in three months.'

(55)

'I've got an idea. I know of one very decent new firm who might well publish your book. When we were in Paris, one of their representatives offered to publish my book if I wanted. Of course, I didn't want. It'd be no use to me. But I just thought of this because the man's in Moscow at the moment. If you like . . . but be careful, if you don't mind . . . You know yourself . . .'

'Thank you. Of course I'll take your advice. I've heard something about this publisher. But I didn't think they did books like mine.'

'I'm not saying they *will* publish it. I'm only saying that it's possible. Anyway, I hope that you've written a proper academic work, not some lousy anti-Soviet rubbish.'

'I'm not an anti-Sovietchik. I don't get involved in politics at all.'

'In that case the thing might come off. Give it a try!'

A few days later Anton turned up with a couple of bottles of wine, and we drank to the launching of the 'enterprise'. I advised Anton not to say a word about it to anyone. And I also asked him to leave our Department before the book appeared and find himself another job.

'Otherwise you'll get us all into trouble. They would destroy us all quite pitilessly.'

My start of an epoch

And what can I remember about those times? In those days I had already become a member of the group of lecturers maintained by the city committee. We were taken to pay our last respects to Stalin without having to grapple with the crowds at all. Vaskin and I were still friends then, and Vaskin said that now our only hope was Mao. I felt myself more attracted by Togliatti. But we were unanimous in our view of Stalin. He published an article about Stalin's work in *Kommunist*—'The economic problems of socialism', and I wrote a series of articles on 'Marxism and problems of linguistics'. Our differences started later, after Khrushchev's speech.

This speech came as a complete surprise to me, even though I was privy to the corridors of the Central Committee, and there were clearly perceptible symptoms that some such event was impending. For instance, we were given permission not to refer to Stalin's works, and in the instructions issued to our group of lecturers, we were directly recommended to avoid quoting him. I believe the highest leadership intended to introduce de-Stalinisation gradually. But who can really know! At the time, Vaskin told me that there was not, nor could there be, any unity within the leadership. One section (and it was clear which one) would try to preserve the status quo, and the other would use criticism of Stalin as a weapon in the power struggle; and this struggle would reflect the real processes which were going on in the country, but not literally and directly, rather through a series of intermediate links and so on. But I did not take this seriously. And later, when it all turned out exactly as he had forecast, I forgot about his predictions. I began to feel that I had known and understood all this myself before that. But all this is an affair of the past. Let historians spend their time digging up this dung hill. My own beginning came much later than the start of the epoch. After Khrushchev's speech to the Central Committee there was a closed meeting of leading ideological workers. Mitrofan Lukich, who took the chair at that meeting (for at that time he was beginning to emerge at the highest level), told us straight out that Stalin had vulgarised Marxism-Leninism and so on, called on us to develop, to move, to raise to a new level, etc., and promised us to promote younger and talented staff. This latter had a direct effect on me. Within a week I was appointed head of a section in our Institute (at that time it was not a department, the department was my own creation later). Then came my doctoral thesis. An apartment. Articles. Books. Commissions. Editorial Boards. Foreign visits. That all came later. And I accepted it all as my right. And when I compared my own position with that of foreign professors, I considered my own way of life as one of penury and servitude. And I was even able to say all that aloud. That was the way times had changed! Everyone talked like that! Even Vaskin.

But there is something else I would like to say here. As I

discovered later, the day after the meeting I have referred to there was another meeting, even more restricted, again under the chairmanship of Mitrofan Lukich, where they talked about hesitations, vacillations, concessions, retreats, and so on, and called for a reinforcement of vigilance, a strengthening of the spirit of the party, etc., and worked out appropriate measures. Vaskin was one of the speakers. And he named certain people who had to be specially closely watched. My name was the first he referred to. I was in no way surprised to learn that two diametrically opposed meetings had been held virtually simultaneously, and that each had adopted measures which paralysed measures adopted by the other. That's in the normal run of things, and I have been used to that for a long time. For example, Stupak's father in one and the same day received the Order of Lenin and was expelled from the party (he was arrested later that night). But I was infuriated by Vaskin's behaviour. And although he swore by all the gods that there had been no such meeting, I did not believe a word of it, because all Moscow was talking about it. After this our ways diverged. This was the beginning of my liberal career, and the beginning of the liberal era. Vaskin had backed the wrong horse. For almost twenty years Vaskin was pushed into the shadows, into anonymity. And throughout all this period I was prancing about for all to see. It is easy to imagine how much he came to hate me! Of course, during the same period Vaskin, too, came to succeed. But he was very much behind me, on a lower scale—forced, one might say, to take a back seat.

New problems

The spaces between the letters proved to be very convenient places for the trysts of the lovelorn young. That was on the side reading 'Long Live Communism'. The other side ('The Radiant Future of All Mankind') which was closer to the 'Youth' café and the wine shop, provided a home for the drinking bouts of the local alcoholics. The spaces between the letters were so arranged that the lovers and the drunks could be observed only from passing motorcars, about which neither party gave a damn. The efforts of the vigilantes and the police to liquidate these centres of debauchery came to nothing, since the lovers and the drunks established friendly contacts with the guardians of the law. Next, a particular sort of young woman began to frequent the area round the Slogan. The word 'Radiant' became a centre for drug-trafficking. And the word 'Communism' was soon taken over almost completely by homosexuals. This was too much for the patience of the workers. It was decided to surround the Slogan with an electrified fence. But the funds set aside for this were frittered away by various planning authorities, and in the end they had to restrict themselves to an ordinary wooden fence with barbed wire on top. But this measure did nothing more than reinforce society's objective tendency to drunkenness and fornication (as Dima observed), since a number of boards in the fence were immediately removed to allow ease of access, and as nothing could be seen behind the fence even when it was light, the Slogan became a seat of debauchery twenty-four hours a day. It became the haunt of foreigners, speculators in currency and clothes, and, of course, informers. It seemed that the Slogan was destined to become a kind of international salon. The famous K G B journalist, Vladimir Couis, became an habitué. The artists of the 'cesspit' school decided to hold their next exhibition in the slogan area, thus demonstrating their loyalty to Soviet power. The city committee held a meeting behind closed doors, where reference was made to Yagoditsyn, and it was resolved that he had not been as wrong as all that.

Sashka

Sashka is my son by my first wife. When we divorced his mother did everything she could to make him hate me. She kept a very close eye on everything I published so as to wring from me everything the law allowed ('her rights'), and she got so much alimony from me that not even a doctor of science could earn so high an income. Yet she kept Sashka half starved and abominably dressed. I tried to give him extra food and buy him a few clothes, but nothing good came out of it. He was forbidden to come and visit me. But gradually he began to slip away from his mother in secret and come to see us. Something seemed to attract him to me. Our meetings became regular. Now he spends most of his time in our apartment. Apparently his mother would now be quite pleased to get rid of him altogether. I have tried several times to get him registered at my address, using my connections at the highest levels, but with no result. It is strange that a father cannot register his son as living with him even when the son is already registered in Moscow! Anton said it was not that that was strange, but the fact that so far I have said nothing about it in my published work.

'It'll soon be time for nominations to higher courses,' I said to Sashka. 'What are your chances? Can I be any help? I know your Dean very well. What about going on to a second degree? If you don't fancy history, maybe historical materialism, or scientific communism. There are quite good prospects in those fields.'

'No, I don't want to,' said Sashka. 'You know, very often the children of people who've been successful aren't motivated to do anything to make a career for themselves. I'm not a child any more. I can put two and two together. All our academic history is almost completely lies and falsifications. And in the odd places where we aren't lying all the time, it's dreadfully boring. What interests me is the real history of Russia in this century. I've managed to read some authentic material about it and I'm certain that there's nothing else I want to do. If you could find me a place where I could study real history, as a real scientist should, I'd go there no matter how little they paid me. You don't know anywhere like that? Nor do I. Amalrik? Gulyaev? But they're exceptions—and dissidents as well. Amalrik has been sent to jail twice, Gulyaev only once. But he's got a good chance of going back inside.'

I tried to explain to him that these days one cannot live directly, straightforwardly, that one has to be flexible, adaptable, to compromise for a time; in general one has to be man. It's not easy for me, either. You've got to live. Otherwise you'll never get anything done. He brought up irrefutable arguments:

What about Solzhenitsyn? What about Sakharov? What about Amalrik? What about Shafarevich? What about Turchin . . .? He reeled off dozens of names, most of which I didn't know. He said that every decent Russian man should know and remember these names. I asked him whether he didn't really want to become a dissident. He said that unfortunately he was too weak for that, knew too little, and understood almost nothing, that first of all he just wanted to live a little, to see and to think. He said that nowadays there were a lot of youngsters like him about. But I don't believe that there are many of them. Where are they? I never see them, despite the fact that I meet a lot of young people and give them every chance to show what they really think, even if it is only by way of discreet hints. The young people swot up their Marxism very thoroughly and get 'A's and 'B's in their examinations. 'C's are very rare, and you hardly ever get a 'Fail'.

'But I'm a model student, too,' said Sashka. 'I've got 'A's in historical materialism, scientific communism and the history of the CPSU. Incidentally, Gulyaev was on a scholarship.'

Potatoes

When I was at the market buying potatoes (I have to admit that happens quite often), a black Volga with Central Committee or KGB number plates drew up alongside me. The man in it, whom I didn't immediately recognise, hailed me.

'Oh, ho!' I said. 'You've become a big boss. Is that your personal car?'

'Why ever not! How are you, old man? World famous, I gather. Too proud to know me. You might at least give me a ring!'

We chatted for a while. When he learnt that I was out buying potatoes, he burst out with an angry speech: how could it be that a professor, almost an Academician . . .! Then he drove off, but without giving me his telephone number.

When I got home I told the story.

'Surely that miserable little twerp can't have . . .' screeched

Tamara. 'It's not possible: There you are, you see, all these stupid creeps have got themselves fixed up, and you . . .'

'Have a bit of patience,' said Lenka. 'When papa's elected a corresponding member, we'll get our pass to the special store. And then we'll live on black caviar!'

My mother-in-law said that there was no point in gnashing your teeth about the temporary food shortages and bad weather. Just wait till next year, when there'd be a good harvest, and . . .

'And they'll open special stores for doctors and professors,' said Lenka. 'Not quite such good stores, of course. And then the year after, when the harvest will be even better, there'll be more stores for masters of science and lecturers. The stores will be even less good, of course. And then there'll have to be ration cards for us all, so that we don't over-stuff ourselves.'

'You're a real viper,' said mother-in-law. 'Just you wait. I'll go to your Komsomol organisation and tell them.'

'You wouldn't dare. Your granddaughter'd be expelled from school. And it'd be worse for you.'

And yet you can't class my mother-in-law as a complete reactionary, nor Lenka as a progressive or a completely committed critic. For instance, on one occasion my mother-in-law came home complaining for all she was worth.

'How dreadful people are these days! Always running, pushing, shoving! Not one of them will give way to let you through. Just try to push ahead of you!'

'It can't be any other way, grandma,' said Lenka. 'If everyone behaved the way you want them to everyone would have to move at the speed of the slowest. You can't have that. Life would grind to a halt.'

I have observed repeatedly that, on a whole range of matters, young people today are much more inclined to be advocates of communism than old obscurantists. The old people still have some idealism left. Young people argue from a basis of facts, which they regard as natural. Even we, for instance, are still exercised by the problems of careerism. The young see no such problems. They only problems they see are those of achieving their own personal position in life. And in this case they don't worry about metaphysics or moral scruples. That is why, in my opinion, all the ideas and efforts of people like Solzhenitsyn and Anton are doomed to failure and oblivion. The natural change of generations will result in mankind accepting the communist way of life almost as an existence pre-ordained by nature. The sufferings and the thoughts of Solzhenitsyn, Sakharov, Shafarevich, and those like them, are merely a reflection of a few ideals of the past and of what still remains of the West in our society which is fundamentally different from theirs. From this point of view those who regard the activity of our dissenters as (in the last analysis) a manifestation of the class struggle, are quite correct. Of course this does not mean that we should fall into vulgarisation and regard Solzhenitsyn, for instance, as a lackey of world imperialism. But fundamentally, there is no getting away from it. That, too, is a real fact.

That is the way that I reflected superficially, but in the cellars of my mind malicious little thoughts were swarming around: you, my friend, you like, you look for justification, you seek a formula for baseness . . . So, what if I do? Haven't I got the right to? Of course I have. All right, then, go on looking. But don't make a fuss about it. Be honest with yourself and become a Vaskin, a Korytov, an Ivanov, a Tvarzhinskaya. And don't whine about it!

On God

'Uncle Anton,' said Lenka, 'Why did people invent God?'

'Ask your father,' said Anton. 'That's his speciality.'

'Papa thinks that men invented God so that the ruling classes could control the exploited classes more easily. Is that what you think?'

'No, I don't.'

'What, then?'

'It's a long story. For a start, gods were invented even in societies which, according to Marxism, were still classless. And secondly, people invented various kinds of gods. And that isn't simply a matter of there being different religions which all have similar functions, or rather let's say enjoying equal rights.

(63)

Among all the gods the Christian God has a special place because it was only in association with Him that Western civilisation was created: a particular social organisation of a multitude of individuals who were conscious of their Ego. In this sense, in inventing God (i.e. inventing precisely this kind of God) people invented themselves as self-sufficient individual personalities. It was a real invention, something artificially created.'

'Where could I find books about all this? I mean, something decent, not all the rubbish that we churn out.'

'There were splendid writers in Russia before the Revolution who dealt with religion in one way and another. Florenskiy, Berdyaev, Merezhkovskiy, the Truvetskoy brothers, Rozanov, Shestov . . . For a start, have a good look at Dostoievsky's "Legend of the Grand Inquisitor" in *The Brothers Karamazov*.'

'Are you a believer yourself?'

'That's a difficult question. I want to believe, but I can't. I cannot take Him into account as a real fact when I'm going about my business, but I try to behave as if He sees everything and I don't want to be ashamed before Him. At critical moments I pray to Him for help, and I have hope in Him. In short, for me, the problem of God is not a Natural Sciences problem. For me it's a problem of my own spirituality, a problem of my I, of my conscience, let's say. I think that the problem's the same for many other people. Marxism rejects religion. That is its right. Religion can be annihilated by the power of the state. But it's not possible to annihilate the facts of spirituality which the Christian religion has engendered in its time without destroying man's vision of his own intrinsic worth. For me, the recognition of God is the same thing as my awareness that I have a conscience.'

'Therefore some kind of religion is necessary?'

'It is possible.'

'But isn't Marxism a religion?'

'Marxism supplants religion but does not replace it. Marxism is not a religion. It is an anti-religion. Not merely that it is hostile to religion as science might be. Marxism is not a science. And today, science is not hostile to religion—for it in no way refutes it. Marxism is an ideology, but an anti-religion, in the

(64)

sense that it is engendered by spiritual phenomena which are opposed to the phenomena engendered by religion, and that Marxism itself cultivates these phenomena. For example, from the religious point of view violence directed against one innocent person cannot be justified by any amount of future benefits for millions of people or for mankind as a whole. By rejecting the absolute nature of morality, Marxism in various ways develops in people the ability to perpetrate this kind of violence while covering itself by talk about the common good. This inevitably leads to falsehood, which can also be justified, and which can hypocritically be passed off as truth. And so it is in all those areas where the most refined products of civilisation affect human personality.'

'But surely the people who fought against religion didn't do so in vain? Some of the finest people, they were! Honest, and wise men!'

'That's another question. In a temperate and sexually continent society it's possible to pass for the progressive avant-garde by preaching free love. It's all very well to talk about the common good when you're sitting in a splendid dining-room at a laden table surrounded by beautiful, well-dressed women. In a society with a highly developed religious and moral conscience, the preacher of atheism can pass for a bringer of light, a champion for the cause of humanity, an enemy of obscurantism. That is one thing. Quite another is a society in which the religious and moral conscience has been totally destroyed and which therefore suffers from a spiritual famine. A hungry man needs bread and not homilies on the mortal danger of overeating.'

This is typical of the kind of conversation that takes place in our home. And often after these occasions I sit alone with Anton and insist that it should stop. We agree that Anton should stop visiting us. But after two or three days we all begin to remark that Zimin hasn't been round for a long time, the children rush to the telephone, and snatch the receiver from one another to yell to Anton that he must come round at once. With Natasha, of course. We've got bored!

Old warriors remember

To mark the last anniversary of the Victory—a good round
figure this time—the members of the editorial board of the wall
newspaper, forgetting the lessons of the past (although it must
be said that these are entirely new people, so there is nothing for
them either to forget or remember), again asked Anton to write
something for them. So Anton, reviving his old memories,
immediately gave them a poem. No one believed that it was an
improvisation. But I know Anton, and I know that he never
lies. Of course the poem was not printed. Here it is:

> They chattered in a constant stream
> Of doing some heroic mission.
> I had a very different dream—
> To sneak from camp without permission.

> To pick up any passing tart,
> And hug and squeeze her all the night,
> To get some booze, and give her part,
> To roll a fag, and have a bite.

> But when the hour of battle chimed,
> They settled back in GHQ.
> Far from the front, in bed they climbed,
> And fought their war with you-know-who.

> Meanwhile, to keep their battles sweet,
> Heroic exploits they required:
> 'Go fight,' they told me. 'No retreat,
> Harry the foe till he's expired.'

> The years they now have swiftly fled,
> It's victory celebration day.
> We gather—all who are not dead—
> No youngsters now, but old and grey.

> And there they stand, their medals bright,
> Their decorations all aglow,
> Recalling how they used to fight
> Heroic battles, long ago.

Russian visitality

Dima proposed the introduction of a new word: 'visitality' (as distinct from 'hospitality') to apply to the specifically Russian pastime of visiting and being visited. Visitality (as he explained it) has nothing to do with hospitality. For example, we are completely inhospitable people, but we regularly go visiting and people visit us just as often. Moreover, we frequently call on people whom we neither like nor want to see. And we often receive visits from people whom we find quite obnoxious. It is a purely social phenomenon. But what is its nature? Here are just a few of its aspects which in part explain it. Going to the cinema is a waste of time. You might see a half-way tolerable film once a year—everything else is rubbish. In the past there were at least quite a few foreign films. Now there are none. The theatre? From time to time there are some decent plays, but it's virtually impossible to get to see them. The tickets go to foreigners, to the bosses and to their friends. There are masses of theatres, but nothing worth seeing, just like the cinema. The same is true of music, of painting, of literature. When by chance something decent appears in print, all Moscow rushes out to buy copies of the magazine which means there are none left on sale or even to borrow from libraries. And anyway very often what's appeared is merely another work of denunciation. There's not much worth spending time on. Television? Ice hockey, football, model workers of communist labour, agricultural shock workers (not that there's anything to eat!), speeches, meetings, departures, arrivals . . . In the past there were at least a few thrillers, foreign films, performances by real singers (ours and from the West). Now hardly at all. The foreigners whom they show us now are hardly distinguishable from our own stars. The Western culture we see now is selected qualitatively and quantitatively so as not to undermine our foundations or to incite us to unwanted comparisons. The restaurants and cafés? For a start, most of them are disgusting. And then there are queues. And the service is dreadful. And you simply can't get into the decent ones. And they're expensive. And they close

(67)

early. In short, look at every side of life, and there's only one thing left to do: go and visit, invite people round.

But visitality isn't merely dictated by force of circumstance—it plays a positive part too: you exchange information you can't get from the papers, you maintain useful contacts, talk business, feel you're needed (which is very important given the general tendency to isolation and the devaluation of the individual), you can find some use for your various creative talents (versifying, joking, yarning, sketching and so on). And of course, there's something decent to eat. Usually people try to put on a show for their guests. There's even a kind of competitiveness about it. The women show themselves off—i.e. their dresses, I mean. There's virtually nowhere else to display them—and they're not cheap! So it would be a sheer waste if no one saw them! And then there's the boost to your self-confidence. Say, for instance, that someone has been abroad. That's a great pleasure, of course. But there's a great deal more satisfaction to be had from letting everyone else know about it, from the thought that you'll be able to talk about the trip and for a time at least you'll be the centre of attention. In short, Russian visitality is a specific social phenomenon. I must say at once that I am not in a position to judge how widespread it is in various parts of the country or in different strata of society. I can merely affirm that it is characteristic of the intellectual-official circles in Moscow. There may well be variations depending on location, stratum, season of the year, national peculiarities and so on.

'What a joke!' said Dima. 'Here we are, people of the twentieth century living in a civilised country, yet we talk about ourselves as if we were describing the lifestyle of some recently discovered savage tribe: they make fire by rubbing two sticks together, live on grubs and roots, the women prepare the food and the men go off hunting with spears . . .'

'There's nothing funny about that,' said Anton. 'It's a negation of a negation. We *are* savages. In some respects we've sunk right back down to the very bottom of human history. We've got to start back again up the path that leads to the emergence and the development of civilisation. But we still don't know that ourselves. And the West even less so. So an accurate description of our daily productive life is a great contribution to our self-knowledge, and our knowledge of communism.'

'Hang on, it's not communism yet,' I said. 'Under communism there'll be none of this. Under communism, as you well know . . .'

'We've had real communism here for a long time,' said Anton. 'From each according to his capacity—that's been done. And to each according to his needs, as well. It's high time to realise that all that is just empty phrases which you can interpret in any way you like. Our society decides for itself what your capacities and needs are. It's a social phenomenon, not a psychological one. We are all put into pigeon holes, into ranks, into cells. And our social position determines everything else which affects our lives. The Korytovs go to Italy on holiday. Couldn't you afford to do the same on your money? Even I could if I tightened my belt and saved up. You're off to Bulgaria, to Golden Sands. It'd be no problem for us to afford that. But . . . compared with you, Kanareikin is a total cretin. But he's an Academician. And wherever the names of our leading philosophers are quoted, you'll find his as well. *Your* name doesn't crop up everywhere. And if you bump into each other, he always takes precedence. If you'll forgive me for saying so, Lebedev is head and shoulders above any of us. But he's hardly ever quoted at all. And if he is quoted, then alongside him you're made to look like a genius. Society knows precisely each man's capacities and needs.'

'You're priceless, Anton,' said Dima. 'We're in a comic situation. Here's the official point of view: scientific communism (i.e. the science of communism) was created a hundred years ago, but communism as a reality does not yet exist.'

'It does show some visible features, some limited manifestations,' I said.

'Rubbish,' said Anton. 'Communist society is conceivable as an empirical phenomenon, not as an abstract system. Every scientist knows the elementary truth: if the object does not exist, then there can be no experimental (I stress experimental) science relating to it. A plan of a house, the blueprint of a machine? A plan is not a science, get that into your head! A plan can be turned into reality with the help of science, but it is not

(69)

itself a science. It is a plan, and nothing more than that. The experimental sciences reveal universal laws for the objects they study. You can draw up a plan for some future society by using science: for instance sciences like sociology, psychology, history, the natural sciences. You can produce a scientifically based plan. But this thing that you call scientific communism isn't even a scientifically based plan. From the very point of view of modern science that is sheer rubbish if you take it literally. And our own experience confirms that it is a purely ideological fiction. But on the other hand, the kind of society which has in fact been formed here (and that I shall call real communism) has never been scientifically studied. What we sometimes say about it (in particular about visitality) is the beginning of our scientific understanding of it. But only the beginning. A collection of facts, nothing more. The very scientific study of this society reveals the fact that in the limited (i.e. the only realistic, or common) sense, all the ideals of ideological ('scientific') communism are realised in it. The state and the parties have atrophied in the sense that they have lost their political character. Morality and law have atrophied as products of civilisation and of the protection of people from one another, and have been replaced by certain rules of 'technical' behaviour suitable to slaves. Everyone has the opportunity to develop his capacities and satisfy his needs, but within the limits of rationality established by society. Here an overwhelming majority of the population exercises oppression over the minority. It is true that in so doing it oppresses itself, while from time to time allowing certain people to drag it in the mire as they wish. But that is sheer triviality. We don't even have money in the Marxian sense. What sense does money make if the same sum will buy you more than it will buy me, or will buy you things which are forbidden to me!'

'I entirely agree with you,' said Dima. 'As a natural scientist all this is absolutely clear to me. It takes more than a starting point of machinery, cars, tractors and the rest to achieve a scientific grasp of society; it requires primarily starting from genuine experimental data. And as far as their mutual interrelations are concerned, they must be discovered and not assumed *a priori*. Who knows, maybe for this society ideology is the determining factor? Ideology, too, is an experimental fact. Marx had many interesting ideas and intuitions—but they have foundered in a sea of ideological claptrap. Now the succeeding generations of Marxists have inflated precisely this ideological aspect of his work. And here, this has been transformed into a state ideology.'

'But we need ideology as well,' I said.

'It's not so much that we need it,' said Anton. 'It, too, is a reality which we have to take into account and which we need to study as part of our experimental data.'

At this point I lost patience. I accused them both of not knowing their ABC: matter, conscience, ideal etc.

'What the hell!' said Dima. 'You'd reckon he was a normal human being. Quite bright really. But just scratch him a little, and he raises such a stink that by comparison even Kanareikin would seem a mighty thinker. Come on, we're not stripping you of your job and your salary. Go ahead and write your books. Be whatever you like. That's not what we're talking about. Between ourselves we can talk frankly. This is the problem: is the present state of society normal or not; is it going to go on reproducing itself in the future, are mass purges the norm, is the absence of freedom of speech the norm, is restriction on freedom of travel the norm, and so on? Your Marxism cannot give an honest answer to these questions. Here we need science, a real science. Why? If for no better reason than to help us plan our lives somehow or other. Maybe even if that holds good for only a small part of society. The people who don't need it have no call to study it. But within our society there is a small section of people who feel a real need for it. You and I've spent more than a year discussing that, and only that. A professional interest? Nonsense! Even for you it's a human interest. What about your Sashka? And Lenka? And me? What fucking difference does it make to me? Yet I lie awake at night thinking about it. The world is worried about the successes of communism and wants to get to the bottom of the problem. Incidentally, it wasn't Solzhenitsyn's books which got people interested in us, but rather the contrary; it was the natural interest of the world in the growing threat of communism that ensured the success of Solzhenitsyn's books and the general interest in us.'

(71)

The television screen began to show a meeting at some factory or other, where practically all the leadership, led by Himself, turned up to hand out some decoration or other.

'Why've they turned out in such a mob?' I wondered.

'What d'you mean, why?' Dima was surprised at my surprise. 'Don't you know that during the congress there was trouble at that factory? Something like a strike. So they're trying to butter them up.'

The picture changed to a shot of the presidium of the meeting—completely identical puffy wooden faces, and medals, medals, medals.

'My god!' Tamurka exploded. 'Just look at those mugs! Where do they find them?!'

'They're home-made,' said Dima. 'Typical Soviet mugs. There it is—the face of communism. Just sit back and admire it!'

Mother-in-law

My mother-in-law is a typical Soviet pensioner, the surest support of Soviet power. She wouldn't be worth a mention if she did not feature among the most essential conditions of the creative activity of a Soviet scientist.

My mother-in-law, then, has been a worthy teacher of Russian language and literature, a woman who is an intellectual to the nth degree. A few years ago she retired (Lenka says she was slung out) to enjoy her well earned rest, adding one more to the already overflowing ranks of Soviet pensioner-terrorists. Ah, the Soviet pensioner!—a phenomenon unknown to human history, never yet described in literature nor studied by science! There is a whole class of Soviet citizens, by no means negligible numerically, who live to a great age but who, long before they retire on pension, have lost the aptitude for anything resembling normal work. It is said that workers retire willingly, since work is not a very easy thing to do. But there aren't very many workers. And as for people in non-manual jobs—and they make up an enormous part of the population—they usually have to be forced into retirement with enormous difficulty. And so the Soviet white-collar workers, including scientists, teachers, doctors, professors, colonels and so on, once put out to grass, still full of energy and a desire to serve, cannot wait to take up socially useful work. Of course, as far as possible, they like to get a decent wage for it. Pensioners of this kind join all sorts of commissions, committees and councils—where they by no means take a back seat. For instance, the campaign against parasites which was conducted some time ago was mainly in the hands of pensioners. And if you need to go on an official visit abroad, you can't avoid coming up against the pensioners. You'll certainly be summoned to meet the commission of the party district committee. And there you will find a pensioner. And that's where the fun begins. Where is Australia? Describe the Belgian social system. What did comrade so-and-so have to say about . . .? And just try to avoid an answer! Or just try being even mildly disrespectful to this senile rat! . . . But back to my mother-in-law.

When she was pensioned off, mother-in-law, in full accord with our propaganda, decided that from now on she was entitled to everything and everyone was indebted to her, because she had worked so meritoriously. And, of course, she was entitled to have people give up their seat to her on public transport. And although she had no need to go anywhere, she immediately decided to exercise her rights. Taking Lenka with her (it was Lenka who told us all about it afterwards), mother-in-law boarded a comparatively uncrowded metro carriage, and marked down her victim—a youngish man with a beard. Having a beard, he must be an intellectual, undoubtedly a scoundrel and probably a lout to boot. Slobs like him needed to be taught a lesson! They've let themselves go too far! A young girl offered my mother-in-law her seat, but that didn't suit her. She wanted a battle! She pushed her way through to her chosen victim, and fixed him with a glare like that of a king cobra. For some time the man did not notice the threat hanging over him (he was pretending, of course!). Then he noticed that before him stood a far from old, quite attractive-looking woman, and he prepared to rise and gallantly offer her his seat. But that was as far as he got.

'You lout!' cried my mother-in-law. 'Look at him sprawling in his seat! Pretending that he cannot see before his eyes elderly ladies who deserve respect! That's what young people are like these days! No respect any more! They think they're entitled to everything!'

Disconcerted by these words, the man forgot his intention of giving up his seat. The polemic spread like wild fire to the rest of the carriage. As most of the passengers were standing, and as there was a majority of middle-aged and elderly people, it was they who took the initiative. Someone demanded the identity of the seated passenger so as to report him to the appropriate authority. Another proposed that he should be reported to his work-place, to his trade union, to the Komsomol or to his party organisation. Another asserted that a satirical piece about him should be sent to the papers. Epithets like 'dissident', 'critic', 'slanderer' and 'ideological deviationist' were bandied about. People began to denounce beards, mini-skirts, maxi-skirts, midi-skirts, tight jeans, bell-bottoms, abstract painters, Arabs (permissible since the Arabs had disobeyed our instructions on some point or other). . . . At the last stop on the line, the man rose with some difficulty, and dragged his completely stiff extremities towards the door, leaning heavily on crutches. The passengers went about their business, and mother-in-law travelled back the way she had come. Back home, she switched on our colour television at full volume and watched with grow-ing interest as Robert Rylov the centre forward of the ice-hockey team 'Dawn of Communism', devoted himself to break-ing the ribs of the centre half from the team 'Yjavakharlalpakh-takairatkor'. From time to time she uttered war cries like 'The puck, you loon!' 'Get stuck in, you fucker!' 'Get him by the balls, Bob!' and so on. When Rylov finally bundled both the puck and the goalminder into the back of the net, mother-in-law almost hit the ceiling, and began to chant in her cracked soprano:

'Only real men play at hockey!
They don't let cowards on the ice!'

Lenka was splitting her sides laughing.

'Grandma!' she yelled through tears of laughter. 'You're tops! You're the greatest!'

(74)

I simply couldn't stand any more of this. I clutched my head (which was stuffed full of categories of dialectical and historical materialism), and rushed to Tamurka in the kitchen.

'Please, I beg you, can't you do something to calm down this . . . this . . . your dear mama? Here I am trying to do some creative work!'

'Well create as much as you like,' said Tamurka calmly. 'She's not stopping you. What's she done? The television? Well, you can calm your daughter down for a start. She spends all day and every day playing these idiotic negro records as loud as she can. The police have already been round. I only got myself out of it by threatening to report them to their superiors: what right have they got to be hostile to our brilliant foreign policy towards the nations of Africa? If they don't like it, they can lump it! That's what I told them. And if you don't like it, you can push off to your bit of fluff.'

My 'bit of fluff', I suppose, must be Svetka. How's Tamurka sniffed her out? But then she's probably sniffed nothing out. She couldn't care less. It's simply that she knows I've got a secretary of that name. And even if there wasn't anything going on between Svetka and me, Tamurka would have accused me of having it off with her just the same. It's just a standard form of family inter-relationships. A polemical gambit, as Dima would say. There's no point in arguing with Tamurka. I decided that on the first night of our life together. On that first night she told me to push off. Now I ran into the corridor, scrambled into my threadbare coat (I'd have to buy a new one, this one's becoming shameful! If only I knew where the money went!) and disappeared round the corner to the Dive—the bar in the 'Youth' café. As I left, there came wafting after me from Lenka's room the chants of the tribes of Africa, throwing off the shackles of imperialism and stepping out on the road towards the construction of socialism. Those are the ones who really have no more respect for anything! They'll have us all by the ears, those blackamoors, just mark my words!

Events

At the Dive, I've got a number of acquaintances who turn up there about as often as I do. I don't know who they are. And they don't know who I am. There's a tacit agreement never to raise the question. One of them is called Victor Ivanovich. He must be only about thirty, but he gives the impression of being a very solid, important citizen. My Sashka won't look as solid as that even when he's an old man. Then there's another called Edik. Like me, he's well past fifty. He's bald, and he seems to have lost half his teeth. Yet he looks like a little boy who appreciates practical jokes and plays them himself from time to time. He knows all the jokes going the rounds of Moscow. I think he probably makes them up himself. Then there's a chap called Rebrov who doesn't turn up quite as often. He's just known as Rebrov. He's usually drunk, and almost never speaks. But you can tell from his eyes that he understands everything, like an intelligent dog. Then there's Lev Borisovich, a very busy, well-informed person. He's always in a hurry. But I suspect that he's not even got a master's degree. And then there are a few nameless people who drop in. I am one of those. I find that quite entertaining. What do they make of me? Nothing very flattering, I'm certain. Most probably they think I'm an informer.

On this occasion I met Rebrov. He asked me how things were going. I shrugged my shoulders—nothing worth mentioning, as usual. There's been a rise in unemployment in the U.S.A. Inflation. An earthquake somewhere in South America. The Egyptians have told us to go and . . . We've infiltrated Angola. Pretty soon we'll get booted out again. Solzhenitsyn's come out with another of his anti-Soviet speeches. Worldwide public opinion . . . While at home it's the same old story of overfulfilled plans, shopfloor initiatives, speeches, creative innovations, space launches and orbits. At this point one of the Nameless ones joined us.

'Boredom is the essence of our existence,' he said. 'Our day-to-day Soviet life is in principle event-free. Nothing out of the ordinary is ever supposed to happen. If it did it would be a deviation from the norm. You know, like talent, or originality, or an independent line of thought.'

'I beg to differ,' said Rebrov, to our huge surprise (so he could talk, after all!) 'Extraordinary things do happen here. And just as often as in the West, only we don't appreciate how exceptional they are. For example, my wife sent me out to the market to buy potatoes at three times the official price. Otherwise there'd be nothing for our guests to eat. So there I am going past the greengrocer's. "Vegetables!" I say with a smirk. Ha, ha, ha! . . . Just think, vegetables in a shop?! . . . Ha, ha, ha! . . . What a joke . . . And fruit! How do you eat fruit? Ha, ha, ha! . . . And then, what do you know, I take a look in the window—and I look again! And what d'you think? Potatoes!! In bags!! And not completely rotten!!! Some were even edible!!! How about that—and you say that nothing extraordinary ever happens! Oh, and I've got another example Believe it or not, this one happened to my neighbour. There he was, walking along Lenin Avenue, and he sees a shop selling instant coffee. Of course, you had to take a kilo of rotten apples along with every jar, but never mind that. The main thing is—it was coffee on sale! And how about this? A friend of mine acquired a real fur hat through knowing the right people. So he put it on, very proud of himself. He was hardly across the courtyard when, bang, a brick dropped on his head! And when he came round, of course, his hat was gone. So off he goes to the police. But when he gets there, it's him they accuse: this citizen, having sold his hat to obtain money for drink, now has the nerve to slander the Soviet people. It was round about this time that the Moscow police had made a socialist promise to reduce the level of unsolved crime to zero per cent. And a crime that has not been committed counts as one that's been solved. For a whole month the entire staff of the Institute tried to extract my friend from his difficulties. They put up bail for him. He was released eventually when he had given a fur hat to each of the policemen. And it was reported later at a meeting that the whole thing had come out all right in the end. The man got off with a caution.'

Nameless listened to Rebrov with evident enjoyment.

'Ah, ha!' he said. 'So you're a thinker, are you? I give in! Of course you're right. I never saw it in that light before. Of course! For instance, it's a much greater triumph for a Soviet intellectual to get his son straight into university from school if he hasn't got friends in the right places than it is for a Corsican lieutenant to become Emperor of France.'

'You sound as if that's a problem you're facing yourself,' I speculated. 'Well, perhaps I can try to help you—of course, not to make him into an emperor but to get him to Moscow university. What faculty does he want?'

'Oh Lord,' said Nameless. 'What difference does that make? Humanities? What the hell! Let's settle for humanities! Even though he hates philosophy and dreams of physics. Just so long as he gets in, we can sort things out later.'

'Just you see,' Rebrov said to Nameless. 'In our great country even miracles are possible.'

When Rebrov had left I decided to take Nameless's telephone number and give him my own. He told me his name and my eyes started out of my head.

'Is that really who you are?' I asked. 'And even you've got problems with the university? Even in physics? That's amazing.'

Then I told him my name.

'I hope,' said Nameless, 'you're not the one I think you are.'

'I'm afraid I am,' I said.

And we had a good laugh about it.

Business

'How are things going?' I asked Anton.

'I'm going to be published. They're looking for an editor at the moment. But it's all going dreadfully slowly. It seems that its not that easy to get published even Over There.'

'It's the same everywhere. Even Solzhenitsyn was kept on ice for two years before the book came out. You've got to be patient.'

'I am being patient. But I still can't make myself believe that the book will ever come out. But thank you all the same.'

(78)

'No need. After all, we are cowardly and mercenary liberals.'
'Don't play the fool. I didn't say that.'

'If you didn't say it, it was someone who looked very much like you. Anyway, it doesn't upset me. What's true is true. Look, take this telephone number. It's the "Forward" publishing house. Ask for Stepan Ivanovitch Trusov. Tell him I told you to ring. I think he's got a job for a senior editor. The pay is twice as much as here.'

Science and ideology

'All the same,' I said, 'I cannot believe that the greatest phenomenon of the spiritual life of mankind is just rubbish, and that the grandiose movement of life itself towards communism is mere degradation. We must observe some limits and show some responsibility to people!'

'Quite so,' said Anton. 'We must be responsible. Have I ever said that Marxism was rubbish? Marxism genuinely is a great phenomenon in the life of society. I am merely saying that it is an ideology, not a science. I don't see anything insulting about that. Ideology is neither better nor worse than science. They are just different. They have different aims, different laws of operation and construction, and different defence mechanisms. An ideology may arise with pretentions towards being a science, on the basis of science, in connection with science, closely interwoven with science, and so on. Its phraseology may use many scientific propositions. Yet from the very moment of its foundation it is not a science. Nor do I consider the actual evolution of the world towards communism to be a degradation. I do not use (or at least, I try to avoid) value judgements. It is a grandiose process; there's no denying it. But what interests me lies in just what it really offers, not in its slogans and its demagogy, and not in its self-adulation and cynical lies.'

'Very well,' I said. 'Let's accept that. But tell me, surely you don't maintain that all its propositions—matter is primary, conscience secondary, that the world is knowable, that space and time are objective, that the world is constantly changing, and that quantitative changes lead to qualitative, and so on—that all these propositions are false? Does not society have an infrastructure and a superstructure, productive forces, productive relationships, classes, parties and so on?'

'At first sight (which is enough for ideology but not for science), all this is true,' said Anton. 'But first, for a proposition to be regarded as scientific it is not enough for it to be true. For a term to be considered scientific it is not enough that it should signify an actual fact. And secondly, if we look more closely, the truth of the propositions of Marxism and the content of its terminology turn out to be illusory. I could take you right through Marxism and show you all this in detail. But for the moment I'll just give you a few curious examples which are useful for limbering up the brain. You say the world is knowable. But is the unknowable knowable? Where does that lead you? Either you have a tautology "the knowable is knowable" or a hypothesis "everything is knowable", and the latter is extremely risky.

'The existence of insoluble problems has been proved. It is possible to prove that one cannot know the consequences of an event which might have taken place but did not. I could give you dozens of examples like that. Of course one can say that here we are talking about something rather different. But what, precisely? Are we talking about the objective content of our knowledge, which does not depend on man or on mankind in general? Very well. In this case I can give you as many examples as you like which will prove the contrary. For instance, what about those symptoms of things which, while themselves non-existent, represent some action of these things on man? Of course, there is in things something which . . . but then we're talking about quite different symptoms! But how do we deal with the former? You only have to dig into the nature of human cognition to see that at the basis of all the products of cognition we find the former element, the "subjective", not the "objective". To learn how to isolate the "objective" we need the "subjective" as the point of departure for everything. Kant, my dear fellow, is not the cretin you make him out to be. He is a genius. That is the point at which you begin your underhand farrago of allegations, accusing all intelligent people of errors, of evil intention, of intellectual bankruptcy. Or here's another example, just as strange. Everything is in flux, everything changes, you say, stealing this banality from the Greeks. But is it everything? For example, the square, the root of minus one, the circular square, how do they change? And can the invariable change? It's clear that we have to find some way out of this. So we say that we were thinking about empirical, material things. Very well. So do ideal objects not change? And do empirically invariable objects change? Does the replacement of certain ideas by others mean that these ideas have changed? One of the vital laws of ideology is that one must never dig into its phraseology beyond the point of constituting a threat to its integrity and its grandeur. All the questions which a reasonable man can ask our philosophers are either "resolved" sophistically or rejected as inadmissible. And, incidentally, people try not to ask these questions—partly because they are afraid, partly because they feel they will not get an answer, and partly from indifference. And mark my words, in time you yourself will be devoured for having infringed this law—not by much, but still an infringement. There's a feeling of this kind of digging too far in your work on socio-economic structure. Do you know what was said about you on this point in the philosophical faculty of the Military Academy?—I've got a friend who works there. They said you were indulging in scholastic logicisation of the categories of historical materialism.'

I found this piece of information from Anton disturbing. I would have to find out in more detail what had really been said. And what in the world had possessed me to get myself mixed up in this analysis of concepts? What need was there?! Fashion! Cybernetics! The successes of logic! The systematic approach! The structural approach! Metascience! Semantics! F—— it all!

'Of course, compared with you, I am a cretin and an ignoramus,' I said. 'But people must be given some *weltanschauung*—some conception of the world.'

'But for what purpose?' said Anton. 'For the sake of their souls, or the sake of their minds? As far as their minds are concerned, the popularisation of science and a summary of its most interesting ideas and results do more than Marxism does.

And that, too, is ideology. Marxism flirts with this ideology, subordinating it to itself only in appearance. As far as the soul goes, Marxism has something to give only to a specific part of the population, and even then only in as far as those people find it profitable to believe in it. Hardly any Soviet citizen (normal, not insane) would go to the stake for his faith in Marxism. You believe in Marxism not as a consumer of ideology, but as a cog in the formal apparatus of ideology. Let's see what song you sing when you're thrown out because you're useless, or even because you're harmful.'

'Don't try to frighten me,' I said. 'I hope that nothing of the kind happens. It's you who need to be thinking about your future. At the Institute I've been asked for full details on you. I don't know for whom. I've got to write a full report on you. What should I write?! By the way, did you make that phone-call?'

'I rang. I went round. I get the impression that at the moment using you as a reference makes people suspicious and puts them on their guard. But don't you worry. As soon as there's the slightest smell of the book, I'll leave at once.'

But I was extremely worried. Not because of the book (I couldn't care less about that!), but because of what Anton told me about the reaction to my recommendation. The bastards must have started a rumour. And now they were putting their united efforts to consolidate it, using all the petty means at their disposal.

On social psychology

'The social psychology of Soviet man (let's call him S, for short) hasn't been studied at all until now,' said Edik. 'And indeed it's hardly likely that anyone will ever study it seriously—it's a very boring occupation. S's feelings, as he stands for hours in a queue? Nothing. Just vacant waiting, and nothing more. S's feelings as he prepares to do down someone close to him? Just a blank awareness of a duty to be done, and nothing more. S's feelings when he gets promoted? Discontent that he has not been promoted still higher, and a blank waiting for his next promotion. And so on and so forth. But there are certain phenomena of S's social psychology which are worthy of attention, if only because people should know what awaits their descendants in the proximate and inevitable radiant future of the construction of partial or complete (which means one and the same thing) communism. Here is one aspect of that future. If S becomes a significant personality who opposes the delights of our reality, that does not mean that he has lived a virtuous life which qualifies him to be enrolled among the saints. If indeed S tries to lead such a life, either he will be rapidly uprooted and liquidated by all available means, or he will develop into a fighter against all the little injustices in his immediate environment and will be encouraged in every way by the Soviet authorities and by propaganda. Such a champion of truth will wage war with the administration of the apartment block in which he lives to get leaky taps repaired, against smoking in public places, against noise pollution from transistor radios, and so on. This kind of champion of justice is one of the pillars of communism. And he will never mature to oppose our entire system. To develop to such a stage of opposition, you have to do something, to live long enough and to think a great deal—and society, for some reason or other, must itself push you into such a role. Of course, traits of character, upbringing and events of your past life play some part in this, and sometimes a decisive part. But not always, and not always visibly. The main thing is that this S must live an ordinary, normal Soviet life, only gradually developing his exclusive nature. For example, Vidov grew up in a well-to-do and totally Soviet family, he was a devotee of Stalin right up to Stalin's death and was driven into the anti-Soviet camp by his fellow artists because of his work. Moreover, he was a friend of members of the K G B, met senior representatives of Soviet power and tried to be loyal to it. Even Rogozin joined the party after Stalin's death, with the intention of fighting the regime actively from inside the party, and that was the only way for anyone who wanted to take part in this cause. It's true that even this course turned out later to be illusory. But that is quite a different question. It's rumoured that even Solzhenitsyn was once an informer. Of course, if he hadn't agreed to this he would soon have been liquidated and he would not have become what he is now. Even more so, there is nothing surprising in the fact that Petrenko (I knew him well) joined the Komsomol as he should, fought as a volunteer in the secondary wars, joined the party early, rose to high rank during the Great Patriotic War (he ended the war as a Colonel with a chestful of ribbons and went on to join the Academy of the General Staff), and was appointed to an important post at the precise moment when the seeds which had lain concealed since his early youth finally sprouted, his eyes were opened, and when he said to himself and to everyone else: No, I can't take any more of this!'

'Tell me,' I asked, 'what are you driving at?'

'Simply,' said Edik, 'that you and I are sitting here eating some crap called beefsteak, without having the faintest idea what kind of dirty tricks fate might play on us this very moment. Maybe I might suddenly launch a public protest. Or suddenly you might become an eminent . . . well, what can I offer you . . .? Let's say an eminent revisionist.'

I felt slightly ill at ease. Although Edik might have scented who I was and decided to have a little fun with me. But it was hardly likely.

'I have lived out my life,' said Edik, pushing aside with distaste his plate of resolutely unchewable meat and mouldy mashed potatoes, all soused in a repulsive sauce made of some unidentifiable filth. 'Just look at what we're eating! And yet this is one of the best restaurants in Moscow, beyond most people's means! What were we talking about? Oh, yes. I have lived out my life, and I have wasted it in studying the ins and outs of the Soviet way of life and its laws. I have completely assimilated the way of life, but as far as the laws which govern it go, I must admit that I've never been able to sort them out. I've got a few ideas, but they're so trivial that I'm ashamed even to speak of them. Thirty-odd years of thought for such a result . . . Recently I visited . . . I was talking to his son. He's an interesting lad. He's a scoundrel, of course, but very far from a fool. You should have heard what he told me about our society! I was literally terrified. It's true that everything he said was tainted by the most filthiest cynicism, and cynicism kills intelligence. But the fact remains that what it's taken me years and years to produce, he knows instinctively. Even on the subject of women I felt ignorant in his presence. I'm over sixty. And how many women have I had? You can count them on the fingers of one hand. He can't be more than twenty, and he's already had more than thirty. And he's not lying, the shit. He's strong, he's handsome, he's witty, well-educated. He's got lots of confidence. You can feel that he's had a lot of experience. No, I'm certain he's not lying. Anyway, the hell with him. I don't envy him or blame him. It's the times we live in! There's nothing you can do about it. That's not what I wanted to talk about. But there is one thing of which I am finally and irrevocably convinced. You're not bored yet? You want to go on listening?'

Edik poured out what was left of the vodka, raised his glass and proposed a toast: to youth, may they be more intelligent and wiser than us! He downed the vodka and swore coarsely.

'What muck!' he said. 'For a start it's a hundred per cent chemicals, and then the bastards water it down. That's the whole essence of our life. The whole problem lies in the human material which composes our society, which our society produces, and which then goes on to produce society. Those human qualities and those human relationships about which our art is completely mute, and which are regarded as secondary in Western art, take pride of place in this country. Our norm comprises the most repugnant qualities of human nature without which it is impossible to survive in Soviet social conditions. And all this filth is veiled by the most grandiose and the most mendacious of ideologies. The rank and file Soviet man is a whole head higher than any Western official or intellectual! No more, no less. One might as well say that as life at the frontiers of biological possibility (in the desert or in the far north) engenders specific forms of creature, so life at the frontiers of social possibility—and that is what our social conditions are—engenders specific kinds of social individual: social bugs, social worms, social rats, social snakes, lizards, scorpions . . . these very social types have a better chance of survival here than the species which emerge in the favourable social conditions of Western civilisation. Social conditions in the Soviet Union are distinct from those in the West in the same way as biological conditions in the desert or in the Arctic Circle differ from conditions in Western Europe and America. That is the first truth which, for me, is indisputable and which I shall never recant. And here's another one for you. You may say that people today do live in the Arctic Circle or in the desert, and don't live all that badly. That is true. But these are people, i.e. creatures, who have been developed in favourable conditions and have support from a world which exists under these conditions. What do I mean? Left to ourselves we would rapidly regress on all fronts, even in comparison with our present life which is so beggarly compared to that of the West. If we cling on to a certain standard of living, it is only because we exist on the ideas and results of our former history and of Western culture. On its own account social progress in the Soviet Union is impossible. It is a social parasite. Do you take my meaning?'

Nameless (who had joined us) shrugged his shoulders.

'I don't know how true all this is,' he said. 'You have used the words "progress" and "regression". But they are very ambiguous. I would have preferred to avoid value judgements for the time being, if only for the time being. I would rather restrict myself to plain statements. Regression, in one respect, is fully compatible with progress in another. For example, year by year we produce more and more vulgar novels and films, but at the same time we learn to dance better, skate better, score more goals and lift heavier weights.'

'That is true,' said Edik. 'But literature and dance do not have the same values as far as the fate of civilisations is concerned.'

'I don't know,' said Nameless. 'Everything depends on the number and the combinations of phenomena of this kind. Here we have no abstract *a priori* rules. It is empirical rules which operate in this area. To discover them we have to observe and to measure. And you must bear in mind that history is an individual process. The world as a whole is an individual phenomenon. Life began at a particular date. Society began at a particular date. The Soviet Union began at a particular date. You may tell me that that can be repeated in different places and at different times. I know. But that is quite a different problem. Here we have to take the process as a whole. So repetitions in

(86)

details are merely details of the whole. I do not claim that our process of life is unknowable. I have racked my brains about this muck as well, and I too have reached certain conclusions. For example, I believe that things are a great deal more serious than you and I think, than Soviet power and its ideologues think, than the enemies and the critics of the Soviet way of life think. I am not prepared at the moment to state categorically either that the Soviet Union is a cancerous growth on the body of Western civilisation or that it is healthy and viable tissue. I acknowledge that the Soviet Union is a regeneration of all the foundations of culture. But is it a *de*-generation? For me, personally, these questions are not clear for the moment. A great deal has been written and spoken on this theme. But everything has been insignificant. At the present time no one, neither the advocates of Marxism, nor its critics, understands what is going on. The world is in confusion. The essential things remain obscure. Hence comes this depressing agitation which everyone and everything suffers from. It is all so trivial.'

'What about Solzhenitsyn, then?' said Edik.

'Solzhenitsyn denounces, he states, he stirs things up,' said Nameless. 'But he does not understand either. What he proposes is irrational. And in our age even irrationalism must be the product of scientific research. What we need is a mystique. But it must be a mystique born from comprehension, and not from ignorance.'

I listened with great interest. It is very strange how our professional work induces a general boredom, while a dilettante conversation like this can keep one's attention for hours on end.

'In my view,' said Edik, 'you exaggerate the importance of science. It's not science that we're short of, it's something else. We've got too much science. And even Marxism claims to be scientific—and at the very highest level. We would be better off with a bit more goodness about. A bit of naivety. Maybe even something childish. A nice fairy story.'

The book

It is a great deal easier to write a book on one's own than with a collective of several authors. And when the collective includes more than forty people, writing a book becomes a nightmare. It took six months merely to draw up a rough plan and a schedule. And we were praised for our speed! Indeed, within the department there were hints that you only needed to hurry when you were catching fleas, and that we would have done better to have considered our plan more fully. The Central Committee also wondered whether our haste might not be some indication of superficiality. And the Academy of Social Sciences roundly accused us of adventurism. Naturally we asked higher authority for two extra months to re-draft the plan. During this time we would be able to attain such a level of idiocy that even the Department of Scientific Communism at the philosophical faculty would praise us. Our plan would be confirmed and would acquire the force of law. And once that happened it would be quite impossible to creep beyond its framework under any circumstances—it would be forbidden. By whom? By us ourselves, of course: the authors, those who had taken part in the discussion sessions, members of the organising committee, and so on—that great host of people who had a vital interest in seeing that nothing intelligent, bright, original or truthful should be said.

We now come to the point of assigning tasks to the various authors. Passions erupted over every trivial detail. Even the totally impassive Anton and the very proper Stupak had a tiff. They both wanted to write the section on the development of science but were in no way prepared to collaborate on it. So we had to divide the responsibility: to one we had to give the development of natural sciences and technology, to the other the human sciences (excluding, of course, philosophy and political economy). The list of authors included two corresponding members, eight doctors, three professors without doctor's degrees (either because of their age or their stupidity), about twenty masters of science, a dozen doctoral candidates for whom participation in the book would guarantee the acceptance of their theses, a few non-graduate research workers (to count the quotations and verify references), and a couple of technical assistants (to retype the manuscript, to run messages for the authors, the authorities and the publisher, to prepare the documentation and so on). These last two have to work in the worst sense of the word, and get paid almost nothing for it. It's hard to see why they carry on with this job. Sometimes it's the prospect of promotion to junior research assistant. Sometimes it's the prospect of getting a rise or some miserable little bonus. And sometimes it's because they're waiting for their pension. I hardly know anything about this category. I give them a job and insist that it be done—and even that I usually leave to my deputy. The work of the non-graduate research workers is easier, but it is still work. Some of them are trying to publish and defend their dissertations. The rest will stay in the same job for life, somehow or other adapting themselves to the limited progress offered by their working conditions: increments, bonuses, fringe benefits and so on. They become a part of the routine life of the Institute (the housing committee, the savings bank, the organisation of paid holidays, cut-price excursions, and so on) and sometimes play an important part in it. The rest of the research group (and here I exclude the external authors who do not work in the department) enjoy a fairly free and easy existence. For them, this book is a chance, and a perfectly legal one, either to do nothing, or to go about their own little personal enterprises which, for many of them, are a great deal more substantial and important than their part in the book. And finally there is me—the head of the entire collective of authors. But that is quite a different story.

Then the work of the authors begins, or, more accurately, work with the authors and work on behalf of the authors. Work on behalf of the authors is only a minor problem. Collective works with a large number of authors usually involve some people who, because of the position they hold, never write their own parts (which are written by others, who generally turn in a decent job). There is another group who fob you off with any kind of crap, or who are not even capable of that. Their participation is taken into account at an early stage. From some point of view they have their uses. Their material is usually written by one of the principal authors who actually do any work, or by the editor himself. Thus I shall be writing Serikov's pieces myself. The first category I listed is very hard to define. Sometimes this group includes respectable authors who, for some reason or other, have made a botch of it. It also includes people like Serikov, about whom hitherto there had been the false impression that there was still some hope. Everything produced by authors like that has to be rewritten from scratch by the principal authors. Work *with* authors is the most difficult part of the book. Among the authors who work independently there is a certain nucleus of principal authors who write decently and carefully (always the same old stuff, of course, but at least they do it professionally). The main thing in dealing with them is to achieve unanimity. That is the reason why the sections, departments and author-collectives are selected in advance to make sure this is the case—or at least to ensure that there is mutual tolerance. If this nucleus is at loggerheads within itself there will be no book. There remains the largest part of the collective of authors. This is dominated by all the worst qualities of the Soviet research worker in the field of human sciences, distributed in a variety of combinations among the various individuals who make up the group: idleness, hackwork, indiscipline, unreliability, trouble-making, arrogance, stubbornness, ambition, a lack of principle, jealousy and so on. And it is within the same group (and only there!) that one sometimes comes across the most abominable traits of these scientific researchers: erudition, originality of thought, talent, boldness. It is true, luckily, that all these are found in only modest quantity. And the large, companionable collective of authors tries not to notice them or to actively ignore them, or, if this proves impossible, to put these little upstarts in their place. Talent, originality and boldness are only tolerable in the group of principal authors, where, fortunately, they are never found.

The work of a collective on a book like ours means months and years of tension which could be the subject of novels truly more terrifying than those of Dostoievsky and Balzac. Dozens—no, hundreds—of meetings of sections, the department, the management, groups, sub-groups, teams, the party

bureaux of the sections, of the department and of the Institute
. . . so many meetings, speeches, notes, reports, accounts,
plans, individual and collective commitments, denunciations,
anonymous letters . . . telephone calls, personal meetings,
group meetings, consultations, receptions, declarations,
demands . . . Add to all this changes in foreign and domestic
policy, changes in the leadership, sessions of the Secretariat and
the Politburo, Plenums of the Central Committee, meetings
within the Central Committee, in the City Committee, in the
Department, in the Presidium . . . Intrigues. Squabbles.
Rumours. The attention and interest of competing organisations . . . My God! If only someone could calculate the sum of
moral, physical and spiritual energy expended so that a year or
two hence (no, too fast—it won't be taken seriously!) we shall
eventually produce a fat, spineless, inconsistent and servile
manuscript and submit it for general discussion! That is still
only at departmental level. But before that there is the discussion of each article and chapter in various departments, sub-
collectives and commissions . . . But now we have the manuscript retyped in several copies and handed over to the Direction and to the Scientific Council (they have now been combined but in the past there were two discussions, one in the
Council and one by the Direction). And all these titanic efforts
will have served for nothing but to produce yet another voluminous candidate for the pulping mills. I could have turned
out a mishmash like this with the help of two assistants, one
scientific and one technical, in six months. But that is impossible since it does not conform to the Soviet principle of collective labour. Moreover, if I were to write it alone, then I could
write better. Glory! Position! No, that is against the rules. And
what would the others do in the meantime? You have to become
an Academician, and have a high post if you want to write on
your own. At all events everyone would realise that either you'd
had it ghosted, or that you had written complete rubbish (like
Academician Ludov, who published the same drivel about
Mendeleev three times in one year under different titles), or
perhaps both at the same time. That would be normal. But for
the time being you must be content to lead a comradely creative
collective.

You think that's the end of the matter? Oh, no! There's still publication to cope with. Then the confidential reports. Then new directives. The return of the manuscript for new revisions. The substitution of certain passages and certain authors. Supplements. Rehashes. Arguments from editors at every level. Editorial in-fighting sparked off by the manuscript. In the end, of course, the book comes out. Then the reviews have to be organised. And then you just wait till someone comes along with some fresh quibble in the light of the latest fashion and directive.

You might well ask why the hell I took this burden on myself? First, because it would have been dumped on me anyway, and the fact that I showed initiative is a point in my favour. Secondly, the plan would at all events have imposed some sort of burden on us, and this one is lighter and more advantageous than the one our bosses had in mind for us. So that's another point for me. Thirdly, if I want to preserve what I've got and to achieve more, there are no other means available to a man at my level. This is my ordinary day-to-day existence. And finally, in doing this, I am working in a good cause. Yes, yes! Just imagine! Once a rumour got about that I was going to leave for a new job, maybe in the Central Committee, maybe higher up in the department, maybe even abroad. And that started up such pandemonium in our group that I almost felt ashamed. Entire delegations sought me out and tried to persuade me not to abandon the 'cause', and all my colleagues. Some even accused me of treason: they had put their fate in my hands, and there I was abandoning them to the mercy of the Vaskins! For there is a difference between people like me (we're pretty thin on the ground) and people like Vaskin (and they are in the overwhelming majority), i.e. between us 'liberals' and them, the 'obscurantists', 'conservatives', 'reactionaries'. Our society is the arena for some vital underground battle which is reflected in our relationships. But what battle in particular?

'That's a trivial problem,' Anton said one day à propos of something quite different. 'There are within us two traditional tendencies—one Westernised, the other home-grown. The Western trend is more gentle, more vivid, more cheerful. Our own is harder, greyer, more serious (gloomier). Usually these days the reference is to China on the one hand and to the West on the other. But both these tendencies are inherent in our system. They're in the nature of our people. I remember once when I was in flying school, during the war, there was a question as to whether we should have our own guardhouse. How could there be any thought of the West or of China at that period? Everyone who took part in the discussion and resolution of the problem fell into one of two hostile groups without any external influences. The groups could be loosely described as 'the holiday campers' and the 'prison campers'. But no one had any doubt that we did need a guardhouse. The only argument was about what form it should take.

Unforeseen circumstances

As it was decided to turn the Avenue of the Construction Workers into a route for government use only (it led directly to the suburban palaces of the highest leadership) all public transport and goods traffic was diverted via the Avenue of Marxism-Leninism. Since the Slogan impeded the traffic flow a number of old buildings and one little fifteenth-century church had to be demolished. No matter about the church, which, left on its own, would have collapsed anyway. But it was a pity about the other buildings. One of them had once been the magnificent mansion of the merchant Behemoth who in his time had been a small bolshevik sympathiser and a protector of modernist painters. A pedestrian sub-way was built. In the course of all this re-building, the Slogan disappeared under a heap of debris, and everyone forgot about it. So the pensioners wrote another letter to the papers. A Saturday of voluntary communist labour was organised. The area round the Slogan was cleared of rubbish. It was decided to leave the fence in position for the time being, just in case, although it was now very difficult to get to the Slogan, and the morally unstable elements of society now gathered on a piece of wasteland closer to the Avenue of the Construction Workers, with the result that the area of the Slogan was left alone. Citizens and visitors once

(93)

again had the opportunity to admire the marvellous spectacle of the Slogan. As the newspapers put it: the workers had been presented with a new gift for the festival.

Business

'Any news about your book?'

'They're looking for a printer. They tell me it's difficult because our people have infiltrated everywhere.'

'That's obviously an exaggeration. We've got into the habit of seeing the KGB everywhere and in everything. There's even a rumour that Nixon was one of our agents.'

'That wouldn't surprise me one bit. He behaved exactly as if we had bought him. The Americans were quite right to get rid of him. But there's something about this business of the printers that I don't like. I know perfectly well that Mirovich sent his book out quite a lot later than I did, and his has come out already.'

'There's nothing surprising about that. Mirovich's book is the usual superficial anti-Soviet rubbish. But your book is serious. And what's more, your judgements are different from those of all our dissidents. You believe that the Revolution was a benefit, that the party and the people are united, and so on. That's not too easy to digest if you're a little western intellectual who protects our dissidents! There are certainly people Over There who think you're a KGB agent.'

'I doubt it. The content of my book is quite clear enough. And there must be people Over There who aren't stupid.'

'Very well, then!' We'll find out in due course!'

The specific nature of Russian tragedy

'The special characteristic of the Russian tragedy,' said Anton, 'is that first it provokes laughter, then horror, and finally obtuse indifference. I was once swapping recollections with a group of perfectly respectable people. I told them that after

Stalin's death the administration of the camp I was in decided to show a bit of liberalism: they let us have a bath. We'd hardly begun to wash ourselves when it turned out there'd been a mistake. They turned the water off and drove us out of the bath-house all wet and naked. And it was thirty below freezing. The thing that struck me at the time was the layer of ice which formed all over my body. And just imagine, my listeners burst out laughing as one man. And later, when I told them that an entire bomber group had flattened a camp holding tens of thousands of people who had allegedly revolted, they were all horrified by the scale of the thing. But they were back to normal within a few minutes. They began to calculate the approximate number of prisoners who had been in camps throughout the whole period of Soviet power. How many of them were guilty, how many innocent. Strangely enough, the figures they got coincided roughly with the ones which Solzhenitsyn produced later.

'So what's the explanation?' Lenka and Sashka demanded, simultaneously.

'There are several,' said Anton. 'The one I prefer is that the Russian tragedy, and the way in which it is received, lies beyond good and evil, outside the sphere of morality. It is a purely psychological, or indeed physiological, reaction to a terrible fact. At the start of the war a friend and I once saw a shell literally blow the head off a quartermaster colonel, and the colonel just carried on standing there. It was very funny, until we realised the full horror of what had happened. That was a reaction outside morality. It lacked any essentially human basis—of moral protest or of moral revulsion.

'But surely the people whom you told about the camp must have understood that all that was wicked, terrible, inhuman?'

'They knew it, but they lacked any moral sense of it. For them, as for most of us, such a moral sense does not exist.'

'Come now,' I said. 'Are you really saying that we're all immoral?'

'Wait a minute, papa. Don't interfere,' said Lenka. 'We're talking about something different.'

'What I have in mind,' said Anton, 'is the fact that there is a mental mechanism which operates even when there are no

(95)

witnesses, no threat of exposure, whether or not there is any danger of punishment, and so on. For instance, a man may refuse to write a denunciation even if no one could possibly know about it, or refuse to kill a victim even if he himself might be killed because of his refusal. Make a dispassionate, objective inventory of your life. Do you find many instances which would confirm the existence of such a mechanism within yourselves? Or can you name many people among your friends in whom you could put complete trust? Well! . . . You see what I mean.'

'What is it that makes us like that?'

'It is because the conditions of our life do not engender any need for moral behaviour and give us no experience of it.'

'What are you talking about?' I said indignantly. 'Thou shalt not kill! Thou shalt not steal! That is exactly what we and our children are taught!'

'Yes, that is what we are taught. We are also taught how to hold our knives and forks, to pay our telephone bills and our rent on time. The things that used in the past to be the basis of moral behaviour are no longer seen as such. Times have changed. Today, in order to be a moral person it's not enough not to kill, not to steal, not to oppress the weak and to give up one's seat to one's elders. Now there is another set of actions which give people a moral definition.'

'And what actions do you regard as moral?'

'That would take a long time to explain. But briefly, they're actions performed by one person towards others without being obliged to by law or custom, which are of no benefit to the person who performs them, and which moreover may even expose him to risk of punishment, but which will be of benefit to the people towards whom they are directed, or at least will cause them no harm . . . Is that generally clear?'

'There is a contradiction,' I said. 'How can an action be free of any norms, if it is executed in accordance with moral norms? Are there any such norms?'

'There are no moral norms. If a norm exists, then there is no morality. What people here describe as moral norms have nothing to do with real morality. There is only one factor in morality: that is the capacity to judge whether a particular action is moral or immoral. So there is one "norm": if you want to be a moral person, be one, i.e. do not commit immoral actions.'

'That is a tautology,' I said.

'No,' said Sashka, 'I'm beginning to understand. You can't draw up a classification of moral and immoral actions of themselves. Morality is a particular component of a person which allows that person (often without thinking about it) to perform actions which satisfy some kind of general and unique moral criterion. Is that it?'

'That's it,' said Anton.

'For instance, a moral person will never denounce anyone, nor betray a friend, under any circumstances.'

'And if that causes harm to others, how can one assess his conduct towards them?'

And we began a crazy, disorganised argument that lasted until midnight. Why is it that discussions of this kind never arise in philosophy seminars?

A good idea

'If I were you,' said Svetka, 'I'd rent a little room to work in. It'd solve a whole lot of problems at a stroke! You wouldn't need to go on so many "business trips", and in general . . .'

I immediately rang Vadim, my deputy. He's a bright lad who picks up every hint. He'd fix it all up in a trice. Although he's a bit of a forelock-tugger, and probably an informer, he's a very useful and necessary man. Everyone in the section was very surprised when I announced my intention to appoint him my deputy. So I sketched out the functions of a deputy and invited them to propose a better candidate. There were no applicants. It's always the same. Of course the job of a deputy has its advantages. But the advantages come at a price! You have to run, you have to sit, you're constantly on the go, you really have to sweat; you have to slave away in the most confused and busy area of our existence. It's hardly surprising that it's only the most committed careerists who are prepared to take on this kind of work. And any decent person who got the job would rapidly turn into a total nonentity. I have proved this by experience. When I was still in charge of a section I appointed a highly respectable and able lad as my deputy. What happened? Within six months he had become such a turd that even I was ashamed for him. The best people for these jobs are devoted self-seekers, who even become a trifle more civilised from their promixity to the higher spheres of culture (if you'll forgive the expression).

To cut a long story short, within a few days Vadim had found me an excellent and comparatively cheap room roughly equidistant from my own apartment, from the Institute and from Svetka's house. About half-an-hour on foot. That would be good for my health, for I was really beginning to put on weight. Vadim came round in his car with Svetka, loaded up all the books and manuscripts I needed for my work, and a few minutes later we were celebrating my house-warming. If you only knew what a blessing it was for me to have, at last, my own separate, isolated room in a quiet, clean and light apartment.

Tamara took my decision as a wholly logical step in the development of our family relationship (in the opinion of our friends we are one of the happiest and best matched families in Moscow!)

'But I won't give you a divorce,' she said, decisively. 'Sleep with whom you like, but no divorce! Divorce is immoral. We've got children, don't forget.'

Sashka took things with complete indifference. Lenka jumped for joy. 'It's great!', she shrilled. 'I'll come and see you in secret, without mama or grandma knowing!'

Then Tamara did some very closely figured accounts and informed me how much money I should have to provide for the family, and how much I could squander on my trollop. It's a good thing she doesn't know about my bonuses, and the odd fees I get. But I must give her her due. The ex-wives of all my friends are screwing blood out of their ex-husbands with the help of specially hired lawyers, letters to the party bureau, and affidavits in court.

Svetka said that she would drop in to see me for an hour or so after work. It's strange, but once I was on my own, what I wanted most of all was for no one to drop in. I never thought that I would find being alone so enjoyable.

My landlady is a neat and welcoming woman of about seventy. She has given me curtains with a pattern of blue flowers, scattered the room with white tablecloths and runners, and insisted that I should drink her freshly brewed tea. And I felt like a child, home with my mother.

All possible variants

'Let's discuss the situation soberly,' said Anton. 'The liberal epoch is over. It is in practice impossible today to publish even the kind of books and articles that were published three years ago. You've obviously felt this yourself. And anyway, it would be almost pointless to do so. They would have no effect. Times have changed, even in the way our work is received. So, what must be done? It's a complex question, but pretty trivial none-theless. Here's the dilemma: either we remain within the framework of Marxism, or we leave it altogether. Let's consider the first variant. Here again there are two alternatives: either one obediently executes every instruction from above, and becomes a jackal like Vaskin, or one seeks to innovate. The first alternative is not for you. Even if you wanted to follow that line, you wouldn't be allowed to. It's too late. In Their book, you're an innovator. And innovation can be accomplished in two ways as well: either you can revise Marxism, i.e. reconsider its essen-tial formulae as no longer responding to contemporary reality, or you can improve it, i.e. "develop" it, adapting it to new conditions without departing by an inch from even its most secondary principles. Now, revisionism is excluded *a priori*. So we are left with improvement. But who is to decide whether you have improved it, or whether you have damaged it? The Vas-kins. Who is to decide whether you have deviated or not? The same people. So whether you are kicked out as a revisionist or as an improver who's slightly overdone it and gone off course, that does not depend on you, but on the Vaskins. From my observa-tions the situation at the moment is that They would rather come to terms with revisionists than with improvers, for these latter are genuine competitors. Vaskin too is angling for a corresponding membership. And his claim is no worse than yours. So if he is offered the slightest opportunity of sticking a knife in your back he will do so without a second's hesitation. After all, you improvers have kept the Vaskins in the shadows for almost twenty years. Now their time is about to come. So the better you do your work, the worse for you. And if you do it badly, you'll only be crushed the more thoroughly, since shoddy work is something They're really good at.'

'That, on the whole, is true,' I said. 'Let's hear your second variant.'

'Very well,' said Anton, 'let's consider it. If you leave the framework of Marxism, that opens the following possibilities: (1) you leave the sphere of ideology altogether; (2) you stay within the field of ideology. The former possibility is not for us. We are too old for that. So we are left with the second. Here again there are variants: (1) to criticise Marxism, to fight against it; (2) to be indifferent to it. The situation here is far more complicated than in the cases we have already considered. I will deal with the criticism of Marxism in a moment. I'd like to start with indifference to it. One can deal with ideology while remaining indifferent to Marxism, for example in the spirit of Buddhism or Orthodoxy. That is quite fashionable these days. I won't discuss this course, for, I think that you will agree with me, this sort of ideological activity is not appropriate to present-day conditions. They signify a flight from the most important ideological problems of our time. That way is not for us. That is for burnt-out cases of inferior rank. So the question arises, is it possible to be indifferent to Marxism if one is dealing with the most important ideological problems of our times? Alas, personally I am convinced that this in fact is impossible. Marxism, old man, is something very serious indeed. You can't get away from it. Whatever problem you tackle, you will find that it has been considered and in a way resolved by Marxism. And whatever you say about it, in one way or another you will come up against Marxist tradition, Marxist protest or Marxist approval. Marxism is a great ideology. And if one works in the spirit of the ideological problems of the age, one cannot avoid coming up against it. That is a fact. I think you take my point. So what remains? The struggle? That's where the real snag lies.

'Just imagine for a moment,' Anton continued, 'that we were given complete freedom of action, that They said, all right lads, attack Marxism as you think fit! Well, what would happen? Haven't there been masses of such unconstrained critics in the West? Haven't they written a great deal? They have. And they have not been fools. And the books they have written have been intelligent. But what has come of it? Nothing. Marxism today is as invulnerable as it has ever been. Not at all because it is right, or wise. The question does not lie there. The problem is that Marxism, like every other ideology, is not a science. It is scientific in form—the tribute it pays to our era. But it is not a science. People have constantly tried to impose on it the status and appearance of a science. That is to the advantage of those in power: everything that happens is the product of objective laws, and not of their own stupidity. They merely discover the laws, forecast and assist their operation. You'll remember that Stalin said: We must saddle the laws and ride them! And that was no empty phrase: it was very seriously meant. They govern in the name of universal laws, and not on the basis of the rules of large-scale gangsterism. And that is an advantage also to the gigantic army of ideologues: they are scientists, not just some kind of priestlings! And it is an advantage to others as well; it is better to think of oneself as being oppressed by the iron-hard laws of matter than by canny self-seekers, pirates and careerists. There are very precise indications of what is a science and what is an ideology. It is a commonplace to say that Marxism satisfies the former criteria, but not the latter. Its alliance with science is an historical peculiarity of Marxism as an ideology. In our age of science and technology and general education it is impossible to get along without that relationship. An ideology which does not claim to be a science, which does not take on an appearance of science, which does not have the means to appear to the broad masses as a science, cannot in our days be an ideology. Marxism, since it is an ideology, and not a science, is invulnerable to scientific criticism. Yet every critique of Marxism of any significance at all claims to demonstrate its scientific inconsistencies. Criticism of any other kind—for instance that which comes from ideologues of Christianity—is almost imperceptible. And against it, Marxism is armed with a most powerful demagogy. But say that we manage to refute Marxism. Then another problem arises: suggest something better of your own! And when we try to produce our own alternative, we will be obliged once again to do so according to the laws by which ideologies are fabricated. And in that case we will produce the same thing all over again, with a few trifling modifications. After all, Marxism did arise on the high road of history. And if we build an ideology in the same place, we will end up with something that looks like Marxism. Must we therefore conclude that we are caught in a vicious circle? No. The period which has just passed was interesting in one very important respect: it indicated a way out. Ideology can be defeated by the facts of the reality which it claims to illuminate. In the given case, that means the facts of that social reality which it claims to recognise, foresee, and theorise about. The facts drive Marxism into its own trap. That is why Nikita's speech and Solzhenitsyn's books dealt a much heavier blow to Marxism than the efforts of all the critics of Marxism through its entire history. This is the path of any real criticism of Marxism—an uncompromising analysis of our society, and the publication of the facts of its existence. And it is the only path. And what is more, it is the only path by which it is possible to develop an ideology more appropriate than Marxism is to man in modern society.'

'So be it,' I said. 'But why do you want to produce this ideology? Forget it! Just go ahead with your study of our society, and leave it at that!'

'It's a question of personal involvement,' said Anton. 'There are people who become doctors so that they can cure the human body. My concern is with the human soul. Not the psyche, but the soul—a purely social phenomenon. So I want to do something for this soul. Ideology is a medicine for the soul. But Marxism has nothing to give the soul—it operates as a purely formal ideological mechanism. An interesting subject, by the way, the nature of the ideological mechanism in Soviet society. In this it differs from Christianity. In Christianity there was also an element of coercion. And in Marxism there is a voluntary element. Yet Marxism is hostile to the soul, to spirituality. It is anti-spiritual. I cannot explain this to you in the abstract. But if you take our society and our people in their reality and not in their propaganda abstraction you will soon see what I mean in every concrete case.'

We had already had several conversations of this kind. But only now did I begin to listen closely to Anton's words, and to find in them a sense which had hitherto always escaped me.

The conference delegation

The scientific section of the Central Committee confirmed the membership of the delegation to an international conference. Theirs is the ultimate decision, if you do not count the KGB who at the last moment always hold several people back and slip a few of their own people in in their place (even though almost all the members of the delegation or of the tourist group are essentially in their pocket anyway). But it's curious all the same, this evolution we've seen recently. Indeed the process between the drawing up of the lists for a delegation or a tourist group at source and the confirmation of the final list by the Central Committee reflects or even represents this evolution. At source (in the sections and faculties) they included in the lists everyone who had done productive work over the last few years and who had acquired a decent reputation—i.e. all the leading liberals of our milieu. Then the list moved up to the level of the administrators and the deans, where a number of the decent people were deleted and replaced by rogues and second-raters. Next, at the level of rectors and academic departments, a few more of the decent people still left were removed and new names added of even worse mediocrity. At ministerial level, and in the governing bodies of the academies, almost all the surviving people of any worth (all the men of the sixties) were struck off and their place taken by scum of a kind which in the past would never even have been admitted to local meetings. Finally, the department of science of the Central Committee took the process to its logical conclusion. But I was left in the delegation, much to my shame. But the lads told me that I had been left on the list because there would have been a general furore if I had been excluded. But I know why I was kept on it.

Academician Kanareikin (the head of the delegation) insisted. Why? For a very simple reason: he had to deliver a report, and the report had to be written, and who better than I could write a report which would both win the approval of our leaders, and at the same time produce a decent impression Over There! Serikov was included in the group of tourists. And that too is readily understandable.

The composition of a Soviet delegation to an international scientific congress is always a matter of the greatest importance to the state. The most varied considerations have to be borne in mind: the interests of a variety of organisations, the proper balance of nationalities, the right age range, a proper balance between the sexes, the numbers of representatives of various academic ranks, family relationships, and so on. This problem takes at least a year and the efforts of many authorities to sort out. The question of the part the KGB should play in such matters has been discussed repeatedly and resolved definitively. But there is one extremely interesting but less well-known aspect. It is clear that any one of us (or almost any one) is prepared to carry out (and does carry out from time to time, either directly or indirectly) missions for the KGB. We are patriots. And moreover, for a reward as considerable as a trip abroad at the state's expense, we are prepared to do even more. But that is not enough for the KGB. They include their own people in every delegation. To what end? Here opinions differ. To carry out tasks which cannot be entrusted to ordinary informer-scientists. To keep an eye on the delegates' behaviour. To stop anyone defecting. There is certainly no smoke without fire. But I incline to the view that the reason is far simpler. The delegates keep an eye on each other's behaviour every bit as well as the professional snoopers. The information they provide is more highly qualified. The special missions for the most part are just a sham. Genuinely serious intelligence work is not done in that way. Some people defect anyway. And those who do get away are trusted and reliable people. Untrustworthy people are simply not allowed out. It is simply that the KGB has the right to take part in all visits abroad and uses it for the benefit of its employees. It is a benefit in the same sense as apartments, rest homes, goods in short supply, tickets for theatres, and exhibitions, and so on. And all this is distributed (I've been able to talk with their 'Boys' once or twice) according to the normal rules by which perks are distributed in the Soviet system. And the KGB agents are just as avid for foreign clothes as the doctors and the professors. But they have one great advantage: they don't need to present a report, discuss it, get it passed by the Glavlit (the censorship), to take part in meetings. Their intellectual level is very much the same as that of the average delegate. At worst, when their crass stupidity cannot be concealed, we pass them off as representatives of the non-Russian Republics or as survivals of Stalinism. In such cases, a poor or totally non-existent grasp of foreign languages is a great asset.

The old rag woman

After work, Svetka 'dropped in'. She complained about her colleagues at the Institute ('all bastards'). She complained about her husband ('that miserable weed') and her mother-in-law ('what a bitch'). She moaned that she didn't have a thing to wear (although she wears a different outfit every day, and the Institute gossips haven't yet been able to make a full tally of her wardrobe). It was very difficult to get rid of her ('I must get some work done'). I spread my books and papers on the table, then stood at the window without a single thought in my head. In the courtyard, I saw a strongly-built old crone in a long, shapeless, black dress. She was rummaging through the dust-bins, every now and again extracting something (it looked like rags or paper) and putting it into her little cart. Her face was very striking: large, purplish-blue in colour, with the shapeless pitted nose of an old alcoholic. But to judge by her expression she might have been given the task of writing the chapter in our epoch-making book on the improving standard of living of the workers. It is impossible to describe this expression. One can only show it and give it a name. But it would be better to do neither.

At first sight, the old rag woman seemed to be incredibly

ancient, well over eighty. But from the way in which she was rifling the dustbins and packing the rubbish in her cart, she might well have been much younger. If at my age I had had to take up this kind of work, (which God forbid!) I would hardly have been able to keep up with her. I asked my landlady who the woman was. She replied that no one knew. They just called her the Old Boozer, although no one had ever seen her drunk. She turned up in the courtyard once a week. No one remembered when she had first appeared. No one had paid any attention to her.

I tried to imagine what her life could be like. No friends. No family. Her only company would be totters like herself. Mere pennies to live on. Quarrels over pennies, swindles over pennies. What does she eat? Where does she sleep? It was like a nightmare. How battered and hacked about her mind must be for her to be able to go on living like this! And what if she still had all her wits and some conception of a better life?! No, that was unthinkable. Judging by her face, she spent all the pennies she scraped together on drink. But what could she drink? It's none too cheap nowadays. She probably gets hold of some kind of meths. That would be why her face was so blue.

I turned back to my papers. But I couldn't get the old woman out of my head. We have a developed form of socialism. We are moving towards communism at an ever-increasing rate. But she didn't give a damn for all that. For her, history did not exist. There were no problems. She would soon disappear. And so would I. And we would become equal in the void. But if some one looked at me from some elevated viewpoint, what would they see me doing? What is the principal difference between my existence and the existence of that old woman? Satisfaction? But who knows, maybe she is happier with her life than I am. I suffer—I want to be an Academician, I want to be awarded a prize. But she may not even envy the tyrant to whom she sells her rags and who always cheats her of half-pence. Could it be a feeling of being useful to mankind? But who can measure my value to humanity? Have I indeed been of any use?

The old woman finished loading her cart and unhurriedly dragged it away by a chain over her shoulder. People passed her without even noticing that she was there. She simply did not exist as far as they were concerned, nor did they for her. It was an example of the co-existence of two independent worlds between which any mutual comprehension was impossible. Why bother to fly off to other planets when there's this old boozer wandering through the streets of Moscow: it is just as impossible to establish contact with her—not that we make any effort to.

I told myself that it would cost me nothing to take from my pocket a sum of money which would keep the old woman going for at least six months. But I did not do so. I don't know why. It wasn't because of the money. I have never been much concerned about money.

The dive

'Let me ask you an indiscreet question,' said Nameless. 'Judging by our conversations, you are not a fool. So how have you been able to write such . . . how shall I put it . . . such peculiar books?'

This was so unexpected that I was taken aback and only managed to stammer out something to the effect that my books are no worse than anybody else's, and that there are people who even say they're a bit better. At all events, they're worth a lot more than anything by Petin, Rimenthal, Kostyukov and company.

'That's very possible,' Nameless agreed in a conciliatory tone. 'I'm only seeing it as a layman. You're in a better position to judge. Can you distinguish one adult louse from another? No. Or at least only by time and space coordinates. But we must assume that as far as they're concerned, they can tell each other apart. There must be talented lice, stupid lice, genius lice.'

I told him that at the moment I was setting up an important section and recruiting the most gifted of the staff. We were working on an enormous book in which we planned to reconsider all the most fundamental principles.

'Oh, revisionists are you?' asked Nameless.

'Not on your life!' I was so agitated I was waving my arms

(107)

about. 'Not at all! We are in the mainstream, in the spirit of and in complete conformity with. On the contrary, we're going to give the revisionists a right drubbing. We shall develop, expand, deepen . . .'

'Just the same,' said Nameless, 'you'll all be attacked as revisionists. Developing Marxism is a prerogative reserved for the Leadership.'

'So what if they do attack us?' I replied. 'All the same some day some one has to sort out what Soviet society really is.'

'My, you're aiming high,' observed Nameless. 'But you'll get precisely nowhere, you and all your bright young men, even if you aren't destroyed, (and I'm sure you will be very soon, they're bound to destroy you!) Even if you're guaranteed absolute security and given permission to write absolutely anything you want. Do you want to know why? Because you are all incapable of moving outside the framework of Marxism, even if you were given permission to become its enemies. And you aren't even capable of doing that—of becoming enemies of Marxism. Formations, infrastructures, superstructures, productive forces, production ratios, classes, the State and so on, all these, my dear Marxist, (or anti-Marxist—because it comes to the same thing) all these things are just romantic images of ideology and not scientific concepts. Scientific concepts are prosaic. And you can't come down out of the clouds of romanticism to the dirty ground of reality and judge it on its merits. You will never understand our society since you have no means of doing so. Or more precisely, you will never understand it until you appreciate the fundamental importance of trivia in our way of life. I repeat, tri-vi-a! The grandeur of our system is a trivial grandeur or a grandeur of trivia—that's the heart of the problem. Your lofty categories are as appropriate to our society as words like "brilliant", "wise", "deep", "perceptive", "exhaustive", "truthful" and so on are appropriate to the idiotic and mendacious speeches of our leaders, which they haven't even written themselves.'

At first, I was quite floored by Nameless's words. But I am a good man and I can never be angry at anyone for very long. And then it occurred to me that Nameless's opinions were clearly those of a dilettante. And the next moment I'd quite recovered my good humour.

'You have a rather superficial judgement of Marxism,' I said. 'After all, to appreciate its concepts and principles as they deserve, you have to be a professional.'

'I understand,' said Nameless. 'Forgive me if I have offended you. Of course I am a dilettante, but if you have no objection, let me try to clarify my thoughts. Maybe my dilettante ideas might be of some use to you as a professional. I say that if you don't understand the importance of trivia, you cannot understand the real essence (I don't mean the ideological or propagandistic essence) of our society. Take any important thread of existence (which of course from the point of view of your elevated theory will be only trivial), pull it and you will always see the same thing appear . . . Take queues, for instance, summer holidays, apartments, theatre or concert tickets, books, travel abroad, food, high quality goods . . . to say nothing of serious medical or legal problems which could crop up for anybody some day. Let's forget about the publication of books, about degrees and titles . . . or the problems of getting into college . . . In short, take any *reality* and not all your faceless productive forces, superstructures and the rest of that clap-trap, (you have to be a well educated idiot in the spirit of our age to take all that seriously!) There was an article in some magazine or other, not long ago, about a lad who'd been sentenced to fifteen years when he was innocent. What must reality be like if even an official magazine can publish things like that? It was all glossed over in the article, all the worst horrors were missed out. The lad served eight years. And the Supreme Court did nothing about it. It was mere chance that saved him. And how many are there like him on whom Chance has not smiled? Do you think that's wholly trivial? And do you remember that gang which included some sons of ministers? Do you remember how that ended? A suspended sentence of one year. They weren't even arrested. Trivial, too? The problem is that the first lad was on the lowest rung of the social ladder, and he didn't have any defence counsel. On the other hand—sons of ministers . . . It's clear enough isn't it? Of course it is. It's self-evident. Terrifyingly self-evident. But why doesn't this find a place in your science? Yet there is no getting away from it: merely by climbing the social ladder you acquire a higher degree of legal immunity for yourself and your family. And in no other way. And that is a lawless society. And people who live in the real world know this elementary truth from their cradle (unlike theoreticians who spend years studying how to avoid noticing anything of the kind). Take queues. To stand in line once is nothing. To stand in line a hundred times is nothing. But if it's day in day out, year in year out? Everywhere and for everything? That's something to drive anyone to despair. Where's the solution? To get yourself into a position where there is no queuing. Where you have special goods, deliveries to your door. Where you've got connections and pull. Now for that, you've got to get yourself into the right kind of job. And for that . . . I believe you're going south for your holidays? May I ask you how you managed to get that arranged? I see! And are your tickets being paid for by this same worthy organisation? Well of course. But I can never get anything like that although I'd like to. I've even got the money by working overtime. No way! . . . But is there any point in going on? You aren't a child, you must understand something of this at least. There is a general desperate struggle for privilege. And it is the most worthless vermin who are winning. They are brought up to engage in this struggle. And if you sum it all up, you can say that there is mass production of a specific type of social individual, a specific kind of human material which serves as the basis of our entire way of life. Everything else (economics, politics, morality, art, the lot) proceeds from this. As you're so fond of the term "infrastructure", there it is—the infrastructure of our entire existence. Even the sweeping purges of the Stalin era, (which haven't stopped even yet) grew out of this. If you are a scientist, you should be making a theory from all that. But do it according to the rules of science, and not the rules of ideology.'

I began to stammer out something about historical difficulties, that the shortages were only temporary, about the metro, about creches, about the sacrifices which we must make for the future and so on.

'Stop,' said Nameless. 'You have touched on the basic question quite by chance, the question of morality, in other words, the primordial foundation of all civilisation. Even if one day you managed to build the Radiant Edifice of Communist Society, in the form of paradise on earth, I will not accept it because it will have been built on the blood of victims, on falsehood, and oppression. Out of elementary decency I would not go into such an edifice. I would prefer to stay among the victims. A victim is forgiven all his sins. To be a victim means to start becoming a man.'

'That is religion, not morality,' I said.

'It is not a religion, but a religious, in other words, a moral consciousness, which is something different. But if you're so keen to stick that label on it, go ahead. It's all the same to me. So let's call it religion. But there is one thing that I am certain of: everything that is bestial comes from nature; everything that is human comes from God, that is, it has been invented.'

The toast

'Uncle Anton,' Sashka asked, 'why were you sent to the camps? For nothing, like everyone else?'

'For something, like everyone else, or nearly everyone else. For a poem about one of Stalin's toasts.'

'Do you still remember it?'

'Of course. You don't forget such things.'

The Leader rose up
      to his puny height,
With a twisted grin
      on his face,
And this
    he said:
      Our toast tonight
Is the glorious
      Russian race.
Their fate
    is the harshest
       fate of all,

Their torments
           too many
                to say,
Without them we
           should now be
Not the bosses   slaves one and all,
          that we are today.

They have given their blood,
                  they have poured out sweat
Until they were
          ready
            to die.
They have starved
          and they've thirsted,
They've been living   and, far worse yet,
          like pigs in a sty.

We have made them to suffer,
                to languish in woe,
Their lives
        are with misery
            fraught;
So that after
        our treatment
            they're bound to know
Even hell
      is a pleasure
          resort.
Have we done them
        the slightest
            bit of good?
I still
    cannot
        comprehend why
They should take
        all we say
            as quite understood

When all we have done
                    is
                         to lie.
What other fools
                 in what other land
Would let us
            over them ride?
Tell me anyone
               else who would raise a hand
To save
        their torturers'
                         hide.
He raised his glass
                    and he sipped
                                   the wine,
Wiped his whiskers,
                    his face serene.
And then his eyes
                  began to shine
. Not a trace
            of guilt
                     to be seen.
Then the whole room
                    burst out
                              in a joyful sound,
And the abject
               Russian nation
Licked their
             tears of joy
                          from off the ground
And made premature
                   confession.

'Oh ho,' said Lenka; 'according to Solzhenitsyn, you ought
to have been killed.'
'They took my military career into account. And anyway, it
was the time when things were moving towards Khrushchevism.'
'So you weren't put inside for nothing.'

'Not for nothing. At that time, it was seldom for nothing. They could always manufacture something.'

'You've read Solzhenitsyn of course?'

'Yes!'

'And what do you think of him?'

'I bow very low before him.'

'So what he writes is the truth?'

'It's the truth but not the whole truth. And partial truth distorts the whole picture. It's not so much truth I respect him for, as for his revolt against falsehood and oppression.'

'If he's right, why isn't he published here?'

'Don't ask stupid questions,' said Sashka.

'It's not a stupid question. What is stupid are the people who haven't published Solzhenitsyn here. If he'd been published here, he wouldn't have achieved such a stupendous worldwide effect, and there wouldn't be this constant interest in his books. It's always better to be open about crimes which you can't conceal.'

'Particularly other people's crimes.'

'And if the crimes are still going on . . .'

Anti-Soviet conversations like that are always going on in my home. And there's nothing that I can do to stop them. And what is worst of all, I don't want to stop them and I even take part in them myself.

Toilet paper

Tamurka came bursting in, running with sweat and her eyes popping out of her head.

'Quick! They've got some toilet paper at the shop! I've got a place in the queue.'

We (that is my mother-in-law, Lenka and I) left the meal we'd just started and dashed off after Tamurka. A couple of hours later, we came back home, happy, swathed in bundles of toilet rolls. I was afraid that passers-by would mock at us. But they took it all with perfect understanding. Many of them asked where we'd got the toilet paper from and hurried off to get some for themselves. There was only one half-drunken loon who followed us screaming that Soviet intellectuals were full of shit. But as he repeated this several times, the initial effect started to wane and some passers-by began to shout him down. Finally, two hefty lads who looked like students got him by the arms, told him to belt up and dragged him off in the opposite direction. Be that as it may, we're sure of clean bottoms for the next six months. I have to admit that in this respect (that of bulk buying of things that are hard to come by) Tamurka is a master. When all Moscow is on the hunt for bicarbonate of soda or washing powder, we almost certainly have plenty in reserve. She even manages to keep two months' supply of onions.

This toilet-paper triumph brought a measure of unity and harmony to our disintegrating, although still healthy and Soviet, family. And we settled down happily to wash the dirty linen of all our friends. Tamurka said that Mrs Korytov always smelt bad. Probably doesn't change her underwear for months. And as for Korytov himself, he always wears an expensive, if tasteless, suit, but cheap shirts and shoes. A typical Ivan. But Natashka is wonderful. It's true she keeps Anton under her thumb, but it's for his own good. My mother-in-law said that Natashka was too stuck up and full of herself. She obviously thinks herself very superior and despises us. I asked her what made her think that. My mother-in-law said it was clear from the formal and excessively polite way she addressed everyone. That's not the way we do it. Lenka said that she wouldn't hear a word spoken against Natashka. On the other hand, look at Novikov's wife—she's a right piece of carrion. Stupid. Rapacious. And thinks herself a genius even though she can't even speak grammatically. Calls herself a PhD!

I used not to like conversations like this. Then I got used to them. And now I have come to understand that there's nothing wrong with them. They're just an expression of a natural need to find one's bearings in one's social environment. It's true that in doing so, we are dealing not with real people, but with characters we have dreamt up ourselves (as Nikiforov puts it, with human models). Yet there is a logic even in that, for people's actions have a meaning not only for them, but also for us, i.e. they are susceptible of a dual interpretation. For

(115)

example let's say that there is a meeting of the editorial board of a magazine to discuss an article by a certain A. I have promised to support him, but then I have fallen ill, and have missed the meeting. For me, this would mean: why should I risk complications after influenza just because of some paltry little article by A? For him, and for many other people, it would mean: I had taken fright, didn't want to tangle with the 'dinosaurs' over A's daring article. As if you could find a daring article in *our* world! I am right. And they are also right, since what is important to them are the consequences of my action as it affects them, and they naturally give it a negative interpretation.

All this is normal, but what really makes me very angry even now is the almost complete absence of benevolence in the way we construe the behaviour of our absent acquaintances and even friends. What dominates is a kind of malice more appropriate to rats than to men. Why should that be? It cannot be that this derives from the biological nature of Russian man. In the past, Russian man was noted for his kindness. But now no trace of any such kindness persists. The dominant attitude of Russian man towards his fellows is now made up of malice, intolerance, envy, *schadenfreude*, hatred and so on. I am not talking about exceptional situations when people are for a time ripped out of the fabric of their social existence, but daily situations of ordinary life (on public transport, in queues, in offices and so on). Yet our book is to devote a special chapter to the characteristics of Soviet man. What shall we write in it? The usual waffle about the elevated moral and other qualities of Soviet man and his superiority over the denizens of bourgeois society? If we were to attempt even the discreetest hint at phenomena which do not even derive specifically from socialism but from the mere fact of a surplus of people and a shortage of goods, we would be putting our heads on the block. For, in theory, we have the finest public-transport system in the world, there is enough of everything, prices are stable and so on. There are of course occasional rare exceptions. . . . In short it's like the old joke: our Soviet dwarf is the biggest dwarf in the world, and the Soviet paraplegic is the most progressive in the world.

The idea of equality

Our dive was closed for an inventory—too much fiddling of the till, obviously. Rebrov, Nameless and I decided to find somewhere else to go. We walked all the way to the Avenue of Marxism-Leninism; but some of the dives had queues outside, others were filthy, others were closed, and so on. And we couldn't get into the Youth Café—there was a queue there as well. Then Rebrov proposed that we each chip in three roubles and buy a couple of bottles and some cheese and sausage. And he knew just the place near by. So that's what we did—decided, as Nameless put it, to go back to the good old days ('it's quite a while since I drank straight from the bottle'). Rebrov led us to the fence around our Slogan, moved a plank aside and we crawled through. The spaces between the letters were crammed, but between the 'U' and 'R' of 'FUTURE', we managed to make a little room and we installed ourselves on some packing cases.

'This is a genuine application of the idea of equality,' said Rebrov, after we had killed the first bottle.

'What's wrong with the idea?' I asked. 'It's a perfectly good idea in itself. An idea can't be responsible for any specific reality.'

'I disagree,' said Rebrov. 'On the contrary, it's very much responsible. And, incidentally, in our country the idea is completely realised. As you know, the idea which grips the masses, and so on . . .'

'Now, hang on a minute!' cried Nameless.

'Why?' said Rebrov. 'Just let me explain what I mean. Here we sit, the three of us, and we can fully realise the idea of equality: we've all chipped in an equal amount, we're all drinking the same amount, we're all eating the same amount and we're all sitting on identical packing cases. But now take an entire nation. Let's say two hundred million people as there are here. Now to realise the idea of general equality even in a single aspect, these two hundred million people would have to be organised in a specific system. You'd have to create a special

(117)

machinery to bring the idea to life and to make sure that everything was done according to plan. Let's even allow that the people are all socially equal, (ignoring distinctions of age, sex, family conditions, physical abilities, desires and so on). At all events, the problem would still arise of how to distribute the people in social cells both horizontally and vertically. There will also be the problem of the distribution of material goods. And they, in principle, cannot be equal. That is an empirical fact for each individual. Remember the army. There's equality for you! Yet even the boots are not identical, even if they are standard. The location of your bed in the barrack room. Remember how we scrapped over the duty rosters (kitchen fatigues or guard duty), and over the postings? Even the division of bread among ourselves and before our very eyes ended up in unequal shares, or so it looked. So what can we say of our differentiated society full of all kinds of temptations? There's really no point in talking about it—it's too banal. Anyway, what's the result: a system of actual social inequality such as has never existed throughout mankind's entire previous history.'

'All very sound,' said Nameless. 'But on your last point, that things have never been worse, surely that can't be true.'

'It *has* been worse, much worse,' I said.

'From what point of view?' asked Rebrov. 'Mark my words, it won't be long before the population will be neatly divided into a race of masters and a race of slaves. It'll even be done on a physiological level. It will be an irreversible process. Science and social selection already make it possible.'

'I seem to remember Adolf Hitler saying something to that effect,' I said.

'Hitler was in favour,' said Rebrov. 'And I'm against. That's one thing. Apart from that, Hitler wanted to resolve the problem on an international scale, and our problem is internal, a purely social problem. Here, we're tackling it from the inside, and that is why success is assured.'

'And who do you intend for the slave race?' asked Nameless.

'I don't intend it, I'm afraid of it,' said Rebrov. 'But I think that there can't be any two opinions about it. It's clear that the Russian people will be the first source. The Russian people is naturally predisposed towards it; it is servile, and inclined to

(118)

mutual hostility and to tearing itself apart. Look back over our history since the Revolution . . .'

'Solzhenitsyn,' I said.

'And what do you propose?' asked Nameless.

'A battle,' said Rebrov. 'Everything depends on the capacity to resist. We're waiting for everything to happen of its own accord. Yet we must fight. The whole course of history depends on whether we fight or not. Let's drink to the fighters!'

'That's a waste of time,' I said. 'I'll join you in a drink, fine! But who are we to fight against? And why? And how? And, what's more, the problems of distributing the functions and obligations of society and its material wealth can be solved reasonably.'

'Now hold it,' said Nameless. 'What d'you mean by "reasonably"? With the help of reason? From that point of view, all human organisation is reasonable, since it is formed with the inevitable participation of reason. Without reason, there can be no human society, there can be only a herd, a flock, a mere concentration like a concentration of cockroaches or bugs. Or does "reasonably" mean in accordance with some kind of public rationality? And who are to be the judges? Stalin and his gang operated in accordance with their ideas of that kind of rationality. Or is it in accordance with some kind of justice? What kind of justice? What are its criteria? Who will enact it? Forgive me, but you've just been equitably allotted a packing case, only there's a nail sticking out of it and you've torn your trousers. It's all words, words, words. What exists is an implacable reality.'

'And what do you propose?' I asked.

'Simply what happens everywhere all the time: a fight.'

On the way to my 'study' I saw the Old Boozer in the courtyard off the Avenue of the Construction Workers. She was bent double trying to heave her overloaded cart. No one offered to help her. And I too lacked the courage.

Lenka

'Papa,' Lenka asked for the hundredth time, 'is it possible that Solzhenitsyn is really telling the truth?'

'Of course,' I said, 'there is a certain amount of truth in his books.'

'But what proportion! Lenka persisted. 'A half? A tenth? How much?'

'I haven't measured it,' I said, 'and now it's impossible to establish it. Anyway, what difference does it make to you?'

'You see,' she said, 'if even one thousandth part of what he's written is true, that's a nightmare. We have to know about it, otherwise it'll be all the worse for us. Sooner or later, we'll find out anyway. Take your Kanareikin, for instance. It's been said of him that dozens of creative workers were shot as a result of his open or secret denunciations and his testimony. And that other man, . . . you remember, the one who came to see us the other day . . . the thin one with lots of hair . . . Uncle Anton said that many people were put inside because of him. He once shared a cell with a man who'd got ten years all because of that man's denunciation. . . . And yet you meet him and shake his hand. . . . How can you?'

'You're still a child,' I said. 'And there's a lot that you don't understand. When you grow up, you'll realise that it's not always as simple as that. You probably don't know that Uncle Anton spent almost half his sentence working in an office.'

'You're talking platitudes,' replied Lenka, 'to say the least. Don't worry, I'm not as stupid as you think. I'm not going to get you into trouble. I'm a model Komsomol member and a first-class student. I have to be for the sake of my diploma and my character reference. But there are certain things that I want to know for my own curiosity, and for the time being, for nothing else.'

If only Lenka had known that her thin man (Ilin), one of our most popular philosophers, had recently been the expert assessor in the case of a group of teachers and students who had written a 'true' history of the CPSU and who had received long prison sentences for forming an anti-Soviet underground organisation!

Once I delivered a lecture on the role of the party at a famous Moscow factory. The lecture hall was huge but very few people turned up. And those who did paid little attention, talked among themselves and walked out quite blatantly during the lecture. It put me in a bad mood and I went home very cross. Over supper, I told them about the lecture. Lenka said it was my own fault. There's a right way to put things over. As for being attentive, we're ready to listen to anything.

'In one club,' she said, 'they advertised a lecture on "The Party and the People". No one turned up. So what was to be done? They asked Abramovich.

'"No problem," said Abramovich, "Put up a notice: Lecture on Three Kinds of Love."

'So that's what they did. The hall was full to bursting. Abramovich began his lecture: "There are three kinds of love. The first kind is homosexual love. That is reprehensible, and a subject not to be discussed. The second kind is heterosexual love. Well, you know all about that, so we shan't discuss that either. There remains the third kind of love: and that is the love of the People for its beloved Party. And it is of this love that I shall speak in more detail."'

Everyone roared with laughter, even my super-orthodox mother-in-law. But I felt uneasy. I hardly dare think how my readers will have dragged my name in the mud! And what can I do about it? I certainly can't sing my lectures to the guitar, like Okudzhava, Galich or Vysotskiy!

On conscience

'You are wrong to talk about Solzhenitsyn and Sakharov here in the Institute. There's already a rumour going that you support them.'

'Rumours don't bother me.'

'But you're wrecking the department. I took you on as a friend.'

'Well, as a friend, I'm warning you: I've no intention of hiding my opinions about the people you mention. So you can take the appropriate steps. I'm looking for another job, but it's not that simple. Do what your conscience tells you.'

'You aren't a child, and you ought to understand . . .'

'And so should you. We are middle-aged men. Not long before we disappear. There'll be barely time to turn round. And what are we going to say to ourselves when our last hour comes? And what will be the last thought before we sink into eternity?'

'That doesn't frighten me. I hope I have a stroke or a heart attack, or go into senile decay. So I needn't bother about things like that.'

'That's a reasonable calculation. But I can't think in that way. I live with the thought that my last hour will come at any moment. I haven't been able to get out of the habit since I was fighting in the front line. It must be that every man has a funny little thing called conscience.'

'Shove your conscience up your ass! I've been summoned to the Central Committee. Do you know how many denunciations have been written against us? That may make no difference to you! You've got your conscience, you see! But I haven't. I've got to rush to the management and from there to the Central Committee, from the Central Committee to the City Committee, and from the City Committee back to the department.'

'Just ignore them, don't go.'

'But some one's got to go.'

'A holy place is never empty.'

'You're right. If I pack the job in, that bastard Vaskin will move in and fire the lot of you.'

'God giveth us life, God feedeth us. We haven't got much chance of a doctorate, and it's not even worth thinking about the Academy.'

How strange people are! What's the harm in my being a doctor? What's the harm in my being elected a corresponding member? I could do more people more good! . . . That's what I thought, but somewhere in the deep recesses of my soul, other little thoughts were agitating. That's all lies, they were telling me. You just want to be a corresponding member and that's all! And why not? Position. Honours. An apartment. Cash. The special privilege shop. And all the rest. Very well, but I'm not as bad as all that. Other people can't even admit it to themselves. And anyway, it would be better for science if they elect me and not some Vaskin or other. But how different are you in fact from Vaskin as a Marxist theoretician? No more than a bug from Ryazan differs from a bug from Tula. Don't try to delude yourself. Consider your work like any job that keeps you in food, but don't try to put your soul into it. The game isn't worth the candle.

For some time now, Anton's existence has been beginning to irritate me. It seems, somehow or other, to interfere with my life. Conscience? What's that? According to Anton (there he is again!) human conscience isn't something absolute. It is always someone else, not himself. That may be the reason why people like Solzhenitsyn and Sakharov are so much feared. People are afraid, not of being unmasked but of acquiring a conscience. To be unmasked does not interfere with ordinary life, but conscience does. But you can't get rid of conscience once it's taken root in you. And I cannot get rid of Anton. I am irresistibly drawn towards him. I cannot live a day without thinking of him. And yet, I have no more acute desire than to be rid of him. People revile dialectics, but you can't take a step without them. Here's an example: liberalism is unthinkable without its opposite—dissidence, and vice versa. The opposite of liberalism in our society is not hard-line Stalinism but precisely dissidence and opposition. Liberalism is merely attenuated Stalinism. As you see, even we liberals can acknowledge this truth.

Our paradoxes

'Does the name Shchedrov mean anything to you?' asked Victor Ivanovich.

'Of course,' we all replied.

'Well,' Victor Ivanovich continued, 'he started his scientific career as a Marxist. First he worked on certain theories in physics where he produced some interesting conclusions which showed a similarity between these theories and Marx's *Das*

Kapital. This was pointed out to him and it was suggested that he could analyse *Das Kapital* from this angle. He got deeply involved in this and produced an extremely interesting and totally Marxist dissertation. At all events, it was of use to Marxism. And what happened? The thesis was rejected when he came to defend it. It was unprecedented; the best thesis for many years, as almost everyone acknowledged, had been rejected, while hundreds of real hack jobs had been passed without a murmur. So what did Shchedrov do? He simply spat on Marxism and addressed himself to the selfsame problems without the slightest reference to the classics or indeed to any Marxists at all. His new thesis amounted to a sharp criticism of Marxist methodology. And what do you think? The thesis was a brilliant success. Today, he is a figure of world reputation in his own field. He could have brought a genuinely scientific form to Marxist philosophy. But he was driven away from that as soon as people perceived his true ability. So how do you explain all that?'

'It's really very simple,' I said. 'I've known Shchedrov for a long time. On a personal level, he's far too sharp and direct. That upsets some people. When he was defending his thesis, he insulted the members of the Scientific Council, treating them as idiots.'

'But isn't that the truth?' asked Victor Ivanovich.

'It is, but there are rules of etiquette just the same. Then there was the usual jealousy of the mediocre towards talent, and there was fear (you never know what might come of this!). But in Shchedrov's case, it all turned out for the best. He wrote what he wanted and had no difficulty in publishing.'

'It's not as simple as you make out,' said Edik. 'Jealousy and irritation and so on are all secondary explanations. It's quite legitimate that Shchedrov should be expelled from Marxism, because Marxism is not a science, and Shchedrov wanted to solve scientific problems by the use of scientific methods within the envelope of Marxism. What I find interesting about all this is something quite different. As Marx himself acknowledged, Christianity has always tried to attract the services of the best brains. In this respect, Marxism is diametrically opposed to Christianity. It has always made a point of getting rid of the best brains and recruiting the emptiest skulls available. That is not a hypothesis. It is an empirical fact which needs a theoretical explanation. So here's my hypothesis: Marxism is the ideology of the most mediocre section of society, created for that section and by that section. It is the quintessence of mediocrity. A boring, unaesthetic ideology. An ideology of oppressors created for oppressors. And for the oppressed as well.

'I really can't agree with you,' I said. 'Have you read *Das Kapital* and the *The Eighteenth Brumaire*? And . . . (I listed a whole series of excellent classical works). Surely they aren't all as mediocre as you make out!'

'I don't deny that Marxism was created by geniuses,' said Edik. 'I am merely saying that when their work became a great ideology, by that very fact, it became the incarnation of mediocrity for the mediocre, that is for the overwhelming majority of the human population. That's the way it was intended. And that is the way it came out.'

'Well,' said Victor Ivanovich, 'Shchedrov is trying to get permission to go and live in the West for the sake of his work. And that means leaving for good.'

'That's a new one!' said Nameless. 'I thought that Rostropovich was an exception. If Shchedrov's attempt comes off, our emigration will lose something of its nationalist-Jewish complexion. What is he claiming as his motive?'

'He's complaining about his total creative isolation.'

'If my memory doesn't deceive me, that's the same reason that Neizvestniy gave. But because he left as a Jew, this reason never came out into the open.'

'But isn't Shchedrov a Jew?'

'How the hell should I know? A Russian only has to achieve some kind of individual success for people to begin to suspect that he is Jewish. You've heard about S. of course? Before the last Academy election, it was decided to reduce the number of Jews. S.'s candidature suited everyone (and of course, as everyone knows, every candidate is vetted in advance by the appropriate departments of the Central Committee of the KGB), but there were rumours that he was a Jew, or at least half Jewish. They checked his documents and everything seemed fine: he was descended from peasants from Vologda.

But you know these Jews are very crafty! So S. was summoned to appear before the appropriate authorities and to explain whether he was a Jew or not. He arrived. And when they asked him about this, he whipped open his flies, took out his penis and slapped it on the table. And the story has it that there were women on the commission. I can imagine the scene. All the same, he was elected. But the really funny part of the story was that he turned out to be a Jew after all. It was simply that his great-grandfather had been converted and become a peasant.

Nothing that is human

Like Marx, I am a stranger to nothing that is human. And I began to daydream. Soon, I shall be elected a corresponding member. Then an Academician, that's no problem. Then a move to the Central Committee, to the department, or perhaps Vice-President. The best thing would be the Central Committee because that would give me a better chance of becoming Secretary for Ideology. And then the job of that feeble old blockhead is well within reach. Of course, no one's ever moved on from there to become General Secretary, but you can always create a precedent. And it would only be justice after all. It's about time there were real scientists in the leadership.

And then I got quite carried away. Radical reforms are needed! The first thing would be to make foreign travel easier. Of course, you can't just let anyone go. You have to be selective, do a few checks. You can let out only reliable people. But it must be done intelligently. Otherwise, there would be too many who wouldn't come back! All forms of repression must be abolished of course. Naturally some people would have to be put in prison, but not just the first comers. It would all have to be done legally. In open court. With evidence. And the papers and magazines—we'd have to put their house in order. Of course, you can't just let them print what they want. If you really gave them their head, they'd end up by bringing out such good journals that nobody would ever read our philosophical review or even *Kommunist*.

At the very peak of my statesmanlike activity, Lenka burst in.

'Here, listen,' she said. 'This is what that boy I was telling you about has written. . . . It's called *The Careerist's Dream*.'

No, not for me the pop star's microphone,
Nor yet the glitter of an emperor's crown.
Up There, right at the heart, I want my throne,
With scarlet drapes behind me, hanging down.
And at my back in gleaming marble white,
Our much-loved leader, our dear guide supreme.
On either side my colleagues, idiots quite,
Sheer cretins, toadies, whatever they may seem.
And out in front, the vast assembly hall
Should roar with joy and burst with sheer delight,
And every eye gaze on me, one and all,
And their 'Hurrahs' and 'Long lives' fill the night.
I want the creeps and villains all around
To acclaim the greatest genius ever seen.
And every blessed day that comes around,
My face must fill the television screen.
From crack of dawn each day I want to see
The gape-mouthed listeners desperate for each word,
While workers in far lands across the sea
Spread flowers before my feet upon the sward.
In armoured limousines I long to ride,
Surrounded by a powerful bodyguard,
And be His equal—as if by his side,
And quite soon too. I want this just reward.
But there's one snag in all this grand design.
What happens if against me all conspire?
If some foul schemer steps right out of line
And spoils this pattern which I so desire?
If some crude villain, who would take my place,
Accuses me of everything and all,
And there, among the tombs, in deep disgrace
I'm lost—no trace, no memory, no recall?
So might it not be better . . .

'That's enough,' I broke in. 'Your boyfriend wants his

bottom smacked; he needs a stint on the virgin lands to find out something about life.'

'But isn't that poem about life? There are all kinds of life. It's not only the virgin lands. But if you really want a poem about the virgin lands, I'll get him to do one for you!'

'Heaven preserve us! Leave me in peace. I've work to do.'

The end of an epoch

At the present time, I can feel myself that the epoch of liberalism is over. And I am obliged to think that it will soon be over for me as well. When? In what form? At all costs I must make sure I'm elected a corresponding member. Otherwise, I can only go downhill. And everything that we've done will turn to dust, and all my pupils will be expelled. I must resist. How can Anton fail to understand that this is necessary not so much for my sake but for the good of the cause? After all, if he has been able to live more or less tolerably, all these years, it is only thanks to us liberals. If they crush us, it'll be the worse for them—for people like Anton. They will be thoroughly pulverised. It is easy to accuse us of self interest and vanity. But how could we behave otherwise? If you want to do something for the common good, and at the same time remain without ranks, or titles, or fame, or material possessions, you will never get anywhere. If you seek the benefit of society, you must attain benefits for yourself. But it must be done in a certain way. And we liberals have instinctively acted correctly—at all events, there was no other course of action possible. And the wider and deeper our power became, the more we had acquired material and spiritual benefits, the greater would have been our influence on society. And the more good we could have done. I have no wish to cast aspersions on disinterested people like Anton. I am ready to pray for them. But they can exist only because we exist. And any influence which they have on society is only possible in the measure that we have influence. That is true in many areas: both from the point of view of their survival and from the point of view of the reception of their ideas. Objec-

(128)

tively, they are nothing but excrescences (even if those excrescences are the summits) of liberalism, and nothing more. And yet they make themselves out to be creatures of a superior race. If one were to weigh what they have done against what we have done. . . . After all, though, what use are these comparisons? It is not even our fault. When we have said 'We' we've included people like Anton, but they have always and in every way tried to distinguish themselves from us.

Today the management has been discussing our outline plan of work. In general, it has been approved, and indeed praised. But it has been completely demolished in detail. In a few words it was proposed to us that we should prepare commentaries and illustrations for the brilliant report of our super brilliant geriatric. What a genius! I remember the line he shot at the outset: Just write me something simple and short, I'm not a theoretician, or a guide, just a simple Party official. . . . And now. . . . One day, Anton counted up all the quotations from Stalin in the most servile number of the philosophical journal printed during the Stalin period, and the number of quotations from our present leader in one of the averagely servile numbers of the same journal. In the terms of such a comparison, Stalin looks like modesty itself. In our section on criticism and self-criticism we had proposed to consider the problem of our dissidents. We were directed to transform this study into a critique of ideological provocations. We were promised help on this from KGB documents. As far as the Jewish problem was concerned, it was suggested that this should be set out in the form of a critique of international Zionism. Literally every point of the plan was handled in a similar way. And finally, they made changes to our editorial board. Since Vaskin had been appointed pro-rector of the Higher Party School, he had asked to be removed from the editorial board, pleading his new responsibilities. It was of course a calculated act: he wanted to free his hands for later. We are all members of countless councils, commissions, editorial boards, but all that makes no difference to how busy we are.

Later, Korytov telephoned from the Central Committee and asked me to go and see him tomorrow for a very serious conversation. I can guess what it's about. Once again, this careerist money-grubbing liberal is going to have to take evasive action. And for what? What would it cost me to put Anton and all those like him, those intrepid, disinterested fighters (for what?) behind me, and live in peace? Is it my conscience that forbids it? If that were all it was! Conscience. Stupidity. Fear. The desire to keep some kind of cover for myself (to appear less dangerous oneself—that's also a valid point of view). But in the end, what does it matter? It's the result that counts. And would that radical of radicals, Solzhenitsyn, have achieved much if it hadn't been for us liberals? Certainly now, after the event, he can drag us in the mud. But why didn't he do it before? Oh God, I've had enough of it!

Business

'What's new?'

'There's another delay. They found a printer. But it seems he's not reliable. So now, they're negotiating with another. I get the feeling that someone is leading me very skilfully by the nose.'

'Nonsense. We've all become a little mad. It's a good thing that they're trying to find a more reliable printer.'

'They've let the moment slip by. Just think if the book had come out before the Congress! That's the time they would have made themselves a packet! And then I've got a distinct feeling that I'm being very closely watched. Surely They can't have got a whiff of it? How? I've not shown the manuscript to anyone except Natasha. Even you wouldn't know.'

'You've got to take yourself in hand. If you go on like this, you'll go right off your head. Just be patient a little longer. By the way, here's a phone number. Ring them and mention my name. It's a first class job. Very quiet. Perfect peace. And the main thing is that it's miles away from ideology.'

The problem of denunciations

We were watching the programme 'Cine Travel Club', one of the very few things on our television that's worth looking at. Meanwhile Sashka and Anton carried on a rather odd conversation.

'How did you get put inside? Was it a denunciation?'

'It's not as simple as that, Sasha. It's only now that we regard that kind of thing as a denunciation. At that time it wasn't denunciation, it was a manifestation of honesty as we understood it at the time.'

'A fine kind of honesty!'

'Judge not, that ye be not judged.'

'But even so, it's very odd!'

'There is nothing strange about it. We—that's me and my best friend—were both members of the party at the time (I'd actually been in the party since I was 22!) And although many of us had a shrewd idea of what Stalinism really was, and we condemned certain features of it, on the whole we were as Stalinist as we could possibly be. If anyone in our unit had had a bad word to say about Stalin we would have torn him into pieces ourselves without awaiting the nod from the Special Department.'

'So what happened?'

'I went on leave to my parents, saw a few things that made me sit up, got angry, and remembered that famous toast of Stalin's to the Russian people and wrote that unfortunate poem. I read it to my friend. And instead of going to the Military Academy I ended up in a camp.'

'What a bastard! If I had been you I'd have bashed that "friend's" face in.'

'There was a time when I dreamt of doing exactly that. But when I was released, I went and thanked him. What would I have been if none of this had happened? A retired colonel on half-pay, or at best a low-ranking general. But as it was, I learnt to understand life and appreciate its true value. That's worth more than being a marshal.'

'You might have changed even without the camp.'

'When? Before Stalin's death I couldn't. And afterward lots of people changed. Even my friend changed. But that's not the same. Those weren't fundamental changes.'

'What about Grigorenko?'

'That variant's not for me. I am not a champion of justice for private life. And anyway, there's nothing I can either prove or refute. At all events in the camps I saw very few people whose basic attitudes changed in any radical way. They left very much the same as when they had come in. It's true that I served my time in pretty good conditions. For five years I worked in an office. It was warm and dry at least. It was there that I made friends with an inveterate anti-Stalinist. I began to understand things as a result of the bitter arguments I had with him. It's very difficult for a person on his own to achieve the truth. You need someone to talk with—it makes no difference whether he is a friend or an enemy; the main thing is that he mustn't be indifferent.'

'And what became of your anti-Stalinist?'

'He was transferred to another camp. And there, after Stalin's death, a fight of some sort broke out, something like an uprising, although I have my doubts about that: I think it was sheer provocation—at least that's what the rumour was. Anyway the camp was wiped off the face of the earth (with all its inmates of course) in a bombing raid. My former colleagues from the pathfinder squadron made a good job of it. If I hadn't been sent to the camps myself, I could easily have been the commander of the squadron that destroyed that camp.'

'What a nightmare,' said Lenka, who'd been sitting silently throughout the conversation on the edge of the divan. 'What an appalling era that was! What monstrous people! It's almost unbelievable. But all the same, uncle Anton, your friend was a complete shit. A traitor and an informer. It is precisely the likes of him who have always been and who still are the mainstay of Stalinism.'

'So what is a denunciation?' asked Sashka.

'It is a simple question,' said Anton 'but it is hard to answer it. More than a dozen times I've been called in by the appropriate authorities and told to write various kinds of explanatory notes. I've been ordered to sign affidavits that I would divulge nothing. I wrote them, and I signed them. I have never turned anyone in, on that point my conscience is clear. But I only recently came to understand that these notes and signatures are essentially a form of co-operation with the KGB. But I have yet to meet a single person who sees things as I do. Now that I am old, when no one is going to call me in (or if they do it will be to arrest me and put me on trial) I have finally happened upon this banal truth. The fact of the matter is that normal life was organised round this system of denunciation. It still is. And a trivial thing like a promise not to divulge anything isn't even regarded as in any way immoral. All the more so since in our society moral conscience has atrophied, exactly as the classics of our theory predicted.'

The gift

It is Dima's birthday. What can we give him? This problem has been plaguing Tamurka and me all week. And it has even brought us together. Problems shared . . .! In the end we decided to buy him an Italian album of one of the officially condemned artists like Chagall, Kandinsky, Picasso, Magritte or suchlike from a second-hand bookshop. Incidentally, it isn't very long since (in the liberal period!) Anyuta brought out a book in which she slated them all. The book was a wild success: in the first place, it was a book about banned modernists; secondly it included a great many reproductions of their pictures. And she condemned them merely for form's sake. Otherwise it would never have been published. Anton instanced this as just another typical idiocy.

'A step forward? In what respect? Do you say this because in the past people simply kept quiet about them or put them on the same footing as enemies of the people, whereas nowadays the decision has been taken to abuse them?'

'But at least it is now permitted to say something positive about them,' Dima objected.

'That's precisely the point—it's now permitted, it's not as if we have won the right to do so,' said Anton.

(133)

'Hang on a moment,' I said, joining in the argument; 'what do you mean by "permitted" or "won the right"? Just take Anyuta's book as an example. A great many people of various ranks and positions, with various convictions and tastes, had a hand in this "permission". You've said yourself that deStalinisation isn't just the action of one man or one group of men, but that it is a social phenomenon. Isn't this exactly the same thing?'

'I understand what you are trying to say,' said Anton. 'But I'm talking about something else, about the very essence of our progress, and about ourselves inasmuch as we promote it. If this is a social phenomenon, then we are playing Their tune. This involves a slice of our goodwill. Anyuta could have written a bolder book and fought for it. That's exactly what Lebedev did, and he broke through. But Anyuta accepted the compromise: the approved text, publication, the royalties, the guarantee of good reviews. But no one wrote a word about Lebedev's book, and he was obliged to forgo his royalties.'

That's how we argued at the time. Without any rancour, by the way. Many years have gone by and now people are beginning to find things to criticise in Anyuta's book. I can imagine what an uproar there will be if Dima applies for an exit visa. But there's still not a word about Lebedev. That's a most interesting phenomenon in its own right. Anyuta's book is completely Marxist. Lebedev's has absolutely no connection with Marxism. There isn't a single reference to the classics. It's a truly excellent book. It's astonishing that it was ever allowed to appear. It was immediately published in the West in several languages. There were sheaves of reviews, and it is still being quoted. But here at home—not a sound. It's as if it never existed. Yet borrowings from Lebedev can be detected even in the works of our mutual friends. It's a characteristic sign of its age that it was published when it was. We, the 'liberals' managed that. I know all this from inside, because I myself wrote a private report in which I acknowledged that the book contained no ideological errors hostile to us. But the fact that everyone kept quiet about the book is also characteristic of its period. A great deal was said about Anyuta's book. It was reviewed and quoted. Lebedev's book was received in complete silence—and by the very same people. They knew—or rather we knew—that Lebedev's book was incomparably superior to Anyuta's. We knew that it was a serious work on an international scale. It was for that very reason that we stayed quiet about it. And that is why we will go on being quiet about it. It is difficult to criticise Lebedev. Any criticism is an advantage to him in that it attracts attention. Nor would it be simple to liquidate him: he is world famous. Anton wrote reviews of Lebedev's book but they were not accepted for publication. I must confess that I myself as a member of the editorial board of my philosophical journal cut out one such review of Lebedev and advised that quotations from him should be removed from another article. Today I can no longer remember how I justified this to myself and to others. Maybe Anton is genuinely right: We, the liberals, have accomplished millions of trivial actions and stratagems which have determined the primitively low standards of the liberal era which has just passed, and have in so doing hastened its end. We ourselves have erected impassable barriers to our own pretensions.

We went into the second-hand bookshop on Gorki Street and drew up a list of all the Western books they had on the seditious painters (which doesn't stop people dealing in them—it's too profitable), showed the list to Dima and asked him which book he wanted (not bad for a little surprise!) Without any hesitation Dima picked the Salvador Dali—the most expensive on the list.

'But do you know how much it costs?' asked Tamara.

'Never mind,' said Dima, 'it won't break you. I only have a birthday once a year.'

Not far from our home we saw the Old Boozer.

'Just look at her!' Tamara dug me in the rubs. 'What a sight! She must drink every last kopeck. Imagine having someone like her for a mother or mother-in-law!'

'What an unfortunate woman!'

'Don't be naive. Do you realise how much she makes by selling those rags?'

'So your trip's been confirmed,' said Dima, 'that's marvellous! So you can take out my letter. They'll never search you. All you've got to do is drop it in a postbox, and that's it.'

'Look—you're going to land me in jail,' I said.

For some reason I really don't want to take his letter out, but I feel I'm going to have to. Otherwise I couldn't look Dima and Anton in the face. Or even Tamara, who thinks me a coward.

'Very well,' I said. 'And what's in this letter?'

'I'll tell you what it's about,' said Dima. 'These days it's none too simple to get an invitation from Israel through the official post. They simply don't let them through, and yet at the visa department they only recognise invitations which have come by post. So I've thought up this little scheme. First, several letters must be posted to me from Israel in the right kind of envelope (if enough are sent, at least one will get through). It doesn't matter what the letters say. They could write that things in Israel are bad, or that they advise me not to come. As for the invitation, you'll bring it back yourself.'

My face obviously must have fallen, because everyone burst out laughing.

'There's nothing for you to be afraid of,' said Dima; 'as long as you go on defending the purity of Marxism and quoting our beloved leader, everything will go swimmingly. The main thing is that you remember to post that letter. And the invitation will be slipped to you so discreetly that no one will notice a thing. Some pro-Soviet Western Marxist will give you some offprints of his articles or something like that.'

'Well it's a funny business,' I said. 'What about you Anton, have you any little task for me? Do you want me to smuggle out your article exposing all the flaws of Soviet society? Or would you rather I took the whole book?'

'Unfortunately,' said Anton, 'I haven't got anything worth-while ready at the moment. But the next time you go. . . .'

'There won't be a next time,' I said. 'This will be the last. So you had better give me what you have.'

'Don't be in too much of a hurry,' said Anton. 'All is not lost. You still have a chance of being elected a corresponding member. You've not blotted your copybook yet. Kanareikin certainly can't do without you, and he is still in charge. Very soon he will see his own affairs going into a decline, and he will do everything he can to promote you as his own man. No one likes Vaskin because he's just too abject. His time is coming, but we aren't quite there yet. And the other competitors scarcely count.'

'That remains to be seen,' Natashka observed quietly. 'In situations like this it's usually some lacklustre, insignificant, inoffensive creature who suddenly breaks through.'

'Natashka's right,' said Dima; 'but you are still in the running. It's a good thing you've got that article coming out in *Kommunist*.'

'Nonsense,' I said; 'it's an abject bit of self-seeking,'

'The content isn't of the least importance,' said Anton. 'It's the fact of publication that matters.'

'But what difference does it make to you?' said Tamara.

'I want your husband to become an Academician,' said Anton. 'It's to my advantage, for a start, because it will be a protection for me. And then he can take my seditious book to the West. And secondly, independent of ulterior motives, I am fond of him. It will give him pleasure to become an Academician, and his pleasure will be my pleasure.'

And then we talked about food shortages, rising prices, the stupidity of our policy in Africa, about the forthcoming trial of Karavaev, Solzhenitsyn's latest statements and so on.

'So tell me,' I asked Dima. 'You've finally made your mind up? But why? You're very well off here, after all. You've got an apartment, a country villa, a car. A job that suits you down to the ground. What more do you want? You're too old now to have real hopes for anything really . . .'

'Shall I tell you what the eighth wonder of the world is?' asked Dima. 'It's a Jewish boy who gets admitted to the Moscow university Mechanics and Mathematics Department this year. My children are growing up. I don't want to have to think that if they don't get anywhere it's because of the Nationality clause in their documents. But speaking between ourselves that's not the nub of the matter—it's a side issue. It's just that for me life here has become quite simply a personal insult. That's not because I'm a Jew, but because I've never been able to become a completely Soviet man. Now since the possibility exists, why not take the risk? Though, I admit, the Jewish problem in the Soviet Union has been grossly distorted, and no one has any real interest in seeing it clarified. The Jews have an interest in appearing to be persecuted, i.e. in looking as if they are simply victims of anti-semitism. The benefit to them from this is obvious both here and in the West. Say a lad fails his exams because he hasn't the ability and knowledge—but he's a Jew! Say Ivanov gets the appointment and not Abramovich—it's because he's a Jew! You've heard the story about the stutterer who failed his audition as a television announcer because he was a Jew? There's a good deal of truth in that. And our authorities have an interest in seeing that discussion of the Jewish problem doesn't go any deeper than the question of the existence of anti-semitism. They can bring powerful weapons to bear against accusations of anti-semitism. What anti-semitism can there be in our country? Take the Academy of Sciences: there are as many Jews as there are physicists and mathematicians. Take the film industry, music, medicine, literature. . . . And yet there are two very important and profound problems about which everyone agrees to keep quiet. The first is the natural process of evolution in which a minority loses its former superiority and becomes ever more strictly subject to the general laws of Soviet life. What do I mean by that? In the past how many scientists, faculties, professors, departments, institutes, theatre companies, musicians, lawyers and so on were there? And how many now? My dear friends, today there simply aren't enough Jews to preserve their former influence and maintain their traditional Jewish solidarity. And what's more, the great host of Russian peoples now provide a sufficient number of able and educated people to compete effectively with the Jews. I agree that the percentage of people of this kind isn't large. But in absolute terms, their numbers are enormous. And even if the Jewish population is not assimilated by the mass of the Russian population as a result of mixed marriages, which are, incidentally, few and far between, the prospects for the Jewish population are extremely gloomy. (Peoples do mix together but mainly by way of movement from place to place and the rupturing of old national ties.) In the end the Jew will have to adopt the same way of life as that of the average Russian. And this natural evolutionary process is paralleled by another, purely social process.

'Which brings us to the second problem. Thanks to their racial solidarity the Jews have established within Soviet society a great many unofficial organisations which are effectively in opposition to state or party organisations. And this solidarity has won to itself a significant part of the Russian population, in particular among the intelligentsia. You know very well that the Russian people, as a great people, is not as much disposed to national solidarity of this kind as the Jews are. Indeed it is disposed rather to national discord, to mutual hostility and mistrust. These qualities are very suitable for the Soviet way of life. The tendency of the Russian intelligentsia towards unification, which was conceived in the recent liberal epoch, derived, not unnaturally from the Jewish community which was already in existence. It's interesting to note that the Jews, who are in principle cosmopolitan, have begun to play an active and patriotic role in Russian culture, while the Russian intellectuals have begun to display significant cosmopolitan tendencies—a fact which supports the thesis that we are facing a purely social problem. It is only because of historical conditions that this problem has come to be regarded as a Jewish problem. In other words, the tendency of the liberal Soviet intelligentsia to consolidate has assumed the aspect of a Jewish problem. There is nothing surprising in the fact that the most extreme manifestation of the liberal tendencies of this period—the dissidents—has taken on a similar appearance. As a result, the unceasing struggle of the authorities against dissidents, opponents and malcontents and so on, and of course against the liberal milieu which has nurtured and protected them, has turned into a struggle against the Jews. Soviet anti-semitism, my friends, is first and foremost the struggle of Soviet authority against a social opposition; as a result, it strikes more openly against the Jewish than against the Russian population. And yet the struggle is directed principally against the Russian intelligentsia. In the long term this latter is a more dangerous enemy of communism than are the Jews—who are a profoundly communist people.'

Then we began to argue about anti-semitism within the population itself. The relative clarity which Dima's discourse had produced was immediately lost. We quarrelled noisily. Then we made our peace. Then we drank to Their speedy end. Then we drank to Their Getting the Worst of it.

On the way home Anton said that we had many important problems which were incapable of solution because of our reluctance to allow ourselves complete frankness. For example take the Jewish problem: there were certain aspects of it about which everyone kept shamefacedly silent for one consideration or another. And a similar situation prevailed in ideology: just get up in any of our opposition groups and assert that Marxism is something serious. They would just laugh in your face! Try telling them that you don't like Solzhenitsyn as a writer—you would be pilloried!

'I can hardly believe that Dimka is really going to leave,' I said. 'It would be a great pity. Our inner circle of friends is being disastrously reduced.'

At home, when Lenka came in to kiss me goodnight she asked me casually what internationalism was. I started to explain, but she cut me short with a wave of her hand.

'That's all out-of-date rubbish. Internationalism is when a Russian, a Georgian, a Ukrainian, a Chuvash, an Uzbek and all the rest get together to go out to beat up a Jew.'

Lenka again

Lenka dashed in from school, flung her satchel into her room and without so much as saying hallo began to declaim a poem.

> When the treacherous onset came,
> A general he—sans troops—became.
> And when the foe was put to flight
> He was—well, not forgotten quite,

But elevated to a post
So far away he seemed a ghost.
But then one day, oh happy fate,
Something you can't anticipate,
Our much-loved executioner's eye
Fell on him—there's no telling why,
And he became some high official,
Though thought of as in no way special.
And then he seized the moment proper
To make his rival come a cropper,
And then, with victory aglow,
Invented exploits long ago,
Which he inflated then so far
He won a tenfold Hero's star.
And then with power and glory sated,
His starving neighbour obliterated.
Then, just to show what he could do,
He crushed another neighbour, too.
And, stirring up some Arab breast,
He took to touring in the West,
And after that . . . to cut things short,
He didn't waste his time for naught.
Speech after speech he ranted out,
With no idea what 'twas about.
And, never mind the actual case—
He's called a genius to his face.

'Guess who that's about.'

Tamurka went into hysterics. My mother-in-law shrugged, turned up the volume on the television and carried on watching her ice-hockey match. As for me, I yelled that it was high time to stop all this nonsense or she'd land us all in jail, but it all ran off Lenka like water off a duck's back.

'Oh good! I see that at any rate you can seize the gist of what I'm saying. Good for you! Well guessed! But our director of studies hasn't twigged. She wants to know the name of the author and who he's got in mind. There's an imbecile for you!'

'They'll find out who wrote it and expel him.'

'They won't find out! No one knows who the author is.'

Lenka went off into her own room. We spent some little time carrying on about modern youth. And then Tamurka (I have to hand it to her, she pulls herself together fast), Tamurka said that this phase would soon end. These days all schoolkids are a pack of wolves, but as soon as they're up at university they tend to become more reasonable.

Agafonov

The laws which govern career-building in our society have never yet been studied. It's a problem which has preoccupied me for a long time. I regard myself as a careerist. But I have never managed to comprehend the finer points of the problem. In all probability I lack the talents of the genuine careerist.

Take Vladilen Makarovich Eropkin. His father was a small merchant from somewhere in Siberia. He adapted himself very rapidly to Soviet power and gave his son the most revolutionary of names: 'Vladilen'—an abbreviation of Vladimir Lenin. He rose to the top of the Cheka, the secret police. He wasn't even shot. Eropkin came to our Institute to take his doctorate, leaving his wife and two children back home. Here he met the daughter of Mitrofan Lukich, Elvira, a student in our department who was as plain and dumb as could be. It was at this time that Mitrofan Lukich began his rise towards the summits of power. Eropkin beguiled this highly enviable young woman, abandoned his wife and children, and married Elvira (declaring cynically at the wedding that science entailed sacrifices). Within two years he had his doctorate; a year after that he was a member of the editorial board and head of a department on the party journal; within a further year he was a corresponding member, and the year following, he was director of the party institute. Now the way to the Academy is open to him. That is a career in total conformity with the laws of the Soviet way of life. I could not have made such a career for myself: I am not mediocre or repulsive enough for Elvira to have taken my bait, and Mitrofan Lukich would not have detected in me a kindred spirit, nor would he have taken me to his bosom as he did

Eropkin; that is all clear enough, and in no way can I fault Eropkin.

But Agafonov has confused all my ideas about Soviet career-ism. He is a handsome enough lad, although not exactly a film star. You can't say that he is particularly bright, but neither is he stupid. He won't say no to a drink. He's not malicious. He is good natured. Idle. A bit sleepy. And he has no family connec-tions. No one to protect him in the way than Kanareikin has protected me. He's published a couple of down-market pamph-lets on philosophy (philosophy for housewives and mental defi-cients, as they were described by such outstanding degenerates as Kanareikin and Petin). And yet he took off like a rocket for no particular reason. He was suddenly included in the editorial board of a leading journal, given a professorship, appointed editor and elected a corresponding member all before my very eyes. I was one of the most famous Marxist theorists, and he was a complete unknown, a mere nobody. Yet without any effort he overtook me. And for certain he has still not reached his zenith. So how is this to be explained? According to Anton, Agafonov is recognised as being totally inept and is therefore not dangerous, while I am seen by our top people as a man of capability and therefore dangerous. But this is no explanation.

Although I helped Agafonov to get his first miserable articles accepted, and indeed corrected them, we have remained on the best of terms. Recently I had the idea of writing a good review on my own book and getting it published in his journal. But I was in no hurry to do this as there was no particular need. But in the present situation it would be sheer stupidity to let such an opportunity go. So I telephoned Agafonov. That evening Tamurka and I went to visit him in his new apartment in one of the luxurious Central Committee blocks in the centre of town. (The Agafonovs had not wanted to go out to Tsarskoe Selo.) I knew that Tamurka would be put into a bad mood for a week at the sight of the Agafonovs' enormous apartment (entrance hall of more than 20 square metres, kitchen of much the same size, and a study of 30 square metres!!) But business demands sac-rifices. We spent the evening as usual at the Agafonovs'. We ate and drank a great deal, indulged in idle gossip, and blankly watched their colour television. The conversation kept drying

up. Agafonov took my idea of a review quite phlegmatically. I
would write the review myself and Agafonov would decide who
to get to sign it. He couldn't do it himself—these days he isn't
allowed to publish without the specific permission of the Central Committee. I suggested that he should have a word with
Eropkin. Agafonov said that was a good idea, and if Eropkin
didn't agree, he would approach. . . . In short, that was not a
problem.

Progress

After its reconstruction, Cosmonaut Square became very beautiful. Flowerbeds were laid out at the foot of the letters. In the
very centre a huge mosaic portrait of Lenin was installed, his
arm raised, his eye winking, and complete with his little cap. In
the evenings the portrait flashed on and off. It was very effective. The eye was the last part to light up. For a short time the
eye appeared to wink in a conspiratorial way, and then went
out, followed progressively (working from the centre outwards)
by the rest of the portrait. Beneath the portrait of Lenin there
were permanent metal frames (also built in a concrete foundation) which on special festival days housed portraits of members
and deputy members of the Politburo. The letters of the Slogan
were replaced by characters made of titanium because for some
unknown reason the stainless steel ones had first of all turned
black and then come out in brown blotches. The story has it
that someone had made a nice little profit for himself by supply-
ing ordinary cast iron in place of the intended stainless steel.
But the Slogan profited by the change. It became a place to be
shown off to foreigners along with the model Kolkhoz 'Champion', the Sovkhoz 'Forward', the factory 'Sunray' and the mink
farm 'Winter'.

The dream of the minor careerist

Once more Lenka brought home one of her friend's poems. I decided that it was about me, and I got very upset. But Lenka swore that it wasn't about me at all, but about Vaskin. She said that everyone appreciated me because I was a kind man while Vaskin was malicious, which could be seen from our books. I said that I was indeed too kind but that her friend was a malicious, and even venomous, whippersnapper. What decent person could write a thing like this:

> My soul is consumed by one burning ambition;
> I've forgotten how long I have harboured this lust.
> I long to become a full Academician;
> 'Corresponding' will do for a start, if it must.
> As Academician, there's no point denying
> I'd have lots of perks, the material sort.
> But, honest to goodness, that's not why I'm trying,
> That's not why the Academy's my only thought.
> Just once in my lifetime, I'm longing to read
> The mute question gleaming in other men's eyes:
> How on earth did this cretinous bastard succeed
> In scaling the heights and purloining the prize?

Mother-in-law observed that Lenka's friend couldn't possibly get better than a C in literature. At all events she would never have marked him higher. Lenka replied that the fate of every great poet was tragic: in their lifetime they got given C's and even D's, but after their deaths they were set up as models of excellence for all good pupils to learn off pat. Tamurka said she liked the poem, and that our shitty existence deserved poems that were every bit as shitty. Sashka said that the poem contained a little pearl and that in time Lenka's friend would turn into a poet every bit as good as Galich. And as for me, Sashka went on, I would never become an Academician, as I didn't take my work seriously enough, and I didn't accord it the tremulous respect that the party demanded. This, he said, could be felt in everything I did. And that of course didn't go down too well.

(145)

He ended his speech by a comparison which sent a chill up my spine. He said that my position in the Soviet Marxist élite was similar to that of Admiral Canaris in Hitler's gang of bandits. Tamurka said that Sashka was aiming too high, and that a better comparison would be that of a brothel in which one prostitute could be distinguished from the rest by her intention to start an honest and healthy family. I said that that wasn't witty. Tamurka said that in the new edition of the collected works of our leader they had planned to print the word 'prostitute', which our leader liked to use, as 'p . . . . e' and add a footnote 'tart'. But later they had decided to stay closer to the original. Lenka asked when they would finally decide to print his collected works in full. Tamurka said if they did they would have to put a warning on the title page: 'Forbidden to children under 16'.

Rogozin

The 'Voices' (that's what we call the Western radio stations broadcasting in Russian for the Soviet Union) broadcast that Rogozin was leaving the country with an invitation to Israel. Although there had previously been cases of Russian cultural figures emigrating with such invitations, they had always been justified in some way or other: either the Russian intellectual turned out to have been at least half Jewish, or his wife was Jewish. But here the case was plain. Rogozin didn't conceal the fact that his Jewish relationships were completely fraudulent. At some hearing connected with his case he was asked the name of the relative who had sent the invitation. From his pocket he pulled a crumpled piece of paper and pronounced syllable by syllable a word with which he was obviously unfamiliar. When he was asked whether it was a man or woman, he answered that he had no idea and that the name itself furnished no clue.

I remember Rogozin well. He began his studies in our faculty, and was expelled for his famous speech (at the time and within our circle) which he delivered when Kadilov was defending his doctoral dissertation. At the time Kadilov was spearheading the campaign against cosmopolitanism in the faculty, and his thesis was on Lenin's contribution to the Marxist theory of knowledge. He had devoted a whole chapter to Lenin's ideas on logic. The submission of the thesis went precisely as required. Kadilov's official opponents praised him to the skies. His unofficial opponents (particularly those whom Kadilov was attacking as cosmopolitans) crawled on their bellies before him. And then suddenly Rogozin took the floor and delivered himself of such an enormity that for some time afterwards Kadilov was left speechless. What Rogozin said amounted roughly to this. The classics of Marxism, and Lenin in particular, were complete ignoramuses where logic was concerned. They hadn't the first idea about the logic of their times. Their thoughts on logic were merely a biographical fact, with no bearing whatever on logic itself. If you don't want to make them into laughing stocks, it would be best to keep silent about anything they said on the subject of logic. For instance. . . . And here Rogozin calmly (for some reason he had not been driven off the platform) dissected everything that Lenin had written on logic (which was not very much), and he did it in such a way that the ineptitude of these ideas was plain to everyone.

Rogozin was expelled from the faculty, but left at liberty. He was even allowed to take a degree in the Department of Mechanics and Mathematics (he was a war veteran, capable, Russian, of peasant stock). In this respect Rogozin's fate was one of the first swallows announcing the summer of the liberal period. His later promotion was characteristic of this liberal period. And his departure was also characteristic of the end of this period.

Where now is Kadilov's dissertation? Where are the results of Lenin's 'brilliant' ideas on logic? Hundreds of people both before and after Kadilov have talked about the vast importance to the world of these ideas on logic. But where has this importance been revealed? While Rogozin (and this is acknowledged even in our country) had made a truly significant contribution to science. Yet he is leaving and from now on his name will never be mentioned anywhere in his native land. His discoveries will be pillaged and profaned piecemeal. And they would be recognised here twenty years hence when they return to us from the West as the discoveries of John, Hans, Georges and so on—if of course the West still survives.

I sat and watched the Old Boozer loading up her little cart in the courtyard, and listened to the 'Voices'. They talked about Solzhenitsyn's latest statement. Then they broadcast a commentary on the subject by one of the 'brother-Marxists' (as we call the Medvedevs). He of course did not agree—it would have been strange if he had. It must be observed, however, that Solzhenitsyn himself seldom agrees with anyone. Our Russian habit of mutual intolerance is the worst scourge of our whole liberal movement, of the whole of our opposition. The Old Boozer tied up some boxes with a piece of string to stop them falling apart, picked up the chain and stood for a few moments quite motionless. Then she slowly ran her eyes along the windows of the house and began to drag her cart away. For an instant I had the idea of rushing out after her and giving her ten roubles, but while I hesitated she disappeared.

Later I met Rogozin on the editorial board of our journal. We had organised a round-table discussion on 'the Psychic, the Physiological and the Logical'. We invited a number of leading specialists. At that time Rogozin was well thought of and we invited him as the only specialist who had elaborated mathematical methods for the study of the behaviour of social individuals. Everyone came out with very intelligent and progressive observations, which were nonetheless flat and noncommittal. Rogozin spoke brilliantly (he had a reputation as a remarkable orator), but it was quite impossible, even in that super-liberal time, to publish anything he said in our journal. So we published the material produced by the round-table conference without so much as mentioning the name of Rogozin. When the editorial board decided to exclude his speech and the discussion which it gave rise to (i.e. the most interesting part) I voted like everyone else for its exclusion. What you sow, so shall you also reap. Now I can feel on my own skin the consequences of millions of actions of this kind for which 'we' are responsible. But at that time could we have acted any differently?

Yet what Rogozin said was very interesting. Agatha Christie, he said, had created a remarkable character: Miss Marple. In her reflections she bases herself on the notion that the laws of human nature are always and everywhere the same. It is precisely these absolute and invariable laws (laws by definition are invariable!) of human nature that are what psychology is all about. It is not the brain and the way it functions, nor is it the logical rules for the use of language, but the general rules of human behaviour. When we speak of human psychology we all intuitively take this as our starting point. When in practice we claim to study, understand and use the laws of the human spirit, that means the laws of psychology. I will give you an immediate example and in a while you will be able to verify for yourselves from this example the accuracy of my psychological analysis. Rogozin then analysed in the greatest detail the situation which would result from the publication of the material produced by the round-table discussion. And he predicted the outcome.

We have at our disposal, said Rogozin, a huge collection of observations on human behaviour, but we need modern theories to systematise these observations; and we need in particular to construct a mathematical theory. But that of course is far from enough. We need experiments and moreover a mass experiment. Now we have such a possibility. In order to isolate psychological laws in their pure state we must learn how to abstract ourselves from the influence of the various products of civilisation, including the influence of religion, morality, and legal restrictions. Inasmuch as in our society these factors of civilisation have been eliminated, history itself has put at our disposal a laboratory comprising an entire society, several million strong. And Rogozin quoted many striking examples which his group had derived from their observations of huge human conglomerations and from the rich sources of information unwittingly collected by our official institutions (complaints, affidavits, testimonies, speeches at meetings, denunciations and so on).

Then came the campaign to discredit Rogozin. This began simultaneously both from below (among his colleagues) and from above (the omission of the passages in our discussion which were connected with Rogozin was sanctioned by the Central Committee). Within two or three years not a trace remained of Rogozin's group. It had taken almost twenty years of dogged labour to create this small group, but only two years to uproot every slightest evidence of its presence in our world of science. It is a striking fact. Today a whole institute founded on Rogozin's ideas has been established. It has a staff of several hundred and is lavishly equipped. But it has produced no results (unless you count those which had already been achieved by Rogozin's own group); yet Rogozin could have become one of the glories of Russian science. He could have become a figure on the same scale as Mechnikov, Mendeleev, Pavlov. He could have done. But he did not. Our system prefers to inflate nonentities into major figures (like Kanareikin, Petin, Bludov) but it cannot tolerate genuinely outstanding personalities.

One more 'birthday'

Six months ago Sashka went to a birthday party of one of his fellow students. He didn't get home until the morning, and in a state of high glee. The party had been a great success. Good company—six boys, six girls. First they had eaten, drunk, and danced, then they had argued until they were hoarse. Finally they had decided as a joke to form a Union to Fight For (for what—that was a matter of individual choice). The aim of the Union was to mark the birthdays of everyone present, with the same participants. As there were some months with several birthdays, and some with none at all, they decided to give each person a month arbitrarily and to celebrate these 'official' birthdays. Now it was Sashka's turn. Only one thing was required of us parents: to clear off the premises and to finance the festivities. After prolonged discussions charged with mutual insults we reached the following conclusions: mother-in-law and Lenka would go to spend the week with her sister in Tambov (Lenka was on holiday from school); Tamara decided to spend the night with her girl friend. And there was no problem as far as I was concerned: I had somewhere to go.

'Take care,' I warned Sashka before I left, 'or this might turn out badly.'

'Don't worry,' said Sashka. 'We'll stay clear of politics. They're a reliable bunch.'

But Sashka's 'birthday' did worry me. I've more than once seen him with Solzhenitsyn's books, *Kontinent* and other émigré publications. I can imagine the kind of things they would talk about at their get-togethers. And where do they get these books from? That's an idle question. Kartoshkin, for example, goes abroad three or four times a year. And he always comes back with a pile of magazines of all kinds and books of that particular kind. His foreign-language anti-Soviet books are now beyond counting; he's got a whole library of them. He has to have this kind of literature for his work. So his son Andrei can read them undisturbed. And he passes them to his friends (in great secrecy of course). Kartoshkin may well be persona grata in the KGB and the Central Committee (or, as Lenka jokes, in the Central Committee of the KGB), but he does happen to be a liberal. He is one of us. Who will evaluate, one day, the enormous benefit which this 'timid' liberal has brought to our society! Do you perhaps believe that it costs him nothing to import all this subversive literature and see from the corner of his eye how it spreads from his home throughout Moscow? It can't last.

It's strange how all these banned books which Sashka brings home are read from cover to cover by every member of the family. And wherever I go I find that people are talking about these books in a way which makes it perfectly clear that the broad circles of the liberal intelligentsia and officials know this literature better than the anthologised Russian classics. Can this go on much longer? Many facts are known which bear witness to the growing power of the old regime. People are gradually beginning to disappear into jail or exile. For the most part they are young people whom no one knows; adults who are more or less well known are being squeezed for the moment by 'domestic' methods. K. is still out of work. Soon there's to be a public trial of Khlebnikov. But he is world-famous. You couldn't hush that up. There are rumours that many people are being locked up in psychiatric hospitals. It seems that several have been opened in Moscow alone. It seems too that new and powerful drugs have been invented. Three injections and your personality is obliterated. And there's no way of fighting back. Anton believes that these are mainly rumours put about by the

KGB with the aim of frightening people. But I think that these rumours are very largely true. Kartoshkin has told me in confidence that the rumours are far outstripped by the reality.

This morning Sashka asked me once again whether it was really the case that everything Solzhenitsyn had written about the victims of the Stalin period was true. What answer could I give him? I said that it was a complex question. But that didn't put him off.

'Give me a straight answer—yes or no.'

'If I told you "no", that would be untrue; if I said "yes", that would do violence to the historical viewpoint.'

'Leave your historical principles out of this. Tell me frankly. Or are you afraid?'

'No, Sashka, I am not afraid. I can answer you "yes" but it wouldn't be that at all. It would not be a lie. Nor would it be the truth. I am not trying to justify anyone. It is simply that this is a more complex problem.'

'Solzhenitsyn claims that Stalinism has never ended; only its forms have changed. He believes that Stalinism is the essence of communism. What's your opinion?'

'Those are irresponsible claims.'

We did not reach any definite conclusion. But the outcome of the conversation was that I applied for a meeting with Mitrofan Lukich.

The historical and the social

There is a passage in Anton's book which is specifically concerned with the relationship between the historical and social aspects of the anlysis of communist society. Here are its basic ideas. The historical aspect. The country is experiencing a decline in its economy, and more importantly in its power system. At this moment a particular organisation is being formed, or already exists, whether spontaneously or under outside pressure (or some combination of all these possibilities in given proportions)—an organisation whose aim is to seize power—'a party of a particular type' ('an organisation of revolutionaries'). The party is composed of people who feel oppressed, failures, adventurers, fanatics, careerists, the ambitious, 'idealists' and so on, i.e. people who for one reason or another can thus achieve their own aims and interests and are thrust by society onto this path. The party embodies general characteristics which are of interest to the social psychologist. It is organised on the principles of gangsterism. Having seized (or having been handed) power with the help of certain strata of society, the party draws into the power system the lower strata of the population, who are attracted by promises of all kinds of benefits, (this can happen during the process of the seizure of power or even rather earlier, when the intention to seize power is conceived); such promises are to some extent fulfilled. If these lower strata include factory workers, the power system which is formed is christened 'the dictatorship of the proletariat'. But the word 'proletariat' can be interpreted in a wider sense, so that the slogan 'the dictatorship of the proletariat' always carries a specific meaning. The renunciation of this slogan by the French communists cannot be considered a serious act—it is more an act of short-term demagogy. The 'historic' process which we are considering is super-imposed on processes which develop according to social laws. That is the social aspect, one which concerns very large (multi-million) human groupings. It affects small countries usually in the form of something imposed from outside by a powerful neighbour, or as something organised after the neighbour's pattern, and not spontaneously, not as a 'creation of the masses'. Under this aspect a social bureaucratic system is formed which organises the broad masses of the population after the pattern of previously discovered models and in forms which are directly perceptible by the people at large.

These two processes go on simultaneously, with the social process gradually becoming dominant. 'The revolutionaries' exterminate each other, disappear, dissolve into the gigantic State apparatus of 'peaceful' power. Generations change. The social hierarchy widens and deepens. Of course this is far from being a painless evolution. The Stalins replace the Lenins. Soviet Stalinism was precisely the period of the formation and consolidation of communism as a social system, but in the given

(153)

historic forms of the revolutionary period and with its possibilities.

In the present case the historical process has nothing fortuitous and temporary about it. Like the social process, it is there for a long time. In the abstract one can ignore state frontiers: but just try to abolish them in actual fact! It may be possible in dreams to transfer Moscow to a new, more appropriate site. But just go ahead and try! Moscow remains and develops on the site chosen by history. It is even more difficult to alter the historic forms of social processes. They, like their social essence, are there to stay for an age. Take for instance the one-party system of power. In social terms this means the liquidation of all parties of whatever kind and the elimination of the very principle of party loyalty. The historic form of the party (and all the corresponding phraseology, demagogy and party organisation) is preserved as a vitally important organisational element in what is essentially a non-party society. In the same way, a totally arbitrary system of lawlessness is realised within the juridical form created by history, a system of immorality within the form of morality, a system of ideological cynicism in ideology, and so on. The difficulty in understanding communist society lies in the fact that it has been formed as an historically individual process, but in forms as universal and stable as its essential connections and relationships. Just as our representation of a being with a highly developed intellect is indissolubly linked with that of the biological entity 'homo sapiens', likewise the profound phenomena which constitute communism are unthinkable without their flesh-and-blood incarnation in the concrete organisation of communist states. To isolate them in their pure state we need precisely that force of abstraction about which Marx spoke and which all Marxist theorists without exception have lost.

And to be perfectly honest I do not have sufficiently powerful arguments to counter this. All I have is a different emotional attitude to it. I merely mark the stresses differently.

The Dive

When I went into the Dive almost everyone was there. They were glad to see me, which I found very pleasant.

'I could easily believe that all this was prearranged,' I said.

'It's a sheer accident,' said Nameless. 'Do you want to know what the probability is? It's no greater than the probability that you and I should become members of the Politburo. Yet, as you see, this chance has actually happened. And since it has happened, there is no way it can be changed. It is a real historical fact.'

As usual this witticism served as the starting point of an interesting conversation. In the past I had taken no account of conversations like this; as a professional with a more or less international reputation I had regarded them as mere gossip of dilettantes and solitary dabblers. But now I noticed increasingly often that real life is as well reflected in these conversations as it is in our lofty theories. And all these 'idealists' and 'metaphysicians' begin to seem less and less the cretins which we have tended to regard them as.

'You have just produced a very detailed criticism of what Nameless has said about history as an individual process which has a diminishing degree of probability,' said Edik. 'Let's say you're right. But allow me to throw in another interesting problem for discussion—the problem of the way that people are fixed to the places where they live and work. I won't consider every aspect of the problem—that would take too long. I'll take just one very simple instance which illustrates my thought well. Our country is large. All kinds of industrial enterprises are scattered over it. And people are needed to operate them. How can they be persuaded to stay? For Marxist theorists there is no problem: the high level of consciousness of the workers, eager to overfulfil production quotas; good food supplies; television; cinemas; theatres; libraries; public transport and so on. We are, after all, moving towards communism!! And when we reach it, well, you'll see yourselves. . . . But there is also the question of specific reality. Food supplies? In Moscow there's nothing to eat, and when you go into the surrounding country, what do you find? Who has ever counted the number of people who flood into Moscow daily looking for food and consumer goods? Do we make many motor cars? And how much do they cost? And who can afford them? What about our roads? What about public services? And what do we see on television? Just try and get tickets for a decent play in Moscow! And that's to say nothing about the rest of the country! Art clubs? Folk dance clubs? Singing groups? Just go out into the country and have a look at what's going on. Drink. Boredom. Punch-ups. Crime. Do you think it's by chance that young people prefer low salaries and bad living conditions here, nearer to the centre of real culture? . . . In the abstract, then, everything is possible. In the abstract one can satisfy the slogan "to each according to his needs". But in reality—give people freedom of movement and a chance of settling wherever they like (for example by abolishing compulsory registration with the police), and then you'll get enormous migrations. Certain places will be totally deserted. At the moment people have to be restrained, have to be tied to where they are by every means possible. We pay no attention to such "details" and yet an enormous process of restructuring of our society is going on before our very eyes both in the geographical and in the "vertical" sense.

'Here's something that might seem unimportant: A boy who finishes his secondary education in Chukhloma has less chance of getting into university. But this is precisely one of the factors compelling people to stay put: keep your great clod-hopping feet out of our sophisticated scientists' world in the capital! Try to get your children into the Institute of International Relations! In theory everything is possible. But in practice do you believe that the children of ministers, academicians, party bosses, People's Artists and so on are going to be prepared to become workers or peasants? Only as rare exceptions. Or for the sake of propaganda. That is our day-to-day reality. But let's accept what you say, that public transport will be developed, that roads will be built, that the aeroplane will become as common as the bicycle, that people will be allowed to go abroad. . . . When is all this going to happen? When that comes

(156)

about our society will have developed a stable, traditional and self-perpetuating social structure. A stable way of life will have been established. It will no longer be possible to reverse the course of this evolution. If such an immense machine takes root as a social entity of a specific type, it will use every effort to preserve itself. It will exploit progress in its own interest, but will not allow itself to change in accordance with your abstract recommendations. The dominant forces and tendencies will not allow any destruction of the stable order which suits them. Motor cars and aeroplanes? Certainly. But of what kind and for whom? Medical treatment and seaside resorts? Yes. But again, what kind and for whom? Travel abroad? By all means, but with the same questions. Do we have any great chance of using our Soviet seaside resorts even if we can afford to? And that's not even going abroad. That's just one example of what history is if you regard it as an individual process. We are in the process of turning ourselves into some kind of animal. And it's a process that only happens once. So what kind of animal? A snake? A jackal? A tiger? A rat? Drop all these romantic Marxist illusions! For a long time now they've been lies, not illusions—they're just a means of making fools of our modern educated cretins. And Marxism itself has already developed into a solidly constituted complete entity which you will never be able to change into anything else. The evolution of complex individual systems is irreversible. I can prove that to you as a theorem.'

'Bravo!' cried Nameless. 'You have expressed my own very dearest thoughts.'

'In Russia,' said Rebrov, 'a traditional way of life has been preserved despite everything. Just as in China. In the last century Russia instituted a movement towards the Western way of life. But nothing came of it. The Revolution threw us back into a state of serfdom, back to the squalid, gory origins of our imperial history. How many victims will there have to be, and what quagmires will we have to plunge into before the abolition of serfdom becomes a real issue again?'

Viktor Ivanovich looked rather strangely at Rebrov, said goodbye and left. Lev Borisovich slipped away unnoticed, leaving only Edik, Nameless, Rebrov and me.

'Don't you have the impression that Viktor Ivanovich is rather odd?' asked Nameless.

'Do you think he might be an informer?' asked Edik. 'Well, the hell with him! We aren't of any interest to Them. We don't act. We're just blabbermouths.'

'Unfortunately they aren't all complete idiots,' said Nameless. 'They know perfectly well by now that words are sooner or later followed by actions.'

Nameless walked me home.

'Our socialist system,' he said on the way, 'combines within itself a very high co-efficient of parasitism with an extremely low co-efficient of utilisation of the population's creative potential. It's dreadful to think how much native wit and talent goes to waste. Take Edik for example. What a great sociologist he could have been. Yet it's certain that he'll vegetate in some editorial job or other, or at best as a senior research worker.'

'Or an Academician,' I said.

And we burst out laughing.

'Look,' I said, 'why don't you and your son drop in to see us some evening? My daughter is just finishing school. They might get acquainted. And I've got a few bottles of wine from the shop for foreigners.'

'I'd love to,' said Nameless. 'And please don't get too angry with us. After all we aren't specialists. And yet we can't keep quiet any longer. I understand perfectly well how theories tend to diverge from empirical facts. And it makes me very angry when incompetent people start sounding off about my own subject. Your philosophers come out with unbelievable rubbish.'

'It's not that which worries me,' I said. 'What I'm afraid of is that my own professional competence may ultimately prove to be on a par with the same philosophical rubbish, with regard to the real science of society—a science which in the present case you and Edik represent.'

Boredom

Sometimes I am lured by the idea of writing. But from the outset I realise perfectly well that my scribbling can provoke nothing more than boredom. I am incapable of entertaining the mass reader. I cannot provide the intellectual élite with food for thought. And anyway, what could I write about that would be of interest? Anecdotes? I can never remember them, and I'm not all that fond of them. 'Underground' facts? I steer clear of them. And after Solzhenitsyn's books in this field, nothing short of verve and professionalism will do. The minor tragedies of life? But they have nothing in common with their description in literature. In all respects our life is terribly grey and monotonous. For every one of us it can be resolved into a comparatively small number of standard elements grouped in combinations which differ from each other only in insignificant detail. We all eat roughly the same, wear roughly the same clothes, say roughly the same things, furnish our homes in much the same way, share very similar experiences. We vary according to our social strata, but only in quantity, not in quality. My wife wears a musquash coat, Natasha wears coney, and Grobovoi's wife has a mink. But these coats play an essentially identical part in the life of each of them. The social role is prestige, aesthetics and so on. I have been able to visit various families, various apartments, various cities. But everywhere has been the same. The cultural level does not increase with social status. People eat better. Drink better. Dress better. The gossip is on a higher level. There is more information. But the boredom is uniformly depressing. The conversations are vile. And their children, with all the benefits of culture, use them in a revolting way. Someone recently said to me that what counts is not the existence of privileged social strata, but their type, their nature—what they look like and the lifestyle they impose on society. Our privileged classes disseminate boredom, greyness, mediocrity, cupidity, decadence, falsehood, parasitism, vanity and so on. They impose on us all a way of life which kills everything which once was the subject of great Russian literature. In our times literature can only be a pitiless description of our reality, which excludes any true literature, even if it is done with the sweep of Solzhenitsyn.

But what am I saying? Who would ever have believed that one of our leading Soviet Marxist theorists (which is to say in principle a boor, a dogmatist, an obscurantist and an oaf) could think in this way! I must stop it at once. This week I have to finish Kanareikin's speech for the congress. I have also to write my own report, discuss it at a departmental meeting and get it through the censorship: that means sending five copies to the directorate with a summary of the minutes of the departmental meeting, get the signature of the director or his deputy supervising our department, hand it all over to the foreign department of the Institute, who will pass it on to Glavlit (i.e. our censorship which has no official existence). In other words a long-drawn-out paper chase. Then I have to organise the translation of the report into English through the presidium of the Academy. I also have to dictate Serikov's speech to him. That'll be no more than five pages. But it's no easier to do than my report. My report has to be official, but Serikov can be allowed a modicum of originality. Something about mass culture. That's in fashion at the moment. But I have been instructed from above to speak on the concept of socio-economic formation, one of the central concepts of traditional (but eternally progressive) Marxism. The theme of Kanareikin's speech is to be historical materialism as the most profound and universal sociological doctrine of our time—no less! The most profound! The strange thing is that they will sit and listen, fascinated, to all our nonsense. They will talk with Kanareikin as with a major scientist. Serikov will pass for a young, highly talented and educated researcher working at an international level. But then why be surprised! It's the same with them as it is with us. It's just that their packaging is rather better. As for me, I've been cast in the role of the conservative, the orthodox. I've got to hold the line! Very well then, I'll show them a thing or two! I set to work and the words came easily. Within a few hours my report was ready. And I even liked it. I rang Anton and asked him to come and see me.

'That's not bad,' said Anton when he'd read the work. 'Not

bad at all. If you were to be freed from the chains of Marxism, you'd become an excellent writer in the social field. But here's my advice: don't give the real thing to the censorship; give them a bit of window-dressing. Or anyway dress it up a bit so that they don't realise immediately what it's about. Otherwise they'll never pass it, and you'll never make it to the Congress.'

'But of course!' I said, elated by my success. 'Don't teach your grandmother to suck eggs! But what do you think of the essence of it?'

Anton began to analyse the essence of the report, and that put me down in the dumps again.

'The concept of formation,' said Anton, 'arose partly out of the comparison between different forms of society, that is clear enough. But we're concerned with the very term "formation", and not with the indicators by which formations are distinguished from one another. It is, I stress, a relative concept. This is very important to bear in mind, since the comparison has its own logical laws which under no circumstances can be overlooked. Say that we need to establish the concept of an animal by comparing rabbits, wolves, bed-bugs, rats, elephants and so on. What does the comparison give us? Thanks to the comparison we discover that one of the objects of the comparison has a given indicator, and the others do not; that certain indicators exist for all the objects of the comparison; that a given indicator has a variety of values or intensities, and so on. If particular cases of the formations are given, then the general concept of the formation should clearly take into account those indicators which are common to all the formations (in other words we must discount the differences between the formations), but which distinguish socio-economic formations from all the rest. Let's remember that. On the other hand the concept of formation also rests on the observation of one type of society in its internal diversity, that is to say, a developed bourgeois society. Hence comes the isolation of such aspects of that society as the forces of production, production inter-relationships, the infrastructure, the superstructure and so on. Moreover for the given society a specific system of human relationships was examined in isolation, a system which determined the overall physiognomy of the society, i.e. which exercised an influence on all

(161)

other aspects of life. In the bourgeois society this was a matter of mercantile relationships, the sale and purchase of labour and so on. The juxtaposition of these two aspects (of these two aspects at least for I am omitting many others), led to such an incredible confusion in our understanding of very simple matters that there is now no possibility of sorting it all out. There is only one possible way, which is to cut through this Gordian knot, i.e. to wash our hands of all this nonsense and get down to serious business. For instance let us take an indicator like the owner-ship of property. In the bourgeois society there exists private ownership of the means of production, in our country there is no such thing. In bourgeois society this is an important indi-cator of the nature of that society as such. Although it could be isolated by means of comparison (by no means obligatory) with other formations, it is significant for the given society indepen-dent of any comparison. But is it a significant indicator of our society that we do not have private ownership of the means of production? If we describe the establishment of our society, it is possible and indeed necessary to take into account the expro-priation of the means of production. But once that society has been formed and has had many years of stable existence, this is no longer a characteristic feature as such, independent of any comparison. The distinctive feature of the snake is not that it has no legs, but that it slithers. It is not that it is untrue to assert that we have no private ownership of the means of production. The assertion is perfectly correct. But it contributes absolutely nothing to our understanding of our society as a society of a specific type. To understand our society as it is we must first of all renounce any comparison with bourgeois, feudal, slave-owning etc. societies, and identify in our own society what it is that determines all other aspects and phenomena of our life. What is this thing? If you set to studying our society not as a glib ideologue but as a true scientist, you will discern that all your high-flown Marxist theory is the purest ideology; that there is nothing scientific about it other than banalities filched from others. And nothing will remain of your concept of formation beyond the general meaning of the term. Different varieties of animal exist, but we can use the general term "animal". We can find indicators which are common to all animals. From this point of view there is nothing to distinguish a bed-bug from a man. There are different types of society. We can introduce the general term of "type of society" ("formation"). We can point to indicators which are common to all societies. From this point of view the society of the Papuans cannot be distinguished even from the communist society of the future. Human society is a linked, stable, conglomeration of people, set at a particular point in space, which has an existence as an entity. That is not a definition of course, but only an element of orientation. As regards types of societies ("formations"), one cannot get away with a classification as stupid as that offered by Marxism. There are hundreds and thousands of them. What we need is some serious research (if it is necessary), and not a rehash of the primitive notions of your great classics. As for our own society, one cannot understand the first thing about it with the aid of Marxist concepts. In a stabilised social system such as ours, from a certain moment in time all these concepts, "primary", "secondary", "infrastructure", "determining", "derivative" and so on, lose any sense. In so far as we are concerned with understanding the society and with constructing a scientific theory capable of providing verifiable predictions, we need to direct our minds in quite another direction. But which? Start from the facts. For example, mass purges, restriction of freedom of movement, the absence of freedom of speech and publication, the shortage of essential products, the squandering of public funds, corruption on a grand scale, careerism. . . . What more do you need? Isn't that enough? There are laws of social existence which flow from the very fact that millions of people are condemned to live together. You could start with that . . .'

We went on talking until just before dawn. I walked Anton home and handed him over to Natasha.

'I beg you, Natasha, don't be angry with me,' I said. 'It was very important. But I'll make it up to you: I definitely promise to help your Anton become a famous dissident. On my own head, of course, but I will help him.'

A conversation with M.L.

No one who has never frequented the corridors of the Central Committee can ever fully understand Soviet society. Not that one can see anything out of the ordinary here. There is absolutely nothing unusual about it. There is a normal (although admittedly very large) office furnished in very bad taste. But this is precisely the point: here there is nothing out of the ordinary to be seen, heard or felt. It is the terrifying drabness about everything that goes on here that is at the root of it.

I showed my party card, was given a pass, climbed to the third floor and walked along a red carpet to the very end of a very long corridor without meeting a single soul. Silence. The soft carpet muffled the sound of footsteps. But to tell the truth there was no need of a carpet: the man who enters the corridors of the Central Committee does not walk in the ordinary sense of the word, but creeps along on tiptoes (those of his hind feet). I knocked on the door of the appropriate office, and hearing a familiar voice say, 'Come in,' I entered. Frol Ivanov, Mitrofan Lukich's deputy, rose to greet me.

'Good morning,' I said.

'Good morning,' said Frol. 'Go on in, Mitrofan Lukich is expecting you.'

And I walked into the office of one of the most powerful leaders of our party, hence of the whole Soviet people, and hence of the whole of progressive humanity.

I have known M.L. for almost twenty years. And through all that time I have seen him no fewer than twenty times. So I had retained no visual impression of him.

'What does he actually look like?' Sashka asked me later.

'Like his portrait,' I said. 'Only forty years older. Stubbier. More malicious and peevish. Evasive little eyes. His hands tremble and they're always fiddling with the things on his desk. A pouting expression of distaste on his face.' And then there's something that doesn't measure up to the role he plays in the party. I think he would look more at home with the KGB in the Lubyanka Building, which is linked with the Central Committee by an underground passage. There was once a rumour that M.L. had asked for the portfolio of Minister of State Security, but he was turned down on the pretext that the country needed a breather. And he was given his present post in the naïve belief that ideology was nothing but words with no important role to play. When the mistake was discovered, it was too late.

I told M.L. that a very important matter had obliged me to turn to him for help. Our book had been assigned an exceptional role: to give a complete coverage to theory underlying the events between the Twentieth and Twenty-fifth Party Congresses. The book would be translated into every Western language and distributed in the West. And yet this period included not only those remarkable events which had been much discussed at the last meeting, but also deplorable events which had been passed over in silence. I am not even talking about the events in Hungary, Poland and Czechoslovakia, where everything is more or less clear. I have our own internal events in mind. Suicides by self-immolation. The assassination attempt that you are aware of. Escapes, one-way trips abroad. The many trials, samizdat, Solzhenitsyn, Sakharov. The Jewish emigration. The departure of famous artists like Rostropovich and Neizvestniy. We cannot suppress these facts or the book will be laughed out of court in the West; and even here we could hardly count on any great success. And it would be even worse to explain all this as we do in our propaganda lectures and articles. Here we must show a great deal more flexibility and maybe even courage. For example in the West the émigré magazine 'New Wave' has published an enormous article full of facts and figures and names. I consulted the K G B and the M V D. Everything was correct. We can of course criticise their conclusions, their interpretation of the facts and so on. But the facts remain and they have to be clarified. We can't do that on our own. We need your help. Directives. General guidelines. For example, how far can we go in explaining all this as the outcome of internal processes and contradictions? For, after all, socialism is a living society and not some abstract schema. It too may have its own difficulties, its own diseases. But we could show very convincingly and without forcing the facts that phenomena of this kind, which arise (albeit in part) as a product of our internal life (under the influence of the West of course), are no more than individual cases and have no effect on the general picture of our society, on its essence.

I spent some considerable time setting out my conception of the book. M.L. listened patiently, constantly rearranging the papers, pencils and pamphlets on his desk. I hinted that it would be no bad thing to publish a book of this kind under M.L.'s own editorship. M.L. did not take the bait, however. He's not a fool, after all. You can't catch a wise monkey with empty peanuts. I could see from his eyes that he understood instantly what was at stake. A book like that would be a trap for him, and he wasn't going to have *his* fingers nipped. I can well imagine the yells that would have gone up in every quarter if such a book had come out under his editorship! The book was a trap for me as well (something I was finally coming to realise!) But who am I? Only small fry. Just another theorist, a famous one, perhaps, but fallible—tending even to make mistakes. I could always be corrected afterwards. That might even be all to the good: see how vigilant we are, see how hard we work! In short, M.L. said that all the commentaries and directives we needed for the book already existed in the appropriate party documents. Make a careful study of the General Secretary's report, and so on.

'How did it go?' asked Frol when I left M.L.'s office.

'Like clockwork,' I said. 'I'm leaving with the same luggage I brought. Look, will you do me a favour? No point hiding the fact that I've spent a whole hour discussing the book with M.L. It's very important for me.'

'Where does M.L. come into it?' asked Frol.

'He's given me permission to refer to our conversation in the sense that all the fundamental problems of evaluating the events of the period are exposed with crystal clarity in the party documents,' I said.

'Clear enough, then,' said Frol. 'You're a crafty type! I bet you a couple of bottles of cognac that you'll be elected a corresponding member. Are you going to Canada? Excellent. You could do me a favour. . . .'

In the corridor I was intercepted by Korytov who dragged me off with him. Korytov is an ex-student of mine, and very mediocre, even for a Marxist. He always addresses me most familiarly, while I speak to him courteously: I've never been able to be familiar with my ex-students. And since I always speak respectfully to my old teachers, whatever their present position, Korytov's familiarity irritates me. Just imagine, a Central Committee instructor who talks as if he were an army sergeant. Korytov regards my attitude of courtesy as an indication of my respect for his position. He even calls our director by his first name, while the director fawns on him for all that he's an Academician.

'Your conduct is unbecoming,' said Korytov. 'Hob-nobbing with all those layabouts. Who's this Zimin? And Gurevich? Take care or you could end up in trouble. Why don't you and your wife come and see us? We're just back from a holiday in Italy. Lots to talk about. So don't forget we'll be expecting you. So long. Forgive me, I can't spare you any more time. Terribly busy!'

Korytov was right of course. He is a careerist to the manner born. Without any experience or knowledge he has sniffed out one of the fundamental rules of career-building in our society: as soon as you get any promotion, the first thing to do is to break off with any connections or acquaintances who might do you any damage or bring you into disrepute, and start up new contacts appropriate to your new position, and try to make useful acquaintances at a higher level. I don't observe this rule, and compensate for it by my books and articles. But that isn't a very sure method. I must find some way of calling on Korytov. Maybe Frol might be there. And anyway it's a sin and a shame to waste opportunities which are available to you without any special effort. Stop, those last words are a lie. It may seem that it would cost no special effort. But more than twenty years of devoted service to Marxism—does that count for nothing? Was it all entirely disinterested? If I'm to be really honest, my devoted service has given me quite a few advantages. Yet all the same I'm not a money-grubber, not even a careerist. I don't overdo it. So just imagine what a man must be like who by Soviet standards is considered a money-grubber, a shark or a careerist! And it's a strange thing that the people of this kind have, with few exceptions, been less successful than I. People say I'm an able man and that I've come up because of my ability. Is that really the case? Are my books so much better than similar works by others? No, that's not the problem. The problem lies in the age. I am a careerist and money-grubber too, but a careerist who's typical of the liberal era, when all this was considered a natural reward for individual merits. And as the liberal period itself was not typical of our society, careerists of this kind do not appear to be careerists. It's simply that I'm not entirely adapted to our society. And that is what has enabled me to rise to the surface in the years past. What will happen later? We must wait and see.

Business

'What about the book?'

'Held up again. This time there's no money. They're looking for a cheaper printer. And time passes. They don't give a damn! They've no idea of the conditions we live in. And Natasha and I are getting to the end of our tether. After all, this is a turning point in our life. And when a turning point keeps getting put off . . .'

I am genuinely sorry for both of them, Anton and Natasha.

'You know, there's something about this story I don't like,' I said. 'Supposing you abandoned this publisher altogether?'

'I'm beginning to think seriously about doing exactly that.'

Even if Anton were to agree immediately to give his book to another publisher, it couldn't come out in less than six months. That is, after the election. And after that, everything else can go to hell.

A typical conversation

I don't know how it is with members of other professions, but in our home a typical subject of conversation when we have guests in is Marxism: we deride it. I try occasionally to make a stand, but I'm always mercilessly interrupted with 'Shut up, you aren't on a platform now,' or, 'Belt up, this isn't one of your philosophy seminars,' and so on. For some years now there has been a constant flow of jokes about Marxism. And there is a vast series about Lenin for any one of which at one time not only the tellers but even the listeners would certainly have been shot. Jokes come out of school (via Lenka), from the University (via Sashka), from the Academy (via all my colleagues), from the Central Committee (via Korytov and Ivanov), from the KGB (via Kartoshkin)—and that's not to mention Dima and my drinking chums from the Dive. It may be that Lenka will shoot out of her room at a totally unexpected moment to blurt out some enormity like this: hanging outside some cave-man's front door is a slogan saying 'Long Live the Slave-Owning Society—The Radiant Future of Mankind'. Or Dima without warning may propound some fragment of Leniniana of this kind: Nadezhda Constantinovna Krupskaya is telling some children about Lenin's kindness. One day, she says, Vladimir Ilyich was shaving. Some children were passing by and they greeted him: 'Good morning Vladimir Ilyich!' And Vladimir Ilyich just said, 'Fuck off the lot of you!' whereas he might have cut their throats with his razor! Dima can go on like this without repeating himself for an hour at a time. Or Sashka might suddenly ask a silly question: what is a revolutionary situation? The answer is: a situation when the led are fed up and the leaders are played out. But the most poisonous stories are those hawked by Ivanov and Kartoshkin. I daren't even repeat them to myself, because I cannot convince myself that you can get away with things like that unpunished. I am not Ivanov or Kartoshkin but, for the moment, merely a candidate for the post of corresponding member of the Academy of Sciences. But even if I'm elected, this kind of little joke will not be without danger for me. So for some time now I have been worried by the direction that conversations in my home have been taking. I try to divert the attention of those present towards clothes, motor cars, villas and trips abroad. Everyone willingly takes the bait. But as soon as they come up against the realities of our system, they begin to revile it with redoubled energy.

(169)

Svetka

On the eve of my departure to the Congress Svetka turned up. She said that she would stay the night. As far as her husband was concerned she's on a three-day tourist trip (the Institute quite often organises trips of this kind to Rostov, Suzdal, Novgorod, Pskov and so on). But where (or rather with whom) does she plan to spend the next night? It doesn't matter a damn to me.

'You know,' she said. 'I've just met a terrible nightmarish old woman. Quite terrifying! I've never seen anything like it; how can such monsters exist! . . . Here, take this. It's a hundred dollars. They cost six hundred roubles on the black market. Because it's you I'll only take five. You can give me them back later. Now here's what I want you to get me . . .' (and she handed me a little list). I was horrified by these dollars and I refused categorically to take them with me. I said I would get something with the money they would give us. Because dollars could easily get you into court. 'You must be out of your mind,' I told her.

'They'll hardly give you a penny,' she replied; 'not enough to buy yourself a bean. They won't search you, don't worry. Everyone does it. Be a sweetie and take them with no more argument. I've been abroad a few times myself. I know the score. They only try to frighten idiots, they know what they're doing.'

I put my foot down, all the same. I refused. I absolutely refused to take the dollars. I confess that I wasn't frightened so much by the idea of the illegal export of currency as by the prospect of having to give her back five hundred roubles. What for? Talk of 'a little present'! I've never even bought Tamurka presents on that scale. Svetka sulked at first, calling me a coward and a fool. But later on she became all sweetness and light and said she'd slipped the dollars to Serikov but would regard the present as coming from me. So I didn't manage to evade this five-hundred-rouble gift after all. Gently does it, though—for if you offer this shark only the tip of your finger, she'll end up by swallowing you whole.

(170)

My good mood had been ruined. I would have been delighted if Svetka had taken herself off with her dollars and gone to spend the night with Serikov. But unfortunately Serikov has a young and jealous wife. And what's more, as far as family life goes he's a bright lad who knows his way around, and he knows what creatures like Svetka are worth. Surely he wouldn't take the dollars?

Svetka tumbled into bed and was soon snoring away. I began to look through the Congress documents, but my thoughts kept turning to the Old Boozer. And it suddenly occurred to me that she was closer to me than this healthy bitch snoring on the bed, who made every man she passed in the street lick his chops; that she was closer to me than Serikov with whom I was writing this book, than Tamurka with whom I had lived for more than twenty years of healthy Soviet family life, than Kanareikin, Agafonov, Korytov, Ivanov . . . my God, but who in real human terms is close to me in this world? Lenka? Sashka? Anton? They are the closest people to me from their point of view. But from mine? I dozed off sitting in my arm chair. And I dreamed an awful dream which I had had several times recently with a few variations: I'd be loading a little handcart with some kind of filthy rubbish, piles of it, my books no doubt. The books kept falling to pieces; I'd heave on the chain but I couldn't move the cart an inch; and then the chain would break. . . .

The congress

I had completely forgotten Dima's letter when he brought it round the evening before our delegation was due to leave for the Congress. And after that I spent a sleepless night. It really is wrong of Dima to force me to do a thing like this. And what's more, if it becomes known that he has applied for an exit visa, someone is bound to inform on me to the party bureau or even higher. My relations with Dima are no secret to anyone. No, it's too much of a risk to take this letter. There are certain to be several full-time KGB agents in the delegation, to say nothing of the KGB part-timers, who constitute practically half the group. I know this specifically because I myself have always been given various little jobs by the KGB, and when I've got back, I've written reports for the Central Committee which were obviously destined for the KGB. Of course all this has been done under camouflage so that no one has anything to reproach me with formally. But with our hands on our hearts we have always been aware of the nature of our relationship with the KGB. So to carry a letter like this would certainly expose me to serious consequences. Not that I would have been subject to overt reprisals—that time has gone by—but people would take note of it and there would be no chance of my going abroad again. So in the end I decided to destroy the letter. Dima is a cunning chap and he is certain to have kept a duplicate. And if later on he sends a letter without having received a reply, I will still have had time to get myself elected a corresponding member. But how am I going to explain that I haven't brought his invitation back with me? Simple: 'I waited but no one turned up to give me anything, maybe the informers intercepted the letter.' Anton, however, had behaved very correctly. He gave me nothing to take out and asked me to bring nothing back.

As always happens they gave us our passports and currency literally a few hours before take-off. So we had to dash straight from the foreign department of the Presidium of the Academy of Sciences, where they kept us for a couple of hours telling us how to behave in the complex congress situation, back home to pick up our suitcases, and then straight to the airport. Some members of the group were not given their passports although they had been prepared. That too is in the normal order of things. Either something had turned up at the last moment, or (and this is more likely) the whole outcome had been decided in advance. These little jokes are all part of our scenario. They have a terrifying and demoralising effect. As a result no one is certain until the last minute whether he will get permission to go. It sometimes happens that people are even removed from the aircraft as it waits for take-off.

The Congress passed as was to be expected—i.e. in utter tedium. We were of course asked why So-and-So and Such-

and-Such hadn't come (naming people who had hitherto played an active part in our philosophy but who were now in disgrace). The newspapers printed articles saying that the composition of the Soviet delegation was very significant, that it bore witness to the return of Soviet ideology towards Stalinism, and so on. There were some attempts at provocations by the Zionists. But it was all very low key and without any particular enthusiasm. As ever, we counterattacked, defended the purity of the doctrine and so on. For most of the time the members of the delegation and of the tourist group were to be found in the shops buying clothes with the money they had saved on their meals. Some members of our delegation managed to feed themselves throughout the Congress on provisions they had brought with them. I just bought trifles, but plenty of them so there'd be something for everybody.

There were two funny incidents. Before the trip we had been thoroughly indoctrinated about relations with our émigrés. The instructor described in highly coloured terms their perfidy and the dangerous consequences that could result from frequenting them. One stupid woman from the Higher Party School took all this very seriously, and she began to tremble with terror even during the briefing at the thought of possible provocations. Then Korytov and Serikov kept building on her fears throughout the journey. As a result she went slightly off her head and refused to leave her hotel room. Someone then told her that when the provocateurs discovered that she was on her own, they would certainly burst in and then God help her! But this had the reverse of the intended effect: the stupid girl from the HPS crawled under her bed. She had to be urgently returned home in the care of one of the 'boys'.

The other incident was rather more substantial. When we went on a visit to Niagara Falls, Shlyapkin (a colourless person from the Ministry) went missing. Someone started a rumour that he had fallen into the waterfall. But that came to nothing. Then another rumour started that he had defected to the United States. Our 'boys' squared their jaws; Kanareikin fouled his pants; Tvarzhinskaya felt instinctively for the place where, during her time with Beria, she had carried her revolver. A general panic broke out, only made worse when a member of

(173)

the Czech delegation claimed to have seen Shlyapkin going off somewhere with a policeman. So there was no possible doubt: Shlyapkin had gone off to seek political asylum. It never even crossed anyone's mind that back in Moscow Shlyapkin had a very cosy nest in the Ministry, a part-time job in the university, a luxurious apartment, a villa, a car and so on, and that in himself Shlyapkin was a complete nonentity, of no use at all to anyone in the West. In fact, Shlyapkin had gone off to look for a lavatory and had got somewhat lost. He was so frightened that he forgot his few miserable words of English and started trying to explain himself in gestures, with the result that he'd been sent off in quite the wrong direction. Following our Russian custom he had turned into a gateway because he couldn't wait any longer. He was caught in the act by a porter who called the police; and Shlyapkin, by this time in tears, was taken off not to the police station as he thought, but straight to the place where the Soviet delegation's coach was waiting. When we finally decided that all was lost and returned to the coach we were greeted by a radiant Shlyapkin who read us a lecture: 'Where have you been? It's time to go!'

When we got back there were a great many meetings at which the members of the delegation discussed their impressions. From their accounts our delegation looked far less pathetic than it had really appeared at the Congress. And that dreadful woman Tvarzhinskaya went as far as claiming that our delegation was at least a head higher than anything the West had offered at the Congress. She politely reproached me with excessive mildness (when I was answering questions which in her view should have detonated an explosion of aggressive hysteria in defence of party principles). One lunatic Czech émigré asked me what Soviet philosophers had contributed to the doctrine of socio-economic formation by comparison with the writings of Marx and Lenin. I calmly explained a few points of my report. I attached no importance to Tvarzhinskaya's remarks, but they kept on going round in my head. That evening I telephoned Anton to ask what it all might mean. He said that in all probability, they were going to start attacking me on this point.

'I did warn you,' he said. 'Why did you start off about this crazy "Asiatic" means of production? Theoretically it's totally

(174)

valueless except as an excuse for a fight. On the contrary, it's pure cloud cuckoo land. You could be accused of revising Marxism at the most central point of its social doctrine. Still, let's hope that nothing comes of it.'

To my great surprise Dima reacted quite calmly when I told him that I had not brought his invitation. He said that it didn't matter, that he wasn't in any hurry. He abused 'them' as hacks. He said that we had a decomposing effect on the whole world, giving everyone an example of botched work. And he promised to come round that evening to listen to my exciting traveller's tales.

The problem of violence

'I've read everything you've written in your books about violence,' said Nameless; 'everything's quite correct. There's nothing I can find to complain about. But there are some aspects of the problem which you've kept quiet about. If you've no objection, I'll tell you briefly what they are.'

This conversation was taking place in Nameless's apartment, after the usual kind of supper—in these times the choice of fare was determined by what the food stores had to offer. Lenka was playing chess with Nameless's son, and to his great astonishment apparently winning: it was the first time he had been beaten by anyone his own age, and particularly by a girl.

'We have to distinguish two forms of violence,' Nameless continued: 'one which is perpetrated for the benefit of individuals and one which causes them harm. In the latter case I prefer to use the word "violation". In practice the two forms tend to merge. The powers that be prefer to disguise the second form under the appearance of the first. But they do not always succeed. Violation is justified by the benefit it confers on others. In future, when I speak of violence, I will be referring exclusively to violation. You Marxists claim that in our society the majority of the population perpetrates violence over the minority. Fine. Let's accept that statement as true. But then a further problem arises. Let's say that there is a country with a

(175)

population of 200 million, and that 101 million are doing violence to the 99 million. What name would you give to that? You think I exaggerate? Perhaps. Let us say then that 170 million oppress 30 million. That has already happened, or even worse. Any objections? Now remember our conversations about the individual nature of the historical process. Thirty million is not a negligible number. You need a huge apparatus of coercion even to maintain the struggle against a mere handful of bandits and dissidents. But we are talking about millions. To deal with that number you need an absolutely gigantic apparatus of violence. More than that, you have to organise the whole of society into a system of coercion. That is exactly what has happened. And what follows? A consequence foreseen neither by the theoreticians nor by the executive arm: the apparatus and the system whereby the majority coerces the minority backfires against the majority itself, becoming an autonomous force which is exploited by social strata very far removed from those for whom the Radiant Future was devised. That is exactly what has happened. Moreover these truths are elementary: you don't have to be a super-genius to predict this kind of little detail in your projected Radiant Future. But now things have gone too far to reverse the process. The apparatus exists. The system exists. They demand to be fed. They have devoured everything for which there was any kind of justification. But what next? There must be victims, if you take my meaning. They're absolutely essential. Throughout all these past years there has been an excruciating hunt for potential victims. But this has failed time after time. There was some minor success with Hungary, Poland, Czechoslovakia. There was a little more success with the people who committed suicide by fire, with terrorists, dissidents, artists, the people of Novocherkassk,[1] the Georgians, the Ukrainian nationalists, and so on. But that was only a drop in the ocean; it lacked the requisite nationwide scale and élan. It lacked any unifying principle. And yet violence needs victims, needs menacing internal enemies. Why? The answer is obvious: they are needed as a target for the hatred of the

[1] In 1962 there was a revolt in Novocherkassk which was put down by force. Many people were killed. (Translator)

(176)

population, a hatred which has accumulated in a huge concentration. (Just walk around Moscow and you can see the hatred brimming in people.) People need victims to justify their own position and their own actions, to discharge on such victims the consequences of their own stupidity, to be seen as a threat to everyone else, to participate in the thrill of power, to realise their own power instinct, and so on. So what conclusions do we reach? They too are self evident: the only remedy against violence is resistance, and the determination of people to resist. And that too is an individual phenomenon. On what does the future history of Russia depend? On something quite trivial: Will Ivanov, Petrov, Sidorov, (i.e. you, or me, or your daughter, or your son) resist (or simply protest) or won't they? And what do you propose from the summits of your brilliant theory? Productive forces, production ratios. . . . For example—the development of a slave-owning society into a feudal society. . . . How many more years do you give us? A thousand? Apart from that you exclude the possibility of a class struggle within our society, you exclude any organisation of malcontents (victims!) into an independent party. And to think that there are theoretical justifications for the one-party system! Surely you must know what in practice this really means: we will stifle this or that! And indeed this is what we are doing. Violence in the name of the majority? Start again from the beginning. It is very sad. It is very sad because everyone understands the situation perfectly well. Yet everyone continues to lie, to dissemble, to justify themselves and everything else. And to what purpose? For their children? But in most cases our children are separating themselves from us, and in two generations they will have become totally alien to us.

Lenka had won three games. We had said everything we had to say. The Nameless family walked us home and promised to visit us again sometime soon.

'Thank you for a pleasant evening,' I said as we parted.

'Social conversation is mankind's supreme achievement,' said Nameless.

'Incidentally,' said Lenka when we got home, 'Nameless junior writes poetry as well. It's not at all bad. Listen to this:'

The other day a miracle occurred.
I met my God, and this he said to me:
'What would you like?'—those were his very words,
'What would you like your future life to be?'
What? Anything? I thought. Well then, why not?
I really haven't anything to lose.
So, 'God,' I said 'if that's the power you've got,
Now this is what I'd really like to choose.
Give me a chance to taste a love that's pure,
From vengeance and betrayal set me free.
Give me a friend of whom I can be sure,
To face life's troubles side by side with me.
Grant that my soul may never show deceit . . .
Nor hide my hatreds 'neath a smiling mask.
Let me remain a man, not take defeat
Before bureaucracy, that's what I ask.
As I mature, let boldness be my guide,
Not the false pleasure that the press proclaim.
Let me admire mad courage, and beside,
Give the oppressed protection that they claim.
And one more thing, O God, one last request,
Give me some daring, so I do not see
Cretins as geniuses, the worst as best,
Nor grandeur in the slough surrounding me.
I said to God—O father, as you see
I don't demand a lot, you must admit.
But if I've asked too much, then I'll agree
To settle only for a part of it!
God did not give an answer straight away.
He paused, then with these words he came straight out:
'If I met your requests, this very day
You'd perish on the spot, without a doubt.'
'Papa,' said I, 'you'd better drop your game,
It seems not to turn out so very pat.
So thank you very much—but all the same,
I'd rather you forgot our little chat!'

The alternative to Marxism

'I'm just back from the Congress,' I said. 'I met all manner of people there, including of course enemies of Marxism. And they all acknowledged that the West has no alternative to Marxism. They can put up nothing against Marxism of equal value or on a similar scale.'

'Well, well, well,' said Anton, 'that just proves that the people you've been talking to are cretins. What kind of alternative are you talking about? Arguing with Marxists is absurd. What can you put up against them? Scientific concepts? Rigorous principles? Proofs? And what do they come up with? Demagogy. Ambiguous concepts and assertions. Fraud. Just you go and try arguing with Tvarzhinskaya! I feel completely powerless in her presence. The weapons she has are so incomparably superior to ours. What does she care for my appeals to the rules for constructing concepts and theories or to the rules of prognosis? Absolutely nothing. And I'm incapable of yelling, slavering and bursting into fits of hysteria the way she does. Me, how many people are there who would understand me and support me? Yet she can count on the support of the most numerous, i.e. on the most primitive section of the population. And we mustn't forget the powerful support she has from the party and the state.'

'And what's more,' Anton continued, after I'd trotted out the usual stereotyped rubbish, 'the problem itself is wrongly posed, on a false basis. An alternative to Marxism does exist: here it is. First of all, there is a schism within the framework of Marxism itself. There is Soviet Marxism. There is Chinese Marxism. The only thing they have in common is their name—"Marxism". Within this common term radically incompatible things exist. It is much the same as if in an age where religion was all dominant, people had tried to find an alternative to religion. It would have been more correct to have talked of an alternative, for example, to Christianity. Now let's look at the possibility of an alternative to Soviet Marxism. That too exists. "Marxism" is merely a name given to the many and varied forms of

(179)

the present ideology. Furthermore the incarnation of Marxist principles in actual life creates realities which rebel against it. From this point of view Solzhenitsyn's *Gulag* and Khrushchev's speech constitute a powerful alternative to Marxism. Under the banners of Marxism (or rather of the Marxisms) is assembled the overwhelming majority of the population of our planet who aspire to our way of life. For most of them our standard of living is a dream. They do not know our real history. The problems which agitate us do not exist for them. Certain strata of the population (and in particular our ruling strata) use these tendencies in their own interest, spouting their propaganda without restraint. Hardly anyone worries about the consequences this will have on future generations. But there do exist in the world forces which resist these tendencies and processes. There are people who in varying degrees understand the essence of actual or impending communism. They understand the prospects which would result from its victory on a worldwide scale. The activity of these people gives the anti-communist forces a certain unity and a certain complexion of principle. That may not be particularly well defined, but it remains a fact. And that's a third alternative, and incidentally one which is very promising. Anti-fascism was not particularly well defined in its ideas either. And incidentally, Soviet Marxism was never really an alternative to fascism.'

'Well, we've talked ourselves into a certain degree of clarity,' I said. 'Tell me now, where is your position?'

'I am not concealing my position. It is obvious. But I do not want to enter into polemics with Marxism. Any polemic against Marxism like an accumulation of texts, words, slogans, speeches and so on merely strengthens it. And I have no wish to strengthen it. I want to tell people what communism is like as a way of life. And then people can choose for themselves whose side they are on. That is the most powerful alternative to Marxism: to create a flood of texts which speak the truth about communism. They might even give birth to an ideology which would oppose Marxism as an ideology.'

'You'll never do it,' I said. 'Despite everything, the world will believe us and not you because it does not want to know the truth. And when it does begin to understand something, it will be too late! You'll never do it—you haven't the time!'

'I'm afraid you're right, but such calculations are not my affair. Even if communism is to conquer the world tomorrow and no one believes me today and my voice remains unheard, I shall still try to say what I have seen with my own eyes.'

'Go ahead and try. But will anyone let you?'

'That is of no importance. I must do this for my own sake. Have you ever heard of a thing called conscience?'

The birthmarks of capitalism

I had not visited Cosmonaut Square for a long time and was unaware of the dramatic events which had taken place there. I learnt of them from an article in the 'Moscow Herald'. It seems that some scrounger from the Ministry of Foreign Trade (the head of the Central Directorate, apparently) had decided to cover the roof of his three-(!!)storey villa (with its own swimming pool!!) in nothing less than titanium. He hired some crooks, who for a healthy fee delivered the first three letters of the Slogan ('LON') to his villa. The crime would have remained undiscovered (for everyone had become accustomed to the Slogan and paid no attention to it any more) had it not been for one old-age pensioner. He had taken his great-great-great-granddaughter for a walk in the square and noticed that something was not quite right.

'I seem to remember,' he wheezed, 'that when I used to stroll round this square with Ilyich, at this point we used to see . . . what was it we saw? . . . well, I know for certain we saw *something*.'

'There used to be a little church there. And over there there was Hippopotamov's mansion.'

'Oh I know all that! That's not what I'm talking about. There was something sort of communist.'

And it was only then that the great-great-great-granddaughter noticed that the letters were missing. Enormous effort went into the investigation of the crime. The story has it that

(181)

cosmonauts in a spaceship noticed the gleaming roof of the villain's villa and reported it to the proper quarters. This was an incontrovertible proof of the practical value of space flight. As there was no more titanium left, the missing letters had to be built of planks and painted grey. But it wasn't quite the same.

The Korytovs

The Korytovs were given a new apartment in 'Tsarskoye Selo' (as we call the area of Moscow where special blocks of flats are built for officials of the Central Committee).[1] The guests at the house-warming party were so high ranking that Frol and I were the most junior. Among them was Kanareikin, who spent the entire evening lavishing tearful compliments on my talent and Tamara's beauty. He had clearly heard rumours that we were heading for a divorce, and he tried in every possible way to persuade me to preserve a treasure like Tamara; he inveighed against all these frivolous modern girls ('predators') and sang a threnody on the moral image of the Soviet scientist. Yet he himself, the bastard, had been married three times and had slept with every cleaning woman, order clerk and secretary in every organisation he had been in charge of. Even the Vice-president of the Academy of Sciences dropped in for half an hour, and then the Director of the Scientific Section. All the time this latter was here we all (including the Vice-president) stood stiffly to attention with unctuous smiles on our faces listening attentively as he babbled on idiotically about the West's slanderous allegations concerning a critical food shortage. The Korytovs' table was groaning under delicacies the very existence of which I had long ago forgotten. I couldn't even remember their names. I was particularly impressed by some splendid fresh strawberries (totally out of season!). And yet Korytov was only a tiny cog in the Central Committee machine.

When all the important guests had left, Korytov led me into

[1] Joking allusion to the famous Czarist palace near St. Petersburg. (Translator)

his luxurious study and showed me his library, an incredible collection by any present standards, and informed me under the seal of secrecy that the Academy of Social Sciences was planning to discuss my latest article.

'Why?' I asked in surprise. 'It's already been discussed. There've even been reviews of it. And it's so long since it came out.'

'It's in connection with your speech at the Congress,' said Korytov. 'Your friend Baranov is trying it on. And Vaskin and Tvarzhinskaya are egging him on. You've nothing to worry about, it's of no importance. You've got the support of Kanareikin and Afonin. And it seems that Mitrofan Lukich isn't too keen on their little game. And of course Eropkin's review is the best support you could have. But just be ready. As you know very well, our life is full of little surprises.'

'Listen,' I said, 'couldn't this discussion be postponed for two or three weeks? I've got an ulcer that's been playing me up, and I've got to go into hospital tomorrow or the day after. And of course I'd like to be present at the discussion.'

Korytov immediately understood what I was getting at. The Academy elections were to be held in a month's time. If the discussion were to be postponed for a couple of weeks, that would automatically mean a couple of months. Just before the elections there would be little time to be bothered with discussions. Baranov was trying to get himself elected Academician, Vaskin would have to be wining and dining the members of the department to win their votes, and so on. In short it was the best course to take.

'I'll try,' said Korytov. 'I think I might swing it. By the way, I've been given a sabbatical to prepare my thesis. It's quite ridiculous—only three months. You live in clover, you lot from the Academy, while we have to graft from morning to night.'

I too instantly understood what Korytov was on about. I told him that we in my section would do everything we could to rush through his thesis as quickly as possible. Korytov gave me a file containing his manuscript.

'Just have a look through those, make any notes you like, think about it,' he said, 'and then you might phone me and we can have a chat.'

(183)

It was late and the metro was no longer running. It took Tamara and me half an hour to get a taxi. The drivers either refused to go to our part of town, or demanded double the usual fare. In the end we persuaded an unlicensed driver to take us. I felt as if I had been swimming in shit, and Tamara was absolutely livid. The splendour of the Korytovs' apartment and the magnificence of their food had driven her mad with jealousy. Her face, which had once been beautiful (and even now people say she's pretty good-looking) expressed her complete contempt for me as a nobody who was not even capable of getting himself elected a corresponding member.

Korytov kept his promise. The discussion was postponed until after the elections. So now I would have to make sure this wily cretin got his degree. Whom should I give the thesis to for rewriting? It would have to be one of the juniors of course with a promise that he would be promoted soon. Perhaps Kantsevich would be the one to give it to. He's an intelligent lad, and he could churn out that sort of claptrap in a month. And in all fairness he ought to be promoted soon. He's been hanging about in a junior job for more than six years.

Sashka and Anton

'Uncle Anton,' said Sashka, 'how does your position really differ from that of Solzhenitsyn?'

'Now don't start perverting my son,' I said.

'I'm not a child anymore,' said Sashka. 'I'm quite capable of perverting myself without any help. Go on, what is the difference?'

'It would take too long to explain,' said Anton. 'Well, by my general method, for a start. I give my opponent every advantage, and I'm ready to acknowledge almost everything he maintains. You think that the Revolution was beneficial to Russia? Agreed. That the party and the people are one? Agreed. That the ideology is right for the society? Agreed. From each according to his abilities? Agreed. To each according to his needs? Agreed. So you see, I acknowledge everything which is regarded as a plus for socialism and communism, and do not reject it. That is just a point of departure. And on the basis of these pluses, I try to explain all our minuses. In short I consider that all the defects of communism (and of socialism) are neither transitory historical phenomena, nor even the result of the disregard of certain principles, but that they derive directly from the realisation of communism's most positive ideals. Do you understand? I believe that the brightest dreams and ideals of mankind, when they are realised in concrete form, produce the most disastrous consequences. But that is not some ideological position or preconceived idea. That is the conclusion reached from a certain method of research into society. Solzhenitsyn simply gives a summary and a description of facts accompanied by certain ideas and generalisations imposed by them. This kind of thing: the purges are no accident, falsehood and corruption reign supreme, there is no freedom of speech, and so on. My method is different. What does it consist of? I shall over-simplify and explain it to you in a word. There are laws of human behaviour which I call social laws. They concern the actions of people towards one another, and the actions of each towards society taken as a whole. They derive from the nature of man and from the single fact that a mass of people are obliged to live together collectively. In themselves these laws are simple and evident. They can be detected by observation, and people discover them for themselves in the practice of their collective life. Imagine a scene like this. In some enclosed space a fairly large group of people is gathered together. They are provided with adequate supplies of food, clothing and accommodation. They are all placed in conditions of equality—that is to say, they are equal from the social point of view. How do you think they will live? For a start, they will discover that they are different and unequal in various other respects. And the social equality I refer to will turn out to be inadequate (and unjust) with respect to their real differences. And very soon the people will divide into groups, choose leaders, work out a system of relative values which will reflect their real inequality—(pierced noses, feathered headdresses, tattooed foreheads and so on). Now imagine that the means of existence put at the disposal of these people come to be redistributed according to the new inequalities. What will happen? The process of restructuring the collective will accelerate and become fiercer. Then introduce a new condition: that the means of existence are not so abundant, shortages arise, there is not enough to go round. And supposing, also, that these means of existence must be acquired by work, and so on. Naturally under these conditions people will carry out actions which have an influence on their own position in society and on that of other people—social action. They do not need very much intelligence to work out which actions will strengthen their position and which will not. For example if man A has the opportunity of performing action x or y towards B, then A will prefer which ever of x or y weakens the position of B, or reinforces it less than the alternative action. So you can imagine in the end, millions of people performing billions of actions, quite literally a society swarming with all manner of little human affairs. And people will work out for themselves and will borrow from previous generations rules of social behaviour which will ensure the most favourable conditions for their existence. That is social life in its pure state. The real history of mankind is such that as human collectives have grown, there has been a simultaneous discovery and development of artificial means which limit and direct the combined action of social laws. These are such things as traditional customs, morality, law, religion, property, art and so on. If you want to know what socialism (or communism) is as a specific type of society, imagine this picture: all the artificial limitations imposed on the action of the social laws (and that is civilisation properly so called) are destroyed, the social laws acquire a decisive importance, subordinating to themselves all other aspects of life, and developing a system of power, ideology, art, and so on which is appropriate to them. Socialism is first and foremost the destruction of all the products of civilisation (which in our country we call the institutions of a class exploiting society) and the creation of conditions under which the laws of collective life become decisive. A grandiose state apparatus is created which corresponds to these conditions, which functions according to the laws of the collective, and which is autonomous. What I've described to you are only the most elementary ideas, and in a highly simplified form. But that should be enough for you to understand the general drift of my conceptions. When Solzhenitsyn criticises Marxism and individual facts of Soviet life, he fails to see all the horrifying normality of communism.'

'So, all in all, communism is sheer garbage,' said Sashka.

'That depends for whom,' said Anton. 'The communist way of life is very profitable for a huge part of the population of the country. Just total up the number of ministers, of deputies, of heads of department and combines, of directors, secretaries of party committees, academicians, writers, painters, officers and generals and so on, right down to policemen, section heads, professors, apartment-block superintendents, warehouse and shop managers, and so on. This society is their society. In our society work is comparatively undemanding, almost everyone's basic needs are met, and a large part of the population lives very well. For the time being this society satisfies the overwhelming majority of the population. Not in all respects, of course, but by and large it does.'

'So it is a good society,' said Sashka.

'It is neither good nor bad,' said Anton. 'There is no need for judgements, which are relative and subjective. It is what it is. And being what it is, as I've said, at the same time it signifies the reign of mediocrity, careerism, envy, corruption, indifference and so on. There comes a moment when all the positive qualities of communism turn against those who defend it and bolster it. It turns out the satiety has been illusory, that good food and good artefacts run short, that artistic and literary standards decline, that spiritual art-forms are driven out by purely mechanical and sensual forms, that literature dies, that falsehood and propaganda suffocate your every step, that the posing and posturing of officials become the very pivot of social life. Inevitably the system of oppression, coercion and constraint increases its pressure. A general ill-humour and irritation becomes the normal background of existence. And people expect the worst. One has to study all the objective mechanisms of our society minutely to attain some degree of certitude and find a programme of rational behaviour with the aim of neutralising to some degree the negative consequences of the positive qualities of communist society.'

(187)

'In some ways,' said Sashka, 'your view coincides with that of Solzhenitsyn. But at bottom (and I don't yet see clearly why) they are different. Couldn't you give our group a more detailed account of your ideas?'

'Group? What group's that?' I asked.

'I didn't put it very clearly,' said Sashka. 'Soon it'll be the birthday of one of my friends. The kids are interested in this sort of subject.'

'You'll get yourself into trouble with these "birthdays" of yours,' I said. 'Didn't you know that several people in the Institute of Technology have been arrested for meetings of this kind, and that the rest have been expelled. And that's not an isolated case. You've got to use your head a bit! At home read what you like, say what you like. You know perfectly well that I don't interfere. But outside . . . Good God! You can imagine how it all might end up if . . . You've got to get your degree first. . . .'

'Yes,' said Sashka. 'And then just try to get a job, or write a thesis. And then your doctorate . . . And then . . . And then . . .'

'Don't blame me, Sashka,' said Anton, 'but I can't come and talk to you. It's not because I agree with your father (because I don't). Nor is it because I'm afraid on my own account, which I'm not. But it would be stupid for your own safety. You must take care. You must behave intelligently to avoid getting crushed at the very outset. Besides, I think at the moment it would be inappropriate to cross swords with Solzhenitsyn. Solzhenitsyn has provided us with such a mass of food for thought that it'll take years to digest it all. I would simply cause harm. Or I would be taken for some kind of KGB agent deputed to criticise and discredit Solzhenitsyn in a very subtle way. He has a lot of ideas which coincide with what I might have to say. Just think for yourselves. . . . And for God's sake don't turn your birthday parties into some kind of political game. You'll be crushed. How many of you are there? A dozen? In that case there must be at least one informer among you. I have no wish to offend any one of you. But bear it in mind. That too is one of the laws of communist society.'

I of course demanded that Sashka should stop attending

these birthday parties. And I brought into play the final, the lowest argument: you might at least think about your family, about me and your mother and Lenka. Sashka promised to think about it.

'There's no need to exaggerate though,' he said. 'Of course we talk, but in such a way that nobody could have anything to complain about. Everyone does it these days. And they can't expel everyone or send them all to jail.'

'How can you tell?' said Anton. 'If they had to, they wouldn't be past jailing everybody.'

Nostalgia

Today it's hard to believe that only a few years ago things went on that these days would be absolutely impossible. In 1968 or 1969 (I don't remember precisely) there was an evening of entertainments at our Institute. The boys put on a first-class show. Nikiforov and another boy (who was later expelled from the Institute for some political affair or other and interned in a lunatic asylum) dressed up, one as a country lass, the other as a yokel. And they improvised philosophical couplets to the accompaniment of the accordion. The audience literally wept with laughter. Kanareikin himself asked for a typewritten copy of the verses. This 'philosophical poem' was published in the Wall newspaper. A couple of years later, some highly suspicious characters turned up poking around the Institute, trying to get hold of a copy of the poem and to find out who had written it. Strangely enough, no one informed on the authors. I had made a copy of this 'philosophical poem'. I have just re-read it and it has made me feel quite depressed. Yes, the better part of my life is past. But it's no longer safe to keep a thing like that at home. I must destroy it. Incidentally I must check out Lenka's room: it's not inconceivable that she may have amassed an entire anti-Soviet library. I must break with the past. The past is something only to be remembered, and even then only in moderation. It would be best not to think about it at all.

Lenka came in and picked up the shreds of the poem I had destroyed. Thinking that I had torn up some of my own writing she regarded this as progress: hitherto I had never torn up anything I had written; I had always written straight off, making corrections only in the typed copy or even in the proof. I know that this has earned me the burning hatred of our technical staff and editors. Lenka reminded me that I had to go to the polling station to vote. I had completely forgotten that it was election day. To elect whom and for what, by the way? What a glaring example of falsehood and hypocrisy, no matter how sincere an expression one tries to put on!—that's what Anton would have said. And Sashka too, probably. Not Lenka, though, because she had absorbed the idea that all our elections are a total fraud along with her mother's milk, and so she had neither a thought nor a feeling to spare on the subject. Just a bit of humour, that's all. This particular fraud had no impact on her life. Incidentally, our book is to contain a section on the development of Soviet democracy, in which we will compare our genuinely democratic electoral system with the fraudulent American system. What kind of democracy can it be, if it can make absolutely no difference whether I vote or not, or whether I vote 'for' or 'against'? Absolutely nothing depends on me. There is one candidate (one candidate to choose from!) and he is nominated via a channel of the power system which in no way depends on the electors. To be truthful, what I said about votes 'against' is wrong. They say that in such cases the person who has voted 'against' is traced and punished. I wonder who could write this section of the book? Edik Nikiforov? Yes he could wriggle his way out of it. He's a very talented boy. He would be able to find such forceful arguments to support the thesis that our electoral system is the pinnacle of democracy that even Kanareikin would ask him to tone it down slightly (to avoid the charge of gilding the lily!) Anton, of course, is right: we liberals only differ from the obscurantists in that we do the same things a little better than they, by slightly different methods and with a greater degree of shame—or cynicism, which amounts to the same thing.

I discovered nothing criminal in Lenka's room. Just this poem:

People accuse us of crimes in our youth,
And urge that we now should stand trial.
But why? for who now can tell fable from truth?
Look how we've developed meanwhile!
—So you think that the past should be now left alone,
No point in reopening old sores?
But history's burdens are never laid down.
That's one of our natural laws.
No matter how guiltless you may try to look,
As though evil has sunk without trace,
The crimes that you thought were by now a closed book—
They're written all over your face.

Could this 'friend of hers' that she talks about be herself? If so, something's got to be done urgently. But what? I'll have to talk to Tamurka. She won't use any kid-glove methods. She'll give her something to think about! . . . I feel sorry for the girl, but there's nothing else to be done. There's no other solution.

The old boozer

On the way to hospital I once again met the Old Boozer. I stopped but she paid no attention to me. If she had shown the slightest interest in her surroundings I would have given her all the money I had on me. But she went on past me with her squeaky little cart, almost as if she were walking straight through me without the slightest suspicion of my existence, as if she were carrying away with her my problem, a very important and unresolved problem. What problem? When I was a child some hamsters turned up in our house. They were engaging little beasts. They irritated me, but at the same time I found them intriguing, as if they were invested with some unknown mystery. I have begun to get a similar feeling whenever I see the Old Boozer or think about her. It is as if I had forgotten something extremely important, but I can never remember precisely what.

(191)

Illness

Our academic hospital is one of the best in the country. The building is superb. The treatment is good. And even the food is edible. But this hospital is primarily intended for healthy people. It is for the huge staff of doctors who for the most part perform bureaucratic jobs. And for people like me who want to spend some time there for some reason or other. As far as medical treatment is concerned, there isn't a great deal of it. They keep a very close eye on us, i.e. once a year we are obliged to go for a check-up. What that means is that at a given time we go from consulting room to consulting room, from the urologist to the optician, from the optician to the stomatologist and so on. We spend hours sitting in queues. The people peer into our ears, look into our mouths, shove a finger up our bums and spend a long time writing down in thick tomes (our medical histories) everything we can whimper out about our peculiarities and our ulterior purposes. If we need a medical certificate to go abroad, we make ourselves out to be in the pink of condition, and they write us down as 'in good general health' even if we've got acute ulcers. If we need to escape for a time from certain little unpleasantnesses, we simulate a malady of some chosen organ, and go into hospital for tests and 'treatment'. A great many people in the Institute use the hospital as a convenient way of solving their problems. But as far as treatment goes there's almost none. Our medicine was not created for that. It exists for its own sake. It maintains its best relations with those who are easiest to treat. And no one is as easy to treat as a healthy person.

I have a private room with a telephone. There are flowers (brought by my devoted subordinates). There's a whole library of books (brought by Lenka, Sashka, Anton and those same devoted colleagues). And I've been showered with fruit and vegetables and such like good and rare delights. The refrigerator is half full of my food reserves. As the greater part of these find their way into the hands of the hospital staff I am allowed as many visitors as I like whenever they want to come, quite against the rules. And I feel very comfortable here. I have the impression of being a good man, loved by all and very useful to society.

But the main thing is that I've managed to do down Baranov, Vaskin, Tvarzhinskaya and the rest of that gang. There will be no discussion of my article until after the elections.

The list of candidates for corresponding member and Academician has been published in the papers. There is a horde of candidates for only three places (two for corresponding members, one for a full Academician). Eropkin will certainly get the Academician vacancy. And two people apart from me have any real chance of being elected corresponding members: Vaskin and the new editor of our journal. Everyone is congratulating me in advance. I just shrug them off with a joke. But underneath it gives me a real pleasure. And some anxiety.

The problem of satiety

Since I have nothing to do I have been thinking about Anton's book. There is one idea in it which has struck me above all others. Communism, Anton wrote, copes splendidly with problems which it has inherited from the past or which are imposed on it from outside: hunger, economic collapse, natural disasters, epidemics, i.e. alien problems. But communism's own problems arise when society achieves relative stability and satiety. It is easier to give a piece of bread to a starving man than to satisfy the appetites of a well fed man who knows the taste of caviar, smoked sturgeon, sterlets, shashlik, etc. It is easier to clothe a man in rags than to pacify a well dressed man who knows the value of fine furs, precious stones, expensive evening wear. . . . It is easier to put a roof over the head of the homeless than it is to alleviate the suffering of a man who has a room of his own or even a small apartment but who knows that other people have huge luxurious apartments and country villas. . . . In brief communism's own problems are the problems of a normal and healthy way of life, and not those which derive from departures from the minimal norms of existence. But history knows no example of a society which has been able to cope by its own efforts with the problems arising from its normal existence. It is possible to cure a sick man, but not a person in good health. Everything which is now decried as the ulcers of Soviet society is in fact the normal manifestation of the healthy nature of communism. In this my conception is substantially different from those of other critics of communism.

Sashka

Sashka has brought me a book by Ivanitskiy published in Paris. It is a kind of anti-Utopia in the style of Orwell. The book has a passage about that period of our history which is regarded as its Golden Age. It was for this passage that Sashka brought me the book.

'Just read it, you might find it comes in handy,' said Sashka; 'the book is pretty boring. It's not Solzhenitsyn, but there are some ideas in it.'

When Sashka left, this is what I read:

What an amazing time it was! At the present the Soviet people have almost constructed exactly what the classics and the wise leaders forecast. As the saying goes, as they have sown, so have they reaped. One can hardly believe that such a time ever existed. Young people dismiss it as old wives' tales. There was meat for sale in the shops? And the potatoes weren't all rotten? And there was no need to stand for more than an hour in a queue? Not everyone who told a joke was jailed? Stop pulling our legs, papa! We're not babies anymore! We've long been out of kindergarten! Just try and convince these young people devoured by scepticism that all this really existed. They, the young, have a devout belief in our marvellous Leadership, which promises that thanks to the uninterrupted improvement in material welfare and the irresistible consolidation of democracy, we shall attain this fruition in the near future. But for the time being . . . In a word, the Golden Age is in the future and not behind us, for that is the directive. Of course the age in which we live at the moment (if of course we are actually alive) is also extremely golden. But the age towards which our beloved and brilliant Leadership is conducting us, towards which we are drawing near aspri . . . apris . . . aripsi . . . oh hell! . . . I can never get that word out without a drink! . . . Anyway the age towards which we are moving, but which we shall never reach, even though it may seem sometimes that we are just on the point of getting there . . . well, that age will be even more golden. It is that age which is truly the Golden Age of our history. It is always ahead of us and never behind us as the slanderers and the critics think. And anyway it is no longer of any importance; these days no one remembers any longer which is the front of our history, and which is the behind.

> It matters not how hard you try,
> The difference you'll ne'er descry.
> Look behind, you'll see a cunt,
> And the arsehole is in front.

So there's no point in racking your brains about it. Now there are no more problems, nor can there be. Obey your leaders, shed a few tender tears and applaud. That is all that is asked of you.

Rogozin's interview

The 'Voices' broadcast an interview with Rogozin. When asked about the position of the cultural world in the Soviet Union he gave the following answer: 'The great majority,' he said, 'are happy and in quite a good situation. There are individuals who suffer. But these individuals are more significant than tens or hundreds of thousands of others. Who are they? Solzhenitsyn. Rostropovich. Maximov. Neizvestniy. I'm sure Solzhenitsyn was exiled not so much for his political activity as because he is a talented writer. In the Soviet Union there are tens of thousands of writers. Tens of thousands of mediocrities. They cannot tolerate the presence in their midst of a genuinely outstanding artist. But if there is still some room for argument in the case of Solzhenitsyn, there is no such room for discussion in the case of Neizvestniy. Neizvestniy was a wholly Soviet man. But for twenty years he was not permitted a single exhibition. Why? Because he was an outstanding artist. His fellow artists, several thousand completely untalented people, chased him out. I do not of course want, nor am I able, to compare myself with these people. But from the social point of view my case is exactly similar. As soon as I began to lead an original group, and as soon as the work of our group began to acquire world-wide recognition, we were broken up. And I found myself in complete creative isolation.'

Curiously enough, I thought to myself, my own case has something in common with that of Rogozin. Our Section comes under fire because it produces a better impression than all the others. And to accuse us of errors is a normal form of battle.

Lenka

Lenka is terribly busy. But she does still occasionally drop in.

'Our idiots,' she said 'have finally gone off their heads altogether. Just imagine, they are making us do a reinterpretation (that's what they call it) of the old fairy story *The Crimson Flower*.[1] On the one hand they want us to make it look like Antonioni, Bergman, or at worst Tarkovskiy. But on the other, they want us to preserve the Marxist Leninist context. Do you know who we are going to cast as the monster? You'd never guess. He turns out to be a progressive young communist, a specialist in land reclamation, who wants to drain the swamp, but a witch who's in the service of imperialism throws a spell on him with the help of chemistry and genetics. And the witch has a plainly Zionist outlook. I must dash. There's another rehearsal today. We're getting it ready for the victory anniversary. It's going to be a magnificent show. I'm playing a partisan. The only trouble is that all our kids are a bit on the small side for fascists. I'm a lot taller than all of them. The headmistress said that that's fine: a Soviet citizen must always be taller than everyone else. It's a symbol!'

[1] A Russian version of *Beauty and the Beast*, as told by Aksakov. (Translator)

'Do you remember, you never finished reciting me that poem by your friend. How does it end?'

'Like this, I think:

I answer: one time among those who are dead,
The rumours were flowing like water—
At the start of our age, and in vain, be it said
You put too many folk to the slaughter.
They said that in vain too much evil was done
Your heaven on earth to create,
And that innocent victims were killed without sum,
While you played benefactors of state.
Well, yes, they reply, that is perfectly true,
But the winners, they never get punished.
Since then, to ensure that our Future comes through,
We've got rid of all manner of rubbish.
Come in, like the rest, do not trouble your brain,
Meet your needs and give what you are able,
And forget those who died—they're the price of our gain,
Their memory no more than a fable.
You admit, I retort, that the butchers were there,
That the stories of victims are true,
So that we can have goodies, and plenty to spare,
Unlike those who would never come through.
I shall never come in to your Radiant House,
I should rather die here at the door.
If we all shuffle in, like obedient cows,
It will happen again as before.'

'He deserves a good hiding, your friend.'

'Thank you,' said Lenka. 'I'll let him know your critique. He's bound to be delighted with such high praise. Do you want to hear a story? Our General Secretary took his grandson along to the Mausoleum. His grandson asked: Grandpa, when you're dead will you live here? Of course, said his grandfather, where else? Then Lenin got up and said, Hey, what do you think this is, a doss house or something?'

And Lenka guffawed. But I didn't find it funny. I was worried. What's going to happen to you, little girl? Will your accelerated growth be any protection? Will you be able to

hold out, to adapt yourself and learn to give back blow for
blow?

Confessions

Some years ago Tamurka and I took our holiday in the Central
Committee rest home in the south. Once we were lying on the
beach. On the public beach people were so packed together you
could hardly walk between them. But on our half kilometre of
beautiful sand there were no more than a dozen. Quite close to
us there were a couple of high ranking middle-aged crooks
who were busy acquiring a tan. They were picking over the
bones of our highest statesmen in much the same way as we did
with our insignificant acquaintances, telling smutty stories
and unfunny anti-Soviet jokes which made them roar with
laughter. They hadn't even noticed that Tamurka and I were
there.

'Do you know what they call a man who never gives his
mistress a present?'

'What?'

'A para-shite! ha ha ha ha!'

'Ha ha ha ha!'

Sometimes they launched into serious matters.

'What's going on is quite incredible, fuck it all! Here we are
mass-producing well-educated, talented, honest and what-
have-you people. Yet wherever you look all you see is stupidity,
ignorance, mediocrity, corruption, bribery, careerism. . . .
Where the hell are we going?'

'Into the shit of course. In time this discrepancy will be
eliminated.'

'I doubt it. Things will get worse.'

'It all depends what you think is worse. If the discrepancy
does disappear, it'll be appalling.'

And they laughed merrily. They could see and understand
everything perfectly. And because of their high positions they
knew a great deal about which we hadn't a clue—including
statistical summaries. And they were no exception. I have never

met a single person of our level or higher who was unaware of the true state of things. As a rule it is people below that level who do not know. And in this sense social awareness is greater at the higher levels than at the lower. Is it perhaps that social awareness is unique and has some real value? Anton is right, we look at our life through a grill of outworn concepts and value judgements. Modern youth is closer to reality. That is why it is alien to us. The Kanareikins and the Tvarzhinskayas are much closer to us. They are on the same plane as we are both in the conceptual and emotional sense. The generation gap is not an age phenomenon. There is no such gap between us and our predecessors. And our children and their children after them will not have such a gap. Somewhere in our recent past there has been a far deeper schism in the life of our society than any previous schisms: we lost our innocence, and resigned ourselves to the reality of communism as to a norm of existence, and rejected all our illusions. And this schism while leaving the souls of the Kanareikins and Tvarzhinskayas intact, as also the souls of our present young people, has stabbed my own generation to the heart. And it has engendered a generation of fantastic creatures—cynical idealists, disinterested thieves, honest crooks and so on. In short, it has created such abject monsters that even we are disgusted with ourselves.

On death

Although I am in perfect health, recently I have often thought about death. Sometimes the thought has kept me awake all night. Sometimes I get myself into such a state that I am on the point of crying out from horror and self-pity. But suddenly, I was struck by a curious thought. Why is it that I feel afraid when I think of death? It is because in imagining myself in a state of non-existence, I am indulging myself in an illicit extrapolation. It is because I am representing the matter to myself as if, after I have ceased to exist, I shall still retain my awareness, and because of this I shall undergo eternal suffering. But that of course is quite simply not possible. When I recog-

nise that, I grow calm again. Now I enjoy a great sense of relief.
I can even laugh as I recall my former fears.

The arrangement of forces

The socio-political structure of our society is not as simple as it
may seem at first sight. For example, it has become the
accepted thing to consider that if a man is engaged in the study
of historical materialism or, even more, of scientific communism, he is *a priori* a conservative or even an obscurantist. But
that is far from being the case. There are just as many obscurantists in the ranks of mathematicians and physicists as there are
in those of the philosophers. They exist even among musicians.
For instance, ask Kolmogorov or Shostakovich to sign any
letter condemning Solzhenitsyn and Sakharov, and they will
scrawl their names without a moment's thought. Yet I know
philosophers who have refused to do this even though they
realise in advance that they will be punished for their refusal.
The physicists themselves will not name more than two or three
people who can be regarded as 'decent' people in the cohorts of
science. They usually name Kapitsa. But what has he really
done? Merely refrained from the most degrading actions. Of
course, under our conditions that is already quite something.
But phenomena of this kind blur the dividing lines in the
socio-political picture of our society.

First of all, we must introduce the concept of the individual
whom we are taking into account. I cannot define this concept
in precise terms. I can only clarify it somewhat. For instance,
recently the workers at a Moscow factory organised something
like a strike. It was a very serious and important action. But
these workers are not individuals who must be taken into
account as individuals (let us say who count in a social sense).
On the other hand, a man like Kapitsa has never undertaken
any political action. But he does count in a social sense. This
type of individual exerts an influence on the country in its
socio-political aspect, either by the very fact of his existence and
his normal daily activity, or by particular kinds of action which

he carries out regularly. The distinctions which follow apply only to individuals of this kind.

The first distinction is between those who are integrated and those who are not (or those who stand outside). This distinction betrays itself in different ways in different fields of activity. For example, among us philosophers, the non-integrated are the people who deliberately choose to ignore Marxism while working on the same problems. There are very few people like this. The majority of them distance themselves so far that to all intents and purposes they change their profession and can usually no longer be counted among the people who should be taken into account. Although they speak scornfully of our philosophy and our way of life, in fact they amount to nothing, since in their new official life they are ordinary citizens of no importance. Those few 'deviants' who remain play a substantial role. They have an influence on the liberals (more of these later). For instance, in the field of philosophy, under the influence of the 'deviants', not only the liberals, but even the obscurantists have tried to reduce to a minimum their quotations from the classics of Marxism, and have quoted the positivists as serious scientists, and so on. These 'deviationists' are, as a rule, people of considerable stature. Sometimes active dissidents appear among them. It is this category that has engendered people like Sakharov, Turchin, Shafarevich, and Rostropovich. Many of them have emigrated. A characteristic feature of the 'deviants' is that they are unwilling or unable to integrate themselves into the Soviet way of life and Soviet ideology.

The second distinction lies within the integrated group. These latter are people who must be taken into account by virtue of and specifically on account of their professional activity. By this criterion, for instance, Shafarevich and Turchin do not fall into this category because their involvement in politics takes place in a context other than that of their professional activity. On the other hand, Neizvestniy, Tarkovskiy, Maximov, Okudzhava and many other artists and writers have become involved in social action by virtue of their professional preoccupations. These 'integrated' figures can be divided crudely into 'liberals' and 'conservatives'. Once again, it is very difficult (if indeed it is possible at all) to give a precise definition of these categories. The borders between them are fluid, changeable, almost imperceptible. But it is possible to give some approximate description and 'examples'. And that will be sufficient. A characteristic example of the 'liberals' is the poet Tvardovskiy. Nesmeyanov is a similar example from the academic world. Another, but less well known, is Academician Rumyantsev. In the past, he was an important party figure, and later Vice-president of the Academy. In the most liberal years, he gave his protection to concrete sociology, and that was his undoing. He was removed from the vice-presidency and from his post of director of the Institute of Concrete Social Research. Khrushchev became a liberal. And even Brezhnev to a certain extent bore a liberal stamp, even if only by inertia. A liberal can be distinguished from a conservative not merely by the fact that the conservative is in favour of putting people in jail while the liberal is against—a liberal can be as good at putting people in jail as a conservative, and there are conservative critics of the 'cult of personality'—but even more so by a purely personal inclination towards greater flexibility, towards rather greater humanity, gentleness, courtesy, delicacy, relaxation—and less discipline.

Just as in the case of the conservatives, the liberals are not all of the same cast. For some of them liberalism is merely a trait of character which it was permissible to acquire or to display in the post-Stalin period. For another group, liberalism is a convenient means of self-assertion and career building. For a third group, it is their tribute to the fashion of the day. For only a very small group is liberalism a matter of principle. All liberals favour the Soviet way of life; they are against only its extremes, and favour improvements to it—and improvements, moreover, whose aim is to consolidate the Soviet system. They accuse the conservatives of being incapable of serving the cause of communism in a proper way (i.e. in accordance with the demands of the age). They believe that they can accomplish this better. There are even liberals within the ranks of the apparatus of the Central Committee and the KGB. There was a time when it was rumoured that the KGB was the most liberal organisation which we had. Liberalism is the striving of Soviet society to breathe a shade more freely, an aspiration which is exploited by a certain category of people to their own egoistical ends.

Among the liberals, there can be isolated a small number of people who for one reason or another are unable to integrate themselves into the Soviet way of life. A typical example of this is Neizvestniy who was driven out of Soviet society by the efforts of his colleagues because he was too gifted and original, and because he had become widely known in the West. Yet he was a Soviet man to the highest degree, and he had a greater capacity than anyone you like for adapting himself to our conditions. Rogozin became a similar case. And in my view, Okudzhava and Tarkovskiy are also in this category although they have not emigrated.

Finally, if we take society as a whole, we see that a very small number of people fall into the role of opponents, champions of freedom, or denouncers. Their names are well known. Their influence on the whole of Soviet society is immense even though everything is done to try to conceal it. The activity of Solzhenitsyn and Sakharov constitutes an entire epoch in the socio-political development of Soviet society. It should be said that Solzhenitsyn was thrust forward as an opponent not only because of the content of his books and speeches, but also because of his talent as a writer. The immense army of our mediocre writers cast him out so that he should not disturb their habitual way of life and their established criteria.

I reflected on all this (the enforced idleness of hospital life tends to encourage this kind of thought) while completely forgetting that my point of departure came directly from Anton's book. When I realised this, I said to myself that Anton really had nothing to do with it, and that I would have thought it all out for myself because these are all self-evident and humdrum truths. But even there I was using Anton's words. In the Preface to his book, he wrote that he did not see his task as the revelation of sensational secrets of Soviet society but as an attempt to introduce a certain system into a number of self-evident factors, and to establish the laws which govern them.

Anton

Anton came to see me. He said that I had been bitterly attacked in the Philosophy Faculty of the Higher Party School. It was still for the same thing, for social formation.

'It was you who drove me off my head,' I remarked jokingly.

'You know what your main weakness is,' he said; 'it's that you go the whole hog. You'll still be attacked just the same. Even after the elections it's quite clear that you'll still be under fire. And what for? For trivia. If you're going to be attacked, it might as well be for something serious. You should have followed your thought right through. Then you might not have been attacked at all. They might have lost their bearings and kept quiet. It wouldn't have been to their advantage to attack you. The same as with Lebedev.'

'If I did stop half way, as you believe, it wasn't from stupidity nor from cowardice,' I said. 'You know perfectly well that I am not a coward. I am not convinced by your ideas! You believe that there are some kinds of universal social laws which are not limited by factors derived from the past history of civilisation, and which define the essence and all aspects of our society. But how come? It still has to be proved.'

'It cannot be proved,' said Anton. 'It can be observed, though. Then society can be studied from this angle. Then we can construct a series of theories according to the rules of experimental science. We can verify this theory empirically, and so on. You know all this perfectly well yourself.'

'But at least give me an example so that I can see what you mean,' I said.

'It's obvious,' said Anton. 'I cannot understand why you can't see it for yourself. You've got a brain that's worth ten of anybody else's. Take any major institution and examine the structure of its workforce. Consider what within this structure serves the interests of the enterprise, and what serves something else. Look at the sectors, departments, institutes . . . what do they have which is conditioned by the laws of physics, biology, language and so on which science is called upon to

(204)

study? Nothing. The interests of the management? Of course! But what is that? Work? That is social life in its own right. And over-manning—does that come from the same infra-structure? And what about idleness? Or shoddy work? Or irresponsibility? Even your productive forces are decisively influenced by the laws of society. If you consider the present state and the evolution of our industry, you will find the imprint of these laws on everything. Even space flights are dictated by them and not by the needs of production. I am not even talking about such things as the monstrous parasitism of a large part of the population, about low productivity, about the way people are prevented from moving freely about the country. Or take the cultural sphere: what will it profit you to know that here we have public ownership of the means of production, that we do not have exploiting classes, and so on? But if you follow the path which I have been pointing out to you for so many years, everything will become transparently clear. Look at the mechanics first. Sixty thousand writers, either completely lacking in talent or of mediocre ability, who live quite well under this system, and who are supported by the powerful apparatus of Party and State, which is also pretty well provided for, will destroy any attempt to create a truthful or original literature. They got rid of Solzhenitsyn not mainly because he unmasked the regime, but because he did it with great talent. And then there's the content as well. There are human problems which arise because of the presence within society of an actively operating system of morality and other problems which arise because of the absence of any such system. Only the former can be the basis of a great spiritual literature. Denunciation, betrayals, deception and falsehood for example, do not engender problems worthy of great art in a society where morality does not function as a significant social mechanism. Great art is the creation of a moral civilisation, and one of its means of existence. That is why we do not have, and cannot have, any great spiritual art. We can force the entire country to dance folk dances, take up figure skating or sing in choirs. But we will not allow great writers like Dostoievsky or Tolstoy to exist. Do I need to say any more? The facts are legion. They beg for scientific study. Yet all we do is try our best to get rid of them.'

News

Serikov, Novikov and Svetka came to visit me. They told me
how things were going with the book. It seems that everything
is going according to plan. And even better. So my absence has
had its advantages. Then they told me all the latest news and
gossip. Sidorov's sheepskin coat had been stolen from the
Department of Ethics. A commission of inquiry had discovered
that Kitaeva had fiddled a thousand roubles' worth of trade
union stamps. The Institute was in turmoil. Kitaeva had
worked there for more than twenty years. She was an old
member of the Party. The management wanted to save her as a
valued worker (or an informer?) but the lower ranks were out
for blood. A delegation had just arrived from Yugoslavia. They
very much wanted to meet me. Tvarzhinskaya smelt something
criminal in this, as all Yugoslavs are well known to be revisionists. Once again, Karasev had been refused permission to take
part in a symposium abroad, and that had caused a minor
scandal. The new scientific secretary had almost drowned the
Institute in a flood of paper. An attack had been launched
against the dialectical materialists, and people were trying to
find evidence of positive error. All in all the process of decay
was going on apace. Everyone was certain that I would be
elected a corresponding member. And people were beginning
to say that it was time to transform our Section into an independent Institute.

'And invite a pogrom, as the sociologists did,' I laughed.
'Before that, we'll have to bring out a couple of serious symposia, a few collections of articles and some monographs. And
then in a year or two we can raise the question of an Institute.'

Then they told me the latest joke about the Congress. Outside the Palace of Congresses, people keep asking the delegates
whether they've got any spare tickets. 'What do you want
tickets for?' ask the astonished delegates. 'To see this marvellous farce that's playing here,' they reply.

'Guess what this is,' says Novikov.

He repeatedly holds up his hand, each time making a kissing sound. Of course I haven't the faintest idea. . . .

'It's the arrival of the government delegation of the Party.'
And Serikov recited a little poem.

'Folk are feeling very sore.
"Can't the Party give us more?"
The Party's not an easy trollop,
Who'll give everyone his dollop!'

In short, we all had a great time. After they'd left, Dima turned up. He brought an enormous quantity of food and a detailed report of Khlebnikov's trial. He got off with a mere trifle: just five years. We began to talk about dissidents in general and came to a unanimous conclusion. Soviet dissidence can only be distinguished in theory from liberalism in general by the degree of its negative attitude to Soviet reality, and not by any positive, matured programme of reform. But we were in complete disagreement in our assessment of their practical activities. Dima regarded them as heroes, while I said that they did nothing but speculate on a particular situation, and that they were not concerned with the good of society but with satisfying their own personal ambition. Dima said it was disgraceful to think like that, but he could not produce any rational arguments. Of course there are heroic figures among them, but it is not they who determine the general picture. Dima said that even if there was only one hero for every thousand worthless ones, that one hero gave the whole movement an heroic quality. I could not understand this, so we began to talk about matters of no importance.

In the name of the people

'We are told to work and sacrifice ourselves,' said Sashka, 'but to what end? In the name of the people, you say? To serve the people? That is sheer demagogy as you know perfectly well. Stalin and his gang committed foul deeds in the name of the people. And hundreds of thousands of his henchmen killed and tortured in the name of the people. And the present generation of hundreds of thousands of thieves and careerists go about their business in the name of the people.'

'But not everyone is a thief or a careerist.'

'Not everyone. But are there many people you know whom you could call anything else? So ask them in whose name they are what they are? And anyway, what is "the people"? Is it the population?'

'No, it's certainly not the population. The people is a social category. You see . . .'

'I can see perfectly well. In the last century, that still had some meaning. But things are different now. The workers? The peasants? The charwomen? The soldiers? The office workers? The students? The teachers? Where is this people of yours, this social category? Is it those who live worse than anyone else? That's a fine category! How are the workers any worse off than Uncle Anton? You have written yourself that the standard of living of the mass of the population is determined by the nature of the social structure. It's true that you wrote also that we have a high and constantly rising standard of living, but what I would like to know is whether you wrote that before you'd been out shopping for potatoes or afterwards! Solzhenitsyn is right: we must radically alter our entire system of concepts, judgements and aims. The demand for freedom of speech is something real. The calls for the ending of censorship are real as well. So are the demands for the freedom to emigrate or to have some means of expressing public opinion. All that is something quite different from "in the name of the people". My opinion is that even "the people" would benefit from it. It is true that those who put forward these demands are suffocated in the name of "the people" for the "people" and by the "people". And work done in the name of society, the State or the Party is purely cynical careerism or dim-wittedness.'

'If you understand everything for yourself, why bother discussing it?! As far as you're concerned, my opinion is tedious, toadying philosophical twaddle. So what more do you want?'

'I don't know. I don't know. That's probably why I'm feeling bitter. Soon I'll finish at university. And then what?'

'Couldn't it be just simply living like everyone else lives?'

'You can't simply live here. And living like everyone else means having to be evasive, to shove people about, to intrigue one's way around. Have you ever tried simply living? That's counting without the rest homes, of course. In this country it's not possible to live without functioning. To "simply live" a man needs a certain degree of independence from society. He needs the freedom to live as he wishes. Even if you live within the boundaries of law and morality, you need a certain degree of independence from the collective to which you belong.'

'But you don't belong to it constantly.'

'Always. Even when you're in bed or on the lavatory. The collective always holds you invisibly under permanent control.'

'That kind of independence has to be won.'

'How? By building a career? That is not independence either. By becoming a genius and making yourself famous? Not everyone is capable of that. What if you're just an ordinary, average man?'

'So what do you propose to do?'

'I don't know precisely. For a start, I might try a few years on one of the big construction projects, say on the Trans-Siberian Railway.'

'You must be mad!'

'So for other people it's an heroic enterprise, but for your son it's madness? That's not honest. Oh, don't worry. I really haven't gone mad yet!'

This conversation disturbed me greatly. Not because of its implications for Sashka's future—he's a solid lad who'll survive. It was more a matter of the problem itself. It's the done thing to regard our ideological propaganda as something completely empty. Everyone knows that it's pure lies whose content leads to a dead-end. It's just a dog barking into the wind. But all that is a profound error. It is to be taken in by appearances to believe that our ideology leaves the souls of our people unaffected, or that it inspires in them scepticism or scorn. The ideological apparatus affects the minds of men quite independently of its content, by the very fact of its existence and its methods of operation. This apparatus works in imperceptible ways to weave a delicate net within human consciousness, a net in which the newborn human 'I' struggles in vain. And when this 'I' matures, it is too late. It is completely imprisoned by this invisible ideological net. There must be exceptional circumstances to permit this net to be torn or to avoid it ensnaring your soul. This opportunity is given to few. Even though Sashka is thrashing about, he has already fallen into this net, and I feel that he will never escape it. Perhaps that is all for the best. He has not got the quality of genius. And as far as becoming a dissident is concerned, it isn't worth the effort. That is boring too.

Tradition and system

I had a visit from Stupak, Nikiforov and a young woman who's one of our junior research workers. They brought a bottle of cognac which we immediately set about draining. They told me about the new system of editorial control of monographs and symposia, and the new system for the preparation and defence of theses.

'Oh ho!' I said; 'now we're going to have to wait five years at least on every miserable little pamphlet, and it will become practically impossible to defend a thesis.'

'That depends on who's defending it,' said Stupak. 'Even the old system was the same in practice. That's not where the problem lies. In the past, we had a certain tradition which had been established despite the formal bureaucratic system. Of course, a lot of villains made a good thing out of it. But once in a while something decent managed to get through. It's a fact that over this period, we've published a few dozen books and articles which were entirely up to world standards. And out of all the people who upheld their doctoral dissertations you might choose thirty or so who could form a first-class Institute, incomparably more productive than ours with its staff of five hundred. This new system means that the tradition of the Sixties will be crushed. The frauds will still get published and win their doctorates as they used to. But now there will be no point in decent people even dreaming of publishing or submitting their theses.'

Then they went on to tell a few jokes. We moved on to price rises, the trial of Khlebnikov, the growing incidence of burglary, and the system of bureaucracy which has overtaken our Institute.

On literature

Sashka brought me a new novel by Tikshin which is the rage of Moscow at the moment.

'You really must read it. It's a shattering book. It has scenes so nightmarish that sometimes even Solzhenitsyn seems drab in comparison. The amazing thing is that he's been able to get it through the censors. It's been published!'

I found the book very difficult to read, and it did not move me to any great enthusiasm. It was in the modern style, as contorted as it could possibly be. Psychoanalysis a little behind the times (as Stupak put it, a Soviet regime behind the times). Neo-realism behind the times by the entire postwar period. The heroes suffer and make each other suffer. Almost all of them are complete nobodies. There are some decent ones, even some able ones. But it is not clear from the book what their decency and their ability consist of. We are simply told that it is so. The heroes are dichotomous and struggle within themselves without being aware of it. The postwar events in our circle are depicted as minor intrigues at the level of Faculties and Institutes. Nothing but envy and the settling of scores. There are allusions of course. I remember all these events very well as I took part in them. Everything was much more simple, more transparent and without any psychology. And nothing surprised anyone. Beat some one up! Certainly! No problem. Whom? That one? Very good. What for? For that? Still no problem. One of the principal heroes of the book, an unprincipled and mediocre careerist, ends up an alcoholic and descends to the 'lower depths'—he goes to work in a furniture shop. That was purely comic. Things don't happen that way. It does not conform to the spirit of our society. There is no need for a careerist with higher education to descend to the 'lower depths'; he can perfectly well become an alcoholic in one of the high positions which we have in abundance. We have a great many people (right up to the very top) who do exactly that—they drink themselves silly in their offices, in their luxurious apartments, in their country villas, and even at official receptions. And what's more, a man who works in a furniture shop is far from being in the 'lower depths'. And anyway, it's meaningless to talk about the 'lower depths' when that is where all of us live.

Anton came to visit, saw the book and laughed.

'So that's what you're up to? I wouldn't be surprised if you soon became an habitué of the "Taganka". What progress!'

'It's not a bad book. Very modern. And bold. And yet you see they've published it!'

'That's exactly it, it's been published. These days quite a lot of that kind of thing gets published. Just look, they're saying, we aren't afraid to show the truth. My dear old candidate corresponding member! You of all people should well know that our authorities, and the censorship which represents them, have a kind of intuition about genuine literature. And if they pass anything, you can look out for defective goods. Of course the book's got a lot right in its details; there is some accurate observation. Some individual images have come off well. But overall it is, at bottom, the usual kind of Soviet falsehood, the kind that is passed by the censorship. There may be allusions and a little bit of discreet snook-cocking, but it's still lies. Its contortions are quite deliberate: it's a way of showing that in real life everything is woven into a complex tangle! What rubbish! In our life, everything is as open to view as in a barracks or in an office. If there is any complexity, it comes from our own confusion and incompetence, and not from principle. Tell me, has it ever taken you dramatic efforts to reach an understanding of our people and our situation? No? Me neither. We got into trouble not because people and situations were complex, but simply because of the element of incontrollable chance in our existence, and because of our own wish to get into trouble. Tikshin's heroes are dichotomous and they fight within themselves, which produces external conflicts and processes. But what happens in reality? There is a struggle between men and between groups of men. It does not derive from the states of mind of the individual but from the very fact of the existence together of large masses of people in the conditions of Soviet society. (Everything an individual acquires comes via the collective, every success, every act of creation is via the collective, he is subject to the power of the collective and so on. Society has no moral consciousness or institutions to support it; there is no juridical protection of the individual; the individual is constrained to live and work in a set place; there are no free elections and so on.) The individual merely reflects the conditions of Soviet life. And in the mass he conforms to them. As for those who do not conform, they perish—a fish cannot live long out of the water. People of course do have their own personal problems. But in our way of life, those problems are simple, transparent, primitive, standard. They are not in themselves subjects for literature. To describe their states of mind is much the same thing as describing the states of minds of people who become bald, get constipated, or lose their virility as they grow old. The object of true literature would be their banality, their greyness, their mediocrity. And in that case, one would have to talk about them rather differently. For example, one could use the research form as Solzhenitsyn in *Gulag*. Incidentally, *Gulag* is not so much an historical document as a brilliant work of literature using historical facts. You and I lived at precisely that time and in the milieu which Tikshin is writing about. Was it like that? No it was not. It wasn't that it was worse or better; it just was not like that. And if you really want to talk about what actually happened, you must speak openly, not in allusions. Yes, there was a plan for mass purges of the Jews, and our acquaintance Khesnokov prepared an entire book to justify it, for which he was promoted by Stalin. But the plan fell apart. Why? Did some dramatic process come into operation far below the surface? Nothing of the kind. It was just a heartless calculation that turned out to be inexpedient. If the signal had been given, the Jews would have been quite cheerfully driven through the streets of Moscow and sent to Siberia. The authorities were afraid of the analogy with fascism. And at the time, we were playing the part of the liberators of mankind! What about the campaign against cosmopolitans? It was a massively organised campaign like all the others. The directive

(213)

from above, the regional authorities ready to put the plan into operation, victims selected in advance and so many enthusiasts, they were swarming on the ground. And it's no use trying to find any psychology except that of fear, malicious pleasure or a desire to keep yourself in favour. One must describe the overall mechanism—that would be the truth. But to try to describe the life of an anthill or a colony of mice through the psychology of one separate ant or one isolated mouse . . . I have nothing against Tikshin. He's not a bad writer. But he is a Lenin Prize-winner after all. People write about him a lot. That is typical. In our society truth and authenticity are killed or passed over in silence.'

'As usual, you're overdoing it. So, according to you, there cannot be any such thing as genuine officially permitted literature? But there is still daily life. Love. The family. Adventures. Romance. In a word, everything which writers usually write about.'

'You are a Marxist, but you do not want to recognise your own principles applied to our society. The family, love, friendship, romance, adventures and so on—all these are the Soviet family, Soviet friendship, Soviet romance, Soviet adventure and so on. Take space flights for example. Heroism! But these are not enthusiastic volunteers who are doing this at their own risk; they are very carefully selected, and above all after a close personal vetting, and for considerations quite remote from the actual business of space flight. We sent up a woman. Why? So that the first woman cosmonaut should be one of ours. That confirms . . . and blah blah! Are there many Jews among the cosmonauts? People might say that the Jews are cowards, as was said during the war. But that is a lie. You know it for yourself. If you launched an appeal saying: "Jews wanted for space flight", there would be a tremendous rush. And then people would say that they're doing it because it's to their advantage. And that's true of course. Have many cosmonauts been killed? And what's the pay like? To be a cosmonaut in our society—that, my friend, is high politics. Friendship? What would happen if all your friends from the Section dropped you straight away? Svetka. Novikov. Serikov. Ivanov. Korytov. Kuritsyn. In Soviet conditions, friendship yields to mutual benefit and the kind of typically Soviet complicity, something very petty and coarse. Something slimy. You know all this better than I do.'

'That's all clear to me. So now a writer has nothing that he can write about? If he writes the truth, he will be killed like a fly. And lying is bad.'

'I'm not forbidding them to write. And they are writing. They're writing a great deal and are very pleased to do so. And they tell their lies voluntarily and sometimes even enthusiastically. All I'm doing is expressing my opinion.'

The radiant future

'What news of the book?'

Anton merely made a weary gesture in reply. And I felt sorry for him. I am, after all, a kindly man—which will prove my undoing. And, to be quite honest, the book isn't badly written. If it comes out one day, it will be a notable event.

Almost a third of Anton's book is about the future of communism. It's a topic we've seldom discussed, and then usually in the form of jokes or threats. I have produced 'witticisms' at about the level of the wit of *Krokodil*; just wait, if we live to be old enough to see communism, then we'll show them our capacities and our needs. In these cases, Anton used to tell me that from this point of view, communism was being built relatively quickly and easily, which was its main attraction for the broad masses of the oppressed, backward and disadvantaged population. But after two or three generations, when the population becomes almost completely literate, when it forgets hunger and exhausting labour, begins to be more or less adequately dressed, and in general acquires a higher standard of living than in the recent past, then the specifically communist problems will make their first appearance. People no longer give a damn about what happened before the Revolution. They base their judgements on contemporary comparisons. Comparison with the past is double-edged. Official propaganda drags everything bad up from the past to try to convince the population that they live extremely well. On the other hand, the malcontents pull all the good things out of the past to underline their present distress. And both parties falsify the past if only by taking simply one side of it and by judging it from a modern standpoint. But that is normal since the past is invoked only to support judgements on the present.

However, as we approached any positive identification of specifically communist problems and the prospect for their solution, our discussions usually broke off or degenerated into petty squabbles over semantic inadequacies. But clearly from Anton's point of view, it is precisely the problem of the future of communism which is central. He only begins at the point at which the critics and apologists of communism have somehow or other left off.

I had skimmed through this section of Anton's book very swiftly, but I was able to gain a certain idea, albeit fragmentary and incomplete, of this part of his thinking. Anton refuses to consider the future of the Soviet Union in the same spirit as did Amalrik. He says absolutely nothing about the historical destiny of such and such a people or state or about the consequences of their relationship. He merely examines tendencies which have already transpired to a greater or lesser degree and which derive from the very essence of communist social structure. Here are the basic tendencies he deals with.

Social stratification, and the hereditary character of the reproduction of these strata (which sometimes goes as far as hereditary professions). The inheritance of one's position in society does not come by birthright, for there is no such thing, but from the practical possibilities of one's parents. The children of people from the highest social strata only descend to lower strata in exceptional circumstances, while children of parents from the lower strata only exceptionally break through to the highest. Of course, mobility from one stratum to another is more frequent between neighbouring strata. It is possible to work out coefficients of such mobility. In as much as there is a hierarchy of strata, the possibility of mobility from stratum to stratum is reduced as the distance between the strata increases. Even under present conditions, where social differentiation is still very fluid, in the Soviet Union the strata are becoming more clearly defined and movement from the lowest strata to the highest, and effective possibilities of maintaining children on a sufficiently high social level, have become much more difficult.

At this point, I thought that I must do all I could to see that Lenka went on to higher education, and not just any kind, but something with a future, and that Sashka got a decent job with possibilities of promotion. Which of our acquaintances' children have become manual workers, junior clerks or school teachers and so on? None of them. The children of our Academicians are, for the most part, mediocre to say the least, yet they are all in good positions. This tendency is plain for all to see. But everyone maintains a decent silence about it.

Anton gives a classification of the strata of communist society. He classes them as Higher, Middle and Lower. And each stratum has gradations within it. He bases this division on the principles of mediatisation and discontinuity. These are rather sophisticated mathematical toys, and I did not understand them. In their simplest form, they mean something like this. The differentiation of social strata is something which is also firmly fixed in men's consciousness and is in part due to this consciousness. As in a large society there is in effect a virtually continuous scale of living standards and way of life, to appreciate one's own distinction from the stratum immediately below, one needs a mediator, an intermediary link which makes the social differentiation clearer. But that is not, of course, the only problem. There are indicators which establish the principal frontiers between the three strata referred to. These indicators concern all the major aspects of the life of individuals: the distribution of material and spiritual advantages, the way one spends one's work and leisure time, medical services, juridical protection and so on. At the present time, one still frequently comes across cases of representatives of a lower class living better than representatives of a higher class. Such accidents will be systematically tracked down and eliminated (as is being done at the present time).

Also at the present time, we can observe some lack of correspondence between the cultural level of representatives of a given stratum and the social rank of that stratum. This shows particularly clearly in the lower and middle strata of a certain section of the intelligentsia, where the cultural level is fairly high, while the cultural level of the ruling upper strata is extremely low. This is a transitory phenomenon. There is already visible a powerful tendency towards the raising of the cultural level of the upper strata (special schools, knowledge of foreign languages, access to the finest works of modern art and so on). Within two or three generations, the principal consumers and connoisseurs of the highest products of culture will almost exclusively be the highest strata of society (as has always been the case in the past). And even now a rigid policy of 'culture for the people' is being promoted, which entirely suits the lower strata of society, a policy which creates lower forms of culture (called higher forms by the propagandists) for the lower strata. It would be foolish to hope that while feeding the 'people' far worse than the privileged strata they would provide the 'people' with spiritual nourishment of a higher quality than they themselves demand. The level of spiritual nourishment of the middle strata (which include the multi-million strong army of doctors, teachers, engineers, technologists, scientific researchers, officers and so on) is rather higher than that of the lowest strata. They receive some crumbs from above. And at the present time, they still manage to seize more than a few for themselves. But everything is tending towards enclosure within the rigid parameters of the culture to which 'they are entitled'. Moreover, these strata do not especially aspire to the phenomena of the highest, or at least to the active, modern culture. Thus we see a tendency to equate the level of culture to social rank.

The enforced territorial and economic attachment of members of the lowest social strata to their place of work; this enforced attachment is now obvious. It also affects the higher strata, although here possibilities exist for evading it: transfers to other jobs, business trips, access to private transport, education, marriage and so on. Communist society has powerful means of keeping the population static, irrespective of the size of the country; the system of housing allocation, increased salaries, premiums, creches and kindergartens and so on. And that is not to mention the system of registration. It must not be forgotten that social processes in society are closely linked with biological processes; the most highly favoured individuals from a biological point of view have more chances of improving their social level (by means of advantageous marriage, athletic success and so on); thus there is a rigorous process of biological selection according to social stratification. It is believed that in time even the highest leaders of the country will look better than they do now. At all events, if one considers the upper strata *en masse*, there can already be observed a certain increase in stature and an improved personal appearance. However, certain phenomena which are survivals of the past exercise a braking effect on the biological improvement of the higher strata (such factors as the advantage of 'proletarian' descent, or membership of a 'healthy' socialist family). In the historical conditions under which communist society was first formed, there are powerful factors inhibiting the realisation of this and other tendencies. But that is merely a question of time. For example, at the moment there is still a directive prohibiting the entry of the children of intellectuals into higher education straight from school. But in practice, this directive does not apply. It merely contributes to the development of a system of bribery and corruption in this most important sphere of our life.

The unification of the system of power. This tendency too is quite evident, inasmuch as the electoral system is pure eyewash. Whether the enormous parasitic institution of 'electoral' power survives or not will depend on circumstances. The system of power is extremely weighty and complex. Why should this be? There are several reasons. In particular, there is the ruling stratum's interest in perpetuating itself. There is also a tendency to make the functions of power as primitive as possible and to eliminate risk (a system under which there is both impunity and an absence of personal responsibility). Already the function of power lies in the hands of at least one-fifth of the population (together with their families). This adds up to tens of millions of people. But the power system is not a social stratum. The distinction between strata is drawn on a different plane. But power itself is divided into strata. For instance, the local policeman is a member of a lower stratum than that of a university professor.

In the same spirit, Anton ran through all the aspects of the life of a communist society. He described the type of economy, the law, art and science, of ideology, of the education system, the system of distribution, personal relationships and so on. When I looked through the book it at first seemed to me that he had deliberately chosen all the worst manifestations of our life and turned them into a law of society. But I soon noticed that in no way did he evaluate this as bad or good, he simply stated it as a fact and developed arguments to support his thesis, according to which all these aspects are endemic to communist society. It is perhaps worth pausing briefly on one further tendency he mentions. But first a few words on communism as a type of society, since I have referred to this problem.

Anton defines communist society by means of its basic cell—each separate self-contained institution (a factory, an institute, an office, a military unit, a school and so on). This cell has its own specific structure. Everyone knows what kind of structure that is. The important thing is that it is through this cell that each individual contributes his strengths to society and receives everything from society. From this point of view, all individuals are placed in an identical position. Society as a whole is the aggregate of these cells. And they are combined into one whole by means of social mechanisms of the same cellular type. Because of the vastness of the social organism, it is differentiated in accordance with the laws of differentiation of large social systems, but in conditions which are common both to the country as a whole and to each individual cell. And then, proceeding from a few very simple rules which govern relationships between individuals within the cells, Anton isolates the inevitable tendencies which I have already referred to in part. Among them is a tendency towards mass purges which is worthy of our special attention. At the present time, following the appearance of Solzhenitsyn's books, it is a major, worldwide topic of thought.

Mass purges. First, they are open and approved. Secondly, they can be carried out with impunity. Thirdly, they are useful in many respects: for dealing with dissidents and rivals, for maintaining order, in the struggle for power, to provide an unpaid workforce, and so on. And fourthly, a modern society is constantly faced with tasks which can be fulfilled only by the use of mass forced labour. That, no doubt, is the most important aspect. This kind of problem is not the result of chance. Gigantic modern societies cannot exist without the resolution of these problems. A partial solution is to disguise the element of constraint in this use of mass labour. We can see this, for instance, in the compulsory drafting of young people into the army and the use of the army as a workforce; the formation of teams of students to work on building projects; the despatch of city dwellers to the countryside for the vegetable harvest; Komsomol appeals for volunteers to work on massive projects, and so on. But these are half-measures and they will never produce the necessary number of volunteers. Moreover, normal work is interrupted. And above all, these people all bring with them their normal prejudices about living conditions which have to be satisfied at least to some degree. And such an army of workers cannot be used for just any kind of work in just any kind of conditions. There is a need for an enormous permanent workforce which is cheap to maintain and which can be used however and wherever it is needed. Now the places where it can be used are widely known. So society must, in one way or another, find a way of meeting its own demand for such a slave army. It has already invented a convenient method of doing this—the method of repression, i.e. of punishment for some crime. This form of approach gives both a 'legal' and a 'moral' justification to the existence of an army of slaves and to the conditions of its inhuman exploitation. Hitherto history has been generous: the Revolution, the Civil War, the war against Germany, and other real facts of our existence have provided both human material in abundance for this army and also a 'legal' and 'moral' justification for its existence. There then followed a hiatus, the reasons for which are widely known. Of course, the repressions never stopped. But throughout all of this last period they have not become massive. There are many people in jail but for the most part they are criminals. And for the time being, their number is comparable with the world average; (for the moment this is a statistical fact). But this situation cannot last for long. Either history itself will provide a convenient pretext and an appropriate form for the coming mass repressions, or society itself will spontaneously provoke events which will produce the same result. The most likely outcome of all will be a combination of the one with the other (as happened, incidentally, in the past).

But the system of mass repressions has one major defect: it involves the creation throughout society of a particular state of mind and of particular organisations to carry out repressions over a fairly long period of time. And that, as experience has shown, is a force which has a tendency to get out of control. And for this reason, the leadership of the country fears the system of mass repression no less than do the liberal intellectuals. This acts as a restraining force. But how long can that last? The struggle for power will sweep away the 'liberal group' and the orientation towards mass repressions (in some veiled form, of course) will serve as an argument for the 'right-wing group' in the struggle.

Next, Anton aligns himself with Shafarevich in saying that communist society has much in common with the societies of the Incas, ancient Egyptians, ancient Chinese and so on. But he considered it more important to stress the differences between our society and the old 'Imperial' models. This distinction relates, above all, to the human material which constitutes the body of the 'Empire' and which summarises within itself historical facts such as science, technology, art and so on. A great part of this human material is condemned to hitherto unheard of spiritual and moral suffering and resistance. And the real aspect which the communist society of the future wears will depend on the battle between its internal forces.

Finally, Anton examines in detail the possibility of an opposition to the dominant tendencies of communism and comes to the following conclusion. Communist leaders must now and for evermore forget any idea about a peaceful and harmonious progress towards the Radiant Future so long as they issue their directives and take their decisions, while the other citizens fulfil and overfulfil quotas and sing the praises of their beloved leaders. The Radiant Future is a fight already begun against the ignominies of communism which are already common knowledge. It will be a bloody battle with many victims. It will produce still more models of the greatest personal heroism, which will be comparable with those of the past. And the first stage of this battle which has already started bears the name of Solzhenitsyn. Anton believes his ideas to be an expression of historical optimism (unlike those of Zamyatin, Orwell and Shafarevich).

When such a book has been written, one has the impression that you could easily have written it yourself, since the author is discussing phenomena which are very familiar to you. But *you* go ahead and write it! And once you've written it, take the decision to publish it. And try to get that decision put into operation! I can never understand what forces motivate people like Anton. Yet I have known him for decades. He reminds me of the Old Boozer. Although we live side by side, he walks past me and through me dragging his little cart in some incomprehensible dimension of life. Where is he going? Why?

In the name of the future

Tomorrow I am leaving hospital. As I dozed all day yesterday I had a sleepless night. First I considered my chances. During my 'illness', I had marked up one or two more things to my advantage. For instance, my book had had excellent reviews in East Germany, Bulgaria and Poland; there had been a discussion in the Institute of Oriental Studies where almost everyone supported my ideas; an article in *Kommunist* included a favourable reference to my name; and my article had been published. On the other hand, certain things had happened to my disadvantage. For instance, there had been a favourable review in Yugoslavia; there was a rumour of a flattering article about me published in the West; I had been attacked in the faculty of the Military Academy, who had sent a little hostile comment about me to the Central Committee, and so on. It may seem that on one side (the plus side) there were major factors, while on the minus side there was nothing but trivia. But in our system, normal methods of calculation are completely inappropriate. For example, your work is being discussed. Ten people vote for it, and they include important, influential people. Only two speak against it. And they are not among the most influential. Has the discussion been to your advantage? That depends when it took place. Ten years ago, ten people for and two against would have settled the matter in your favour. But now? In the general situation we are fast approaching, even one adverse vote leaves the impression of a danger signal: everyone begins to think that there's something not quite right about you. Rumours begin to circulate which have the force of public opinion. And sometimes this kind of rumour provokes a decision which was never initially foreseen.

Thinking along these lines, I came to the conclusion that at the moment, no one could forecast the result of the elections. The whole thing could be decided by some totally unforeseen triviality. I had a good chance, a chance better than I'd ever had before and which I would never have again. Exhausted by these electoral considerations, I returned almost inadvertently to Anton's books. And I remembered my last conversation with him.

'We're funny creatures,' I had said. 'We rush about, we make plans, we suffer . . . but it may be that the whole of human history has got only one meaning: it will become impossible to live on earth, so people will build a mighty space ship, select a thousand of the most important people on earth, find a good spot to fly off to and settle there. And they will create a new civilisation. That will be real communism.'

'That is a consolation for idiots—or maybe a demagogic ploy suitable to a teacher of amenable fools. The slogan "Live for a Radiant Future" is nothing but a badly camouflaged demand to live with an eye on the privileges of the topmost ranks of society. We must live today. Here. For the sake of our worldly ambitions. There is no other life. The future is merely what results from the present. "In the name of the future" is necessary to those who live well today, or to those who have no chance of living decently today or indeed of living at all. For the former, it is a mask of falsehood; for the latter, it is a final consolation.'

I had got thoroughly bored in hospital and I left with pleasure.
Outside, the weather smelt of the approach of spring. Sparrows
were flying in all directions as if demented and I could hear the
chirruping of some little birds which I had never even noticed
before. Big bellied cats stretched in the thin sunlight, their eyes
half shut because of the warmth and their agreeable memories.
Young girls had begun to unveil their irresistible charms. I'll be
damned, but it seemed that Moscow had suddenly blossomed
out with a whole crowd of attractive young women. Life is
beautiful! Long live life! Life is good even in our radiant
communist society. It is better to be alive under communism
than not alive in a democratic and joyful society. I must get
some new clothes because I really am dressed like a retired
colonel. It's enough to make even me feel sick. After all, I'm not
yet old. And judging by certain signs, I can still count on a
certain degree of success. Svetka once said to me that she
fancied me quite regardless of my fame and my position, and
that at first she didn't even know who I was. But Svetka is a
first-class bitch, and what's more, our affair is coming to an
end.

I decided to walk part of the way home. My route lay through
Cosmonaut Square. Even from far away, I could see that not all
was well. The Leader had lost an eye, and his face now gave the
impression not of arch joviality, but of sheer ill temper. In the
past, he had looked as if he were saying, 'You're going the right
way, Comrades!' but now he was saying something else: 'Where
the hell d'you think you're off to, you mother fuckers?' But that
was perhaps only my post-hospital impression. The boys and
girls who were walking past me also noticed the Leader's missing eye and the change in his expression, but they declared
unanimously that it was a great improvement.

As I drew closer, I was shocked to the bottom of my soul.
Some of the letters of the Slogan had disappeared altogether to
some unknown destination. Others had fallen down, and the
rest had been so bespattered by the pigeons that not even

mathematical linguists could have deciphered them. I was over-taken by a feeling of impending doom. My idea of walking home vanished. I caught a taxi. All the way the driver cursed the idiots who had cluttered up the road with all this rubbish (it was our Slogan that he was referring to). Before we turned onto the bridge, we were stopped by a traffic policeman and the driver had to slip him a rouble. For the rest of the way home, we both attacked our way of life in chorus and with redoubled strength. For the first time, in all my taxi-hiring life, it was a positive pleasure to tip the driver.

The congress: a summary

When I got home from hospital I found on my desk the latest number of 'Problems of Philosophy'. It included an article by Kanareikin (i.e. the Congress Report I had written for him), one by Tvarzhinskaya criticising the principal tendencies of anti-communism, a paper by Vaskin criticising the most impor-tant tendencies of modern revisionism, and an account of the Congress signed by Serikov but written by myself. Serikov had introduced only one correction into my account: he had drop-ped the passage about my own speech and extended the pass-ages on those by Tvarzhinskaya and Vaskin. And yet my speech had been the only one from the Soviet delegation which had led to any lively discussion. That Serikov really is a bastard. That is something I shall not forgive him for. You mustn't force the pace, my lad!

But this had destroyed my good mood. I bought a bottle of cognac and something to eat and went off to my 'office'. I rang Svetka. She said she was busy. She's not much better than Serikov, the cow! I drank the bottle on my own and got pretty drunk. But at least I fell sound asleep. I slept fully dressed until the morning, and I was very nearly late for the Saturday of Voluntary Extra Work.

On romanticism

This time Lenka brought home a poem on romanticism. I said that her friend should have gone on to this kind of theme a long time ago, and settled down to listen.

> The meeting has run on three hours and more,
> I sit and gape, yet I forbear to snore.
> I'm stifled by the horrid stench as well as
> By all the speeches of these brainless fellows.
> Romantic dreams take shape within my mind
> Of storms, not sea-storms but another kind.
> No cries of pirates leaping to attack,
> Nor cutlass clashes as the crew fight back.
> My dream is not like boys' dreams used to be.
> I dream of being the First Secretary.
> The party tribune's what I want to swing.
> No storm I fear, but saying the wrong thing.
> No hidden treasure on some coral beach—
> My treasure's in my briefcase—it's my speech.
> Ah yet, romance . . . I'm not a simple loon.
> Just wait, I'll get some high position soon.
> When I command, the ocean will be mine.
> Marshals I'll make—not captains of the line.

I grew angry but could not sustain this emotion and ended up by bursting into laughter in concert with Lenka.

'It's just the same thing with you!'

'Of course it is! We're well used to it already. You should see what happens to the first years. You can just imagine how they're made to stuff their heads with all the Congress material. But it must have been exactly the same when you were at school.'

'Very similar. But in my time *The Brigantine* had just come out. By the way I knew the author. We were at school together for a time.'

'How marvellous! Tell me what he was like.'

(**227**)

'A model young communist. A Stalinist. A patriot. In short, like we all were.'

'Impossible. Probably he simply didn't have time to change. If he'd lived long enough he would have become different.'

'Who knows?'

The communist saturday of voluntary labour

The caretakers were idly tidying up a heap of rubbish left over from the winter. A few militant pensioners were demonstratively raking together last year's fallen leaves and cursing young people and Jews. Out in the streets citizens in leisure wear were hurrying to their factories and offices, where they faced the prospect of displaying their enthusiasm for work and their genuinely communist attitude to labour. The women had made an extra-special effort. They had taken the opportunity to encase their powerful forms in tight-fitting trousers and brandished their hips in every direction. It was a disturbing spectacle.

In the Institute the technical staff were shoving cupboards about raising huge clouds of dust, and ripping the winter sealing strips from the windows. The scientific staff were wandering about their sections and departments filling in the time as best they could. Some of them were holding trades union meetings, others party meetings, and others again production seminars. Other groups were having section meetings, some were holding a session of the authors' collective, and others yet again group discussions. But the only difference between these various occupations lay in their titles. In every case they were blathering about anything that came into their heads, telling jokes and gossiping, or simply fooling about. Then they made tea and looked repeatedly at their watches: how much longer would this nonsense go on?

'See how far a noble idea has been degraded,' I said.

'Why degraded?' objected Anton. 'It's the very opposite, the idea has actually been realised. What more do you want? A genuinely communist attitude to labour! Well, my friend, it's all there before your very eyes: we're working without pay; skilled workers are performing the duties of charwomen; and so we're all going through a pretence of work, a downright deception.'

Then we were all herded into the main hall where there was to be a trade union meeting to hand out 'Communist Shock-Worker' badges. Tvarzhinskaya delivered a speech on behalf of the recipients.

Oh God, it's enough to make you die of boredom!

The following day every newspaper printed accounts of the results of the Voluntary Saturday. They all said exactly the same:

The communist Saturday was extremely well organised and demonstrated great political enthusiasm and eagerness to work. It was marked by highly productive shock work in all branches of the city's economy, and in the scientific and cultural sphere. It became a mass festival of communist labour, a vivid demonstration of the triumph of Leninist ideas about the living, creative participation of the broad masses of the workers in the construction of the new society. Pursuing and developing the glorious traditions of the Great Initiative, the workers responded actively to the appeal of the communist Saturday of Voluntary Labour, working with self-denial and thus demonstrating their elevated degree of consciousness, their patriotism, and their unswerving devotion to the ideals of communism. The 'Red Saturday' became a new and vivid demonstration of the indestructible unity of the Party and People, of the indestructible unity of the workers round the Communist Party and its Leninist Central Committee. Before the Saturday even began there were mass meetings in every factory and organisation. There the workers declared their complete and limitless support for the policies of the CPSU and the Soviet state, their unanimous approval of the solid and many-faceted activity of the Central Committee of the CPSU and of its Politburo under the leadership of the General Secretary of the Central Committee of the CPSU, Comrade . . .

I read all this, spat in disgust, and said to myself: 'that's exactly what you deserve, you crook! You're responsible for quite a lot of that!'

Six million two hundred thousand workers took part in the Voluntary Work Saturday. All the workers employed in the area of production and service industries worked at their normal work places. Their efforts were aimed at achieving the highest possible level of productivity. . . . Workers in scientific research and planning organisations, and in state institutions also made their contribution to Moscow's communist Saturday. Thus, in the Institute . . .

I raged, spat, cursed, and raged again . . . In this way I went through all the newspapers, something I had never done before. I knew that everything they wrote was rubbish, so I never read them. But on this occasion I had absorbed an unaccustomed dose of our press and I was horrified. Surely all this cannot really be read?! Yet it is read! And it has an effect!

I tore the newspapers into shreds, rushed into the street and headed straight for the Dive.

'I've had enough,' I thought, almost speaking my thoughts aloud. 'As soon as I get to be a corresponding member I'll put an end to all this. The years are going by and I still haven't done anything really important. While I've still got my strength and the power of thought, I must do something.'

Near the Dive I met Edik. And then we were joined by Nameless.

The lessons of history

'It's not true to say that history teaches us nothing,' said Edik. 'For instance Hitler gave Germany such a lesson that the Germans will never again be counted among the leaders of world history. And that is not because their defeat put them in an unfavourable position. It is because they will always be subject to historical memory which can never be wiped out by any means at all. Do you know why we no longer have mass purges as we did in Stalin's time? There is still a desire to put people in prison and there are plenty of camps. There is enough work and more which prisoners could do. And yet people are no longer being jailed on the same scale. That is because people are so

(230)

afraid of historical memory. There's a lesson for you! And although people here keep quiet about the past and are gradually rehabilitating Stalin, historical memory still operates through invisible and uncontrollable channels. For example I know a very senior K G B official. He carries on a continuous battle against people who read *Gulag*. Yet his son knows *Gulag* by heart. What's the use of fighting in conditions like that! We underestimate the part that Solzhenitsyn has played in our history. He has elevated historical memory almost to the status of a religion. That is now an historical fact. It's a new starting point for calculating the calendar. He has driven such a stake into the tomb of Stalinism that now there can be no going back. Khrushchevism? Maybe, but all the same, that's better than Stalinism.'

We wandered slowly towards Cosmonaut Square. Our Dive was still closed. Rebrov had promised us a bottle of cognac today—he had received a fee for an . . . unpublished pamphlet.

'It's the fourth time I've had a fee for this pompous rubbish.' He said. 'Now I'll take it . . . Over There . . . there's still one place left. I'll sign a contract and pick up another fee. How do I manage to do that? No problem. No, I haven't got any well-placed friends. And I don't go in for bribery. I've got another method. I pick out the right kind of institution. My subject is one that's always of current interest. I propose it. I submit a few testimonials from leading lights—that's no problem. I've got plenty of them. And they immediately include me in their publishing plan. It's a green light all the way. But I've no desire to have this crap published. I'd be too ashamed of it. And it wouldn't be to my advantage. So I organise a little letter. The letter is of such a kind that once they've read it they're afraid of printing the book, yet they have no apparent way to avoid doing so. Then they try to find a way out. And I wait patiently and that's all I do. I end up by taking back the book with the right of publishing it elsewhere (they usually advise me themselves where to go), but as a sort of moral damages, they pay my fee in full. They've got clauses to cover that, so everything's legal.'

'But it's immoral,' I said.

'Why?' said Edik. 'What's your salary?' he asked Rebrov. 'So you see! Cleaning women earn more than that here. Just you try

(231)

to live on that kind of money. And then you've got the rent to pay on a co-operative apartment, I imagine? I can see from your face that you don't get a penny out of your employers for that. And how much have you managed to make out of your little trip?'

Rebrov named a figure, and I felt embarrassed. Edik roared with laughter. Nameless spat and cursed vigorously.

'You've just used the word "immoral". Do you know how much Mzhavanadze and his family got away with?! Or Nasreddinova?![1] I've got a relative who recently was a member of a special group investigating an extraordinary case of embezzlement of public funds in a southern republic. They had their work cut out. Multi-million rouble thefts are commonplace. The investigation was stopped because if they'd gone on digging they would have had to jail the entire party and state apparatus of the republic. And there you are, talking about immorality!'

This time we had the patience to queue outside the 'Youth' café, and got a table to ourselves. After about an hour a waitress, who was still young but already running to coarse fat, was kind enough to take our modest order with a martyred air.

The birthday

To my dismay Tamurka remembered that my birthday was drawing near.

'We must celebrate it properly. And at the same time we can mark the anniversary of our happy family life. It's got to a round figure this year. We'll ask useful people. We mustn't let a chance like this slip. Vaskin organised a full-scale banquet. If he can do that, why not you?'

I tried to resist in every possible way, recalling Anton's advice: keep quiet, keep your head down, lie doggo for a time as if you didn't exist, no fireworks, don't attract attention to yourself. But I had to give way to the pressure from Tamurka

[1] Two local officials who were dismissed for corruption. (Translator)

and my colleagues in the department, who were very keen on the idea of eating and drinking at someone else's expense.

The problem arose as to whom to invite and how to deal with our closest friends, the Zimins and the Gureviches. We decided to act according to all the rules of Soviet careerism: divide them up! And that is what we did. The Zimins and the Gureviches came round for an 'intimate family evening'; the party was boring and uneasy. They left early on the pretext that they were very busy the next day. The second party—'for the others' —was a very grand affair. We had the Kanareikins, the Bludovs, the Agafonovs, the Korytovs, the Ivanovs and other influential people. There was a great deal of eating and drinking and loud talking. After the departure of the old Academicians everyone let their hair down completely. There was slanderous gossip and anti-Soviet anecdotes. Korytov launched into a whole series of stories about the life of Lenin. We talked about Solzhenitsyn's book *Lenin in Zurich*. And people came out with such things that if I hadn't heard them with my own ears I would never have believed them. It was the best informed people who really excelled themselves—Korytov, Ivanov, Nikiforov and even Serikov. To listen to them one would have thought that Lenin was a complete nonentity, a boor, a mental defective, a crook and so on, and that our Revolution had been organised with German money. And what's more, everyone showed off to each other by producing so called 'secrets' which even the most passionate enemies of Lenin had never even dreamt of. It's a good job that Anton wasn't there. I can't bear to think what would have happened. But at this point Novikov suddenly joined in the conversation.

'All this is nonsense. What does it matter who said or did what to whom? What does it matter if certain things happened? That doesn't explain anything at all. That's not the root of the problem. The main thing is that Russia collapsed right to its very foundations. And it could only carry on at the most primitive level of social organisation. Either Russia would have perished altogether, or if it were to continue, it could only be in a communist form quite independent of whether there had been Marxists before or not, or whether Lenin and the party were already in existence. All these wonders would have emerged spontaneously anyway, merely as a result of the action of the laws of social organisation on large masses of population in conditions of a comparatively complex economy.'

Novikov's words produced a strange impression. Although Korytov, Ivanov and the rest had to all intents and purposes discredited the Revolution, the party and Lenin, while Novikov appeared to be defending all this, in their diatribes there was no feeling of any great hostility to what they were attacking, while Novikov's speech in defence was taken by everyone as an enemy attack. Why? Their diatribes were just ordinary dinner-table chatter, a permissible drunken relaxation which these days wouldn't even lead to a reprimand. But what Novikov had said went right to the heart of the problem.

'The problem isn't what kind of person Lenin was,' he continued 'or who joined the party, or where it got its money from and so on, but what the Revolution really gave birth to. And our position would be a great deal stronger if we admitted that the Revolution was made by geniuses and heroes, by the best people, the most honest, and so on. If vile people produced a vile thing, that is in the natural order of things. But if a vile thing is produced despite every possible and imaginable virtue, that's something worth pondering over.'

'It was a mistake to start off on that tack,' I said to Novikov later.

'Forgive me, but I couldn't restrain myself. Lenin, the party, the Revolution and all those things—they talk about them as if they were their own private property. They praise them to the skies, or they vilify them, just as the mood takes them. They regard them as their own chattels. Essentially they have no quarrel with Solzhenitsyn's interpretation of Lenin. What drives them wild is the fact that he has infringed their right of interpreting Lenin in any way they like. Or perhaps it's even simpler: perhaps they were afraid that I was going to tell on them. And that's exactly what they need! And what fun that would be! I'm willing to bet that even now they're still waiting and trembling. And I'd also bet that they've prepared denunciations of me and each other, just in case. And of you, of course.'

I felt very ill at ease after this conversation. And all my

magnificent and expensive birthday party suddenly seemed to me like some sort of provocation. Self-provocation is also a specifically Soviet phenomenon. Novikov had certainly stirred things up! But if it hadn't been him, it would have been someone else. In any large group of people you will always find one who contradicts the others. So our Soviet opposition is indestructible if only because it is a fact of social analysis (is that something else I've got from Anton?!).

Anton wasn't in the least surprised that Novikov had taken on his own dissident function. Nikiforov might have done so just as easily, as might many others. A rumour began to circulate in Moscow about the splendid banquet I had given, at which, so the rumour had it, M.L. himself had been one of the guests. The first question Kanareikin asked me was whether it was true that after he had left we had discussed Solzhenitsyn's book. I said we had not discussed it, but violently criticised it, and that Novikov had suggested writing a smouldering criticism of it. Kanareikin said that that was worth thinking about. It was high time, it was even necessary, to put forward a high-level riposte to this criminal. But on the other hand that would attract attention to his disgusting little books. If we keep quiet, though, people may think that he was right. And Kanareikin got himself thoroughly confused in this trivial problem.

How to educate our people better

An ordinary newspaper. An ordinary article by an ordinary headmaster of an ordinary school. Ordinary rubbish about the historic significance of the Congress and the application of its guidelines in school. But it is in this very ordinariness that recently I had begun to suspect the great significance of all that has happened.

'The materials of the Twenty-fifth Party Congress, with the multitude of new and profound ideas, theses and objectives which they contain, have given a powerful impulse towards the rethinking of the entire process of instruction and education in our schools, and to the search for new forms and methods of work with the pupils.'

And that is no empty phrase. I can just imagine the chaos going on in the schools! Those poor teachers, they must be feeling quite sick and bewildered!

'Meetings, seminars, gatherings of the Young Pioneers and the Komsomol are now being organised very frequently in the schools. Their theme is the Party Congress and the new Five-Year-Plan. Pupils from all classes are currently engaged in this work.'

That's exactly it—from all classes. Including the very youngest. I can just imagine the bucketfuls of propaganda slops which are being currently poured over the children's heads!

'In this huge educative work, it is the classroom lesson which should be exploited first and foremost. If the teacher approaches the subject matter of his lesson creatively, he succeeds in broadening the mental horizon of the child, and finding a method of approach which will afford greater immediacy to the historic transformations going on in the country, making them more comprehensible to the pupil.'

In every lesson! Even lessons in mathematics and physics are to be transformed into emetic demagogic sermons! And that's to say nothing of literature and history!

'At the present time the entire education system is imbued with the ideas of the Congress. And a start has been made on serious concentrated study by school pupils of the materials of the Twenty-fifth Congress of the CPSU. But already it is contributing to an improvement in the pedagogical efficiency of education.'

That is very true. Everyone without exception (from the headmaster down to the dunce in the elementary class—as also the cleaning woman) is sick to death with the overall penetration of these ideas. But just try not to let yourself be penetrated! In the first place, Higher Authority will force them down your throats. And then everyone will set to butchering each other. And what's more, an entire system of concrete measures which waste everyone's time, energy, intelligence, talent and temper, has been developed and applied to school work. What, for instance, can one make of this measure:

(236)

'"The Journal of the Five-Year Plan"—that is the title of a voluminous exercise book containing cuttings from newspapers and magazines neatly stuck into place, notes and drawings which speak of the creative work of the Soviet people. From the fourth year onwards every pupil in the school keeps such a journal.'

So from the fourth year on the future Soviet man is already being actively moulded into a creature whom it will be hard to distinguish from any old party dogsbody pensioned off on account of sheer stupidity. I asked Lenka if she too had to keep one of these 'Journals of the Five-Year Plan'.

'It's a pure formality,' said Lenka; 'they tried it in our school, but nothing came of it. Our school is privileged—remember? One of the parents heard about it, called the headmistress into see him (I can't remember whether it was at the Central Committee, or the Council of Ministers or at the KGB) and told her to stop this nonsense.'

Lenka's story discouraged me still further. So even from the point of view of stuffing the heads of children with our progressive, brilliant and super scientific ideology, the children of the privileged classes have an advantage. But why should that surprise me? I've noticed several times in the past that students in privileged higher educational establishments pay less attention to Marxism-Leninism, regard it much more lightly, and sometimes even deride it.

In short, from whatever aspect we examine our life, everywhere we see the efforts of certain strata of our society to guarantee themselves the possibility, even if only in part, of evading the laws of communist existence and enjoying a more comfortable, free, happy and agreeable lifestyle. And a bitter struggle goes on within society to gain access to these strata. It is one more paradox of our life: one of the fundamental tendencies of the communist way of life is the attempt to escape from the rules of that very way of life.

I was rather pleased to have uncovered such a well turned formula, and I told myself that I wasn't all that stupid after all, and was indeed capable of some degree of thought. But my pleasure was destroyed when I recalled that this idea too was derived from Anton's book. The hell with this book! Am I

(237)

never going to be able to escape from its claws? Whatever I think out for myself, whatever truth I formulate, every time I find myself in the position of a plagiarist. And a plagiarist of whom? Of a man who has never published a single article worth a damn. Of an author whose book will never be published. But that is unfair! I myself am capable of reaching the same conclusions. But why are you getting so worked up about it anyway? Reach as many conclusions as you like! Publish them! But that's where you come to the main snag. Works like that of Anton can hang around for years, anyone can steal from them, but no one ever does—why not? It's easy to talk about stealing from books like that! But who will dare to publish that sort of thing? And even if anyone does dare, each thought taken on its own is completely trite. Besides no one but the author is capable of putting the whole thing together.

A typical case

Golubkina telephoned. She used to be a student of mine and wrote a pretty good thesis. Then she took her doctorate and turned into a puffed up and phenomenally stupid goose. But towards me she retained feelings of the deepest affection (she herself told me many times, which I found quite agreeable). She said that Barskiy had told her to write a review of a book which included the materials of a symposium held the year before the year before the year before the year before last. The book has only just been published. And what's more, Barskiy had made it a condition that Golubkina should be highly critical of my contribution, and he had indicated the points which she should attack. And now Golubkina did not know whether she should refuse or go ahead and write the article but water down the passages about my contribution. As she had the highest regard for me, she was asking me what to do. If she refused, the review would be written by Sobakina. And that bitch was only waiting for the opportunity to do me dirt. But if Golubkina agreed to write the article, she wanted to know how best to write the passage about my contribution while taking Barskiy's demands into account. Barskiy had told her that he had cleared his demands with the appropriate authorities.

Frankly, she caught me rather on the hop. Only yesterday Barskiy had telephoned and chatted with Tamurka (at the time I was in my 'study'); he had praised my contribution to the skies, saying that it was the only thing in the entire book worthy of attention. Tamurka had immediately told me that she was certain that Barskiy was up to no good, because she had this feeling for people. And I had accused her of always thinking the worst of people. 'Of course Barskiy is a slippery customer. But on the whole there's nothing wrong with him, and he thinks highly of me.' I simply didn't want to imagine that anything unpleasant was afoot. But now I could see clearly that Barskiy, who had always been jealous of me and envious of every book or article I had written, of every quotation from my work, of every reference to my name, had decided on this occasion to take the opportunity to stab me in the back. But—as was his nature—by someone else's hand. He himself wanted to appear clean and decent. And more than that, he would act in such a way as to make it seem that he had put enormous efforts into trying to save me from attack.

But now take Golubkina. Whatever happened she would write the review. She had certainly already accepted. And she had telephoned to salve her conscience, or perhaps from even murkier motives. She too, she would say, had done everything she could. And what's more, she would broadcast our conversation all over Moscow. And it would begin to look as if it was I who had denounced myself. And people would say what a wily old fox I was.

That is a striking example of the way the liberal epoch has evolved into something quite different. In the past a louse like Barskiy wouldn't have dared attack me, even in thought, no matter how much or how often he might have wished to. But today even nonentities like Golubkina or Sobakina (who incidentally are both very progressive by contemporary standards) are prepared to bite me in public. But we still have one foot in the liberal epoch: I have been asked to choose for myself the way in which I would prefer to be torn apart.

All this passed through my mind in a flash. I performed a

simple calculation and worked out that even if the article went very rapidly through the processes of writing, discussion, scheduling and so on, it could never be published before the Academy elections. And after that, I couldn't care less. Indeed from one point of view it would be quite agreeable: I would be classed among those talented people who are persecuted by reactionaries.

'Do whatever your conscience tells you,' I said to Golubkina. 'I can't give you any more concrete advice.'

But all the same I felt dejected. It's all very well knowing that Soviet man is capable of behaving appallingly with striking ease, or that you can expect even the people closest to you to behave in this way; when it actually happens it always comes as a complete and appalling surprise. What harm have I ever done Barskiy? What harm have I ever done this Sobakina, whom I've seen no more than once in my life, and even then at a distance? And as for Golubkina, without my help she would never have even got her Master's degree. Whence this irrepressible desire to do harm to others? What good will Barskiy or Golubkina get out of it? I really can't understand! . . .

On socialist realism

The lists of the new Lenin Prize winners have been published. The literature prize, of course, has gone to Malkov. As Lenka puts it, he's won it for his idiotic poems for babies at their mother's breasts.

> Hush my baby, lullaby,
> The party we must glorify.

And for pre-school infants:

> Even mummy's littlest man
> Helps fulfil the Five-Year Plan.

Malkov, however, is the head of the Moscow writers' union with several thousand members. So it is in the nature of things that Malkov should get a prize. But the fact that Khvostov has got one as well defies comprehension. In the past, too, prizes were given to people who had done good service to the party and the Soviet state, and not to people of talent and intelligence. But at least they were given to people who genuinely had given better service than others. They had to be earned! But now? Khvostov is a classic example of this. He has been awarded the prize for his novel *The Steppes of Kazadzhikstan* which is devoted to current fundamental problems: socialist competition, both personal and social, duty, love, the family and so on in the conditions of the developed socialist society. It is as the reviewers put it, a novel on many planes. One might even say it was polyphonic, like the novels of Dostoievsky. Among all the multifarious crappy novels of this type, Khvostov's cannot be regarded even as average. Even my mother-in-law said that it was tripe. It is nothing more than the work of a semi-literate idiot with pretensions to outdo the classics. It must be (my mother-in-law added) that he's getting a bit of help from Up There. He must be Someone's son-in-law. But that's not the case, I know for certain that he hasn't got any such support. He's a bit like our Agafonov. And he's got the prize precisely for his wholly inept attempt to look like a genius, for something which is deeply hostile to the slightest talent.

When Khvostov's novel came out, it became a sort of best-seller. It seems that on the black market it costs as much as Solzhenitsyn's books. The whole of Moscow mocked this phenomenally stupid and pretentious book. Certain phrases from it went the rounds of Moscow just as though they were jokes, as examples of sheer vulgar idiocy. The novel starts in the boundless steppes of Kazadzhikstan, with the protagonist driving through the wide open spaces. He is a doctor of philosophy(!!) who has agreed to become the chairman of a collective farm to till the virgin soil of the steppes of Kazadzhikstan. In our philosophical circles, we had a great deal of fun out of the fact that the hero was a doctor of philosophy—philosophy, really! We are in the best place to know that if any individual has decided to devote his life to philosophy, and even more so if he has managed to get himself a doctor's degree, he is by definition destined to a quite different kind of life: he will use every effort to ensconce himself in the life of the capital, or at worst in some other major city, and get his teeth into the tastiest parts of the social cake which is devoured by all kinds of parasites. But be that as it may our hero—chairman—philosopher drives through the steppes thinking along these lines: nothing could be more beautiful, he says to himself, than the Kazadzhikstan steppe. No matter where one looks there is no sign of a hill, of a tree, of a living soul. For a brief moment a gopher may spring out of its burrow, stand on its hind legs and look at you in amazement, and disappear just as quickly. Not a cloud in the sky. The sun is so hot that not even a dozen quilted kaftans and a hat made from the fur of the Astrakhan lamb can protect you. Great beads of sweat run down your nose and fall into your mouth, they trickle, pleasantly cold, down your back and your legs right into your boots. And you have only one desire—to boil up a pot of fresh spring water, throw in a handful of salt, a leaf of green tea and a chunk of fresh mutton fat, and drink, drink, drink . . . but alas, there is work to be done.

It has never even occurred to this chairman-idiot to ask himself what super-idiot managed to dream up the idea of abandoning the cultivated lands of European Russia close to major cities, transforming these steppes, which used to feed millions of cattle and provide meat, into a barren and dusty wilderness—as wise specialists and old men have forecast it will become in the near future. And then there will be neither bread, nor meat, nor wool. It should be said that our system does not merely have the capacity to lift a country out of ruin to a tolerable level of existence; it can also reduce entire areas of the economy to a state of ruin. (Anton maintains that the entire communist economy tends to be an unceasing battle against ruin and the leading of the country into ruin, and that the 'capitalist encirclement' is the only factor which sometimes maintains us at a certain level, and so on.) It must be admitted that Khvostov's book contains (quite unwittingly from the point of view of the author, who was trying to say something quite different) a first-class description of the blind, destructive force of the system—this mania for gigantic undertakings, and the inflexible 'will' to carry them out no matter what the price.

Later in the book the hero launches into a long and tedious

philosophical disquisition on the miserable existence of the people of Western Europe and America. The book as a whole is constructed after models which used to be fashionable in the West: the principal hero and his 'foil' ride along in a car, delve into their memories, and discuss the acute problems of our age—whether or not to sleep with one's fiancée before marriage, whether or not to help one's children to get on, whether or not to admit openly the truth about one's shortcomings, and so on. Our hero's companion and 'foil' has landed in the collective farm against his will, sent there by chance when jobs were being handed out. He is the son of a highly placed official. But shortly before he finished his university course his father was dismissed for some major offence. Their luxurious apartment was taken away. And any thought of going on to a further degree, as the companion himself observes, was out of the question. Our principal hero points out that this is the best thing that could have happened to him, despite the fact that our hero has kept on an apartment in Moscow and is himself planning to take a further degree. In actual practice the people who took such ultra-patriotic decisions as going to work in the virgin lands were the most mediocre careerists who could otherwise see no way of advancing their career in Moscow.

The young specialist is clearly infected by the Western virus, and is discontented with the Soviet system which has deprived him of the benefits of civilisation. When the protagonist proves to this occidentalist, with the help of quotations from the national newspapers (from the column 'The Way They Live') that people in the West are suffering, his interlocutor says that *he* suffers from the fact that he cannot suffer in the way that people suffer in the West. And our hero sees clearly that this young specialist is an internal émigré. This part of the book is an open denunciation and provocation. The author declares without any right of appeal that all our forms of opposition (including the dissident movement) derive from the following facts: (1) young people do not know how badly people live in the West; (2) young people do not know how beautiful our life is; (3) they listen to foreign broadcasts, read foreign books, and go abroad (wait! I thought people lived badly Over There!); (4) they don't know how lucky they are; (5) what they need is a bit of discipline; (6) they are over-educated (you know, these days, one in five of them can babble in English, while before . . . if you take my meaning! . . .), and so on in the same vein. And through the lips of the hero the author produces this rational and 'well founded' proposal: re-education by imposing a general obligation on everyone to work for three years on the great construction sites and in particularly 'difficult' areas.

At this point the car stops: it has run out of petrol. It turns out that the young specialist has forgotten to check the fuel tank (that's our Western-influenced youth for you!). There's no food or water. It's at least three hundred kilometres to the nearest village (what, one wonders, are they doing out here in the first place?!). The young specialist takes fright(?) and suggests that they should set off on foot. The hero regards this as desertion. It appears that they are delivering some extremely valuable filth to the next collective farm, and if they leave it unprotected the gophers will come along and eat it. So to cut a long story short the young specialist sets off and our hero stays behind to guard his precious filth from the gophers. The young one makes it and saves his skin(!!). But the hero dies—he loses consciousness and the gophers gobble him up. It would be interesting to know whether real gophers gobble up real doctors of philosophy. I must ask Lenka. Anyway as a result the young specialist falls into a state of moral bankruptcy. His fiancée refuses to marry him and contracts a posthumous marriage with the hero. That's no doubt a unique invention not merely in our native literature but in the literature of the world. On the spot where the hero perished there grows up a new city with all modern conveniences which becomes the mecca for progressive youth. And the wheat harvest in the steppes reaches such proportions that people simply don't know what to do with it and have to sell it off cheap to the starving Americans. As one of the reviewers commented, here we see a total affirmation of one of the most important principles of socialist realism—to depict life in its revolutionary development. The author has shown the immediate future of our countryside. And that—after our scandalous purchases of wheat from that self-same 'starving' America!

Sometimes one gets the impression that somewhere in the

depths of our life there is a constant output of a dense, clinging and viscous stupidity. It starts off by building up within and then begins to invade the world outside and obstruct every pore of our society. And there is nothing one can do about it since this stupidity is the natural product of our own life.

The mad house

When we learnt that Ilyich II (that's what we call Himself in our home) had been awarded the title of Marshal, even my mother-in-law could not restrain her laughter.

'A brilliant military career! I wouldn't be in the least surprised if next year they dubbed him Generalissimo.'

'And gave him the Victory Medal and his tenth Hero's Star,' added Tamurka. 'My God, what's going on! It's a mad house! They're off their heads!'

'Why are you making a song and dance about it?' said Lenka in surprise. 'Let them have their little pleasures! After all, they are old fogies, and old people are like children.'

'Not all old people fall into a second childhood,' observed my mother-in-law, regarding herself as an exception.

'It's not bad for a joke,' said Sashka. 'What if there's a war? Once again we'll be led by geriatric marshals. I don't think the country could stand a second dose of that.'

'But it won't happen,' said Lenka. 'In the next war only one thing will be asked of the High Command: all they'll have to do is to hide deep down in their well-appointed shelters and give the order to press the button. You don't need much intelligence for that. And no one knows what will happen afterwards.'

'This isn't a family, it's the General Staff,' I said. 'You have to be a specialist to form judgements about serious things like that.'

'I don't seem to have noticed any particular professionalism in the speeches of our military experts and politicians,' remarked Sashka. 'They all reduce everything to the most trivial level.'

'And anyway,' Lenka said, 'these days you don't need any

intelligence or special training to command an army or rule a state. All you need to do is worm your way to the top and seize power. And since decent, able and intelligent people aren't attracted by that kind of life or have poorer chances than the rest, we find ourselves led by . . .'

'Just you watch what you're saying,' my mother-in-law exploded. 'For words like that . . . for words like that . . . words like that . . .'

'These days, words like that won't get you into any trouble. Everyone's saying that everywhere. It's common knowledge so there's no point in keeping quiet about it! . . .'

The following day Lenka brought another of her friend's poems home from school:

> Epochs begin each time he waves his wand.
> He takes a step—the sun stops in the sky.
> A theoretician with no ideas to hand,
> A general who has won no victory.
> His slightest word's a blinding revelation,
> An insight into life's great mystery,
> A major scientific observation,
> Something to change the course of history.
> From year to year this lunacy goes on
> Yet no one dares to state the simple fact:
> He's just an idiotic babbling man,
> Scourging your hides with every drunken act.

In complete silence Tamurka took the poem from Lenka, tore it into shreds, slapped Lenka's face and said that if this happened again she would throw Lenka out of the house. Lenka said that that was illogical and that she would never forget it. And without even wiping away her tears she stormed out, slamming the door behind her. My mother-in-law laid into me ('there you are, that's the way you've brought them up'). I said that it wasn't I who had established Soviet power, nor had I given Ilyich II the title of Marshal. Tamurka picked me up on that and said it was I who had promoted the idiot to the rank of genius. I declared that this was not a family but a mad house, and withdrew to my 'study'.

On ideology

On the way to my 'study' I came to the conclusion that the real ideology of the privileged classes of our society is cynicism. And as always, this was not an original thought. Anton's book distinguishes between real ideology and formal ideology and describes all the types of the former for the main categories of the population. And he described cynicism as well not as a trait of human character, but as a form of ideology which in practice controls human behaviour. In the formation of individual personality this ideology is attained via the recognition of the truth, the choice of one's position and a certain emotional paralysis. Judging from all the evidence, my children are following this way. And here unhealthy phenomena may appear. But in the vast number of cases they are only a statistical fact, a very small percentage. What happens, though, if this tiny percentage happens to affect you? Better not to think about it. And people do not think about it, any more than they contemplate the possibility of producing a monster when they decide to conceive a child. Cynicism is in every respect a rationalist ideology.

One of its necessary conditions is a comparatively high level of education and information (not the kind of information you get from a newspaper of course). So it cannot be an ideology for the lower strata of population. If we add to that a factor such as the degree of protection against the authorities and the pressure of the collective, then this conclusion becomes self-evident. What is taken to be the cynicism of the lower strata towards ideology is merely a particular attitude towards official ideology, and not an ideology in itself. Ideology is a relationship to social reality to one's own position in it, and not to ideology in itself. The lower strata of the population, like the higher strata, may be indifferent to official ideology, may have a humorous or even a critical attitude to it. But this does not in practice define their ideology. The practical ideology of the lower strata of the population is formed under the influence of factors such as the shortage of essential products, disinformation, a fear of worse to come, the desire to hope for better things, a lack of protection against the authorities and so on. In other words, if you describe the most substantial negative conditions of existence of a specific group of the population, if you establish acceptable and natural means (from the viewpoint of the individual himself) by which he can protect himself from them, if you define the way in which these means of self-defence can be perceived in the given historical context of the culture, you will discover the real ideology of this group. Your prognosis will certainly coincide with the empirical facts, since even in their most subtle phenomena, people are subject to the general laws of analytical combination and self-conservation.

Formal (or official) ideology is a hypocritical but very convenient form which conceals the ignoble essence both of 'directorial' and of 'popular' ideology. Discussions of honesty, mutual aid, industriousness, self-sacrifice and so on have nothing to do with ideology, nor even with morality. These days their role is only to impart information about the sanctions society can employ towards individuals if they commit actions of a specific type. They do not bring to real ideology or real morality anything corresponding to their textual content, since they contradict real ideology and morality. They are merely elements of social knowledge.

I deeply regret now that I did not make a note of Anton's words in the past. I did not think that they were important. It is also a pity that I was not given the book for at least a couple of days. Now, of course, I would have made all the notes I needed. But now there's nothing to be done about it. No matter how long Anton's book is delayed, sooner or later it will appear. And I shall not have the time . . . and anyway how could I use all this? In some form of criticism? And to whom should I attribute these ideas? And then I would need time to systematise all this. A year at least. Oh God, what a fool I've been! On dozens of occasions Anton has explained his ideas on every major problem of communism and I did not trouble to note down even the major points. And what I remember now are merely random crumbs . . . What if I were to ask Anton to lend me his manuscripts? That's an idea! But what if he doesn't have a single copy? And anyway, what would he think? No, that won't do. I shall have to reread the works of our dissidents. Now there's a situation for you: one of the leading theoreticians of orthodox Marxism and communism scratching up ideas from the amateur works of the enemies of Marxism and communism! Could Anton be right in this too: that Marxism (and communism) as an ideology is a plagiarism accompanied by a destruction of the sources which have been plundered and are still being plundered, while real communism as a social structure is a parasitical growth on the body of Western civilisation, a secondary by-product of that civilisation, a parasite which kills the being which has given it birth and nourished it and which still feeds it? Will this parasite be able to develop within itself a creative potential, or will it lead mankind into a cul-de-sac like an anthill or like the empire of ancient (or maybe modern) China?

One day Anton and I were talking about the passion of a certain part of our society for spiritualism, parapsychology, yoga and so on. Anton said that as stable ideological forms these phenomena were futile, but he added that they were not the product of chance. Later I was able to skim through what he had written on this subject in his book. I remember one interesting idea. In our society, Anton wrote, one can feel how impotent the individual or any group of individuals is to resist the negative phenomena of communism—whether it be communism in the bud or communism which has already established itself and is gaining strength. Hence we see a natural attempt to win security or at least in part to protect oneself within one's own personality (which is a predictable probability), to develop a system of rules to avoid the harmful influences of society on the individual, or to neutralise such influences. This tendency penetrates all strata of society and leaves its traces on all the aspects and forms of real ideologies.

If we add to this the mutual interpenetration and influence of social strata, we can in a very general way forecast a tendency towards the formation of a certain unified real ideology of communist society. It may be divided internally, but it is unified despite that. From this point of view the ideology of cynicism in the sense we have given this word is, for example, a component part of this unified ideology. And the panicky swings from extreme faith in demagogic slogans to complete scepticism also affect the higher strata of society, sometimes provoking crises of mass hysteria.

It is perfectly clear to me that Anton's reflections are largely those of a dilettante. But they are sincere and honest. And it is only on the basis of such dilettantism (and not from the fashionable books of Western sociology, Sovietology, anti-communism and so on) that a genuine science of our society can begin. I am certain that if Anton's book is published it will not be obtainable in any one of our libraries, not even the most top-secret, while any Western 'hostile' literature is already to be found in the offices of many of our senior research workers.

On personality

'Uncle Anton,' said Sashka; 'our books and films about the war always show marvellous relationships between people. Is that all lies?'

'No, it's almost all true.'

'Well then . . .'

'What do you mean "well then"? Have you ever been inside a rest home? What sort of relationships did you find there?'

'Excellent. But war isn't a rest home.'

'War indeed is no rest home. But they have common characteristics. In war there are many cases reminiscent of a rest home, in this sense: in both cases the constant action of social factors is removed. For example under normal circumstances no one is trying to make a career when they're in a rest home or when they're at the front. But introduce a powerful social factor into these situations, and the picture changes. Have you ever had a little flirtation when you have been staying in a rest home? Let's say that you're attracted by a particular woman and she likes you, so you have a pretty good chance. But then some high-ranking official turns up in the rest home, someone who will have a say in the fate of the girl you're interested in. And he lets her know that he wouldn't say no to having a little fun with her. Who do you think she's going to prefer? It's pretty clear isn't it? And then what'd be left of your idyllic picture of excellent relationships? Not a thing. Or here's another situation for you. The commander of a large military unit has a choice between two courses of action. The first choice will involve a senseless loss of men but will guarantee the approval of his superiors and will bring promotion and other rewards. The second possibility avoids the casualties, but involves a risk of angering the top brass and maybe even a risk of demotion (or perhaps merely the risk of delayed promotion). Which course will the commander prefer? The former, of course. Exceptions are conceivable, and they are sometimes thrust before our eyes in books and films. But I have never come across any in real life. Our films and books lie, but always in a very special way: they give an accurate picture of situations beyond the reach of constant social factors, i.e. exceptional and provisional situations; and even if they do touch on the action of the social laws, they depict those laws as something isolated, occasional, generally condemned and set aside. It's not too difficult to give a true picture of a battle, of a rest period between battles, of a military hospital, and so on. But that is not the truth about war. The truth about war is the executions of military commanders before the war, the millions of prisoners taken in the first few weeks of the war, the enemy on the banks of the Volga, one soldier in five killed, the dispersal of people in the rear, in headquarters, in warm and well-fed safety, the innumerable decorations handed out to replete parasites who have never seen the enemy, and so on. Do I make myself clear?'

'You do. So they are lies just the same.'

'Yes, they're lies. And what's more, in real military life there was not the same perception of time, of the importance and the subjective value of events, as is shown in books and films.'

At the time we were watching a war film on television, a film with some pretensions to truth and a certain critical approach.

'Just look how this attractive major sets about courting his girl-friend. How gallant he is! The time he takes! The words he uses! How pure and civilised it all is! In actual fact it would have been enough for him to give her an order and she'd go and sleep with him without a word. That's the way it usually happened.'

'I don't see anything awful about that,' said Tamurka.

(251)

'Nor do I,' said Anton. 'I'm merely saying that the film is lying.'

'Of course it's lying,' said Tamurka; 'but if they showed the truth it wouldn't be interesting.'

'It all depends for whom,' said Lenka. 'I'd have preferred the truth.'

'That's because you're too young and too silly,' remarked Tamurka.

My mother-in-law, Lenka and Tamurka launched off into a boring quarrel which didn't stop them from watching the film and making comments on it. I listened with half an ear to what Anton and Sashka were discussing.

'Just watch,' said Anton, 'how they make the distinction between "our lot" and the Germans. Ours all have a name, a face, a character and a fate. They'll all get killed in the end, of course. But before that they will have lived individual lives in our eyes. Let's say that they are personal lives. They are distinguished for us as separate and complete personalities, each with his own "I". And we attribute to them our image of them, as if they were actually personified in themselves and not merely in our minds. That is one of the laws of perception of works of art. Now look at the Germans. Can you distinguish their names and faces? Does any one of them suggest to you a personality or an individual fate? Look, they pop up suddenly and accidentally like spectres. Bang, one's dead. Bang, that's another one dead. They are not personalised. Try to put yourself in their place. Imagine that you are one of them, but one precisely like the ones we are being shown here: you flash onto the screen, there's a shell-burst, and that's the end of you. Well, the biggest falsehood of our art doesn't even lie in what I've been saying. It's a fact that for the overwhelming majority of people (in war as well as in peace!) there is in reality not even as much personification as our art depicts. And if such personification does exist for a minority, it doesn't assume these forms. So what forms does it take? Servility, for example, and fawning on the bosses. Attempts to attract attention. Buffoonery and so on. Heroism? Sometimes. But what kind of heroism can there be for the great mass of people who are destroyed without distinction by air-raids or by tanks or by artillery fire? And what

(252)

is heroism anyway? Say there's a squadron in combat formation. The lead aircraft is shot down but I survive and I get a decoration. Where's the heroism? It's pure chance. We even speak about mass heroism. What's that? In reality it's mass suffering. It's a huge problem, my friend.'

'But it was like that in the past as well. And it's the same in the West.'

'It was. And it is. But there is a difference in principle: Western civilisation, which has developed the personification of the individual to a high degree for a majority of the population, has developed it now to some degree for the whole of society. You mustn't forget, incidentally, that a believer is already personified at least to some small degree: he is personified in the eyes of God, which means in his own eyes as well. Even a shepherd used to be more personified than one of our directors, (let's say of a section), or a secretary of a regional party committee is today. Our society is in principle a society which produces a general depersonalisation of individuals. We have a dominating social tendency according to which the degree of the personalisation of the individual depends on his social level. That is why all these "cults of personality" are no accident. That is why this desperate self-assertion and self-promotion penetrate all aspects of our life and all levels of society. As a result of biological heredity people have developed an innate desire to distinguish themselves from society and consider themselves as individual personalities, that is as having some intrinsic value. The later history of civilisation has developed this capacity to a high degree. Contemporary culture, without which contemporary society (even ours) could not exist, is a strong stimulant to this capacity. But on the other hand, the social structure of our life necessarily engenders a tendency to the depersonalisation of the whole (and I mean the whole!) of society. Whence flow, naturally, all our monstrous forms of self-assertion. All these nonentities who are inflated into geniuses. All these interminable self-decorations, all these titles. When employees in our offices fight bitterly among themselves for some trifling wage increase, it's not the size of the increase that matters but the very fact of getting it. The desire of the head of state to cover his chest with medals and orders, to acquire titles, to be all over the papers and television screens and so on is, from this point of view, no different from the desire of the book-keeper to be congratulated by name in some official notice. Neither the one nor the other is a genuine personality, but each strives his utmost to look like one in his own eyes and in the eyes of those about him. They're not striving to be personalities, mark you, (that possibility is out of the question for both of them) but to look like personalities. And that produces false personalities, sometimes of a quite grandiose falsity. Stalin in particular experienced the influence of this law to a high degree, but it is our present leaders who provide us with the purest example of its operation.'

I remembered the lines by Lenka's friend:

A theoretician with no ideas to hand,
A general who has won no victory.

And who am I? Am I too a false personality? And what about my ambition to get into the Academy? Is everything I say about 'the good of the cause' just deceit? Is it self-consolation? I search feverishly for a way out of my situation. And I find it.

'The problem is not the destruction of the individual,' I said, 'but the alteration of the form it takes. It is simply that communism engenders another status for human personality and other ideas about it. That is an elementary truth.'

'You are right,' said Anton; 'but only in the sense in which poverty is a variety of wealth, stupidity a form of intellect, death a form of existence. Moreover everything I have said is in complete accord with Marxism; personification is a phenomenon of the superstructure which, as everyone knows, may be rejected.'

The film was over. The attractive, sympathetic major had perished without having managed to seduce the impregnable nurse.

On education

Anton has an astonishing capacity: whatever we are talking about, he always finds some aspect of the matter which no one has noticed and which turns out in the end to be a decisive factor. This is a faculty to see the truth immediately; it distinguishes the born genius from the mediocrity. For instance Dima came to see us, and he told us how his daughter Marinka had been tormented at school and at the regional Komsomol office. (It appears that to apply for exit documents, senior-school children must submit a character reference, which entails a whole series of meetings at which the child is denounced as an enemy of the people and a traitor.)

'The idiots,' said Dima. 'It is themselves they harm by this. They force all Marinka's friends to pour all kinds of filth over her. They don't believe a word that they are saying. And when they get home, they are disgusted with themselves, I know that for a fact. And the children lose faith. So they are taught cynicism, hypocrisy, and a propensity to betray their friends, rather than high civic qualities.'

'But why are they idiots?' asked Anton. 'They're doing exactly what is needed: they are using concrete examples to inculcate in the children the qualities of a genuinely Soviet person. They are educating them. They are training them. In the same way that we too are trained, constantly, so as not to lose the habit of being genuine Soviet people.'

'Good God,' said Dima, 'you're right. They are setting about their business with a serious pedagogic approach. No, my friends. Say what you like, but I must get out of here as soon as possible. Soon my Vitka will be reaching school age, and when I think what he can expect my head spins. I don't want him to be a pioneer and a Komsomol.'

A little theoretical problem

There was an article in the newspaper about a brothel which had been organised for their own use by the management of that famous construction project in the Volga region. It was a luxurious brothel, with young girls, food and drink fit for a king, a swimming pool, and a sauna. And all for free, of course. It is the talk of Moscow at the moment. There was a trial. And, as was to be expected, the small fry ('bath-attendants', 'waitresses', 'store-men', and so on) got long sentences while the principal actors remained in the shadows and were not even mentioned in the depositions. And of course there wasn't a single word about all the medals, decorations, and prizes, and the delegations which a large number of the managers and communist shock workers of the enterprise (they too had had access to the brothel) had enjoyed not so long ago. Their portraits had been seen in newspapers and magazines, and they had been shown on television and in newsreels.

'What swines they are,' said Lenka. 'Shooting's too good for them!'

'Who do you mean?' asked Sashka, 'the bosses or the "bath-attendants"?'

'Things like this are an exception here,' said my mother-in-law, 'and we fight against them.'

'What nonsense!' said Tamurka. 'All that's exceptional is the fact that there's been a trial and stories in the press. Why they've started this particular hare is anybody's guess. Probably they had a row among themselves. Or maybe the workers down there weren't getting fed. This disgusting business went on for two years in the full sight of everybody but nothing was done about it. Is that an exception as well? I'd bet my right arm that some of the biggest bosses from Moscow have been invited to enjoy the delights of their establishment. KGB officers and court officials too, take my word.'

Any my entire family, including my mother-in-law, plunged into recollections. They recalled Mzhavanadze, Nasreddinova, the events in Lvov and Ryazan.

'But do you know what's going on in Azerbaijan?' said Sashka. 'Our Russian hooligan officials are like choir boys compared with your average Azerbaijanis . . .'

The conversation continued in this vein until well after supper. That was almost always the case when we were together. We never talked about masterpieces of literature and art, for they do not exist in our country. Nor about films which raise problems or provoke emotions, for we have none of them either. We talk about all the dirt in our life, for we have plenty of that. And even the official press sometimes gives in to the pressure of these events, thus creating an illusion that in our society they are exceptional and accidental, and that we wage a pitiless war against them.

Then the Zimins looked in and asked us out for a stroll.

'Dima's mother-in-law has refused to sign an authorisation for Anyuta to leave the country,' said Anton. 'The authorities have praised the mother-in-law (after having first persuaded her to refuse, of course), saying that she is a true citizen and a patriot. Anyuta has been abused in the worst possible terms (she is Russian after all!), and accused of treason. The mother-in-law is 75. She's had two heart attacks and is completely senile. Apart from Anyuta, she's got two sons and a daughter whom she lives with. Anyuta has paid her a pension exactly as if she were the only daughter. And the mother-in-law's got a perfectly respectable pension of her own. And yet there she is, a model of civic conscience. Anyuta has written quite a number of high class essays and articles, she's at the height of her creative powers, with a Master's degree. And yet she's accused of being mentally ill! Just imagine, she's got relatives and colleagues who are seriously talking about putting her into a psychiatric hospital. So there's a little problem for you! You solve it! You know Anyuta, and you know her mother. So solve the problem! Maybe your science can come up with the answer?'

'My science doesn't solve that kind of problem.'

'I know. When you come up against a little problem which isn't very nice, your science says that it only operates over entire epochs. But when some poor little beggar who's been working his guts out for forty years is allotted a two-roomed flat to house

(257)

a family of four, your theory's right there waiting: "There you are you see! What progress! That confirms the theory!" But tell me, what you would say about a theory which provided a method for solving *this* kind of little problem?'

I shrugged my shoulders (what else could I do?)

'There is no such theory.'

'Why not? There is one, at least a partial one. And you aren't entirely unfamiliar with it. From the standpoint of this theory, this kind of problem is only fit for beginners.'

I was struck dumb. Could Anton suspect something? If so, why did he go on seeing me? It was all very strange. And why did I go on seeing him? I wanted to know what he thought and said about me. I felt as if he and I were one single person divided up in a most absurd way. At all events there is something Anton-like in me. Is it not something of the dialectic? Dialectic is always being reviled, and yet those who revile it live as classical examples of it. Only they conceal it. And does Anton have within himself something like me? I waited for the right moment to ask him if he had ever wanted a degree, a title, a position, a good salary, decorations, fame and so on.

'That is beyond the threshold of my consciousness,' said Anton. 'It is society that makes a social individual of a person and does so despite his own wishes; but if a man becomes a personality, he does so by his own will and against the wishes of society. That is why a man as a social individual is divided, and your dialectics have no bearing on the matter, while a personality is always one and has a tendency to completeness. I can guess what is worrying you. But believe me, my attitude to people is based wholly on sympathy and antipathy, without any rational calculation. That is why incidentally I don't maintain contacts with our dissidents. I am sickened by their intolerance, their incompetence, their self-esteem and other very Soviet qualities. Our dissidents are the flesh and blood of Soviet society, they bear the features of this society in a hypertrophied and pathologically caricatured form without being aware of it themselves. And I prefer simple people.'

'How good it would be if we could get away from all our miserable little problems and affairs and just live a few years simply as human beings.'

'You know yourself that that is impossible. And unnecessary. Let us bless our fate for having given us a long life and our "miserable little problems"; it's a good thing that they exist. Remember that in the past we didn't even have that. Where there are problems there is life.'

Our good mood was ruined by some young drunks. They began to pester us for no good reason because they'd nothing better to do, and on the excuse of asking us for a light. They began to hurl abuse at us. Anton knocked one of them off his feet and twisted the arm of another up his back. The rest took fright. Then they apologised, wanted to kiss and make up and asked us to have a drink with them. It was very difficult to get rid of them.

'What scum,' I said.

'It's funny,' said Anton. 'It's easy to defend oneself from the threats and insults of the Soviet people but impossible to defend oneself against its love. The Soviet's love for his neighbour—that's what will suffocate the world.'

The Russian people and the future

Our Dive had been taken over for some office party or wedding reception, so we walked the whole length of the Avenue of the Construction Workers without being able to get into any bar or restaurant.

'Moscow really is a prodigiously boring city,' said Rebrov, 'a completely cheerless town.'

'Mediocre' added Nameless.

'A massive mediocrity,' observed Edik, 'the kind that is sponsored by the State.'

'Yet the Russian people are extraordinarily talented,' I said.

'Of course,' said Edik, 'but very much in a way of its own. In a petty and incoherent way. Unproductive. Take my neighbour for example. He's an engineer. An inventor. He's got a whole heap of patents. You can't get into his room for bits of wire and tubes and cog-wheels. He did something heroic when there was some kind of accident in his factory, and he got an invalidity pension. So now he is a clandestine legal adviser. He's incredibly intelligent and inventive. But up to now he's not been able to organise himself an apartment or a car. And that's not because he's an enthusiast without any self-interest. Quite the contrary, he's a very grasping and calculating rogue. It's simply that he can't. All his talent goes into unproductive trifles.'

'All that,' said Rebrov, 'is because we haven't been allowed to develop individual initiative in our society. If we had stopped in February 1917, the Russian people would have developed in all its strength and capacity in every field of culture.'

And we launched off into an empty argument about what would have resulted if certain things hadn't happened and certain others had.

'All the same,' said Edik, 'I think that our incompetent and unproductive nature doesn't derive from our biology but from our history. Every nation has a certain co-efficient of productivity. That is a characteristic of its historical individuality. Take the Germans: almost every German individually is stupid and blinkered. But collectively they are a nation of geniuses. Almost every Russian taken individually is a Lomonosov. But collectively we are glaringly mediocre.'

'What we need is a real Russian nationalism,' said Rebrov, 'no matter what the kind. Even if it's the worst kind of "Black Hundreds". Otherwise Russia will never recover and the Russian people will always remain trodden down and exploited by every kind of villain.'

And we launched off into another absurd argument, this time about nationalism, internationalism, anti-semitism and zionism.

'In every conversation we have of this kind," Rebrov said after a while, 'there's something hypocritical, something shameful and cowardly. And yet a nation that wants to play an active and independent part in history cannot get by without nationalism. Nationalism flourishes in all our republics, and we recognise it as legitimate. But for the most miserable and oppressed nation in this country—the Russian people—we don't even allow the thought of nationalism. That, my dear friends is nothing more than the betrayal of our own people!'

'I am quite prepared to accept Russian nationalism,' said

Nameless, 'but only on a purely social programme. Otherwise Russian nationalism usually degenerates into one single idiotic incantation: the Jews are responsible for all our ills.'

'And what do you mean by a social programme?' I asked.

'Western culture and a Western way of life,' said Nameless.

'That is a profound error,' said Rebrov; 'the Russian people are not of a Western type. They're simply Russian and that's all. They are their own model, like any great nation.'

Then we parted without having found anywhere to eat nor any measure of agreement about Russian nationalism. As far as I am concerned, I have never felt myself to be a representative of the Russian nation. I have always thought of myself as a Muscovite—a representative of a very special kind of cosmopolitan conglomeration comprising people of the most varied nationalities, and more precisely of that part of that conglomeration whose representatives are always suspected of being camouflaged Jews or half-Jews. Moscow, which is the incarnation of all our huge country in all its variety, is at the same time in a certain sense distinct from it, in the same way that a completely new and universal creation would be distinct from a remote semi-Asiatic province. And at times I see something more significant in Moscow's greyness and gloom than in the lively vividness of West European cities. Now I see in them something comparable to an oriental bazaar. Moscow has a future, while the West has a past. And if we must talk of a role of the Russian people, the only problem which appears to me to be really genuine is this: once it has disappeared from the face of the earth, what can the Russian people bring to this new community? For the Russian people is in practice disappearing as a nation. The Revolution, the Civil War, collectivisation, the innumerable purges, the Second World War, they all have shattered Russia as a nation. Russia ceased to exist long ago, and will never exist again. What remains is the Russian population, raw material which can be used for something else, but not for a nation. I am convinced that for the Russian population nationalism would be extremely reactionary. It would be a way back, not a way forward. Here is an example of dialectics: those who have harmed Russia as a nation (but was there ever such a thing?) have by the same token benefited the Russian popula-

(261)

tion by forcing it to live in a different and more modern community. From this point of view the Jewish immigration, the revival of Jewish nationalism and anti-semitism have caused enormous harm primarily to the Russian people, since the Jews played an enormous part in the integration of the Russian population into this new community (at least in Moscow). If Russian nationalism can find support and reinforcement, that could cause a great slowing down of the present evolutionary process of the Russian population. I have been Russian for tens of generations. But I would like to see my people living a good life. And so I am against every kind of nationalism, and I welcome what I can see happening before our eyes. And then everything is far from being as simple as my interlocutors and opponents claim. Despite everything, I remain at bottom optimistic about the future of communism. I feel sure that people will find antidotes to its negative aspects and will live better than we do.

When I got home Lenka rushed in to see me all excited.

'The flat on the fourth floor has been completely cleaned out. The Semyonovs. Just think, they took five fur coats, two of them mink. And two thousand roubles in cash. Why in the world did they keep that amount of money in the house! They only took half an hour while the servant was out shopping. People are saying that it must have been friends of the family who gave the robbers the tip-off.'

After all my optimistic reflections this struck me as funny, and I couldn't help laughing.

'You may think it's funny,' said Tamurka, 'but what if it happened to us? I've been telling you for a long time that we need a burglar alarm. Burglaries have got very common in Moscow. Because money isn't worth anything any more, people are investing it in valuables they can keep in their homes.'

'Our history teacher once said that robbery as a mass social phenomenon appeared at the same time as the division of society into classes, with people being divided into the rich and the poor,' said Lenka. 'And he said that robbery would disappear the moment classes were done away with.'

'You have to know how to use dialectics,' said Sashka sarcastically. 'The state perishes by growing stronger. And robbery diminishes by becoming more widespread. When everything has been stolen, then . . .'

'In my opinion,' said Lenka, 'robbery is much closer to the essence of communism than . . .'

'Stop this anti-communist farce,' screeched my mother-in-law. 'There are limits after all! I'm going to write to your Institute about you, to the party bureau! Understand?'

It's hardly difficult to understand! A cow like her is capable of anything.

On disinterest, self-denial and so on

Nameless and I went to the 'Cosmos' café for a cup of coffee and there we met a friend of Nameless called Vadim. When Vadim had left, Nameless told me about him.

Nameless was in the process of preparing for his Master's degree and ran a small seminar for second year students. This Vadim was among them. He seemed to be quite a capable lad. He was interested in the subject, and soon he became a disciple, indeed a close disciple, of Nameless, who had already achieved some success. One day Vadim told Nameless that he had been summoned to the KGB (the MGB as it was at the time) and invited to become an informer. Vadim wanted advice on what to do. Nameless immediately realised that Vadim had already agreed, and was being so frank about it either under the influence of his emotions, or because he had been instructed to be so; he had advised him, therefore, to accept. At least, he thought, I will have an informer I can trust. The years went by. Vadim turned out to be a very mediocre scientist. He had some small success—he upheld his doctoral thesis and got a good job. He went abroad frequently. Recently Nameless had accidentally discovered that Vadim was keeping an eye on all his activity for the KGB. Vadim became an inevitable member of all kinds of international organisations and published a number of very shallow but apparently modern books. In short he became an influential and well-known figure in their circles. Who was he? A KGB agent? Not quite. He was regarded as an eminent scientist, well-known abroad, with access to high places at home. A scientist? By no means. Of course over all those years he had acquired a certain veneer. He had learnt foreign languages. He had learnt how to make compilations and throw dust in people's eyes. That is a fairly typical phenomenon of our society where a party, state, or KGB official (which are in fact all one and the same) plays the part of a scientist, a writer, an artist, a composer and so on. Besides, he is specially trained to become a scientist, writer or what-have-you, and even sometimes achieves a significant success in these fields. And yet he has been trained not as a scientist or as a writer but as a party or KGB official. And that does not happen with impunity. One man of this kind is capable of destroying the creative spirit in a whole area of culture since he attacks the most delicate and profound threads of creative activity. Once Nameless had analysed and summarised Vadim's activity over many years, he was horrified at the scale of his destructive influence. And the worst of it was, there was nothing concrete to reproach him with. In any formal way he was as pure as the driven snow. Nameless told all his colleagues abroad that Vadim was a KGB agent. No effect. It seemed that this was not of the slightest importance to them.

'You've seen for yourself,' said Nameless. 'He's a very well-mannered, pleasant, educated man. Yet he is one of the most ignoble individuals in our circle. A striking, well-defined product of our educational system.'

'I think you're going a bit far there. There aren't many such Vadims about.'

'I'm not saying there are a lot of them. I'm merely pointing out that they are no accident, that they are part of the scheme of things, that they are significant. Sometimes even one such character can be an indicator of the system.'

'I can't agree that he is a product of the educational system. You surely won't deny that it is the aim of our entire system of education to develop people's positive characteristics. Let's say their propensity to heroism, self-denial, disinterestedness and so on. And that is a good thing!'

'For a start, I'm not trying to say that Vadim has nothing but faults, and no good qualities. Indeed, he's irreproachable. And

(264)

secondly, there is a real system of education, and there's a demagogy which glorifies the qualities of a "builder of communism". It's the former that I'm talking about. And thirdly—you said "and that is a good thing". Good for whom? It suits careerists and profiteers to be surrounded by people who are disinterested, modest and so on. But who profits from heroism and self-denial? The people who display those qualities? They're usually in a situation where they have no choice. For some people they are means of self-assertion and career-building. It's useful to the authorities if the people display mass heroism and self-denial: that might to a certain extent counter-balance their stupidity and ineptitude. And anyway, you know perfectly well yourself that in our world heroes are selected. You think that people don't understand that? Everyone sees it. That's why you get this total hypocrisy among the overwhelm-ing majority of the population, and the makings of a spiritual drama among the few. For example, in our society an able scientist has necessarily got to make a career for himself, to achieve a position and power. Otherwise he'll be totally chewed up and destroyed. If he has power, he'll have pupils, suppor-ters, disciples. He'll be quoted, take part in public life, be recognised. If he has no power, then what recognition there is will be silent and behind the scenes, after which all reference to him will be positively hushed up, and then . . . In short, either you set yourself on the road which will lead in the end to people talking about you and saying that you're a pretty capable chap but a typical Soviet careerist—or you simply won't exist. Is that how things are shaping in your case?'

At this, I poured out my soul to him. My God, what didn't I say? I told him everything that had been piling up in me for years.

'Forgive me for weeping on your shoulder like this. It all boiled over. I can't stand any more of it.'

'All this is new to me. I never thought it was the same in your circle.'

Malice without a cause

Some insignificant question was being discussed at the Faculty of Philosophy in the Institute of Medicine. Someone mentioned my name. And then, to everyone's surprise, K-ov delivered a long speech. I was told later that he attacked me with totally unconcealed malice. I cannot understand what it's all about. We have always been on excellent terms. I have always helped K-ov. I have got some of his articles into our journal. We met quite recently. He was abusing Vaskin, Tvarzhinskaya and the others. And suddenly this . . . What can be the meaning of it?

'Do you want to know what I think?' said Anton. 'It's really very simple. This man has a certain volume of malice built up within him. It must find some way out. Whom it lands on depends entirely on circumstances. It won't necessarily be on anyone who's caused him harm. As a rule, it's directed against someone who's suitable from a different point of view, usually someone without many defences. Or on someone who's promising in the sense that an attack on him might turn out useful to the attacker. It's quite clear that K-ov must have got wind of something building up against you. And on top of that, you've got a chance of getting into the Academy. And who wants that? You'll get all manner of privileges and honours, and he won't get a thing. And, he thinks, I'm no worse than he is. And so this man is ripe for an explosion, and it only needs something quite trivial to trigger it off. Someone mentioned your name: he pushed the button, and the balloon went up. That's what happened to K-ov. As far as the others are concerned, they might be attacking you in a calculated way. K-ov is an example of a psychological derailment. But what's interesting here isn't so much that as whether phenomena of this kind are typical or widespread in our society.'

Anton began to expound some of his views on this subject. I couldn't listen, plunged deep in my own thoughts. If even people like K-ov could allow themselves to go off the rails like this, what might others do? It was quite clear that I was approaching the critical moment. Yet why was I surprised?

What happened to Skopin when he was on the point of getting into the Academy? A year before his election a campaign of denigration, both secret and public, opened up against him. Skopin managed to come through. But can he really be said to have succeeded? He was elected, but soon afterwards he was taken into hospital and died. Will I come through? I must. But I won't be sent to hospital like Skopin. My character's quite different. People who've got powerful support in the wings are very lucky. A father-in-law who's a big wheel, for instance. Or people for whom the decision's all cut and dried. For instance, when Agafonov was elected, all the people on whom his election depended were summoned to the appropriate place for a long and private conversation. And after that, just you dare try to vote against! In a word, the situation is rather as if you're running up to make your jump, with all sorts of creatures tangling round your feet; you have to be able to swerve and sidestep and jump in such a way that they don't hold you back and drag you down as you leap. Well, we shall see who is the strongest!

My brother

My brother flew into Moscow for some super-secret meeting. He was accompanying one of the leaders of the Volga region. He called on us late one evening. We drank, without getting drunk, and talked until dawn.

'What's your meeting about, if it isn't a secret?' I asked.

'It is a secret. A secret for idiots. It's always the same subject: there's nothing to eat, and no prospects of anything turning up.'

'Who's delivered the report?'

'Himself. God, what a cretin! For an entire hour he played the revolutionary (in a revolution that happened sixty years ago!) and blathered on about our outstanding achievements. It was only right at the end that he referred in passing to the fact that our growth rates were slightly lagging behind the plan. In other words, we live like pigs and it'll get worse.'

(267)

'And how are things with you?'

'Worse still.'

'Do people ask you why?'

'They do. We lie, and talk about crop failures.'

'Do they believe you?'

'Of course not. Do you think people don't see anything or understand anything?'

'But can't you take some sensible measures?'

'There are measures that can be taken. And we take them. But not sensible ones. Not in any circumstances. It's a vicious circle, old man. Whatever you do, you get the same result. The whole system needs to be radically rebuilt. As for measures . . . that's all we do, take measures. And the result is that there are always more officials, more parasites, more layabouts, more crooks, more idlers, more profiteers, and less and less grain and meat.'

I listed all manner of possible reforms. My brother demolished them in quick succession.

'Everything's interwoven. You pull one thread, and the whole lot comes with it.'

'But there must be one main thread, as Lenin said, and if you get hold of that . . .'

'Maize? Virgin lands? How many of these main threads have there been in the past? What's happened to them? And they were all main threads once. Now where are they? Now everything's a main thread. In the past the problems we had to resolve were all large-scale, coarse. If you were short of a little screw, or if it was badly made, it didn't matter too much, you got by without it. But now it's not the same. The mechanism of our life has become too complex. The screws have got to be properly made. If they're not, the machine won't function. Every part has got to be precision-made. If it's not, you might as well stuff the whole thing up your . . . You know, even out in the provinces we're not just out of the trees: we're capable of understanding things for ourselves. If we're to solve the little problems we face, we need to be honest, conscientious, motivated, skilful, economical, thrifty. And where do we find these qualities? All we produce in abundance are irresponsibility, bluff, trickery, humbug, extravagance and incompetence.'

'So what's the solution?'

'Everyone's looking for a solution for himself. Why do you think I'm here? To listen to that idiot? No, to try to get myself off the hook. To throw a bit of dust in their eyes. To make promises. Just so long as the leaders are happy. Just to keep my job.'

'And the problems remain.'

'The problems are getting solved. How? On their own. Time passes. People run from queue to queue. They get together in groups and send their "representatives" to Moscow for foodstuffs. Somehow or other they get by. They go on living. And time passes. And something gradually emerges all on its own. It's one thing to have measures, decrees, appeals . . . the natural progress of life is something quite different. That has its own laws, and its own measures.'

Then we talked about the system of payment for labour, of the drain on the labour force, of the compulsory restriction of movement of population. And I was struck by the similarity of my brother's views with those of Anton. There is a passage in Anton's book which deals indirectly with the subject of our conversation. Here in a few words are his ideas. Communism's profoundly rooted tendency towards the complete enslavement of the individual is opposed by the equally organic tendency to give individuals in general and certain categories of individuals in particular a certain degree of freedom of action. If the former derives from the profound relationships which exist in primary collectives, the latter derives from the relationships between a large number of collectives, from the differentiation of society, from the interests of society as a whole. A characteristic example of these two tendencies is to be found in the system of strictly controlled wages: an individual by law receives a specific sum for his subsistence merely because he holds a particular job. There are some exceptions to this rule, but they are not of any consequence. The important thing is that the individual receives a certain legal minimum wage to live on which makes him to a certain extent independent of the collective. Attempts to make wages paid to an individual entirely dependent on the power of the collective (for example the 'Karpov system') have not been successful. (The 'Karpov system' also preserves a certain minimum wage which does not depend on the power of the collective.) The complete enslavement of the individual by the collective is disadvantageous to society as a whole. And there are other factors inhibiting total slavery. For example, hostile groups, competing organisations, the possibility of changing jobs, personal connections, protection from above, the state of the market, the shortage of useful people (and a superabundance of parasites), the independence of bosses from the will of their subordinates, and so on.

A social organism is a system which involves a complex equilibrium in its details. Things which may sometimes seem absurd taken on their own, turn out to be extremely sensible from the point of view of the whole. And things which may seem to be absolutely brilliant in themselves are wholly ridiculous for society as a whole. And it is far from easy to solve social problems of this kind by simple legislation. Social life is an experiment which has no end. The equilibrium between the detailed parts of a social organism is achieved—and is constantly disrupted—by the progress of life itself. For the authorities, these details are little toys, an arena where they can satisfy their love of power and their vanity. For the others, they are the only drama of real life. And the main driving force for the improvement of the social organism is not the illusory wisdom of the leadership, but the practical capacity for resistance on the part of those involved in the living drama.

I told all this to my brother.

'That's true,' he said. 'Your friend is no fool. We need strikes. More strikes, and that'll get things moving. But I'm afraid it takes extraordinary circumstances to get our Soviet man to come out on strike.'

'There've been rumours of strikes in your part of the world.'

'Oh, they didn't amount to anything. We're not like Moscow. Not in the full sight of everyone. They were put down in an instant, and no traces, just rumours. And rumours run around for a little and then they're forgotten. Besides, we sling people inside for rumour-mongering as well. That's anti-Soviet slander, lad, that's what!'

'Hey, that doesn't add up: you admit yourself that strikes are

(270)

necessary, and yet you take steps to make sure they don't happen.'

'Ask me something harder than that! In our society, even the strikers themselves know that they have to be crushed. Otherwise there'd be nothing to eat.'

On morality

Dima looked in. He had finally got his exit permit.

'Would you believe it?' he said. 'Among the people you gave my letter to, there turned out to be one of our . . . shit, THEIR men! But I set everything up through another channel. Don't come and see me off, old man. I'm not a child, you know. It might do you a lot of harm! Even without that, in my opinion you're getting pretty close to the edge. My God! What a country! People having to conceal years of friendship so as not to damage their official life! And that's a betrayal! And a betrayal of a specifically Soviet kind—both the betrayer and the betrayed go into it voluntarily, and accept it as a norm of Soviet life. And no one could give a toss for our real relationship. What matters is that formally things should appear to be the way the society officially wants them to be: if you don't come to see me off, that means that our friendship of thirty years never existed.'

We talked about émigrés and their fate in the West. We recalled the artist who had recently left for good and was now holding triumphal exhibitions throughout the world.

'I know him well,' said Dima. 'He's an interesting case in many ways. He's being represented there as a morally crystal-pure champion of non-violence and so on. But that simply isn't true. He was a perfectly worthy partner in our system. If he had been the kind of Simon-pure archangel he's made out to be he'd have been thoroughly crushed in his youth. Our system even forces certain general traits on its victims: an ability to cheat, to lie, to play a double game. Either you fight on the ground of complete immorality, or you perish at the outset. Or do you remember the writer, ———? He was ready to do anything to

(271)

gain their confidence. He wrote some rather nasty books. He wrote repulsive little articles. He was a party boss. Why? So he could get abroad, stay there and publish his book, which he thinks he's written honestly and sincerely. The only honest book of his whole long career as a writer!'

'But take our own circle,' I said. 'For every ten sharks, careerists, party functionaries, administrators, sons-in-law and so on who get into the Academy, one decent scientist does get elected. Why does he get in? So that our Academy should not look like a lucrative place for the satisfaction of vanity, ambition and greed, but like a temple of learning into which only great minds and morally impeccable personalities are admitted. And the lengths that people will go to in order to get into this temple! And it's the same everywhere. The same with prizes. Believe it or not, but we're going to nominate Baranov, Kanareikin and Tvarzhinskaya for their three-volume work *The Triumph of Communist Ideas*. You should have a look at it! It'd make you bust a gut laughing!'

'What really gets me is that we understand all this perfectly well, yet we voluntarily take part in this orgy of falsehood. One of the main reasons I'm leaving is to get myself out of this dung-heap. I've had my belly-full here.'

'And what about the people who've got no chance of getting out? We're very well aware of what the dung-heap's like. We know about the possibility of something different, something better. But from our very childhood we've been deprived of the ability to live outside of it. All that's left for us is to blunt our sensibilities, abase ourselves, and shape ourselves candidly for life on this dung-hill. Otherwise there's no way of going on living.'

'I hope we'll meet again. If you come to a congress anywhere, let me know. I'll come and see you no matter where I am.'

But all the same . . .

'Very well,' I said. 'Let's say you're right. But imagine that a miracle has happened, and you're back in the days of the Revolution and the Civil War. And you know in advance what's

(272)

going to happen. You know that there's going to be a Gulag Archipelago. What would you do? Which side would you choose?'

'That's a different question. There's no problem of choice for me. I would have gone with the reds even if I'd known that the next day I would be shot. There's no problem of choice for me even today. If anything were to happen I would defend this country and our way of life to the last drop of my blood. I don't want to put the clock back. I want to go on going forward, accepting what has happened in the past as an indisputable fact. Criticism of communism on communism's home ground is not a battle against communism. It cannot in principle lead to the restoration of the pre-communist order. It's rather the opposite; it is precisely the suppression of the criticism of communism which tends towards such a restoration, or in the extreme case it tends to a metamorphosis of communism within the spirit of such a restoration. Incidentally, no one here is doing more to discredit communism than our own highest officials. And Stalinism was, incidentally, the most classic of counter-revolutions. And do you know what our privileged classes instinctively feel behind criticism of the Soviet system? The threat of revolution, in other words, a threat to their own prosperity. Those are the kind of tricks that history sometimes plays on us. Here everything is inside out, upside down, distorted. I just want to get down to the heart of the matter. I want to discover the start of a new path. Now tell me truthfully, after the Revolution, what side would you have taken?'

I could not answer this question. It was not that I was afraid: with Anton I could safely say anything I wanted. It was simply that I had no answer. And I did not want to search for one.

'There you are, you see. And yet essentially it's a simple matter; it's the eternal problem of the haves and have-nots, the oppressors and the oppressed. I'm a have-not. You're a have. What could be simpler? The idea of communism was given birth to by the have-nots or in the name of the have-nots and in the name of the victims. And it is in the name of the victims that today criticism of communism as a given reality is on the upsurge. And now and for evermore, criticism of communism

(273)

is every bit as serious a matter as communism itself. Anti-communism is a reality of communism, and its eternal companion. So what are you afraid of? There's a brilliant example of your dialectic for you. Or do you permit it to be used only towards other people, not towards yourself?'

'You said "anti-communism". But by that we mean something different from what you mean by it. We mean criticism of communism from the capitalist point of view.'

'Rubbish! In reality, there's no such phenomenon. You're operating with schemes of your own devising. Any criticism of communism in an age in which communism triumphs and flourishes is anti-communism, whatever sources that criticism comes from and wherever it draws its inspiration from. Quite a different matter is the struggle against the Soviet Empire and its satellites as a group of states. Inasmuch as these states are communist, this struggle takes on the form of anti-communism. But they are not the same thing. They are deliberately confused, by both the one camp and the other. The West, whom we menace, finds it convenient to represent the threat we pose as the threat of communism, and not simply a threat from the nations who inhabit the countries of our bloc. We find it convenient to represent the resistance to our westward thrust as anti-communism, and not as popular resistance to insurgents coming along with another way of life (what way of life is immaterial). Certainly our pressure on the West contains a social element: to liquidate a basis for comparison and criticism of our way of life. But that's not the main element. What is more important is the struggle which derives from the relationships between peoples and states for existence, security, supremacy and so on.'

'So you see, you admit yourself . . .'

'I'm prepared to admit anything you like. There is only one thing I want: to isolate specifically communist phenomena in their pure state, as Marx did for capitalism, and subject them to objective study. That is all.'

'Well, that's quite an ambition! You want to strike straight to the heart. You want to unveil the secrets of communist exploitation. And you say that's a very modest aim.'

'I'm not claiming to unveil this mechanism. I know my

(274)

limitations. I claim only one thing: I want to convince even one single person that such a mechanism exists.'

'That amounts to the same thing. That still means a fight to the death.'

'I understand that. Unfortunately, I understand something even worse as well. Marx had a great advantage. By the time people began to realise his intentions, he had already accomplished his work. But we have an entire army of ideologues and theoreticians who perceive this kind of enterprise well in advance, and a powerful apparatus capable of killing it in the egg. Communism intends that the laws of its nature should be the most taboo secret of all its future existence.'

'I think you're exaggerating. As soon as communism feels itself to be in complete security, it will reveal its secrets in the most cynical way.'

'It will never feel totally secure. Fear for its own existence is one of its essential qualities, and will remain so even if the world becomes just one single country. Do you know why you'll lose these elections?'

The question was so unexpected and so unpleasant in its implication that it quite floored me.

'Well, you will not be elected because you are well known, and They are aware that you have a certain desire to understand communism scientifically, i.e. objectively. At all events, They know that you do not have that firm, unshakeable resolve to oppose with all your strength the understanding of communism. You, like They, put obstacles in the way of understanding, but you do it in such a way that it might seem that you are keeping something to yourself. Just in case it might come in handy one day.'

The elections

I waited impatiently for the telephone to ring. As soon as the meeting of the department of the Academy ended, the results of the election would be known. The full meeting was a sheer formality. The main thing was the department. That evening

(275)

Serikov was the first to ring with the sad news; I had been passed over, and Vaskin elected. Later many other people phoned. I had been defeated by one vote. And that was the vote of that geriatric Kanareikin. He had decided to sacrifice me, and at that price prolong . . . Prolong what? You cretin, your days are numbered anyway. This won't help you. You'll be devoured within six months at most!

It appears that Kanareikin spoke, saying that I was a capable scientist but that I got carried away, that I was still young and could wait until the next election, that I had committed certain errors which should be corrected, and so on. Kanareikin's speech caused some surprise, but in any case several of my supporters (and my friends, of course) voted against me.

So the comedy is over. And I feel relieved. I am even in some ways pleased: now people will begin to whisper in corners that that bastard Vaskin has been elected, and I, a respectable scientist, have been passed over. It's now that the heat will start being applied. I'll be torn to shreds in the Academy, in the Higher Party School and in every faculty where I have the reputation of being a revisionist. My section will be disbanded. All our books and articles awaiting publication will be returned. Doctoral theses will be postponed or cancelled altogether. Trips abroad will be cancelled. The journals will begin sticking the odd pin in me. At first it will be indirect, very quietly. Later it will be straight in, with huge fanfares. Our names will be bandied about at every conference, meeting and assembly. And there will be clauses about us in every resolution adopted at every level of authority. This will go on for a couple of years at least, assuming, of course, that nothing out of the ordinary happens. If something does, and it's anything to do with us, we'll be attacked with redoubled force as the guilty parties.

As I thought about all this, for the first time in all this crazy period I fell into a peaceful sleep and didn't wake up until after breakfast. Well then, I can start living like a human being now. I'll get some rest, read a few books, wander round the museums. No one may believe it, but for the last twenty years I've never gone skiing, never been to an art gallery or a concert. I've been to the theatre no more than two or three times. And even then it was by accident. I'll spend more time with Sashka and Lenka. Marvellous!

Yet all the same, what they've done is unjust. So how did it all come about?

The decision

There is an intangible yet totally real mechanism which determines the fate of a man in our society. This is not a decision in the proper sense of the word, for that presupposes personalities endowed with will and consciousness. It is rather a kind of behaviour or a reaction of part of society towards oneself, a reaction which determines decisions as purely formal consequences. Nor is this mechanism a mechanism of public opinion—for no such thing exists in our society. It is something else, something specific to our society. It is hard to say how such a mechanism operates. Here we need specific scientific research. And of course, it cannot be described at all within the framework of Marxism.

Who can tell how all this began? Maybe somewhere or other Kanareikin overpraised me, saying that I would go far, and someone became jealous or angered. Maybe M.L. screwed up his nose at the mention of my name, or waved his arm, and Frol told someone or other in secret, adding a few words of his own. Or maybe Korytov hinted to Kanareikin that Up There they think that . . . Or someone might have written to the appropriate authority a note about my relationship with Dima. Or with Anton. Someone wrote, or said, that I protected Jews and dissidents. Who knows? Now it is impossible to establish the truth. We come into this world bearing within ourselves the seeds of our own death.

Now comes the period of quantitative accumulation. Here there are allusions to you. There a reference. Here abuse. There demands. But for the time being this is of no consequence. It's just the norm. Every successful individual must necessarily be the object of accumulations of this kind which can be used against him if the need arises. There have to be more serious reasons before the mark is overstepped, and the quantitative accumulation becomes a qualititative one. What kind of reasons? Once again it's impossible to give a definite answer. My works on social formation? Rubbish. If there hadn't been those, they'd have found something else. So what then? The answer is clear. I am a man of the sixties by every indication, and the sixties were an error. Errors must be corrected. The inertia of the sixties kept me in the ascendant. And the state of society which brought an end to those years has now tripped me up. This is just one of the areas where the errors of those years have been corrected, albeit with a certain delay. And that is natural. It would have been contrary to nature if I had been elected. I timed it wrong, that's the essence of the problem. All the rest is just window-dressing. My books have nothing to do with it. In everyone's eyes I am closely linked with that period, and that period is over.

It remains to discover the pretext which was used to trigger off this pitiless mechanism. There is such a pretext: my timid attempts to bring something new to the Marxist doctrine of socio-economic formation. The discussion of my article at the Academy of Social Sciences, with the collaboration of the Higher Party School, my own Institute and representatives from various Moscow faculties was, as might have been expected, on a high theoretical and ideological level. It is interesting that I was praised rather more than I was blamed. I was defended by Afonin, Kanareikin, Eropkin and many other major figures. Even Vaskin threw in a few words of approbation. But all this had something of the feel of an obituary about it. I spoke myself. I acknowledged certain errors, rebutted a few accusations. I tried to maintain my positions. Why? A matter of habit. A desire to preserve my section; if I get the push, the section will be dispersed.

But my fate was sealed. Only the manner of my fall remained to be discussed. It is possible that I might have managed to hang on to my job with no worse consequences than the loss of my university post and of my position on the editorial board of the journal, had it not been for an article in a western review, in which, compared with the conservative Kanareikin, I was considered an innovator, seeking to push forward and take account of the spirit of the times (the article being about the recent Congress). As a result, the Regional Committee of the party proposed the establishment of a special commission to examine the situation within our section.

The commission, the meeting and so on

The subsequent course of events held no surprises, with the exception of one minor detail. At the party meeting summoned to consider my case, one young lad made a wholly unexpected outburst. He was a very quiet, discreet boy, not even a member of our section, but after what he said he was immediately expelled from the party and fired from his job. While I, the guilty party in the case, got off very lightly: just a reprimand to be entered in my personal dossier—not to mention my dismissal from my post.

The chairman of the commission was Baranov's deputy. My own Institute was represented by Tvarzhinskaya, Nikiforov and Serikov. Apart from gross theoretical errors committed by myself and other members of the section (one must always go for the group!) the commission noted a gross violation of Leninist principles in the selection of my staff (they managed to uncover some departures from the proper formalities in the appointment to the section of certain junior research workers, including Anton). At the party bureau some voices were raised in demands for my expulsion from the party. But they took my previous services into account, and confined themselves to a reprimand. The meeting rolled smoothly on, as meetings of this kind are supposed to do, with denunciations, promises, appeals and so on. If only that lad hadn't spoken up! He intervened quite in vain and only managed to muck everything up. The representatives of the regional and city committees were already coming round to the view that I deserved only some mild punishment, when there was this sudden incident! After that it was such a witches' sabbath that it makes me shudder when I think of it. There'd been nothing like it since Stalin's time. As a result, I was at first expelled. It was only later at the regional party office that the sentence was reduced to a reprimand and a warning. And then the Party Control Commission of the Central Committee reduced it still further to a simple reprimand. The Commission recommended that I should be relieved of the responsibilities of head of section. The section itself was totally reorganised—its name was changed and all posts in it were opened to competition. The staff members were dispersed to other sections; some of them were dismissed (they were advised not to reapply for their jobs, and they left of their own accord). Thanks to Kanareikin's intervention, I was found a job as a senior research worker in a little backstreet institute, unofficially recognised as a place of exile for all manner of offenders. Svetka, of course, disappeared like a puff of smoke, transferring her affections to the new director. I did not regret her departure. Tamara started divorce proceedings and demanded the division of our apartment. As for me, I tasted all the joys of the life of an ordinary senior research assistant: I slept as long as I liked, did my morning physical jerks, wandered the streets, dropped into the Institute a couple of times a month to pick up my pay. And I began to think about a new book which I decided to write with all the appropriate sincerity and sobriety.

But troubles never come singly. Lenka died.

The balance sheet

I have only a confused recollection of this period, and I have no wish to recall it more clearly. What good would it do? Nothing in it can be changed. And if I could remember the details, it would be impossible to go on living. Is it not much the same as the attitude of our entire society to its nightmare past? It is not true to say that our authorities try to conceal our past from the young. Or if that is the truth, it is only a partial truth, and not the most important part. The important truth is that almost the entire population of the country does not want to remember the past, because they want their present life to be at least a little bearable. The only people who recall the past are those who

(280)

have made it their profession (Solzhenitsyn, Anton) and those few people who have fallen under their influence. Very late in the day I realised that my own children had become victims of that memory. And I bear my share of the guilt. I underestimated the dangers, I thought that all this was unimportant, and that real life was more powerful than the ephemeral words of failures.

Later I was ill for a long time. Sashka and Anton brought me out of hospital. I was still in such a poor state that Sashka decided to come and live with me for a time. Anton and Natasha often came round with gifts of tempting food. Where did they get the money from? Anton was still out of work. Natasha said that they were living better at present. She did some typing. Anton, as in the old days, was doing translations and abstracts at second hand, brought to him by intermediaries who took at least half of the fees he earned. But still they refuse to give in. They say they get by. They await the publication of the book. Naïve people!

One day I asked Sashka how it had happened.

'She did it herself,' Sashka replied.

'But why?'

'She found out everything.'

'How?'

'Quite by chance. She and some of the kids from her school went to the Military Affairs Office to invite some war veterans to the Victory Day celebrations. And they found out accidentally that you and Uncle Anton had been in the same regiment. I'd guessed that long ago. But I swear I never said a word about it to anyone. After all, I can understand. But she was only a little girl!'

A hymn to Moscow

Force of habit pulled me back to the Old Square. I had decided to seek an interview with someone. With whom? I don't know. Why? I don't know that either. My only principle was 'you never know' or 'who knows, something might turn up' . . . But then I changed my mind and I wandered off to the Centre. By the Metropol Hotel I came across Victor Ivanovich. He was clearly pleased to see me. I suggested we drop into the café and have a meal. He said that the food there was awful, and suggested instead that we should go to the 'Uzbekistan'. I said there was no point in that because there was always a tremendous queue. He said there was no need to worry about queues, they wouldn't be a problem for us. And indeed, half an hour later we were sitting in the 'Uzbekistan', with Victor Ivanovich pouring out a bewildering stream of orders to the obsequiously stooping waiter, and me going anxiously through my pockets. Victor Ivanovich told me not to worry—he was my host this evening.

Then we began to talk. I started by moaning about Moscow—all the hurry, the pressure, the greyness, the boredom, the irritations of life. In short, I said everything which is usually said about Moscow in intellectual circles.

'I can't agree with you at all,' said Victor Ivanovich, after I had said my say. We had started off with a glass of vodka each, and were now setting to on a range of regal hors d'oeuvres, the like of which I had not seen since my last visit to the Korytovs. 'You simply don't know Moscow, you're not aware of its real life. Moscow is a great city. One of the greatest cities in the world, in every respect. And if we take into account the intensity of life here, it might even be *the* greatest. Today the pulse of the world beats here in Moscow. Moscow is anything you like, except a provincial city, as you suggest. Paris and London are more provincial these days than Moscow is, and that's even more true of Rome, Vienna, Madrid or such like European cities. No, Moscow is far from being provincial.'

I felt slightly drunk, not from the wine, but from the unaccustomed delicious food, and the general excitement and animation of the restaurant. Victor Ivanovich dealt with the wines, the food and the waiters like an experienced habitué of such places. There was little trace of the old Victor Ivanovich, my former drinking companion in the Dive.

'You think I'm joking,' he went on. 'Not in the least. In Moscow you can find absolutely anything you want. Any wines, any food, any kind of girl. The girls in Moscow these days are better than any you'll find in Paris. Girls of any age, any appearance, any intellect, every temperament. There's everything in Moscow. Drugs. Syphilis. Spies. Foreigners. Currency dealers. Prostitutes. Buddhists. Geniuses. Sharks. Homosexuals. Seekers after God. Parapsychologists. Absolutely everything in Moscow.'

'But all the same, it's grey, boring, colourless,' I said. 'You only have to compare it with the life style you'll find described in, say, Balzac or Maupassant.'

'All right. Let's do some comparing. Women? I assure you that the good ladies of Moscow are more than a match for your Parisiennes. Some of them are even better. The only problem is that you haven't got access to them. We've got twenty times more ballerinas and actresses than they have, and they're chosen from a far wider range of human material. And I promise you there's been great progress in this area. Food? If you only knew the kind of things people stuff themselves with in Moscow, you wouldn't believe your eyes. You don't even know the names of things you'll find on the tables of our upper strata. Apartments? Houses? Palaces? Even Balzac's heroes didn't live at Versailles or in the Louvre. And these days as far as apartments and villas are concerned, we're no worse off here than the French in that golden age. I've been to Paris, after all, and I've been in their homes. There's no comparison! If we had the time I could show you some apartments here in Moscow that would make you gasp. Jewels? You don't believe they exist any more? Yet we've got people here who live like Western millionaires, just as many as there are in the West. Just look over there! You see that fat old cow in black? Each of her ear-rings is worth a mansion. And look at her paws! There are scores of people like her these days. Entertainments? My dear man, they may be inaccessible to you, but for people who know their way around there's no need to be bored for a moment. There are a hundred times more cinemas and theatres in Moscow. And for those in the know, in Moscow you can see any foreign films you like, listen to any foreign music, read any book that's published. Conversation? Do you believe that the heroes of Balzac and Maupassant had more interesting conversations than we do? That's nonsense, and I've made a special study of the subject.

(283)

In Moscow literally hundreds of thousands of people have conversations on a far higher intellectual level. And there's not enough going on, you say? Who was it who told you that Moscow life lacked drama? You just ought to go round the courts! Or read the letters that pour in to newspaper offices! And the dramas of Moscow are no less dramatic than those of Balzac.'

We were eating exquisite Asiatic dishes and drinking wines which had long been impossible to find in the shops, and as we emptied bottle after bottle we progressively lost contact with the mire of our existence as it was, is now and ever shall be beyond the walls of the golden oasis where we sat.

'Moscow has become the centre of attraction for many millions of people,' pursued Victor Ivanovich. 'Do you know how many people pour into Moscow every year despite every kind of ban and prohibition? And many of them are successful, I'd have you know. Just look at our statesmen, our generals, our top writers and artists, our actors, our sportsmen . . . are many of them native Muscovites? What's happening today in Moscow isn't just an analogy with the Paris of Balzac and Maupassant. There are a thousand such Parises here. That might be the one defect of our life: too many Parises. No feeling of exclusivity. But that's another problem.'

We sat in the restaurant until it closed. We had drunk all kinds of wines, yet we left the place completely sober.

'That's what it's all about,' said Victor Ivanovich. 'The main cause of alcoholism is poor-quality liquor and no decent food to eat with it. The amount we've knocked back tonight would have been enough to put a dozen ordinary alcoholics on their backs.'

At night, when it is deserted, Moscow looks quite different from daytime. The dimly illuminated streets look beautiful and full of promise. The lit windows (God, how many!) create an illusion of mystery.

'You're right on one point, I agree,' said Victor Ivanovich. 'Moscow hasn't got enough poets. Writers like Balzac and Maupassant. If only we had a literature on that level, Moscow life would appear in quite a different light. And it would genuinely become different. It's not enough just to dress well, drink and eat, sleep with lovely women, go to shows and have witty and inspiring conversations. Those are necessary elements of a decent life. But that's not all. We ought to be specifically aware of all these benefits, and in a socially recognised form. We've just had a first class meal. But alas that's just a physiological fact, not a social fact. And in particular it's not a literary fact. Moscow needs its own great poets. But will they appear? While we wait, we must still go on living. We must live, d'you understand? Live!'

We came out on to Gorki Street, crossed Red Square and reached the river embankment.

'Have you ever happened to watch a man quite unashamedly and successfully going about the business of making himself a career? You see him as a cynic, an intriguer, a careerist, a trickster. He makes you sick. But you're attracted by him. And sometimes you even admire him: that bastard's really making it! Moscow puts me very much in mind of that kind of creature. The city is openly and successfully making a career for herself. She may be grey and mediocre, but all the same she's crawling through into the number one position. And which of our leaders didn't seem to be grey and mediocre in the beginning? In a hundred years or so, the history of Moscow will intrigue people just as much as the history of Paris at the time of the French Revolution. People will pore over the biography of Brezhnev. While Solzhenitsyn will be forgotten.'

My interlocutor was right. But it's a pity!

'Why's it a pity?'

'It's a pity that Brezhnev's biography will be studied and people will forget Solzhenitsyn.'

And that's me saying that, a man from Brezhnev's party!

'There's nothing you can do about it! That's life.'

Long live communism

Anton's book has still not come out. He's afraid that someone's making a fool of him. He has decided to give his permission for publication by any anti-Soviet firm. He says there's no

(285)

alternative. They themselves are driving him to it. Well, that's perfectly logical. It's much easier for them to cope with straightforward anti-Sovietism (particularly since it's gone out of fashion) than with a calm academic analysis of the basic problems of our society.

In the conclusion to his book Anton wrote that communism is a completely natural and normal social structure. There is less artificiality in it than in the societies of Western civilisation. This part of the manuscript was circled in red pencil, and someone had written 'Quite right!' in the margin. The aim of the book is to give an objective description of communism as it really is from the point of view of its deepest underlying laws, its tendencies and its future prospects. What attitude to take up vis-à-vis this society is the personal affair of each reader. The author is not trying to dictate any line of response to him. The only thing he can advise is: if you are not content, if you don't like it, fight against it. How? However you are able. For the best forms of struggle can only be found from experience of the struggle. And for the moment there is too little such experience for useful conclusions to be drawn. This passage in the manuscript was encircled in black pencil, with a note in the margin 'This is dangerous!'

My period in purgatory came to an end. I was offered a chair in a Moscow institute. It is a miserable little faculty, but within three years I'll be able to turn it into something decent. So all is not yet lost.

One evening I went out and wandered aimlessly. I came to our Institute. (I still can't stop myself calling it 'ours'!) I looked up at the darkened windows of our section. I sighed a little. And then I wandered off along the avenue that leads from our Yellow House to the far off bright lights of Cosmonaut Square. To our Slogan.

'No, Mr. Zimin,' I thought aloud. 'Our struggle is still not over. It is only just beginning. Wait till your book comes out, and we'll talk about it again. In the open. It may not be a bad idea at that. They're sure to give me half a page in Pravda. Then an article in *Kommunist*. And I suddenly wanted Anton's book to come out as soon as possible. And I even felt sad that we hadn't met for so long. Cosmonaut Square was brightly lit.

They had begun to repair our Slogan. The letters were covered in scaffolding. I can imagine how Kanareikin will be trumpeting about it all over the department. He has been removed from the job of director and appointed Academician Secretary of the department—fired by means of promotion, as quite often happens here. For sure this degenerate will organise a special meeting devoted to the reconstruction of the Slogan. I can see him on the platform: our beautiful Slogan, like the phoenix, rises each time from its ashes, etc. etc. God, when will someone decide to get rid of all these idiots and replace them with some worthwhile people?'

I stood for a while in the square, and then retraced my steps. I have begun to drag one leg a little. And my heart troubles me from time to time. But that's of no matter. It's the attacks of constipation that are the worst. Those old piles. God knows! Here we are, flying to the moon. People say they can cure cancer now. But they still can't cope with these miserable piles!

'Yet we *will* build it. We *will* build communism.' I thought I was talking to myself, but somehow the words came out aloud.

I was afraid that passers-by would look at me and laugh. But no one paid the slightest attention. I walked past them dragging my meaningless little cart, walked through them, in some sector of existence of which they were unaware. But where to? . . .